Anne of the Island & Anne of Windy Poplars

Lucy Maud Montgomery

Nimbus Publishing, 2025
Anne of the Island - First published 1915
Anne of Windy Poplars - First published 1936

All rights reserved. No part of this book may be reproduced, stored in a retrieval system or transmitted in any form or by any means without the prior written permission from the publisher, or, in the case of photocopying or other reprographic copying, permission from Access Copyright, 1 Yonge Street, Suite 1900, Toronto, Ontario M5E 1E5.

Nimbus Publishing Limited
3660 Strawberry Hill Street, Halifax, NS, B3K 5A9
(902) 455-4286 nimbus.ca

Artwork copyright Briana Corr Scott
Printed and bound in China
NB1807

Nimbus Publishing is based in Kjipuktuk, Mi'kma'ki, the traditional territory of the Mi'kmaq People.

Library and Archives Canada Cataloguing in Publication
Title: Anne of the island ; & Anne of Windy Poplars / L.M. Montgomery.
Other titles: Anne of the island (Compilation) | Anne of Windy Poplars
Names: Montgomery, L. M. (Lucy Maud), 1874-1942, author. | Container of (work): Montgomery, L. M. Lucy Maud), 1874-1942. Anne of the island. | Container of (work): Montgomery, L. M. (Lucy Maud), 1874-1942. Anne of Windy Poplars.
Description: Collectors' edition bind-ups. Identifiers: Canadiana 20240535456 | ISBN 9781774714294 (softcover)
Subjects: LCGFT: Novels. Classification: LCC PS8526.O55 A657 2025 | DDC jC813/.52—dc23

Nimbus Publishing acknowledges the financial support for its publishing activities from the Government of Canada, the Canada Council for the Arts, and from the Province of Nova Scotia. We are pleased to work in partnership with the Province of Nova Scotia to develop and promote our creative industries for the benefit of all Nova Scotians.

Anne of the Island

Contents

Chapter		Page
1	The Shadow of Change	1
2	Garlands of Autumn	9
3	Greeting and Farewell	16
4	April's Lady	22
5	Letters from Home	35
6	In the Park	42
7	Home Again	49
8	Anne's First Proposal	57
9	An Unwelcome Lover and a Welcome Friend	61
10	Patty's Place	69
11	The Round of Life	77
12	"Averil's Atonement"	85
13	The Way of Transgressors	92
14	The Summons	102
15	A Dream Turned Upside Down	110
16	Adjusted Relationships	114
17	A Letter from Davy	125
18	Miss Josephine Remembers the Anne-Girl	128
19	An Interlude	134
20	Gilbert Speaks	137
21	Roses of Yesterday	142
22	Spring and Anne Return to Green Gables	146
23	Paul Cannot Find the Rock People	150
24	Enter Jonas	154

25	Enter Prince Charming	160
26	Enter Christine	166
27	Mutual Confidences	169
28	A June Evening	174
29	Diana's Wedding	179
30	Mrs. Skinner's Romance	182
31	Anne to Philippa	186
32	Tea with Mrs. Douglas	188
33	"He Just Kept Coming and Coming"	193
34	John Douglas Speaks at Last	196
35	The Last Redmond Year Opens	201
36	The Gardners' Call	207
37	Full-Fledged B.A.'s	212
38	False Dawn	218
39	Deals with Weddings	223
40	A Book of Revelation	231
41	Love Takes Up the Glass of Time	235

Anne of Windy Poplars

Contents

The First Year
243

The Second Year
373

The Third Year
451

1
The Shadow of Change

"Harvest is ended and summer is gone," quoted Anne Shirley, gazing across the shorn fields dreamily. She and Diana Barry had been picking apples in the Green Gables orchard, but were now resting from their labors in a sunny corner, where airy fleets of thistledown drifted by on the wings of a wind that was still summer-sweet with the incense of ferns in the Haunted Wood.

But everything in the landscape around them spoke of autumn. The sea was roaring hollowly in the distance, the fields were bare and sere, scarfed with golden rod, the brook valley below Green Gables overflowed with asters of ethereal purple, and the Lake of Shining Waters was blue—blue—blue; not the changeful blue of spring, nor the pale azure of summer, but a clear, steadfast, serene blue, as if the water were past all moods and tenses of emotion and had settled down to a tranquility unbroken by fickle dreams.

"It has been a nice summer," said Diana, twisting the new ring on her left hand with a smile. "And Miss Lavendar's wedding seemed to come as a sort of crown to it. I suppose Mr. and Mrs. Irving are on the Pacific coast now."

"It seems to me they have been gone long enough to go around the world," sighed Anne. "I can't believe it is only a week since they were married. Everything has changed. Miss

Lavendar and Mr. and Mrs. Allan gone—how lonely the manse looks with the shutters all closed! I went past it last night, and it made me feel as if everybody in it had died."

"We'll never get another minister as nice as Mr. Allan," said Diana, with gloomy conviction. "I suppose we'll have all kinds of supplies this winter, and half the Sundays no preaching at all. And you and Gilbert gone—it will be awfully dull."

"Fred will be here," insinuated Anne slyly. "When is Mrs. Lynde going to move up?" asked Diana, as if she had not heard Anne's remark.

"Tomorrow. I'm glad she's coming—but it will be another change. Marilla and I cleared everything out of the spare room yesterday. Do you know, I hated to do it? Of course, it was silly—but it did seem as if we were committing sacrilege. That old spare room has always seemed like a shrine to me. When I was a child I thought it the most wonderful apartment in the world. You remember what a consuming desire I had to sleep in a spare room bed—but not the Green Gables spare room. Oh, no, never there! It would have been too terrible—I couldn't have slept a wink from awe. I never *walked* through that room when Marilla sent me in on an errand—no, indeed, I tiptoed through it and held my breath, as if I were in church, and felt relieved when I got out of it. The pictures of George Whitefield and the Duke of Wellington hung there, one on each side of the mirror, and frowned so sternly at me all the time I was in, especially if I dared peep in the mirror, which was the only one in the house that didn't twist my face a little. I always wondered how Marilla dared houseclean that room. And now it's not only cleaned but stripped bare. George Whitefield and the Duke have been relegated to the upstairs hall. 'So passes the glory of this world,'" concluded Anne, with a laugh in which there was a little note of regret. It is never pleasant to have our old shrines desecrated, even when we have outgrown them.

The Shadow of Change

"I'll be so lonesome when you go," moaned Diana for the hundredth time. "And to think you go next week!"

"But we're together still," said Anne cheerily. "We mustn't let next week rob us of this week's joy. I hate the thought of going myself—home and I are such good friends. Talk of being lonesome! It's I who should groan. *You'll* be here with any number of your old friends—*and* Fred! While I shall be alone among strangers, not knowing a soul!"

"*Except* Gilbert—*and* Charlie Sloane," said Diana, imitating Anne's italics and slyness.

"Charlie Sloane will be a great comfort, of course," agreed Anne sarcastically; whereupon both those irresponsible damsels laughed. Diana knew exactly what Anne thought of Charlie Sloane; but, despite sundry confidential talks, she did *not* know just what Anne thought of Gilbert Blythe. To be sure, Anne herself did not know that.

"The boys may be boarding at the other end of Kingsport, for all I know," Anne went on. "I am glad I'm going to Redmond, and I am sure I shall like it after a while. But for the first few weeks I know I won't. I shan't even have the comfort of looking forward to the weekend visit home, as I had when I went to Queen's. Christmas will seem like a thousand years away."

"Everything is changing—or going to change," said Diana sadly. "I have a feeling that things will never be the same again, Anne."

"We have come to a parting of the ways, I suppose," said Anne thoughtfully. "We had to come to it. Do you think, Diana, that being grown—up is really as nice as we used to imagine it would be when we were children?"

"I don't know—there are *some* nice things about it," answered Diana, again caressing her ring with that little smile which always had the effect of making Anne feel suddenly left out and inexperienced. "But there are so many puzzling things, too. Sometimes I feel as if being grown—up just frightened me—and then I would give anything to be a little girl again."

"I suppose we'll get used to being grown—up in time," said Anne cheerfully. "There won't be so many unexpected things about it by and by—though, after all, I fancy it's the unexpected things that give spice to life. We're eighteen, Diana. In two more years we'll be twenty. When I was ten I thought twenty was a green old age. In no time you'll be a staid, middle-aged matron, and I shall be nice, old maid Aunt Anne, coming to visit you in vacations. You'll always keep a comer for me, won't you, Di darling? Not the spare room, of course—old maids can't aspire to spare rooms, and I shall be as 'umble as *Uriah Heep,* and quite content with a little over-the-porch or off-the-parlor cubby hole."

"What nonsense you do talk, Anne," laughed Diana. "You'll marry somebody splendid and handsome and rich—and no spare room in Avonlea will be half gorgeous enough for you— and you'll turn up your nose at all the friends of your youth."

"That would be a pity; my nose is quite nice, but I fear turning it up would spoil it," said Anne, patting that shapely organ. "I haven't so many good features that I could afford to spoil those I have; so, even if I should marry the King of the Cannibal Islands, I promise you I won't turn up my nose at *you,* Diana."

With another gay laugh the girls separated, Diana to return to Orchard Slope, Anne to walk to the Post Office. She found a letter awaiting her there, and when Gilbert Blythe overtook her on the bridge over the Lake of Shining Waters she was sparkling with the excitement of it.

"Priscilla Grant is going to Redmond, too," she exclaimed. "Isn't that splendid? I hoped she would, but she didn't think her father would consent. He has, however, and we're to board together. I feel that I can face an army with banners—or all the professors of Redmond in one fell phalanx—with a chum like Priscilla by my side."

The Shadow of Change

"I think we'll like Kingsport," said Gilbert. "It's a nice old burg, they tell me, and has the finest natural park in the world. I've heard that the scenery in it is magnificent."

"I wonder if it will be—can be—any more beautiful than this," murmured Anne, looking around her with the loving, enraptured eyes of those to whom "home" must always be the loveliest spot in the world, no matter what fairer lands may lie under alien stars.

They were leaning on the bridge of the old pond, drinking deep of the enchantment of the dusk, just at the spot where Anne had climbed from her sinking Dory on the day Elaine floated down to Camelot. The fine, empurpling dye of sunset still stained the western skies, but the moon was rising and the water lay like a great, silver dream in her light. Remembrance wove a sweet and subtle spell over the two young creatures.

"You are very quiet, Anne," said Gilbert at last.

"I'm afraid to speak or move for fear all this wonderful beauty will vanish just like a broken silence," breathed Anne.

Gilbert suddenly laid his hand over the slender white one lying on the rail of the bridge. His hazel eyes deepened into darkness, his still boyish lips opened to say something of the dream and hope that thrilled his soul. But Anne snatched her hand away and turned quickly. The spell of the dusk was broken for her.

"I must go home," she exclaimed, with a rather overdone carelessness. "Marilla had a headache this afternoon, and I'm sure the twins will be in some dreadful mischief by this time. I really shouldn't have stayed away so long."

She chattered ceaselessly and inconsequently until they reached the Green Gabled lane. Poor Gilbert hardly had a chance to get a word in edgewise. Anne felt rather relieved when they parted. There had been a new, secret self-consciousness in her heart with regard to Gilbert, ever since that fleeting moment of revelation in the garden of Echo Lodge. Something alien had intruded into the old, perfect, school-day comradeship—something that threatened to mar it.

"I never felt glad to see Gilbert go before," she thought, half-resentfully, half-sorrowfully, as she walked alone up the lane. "Our friendship will be spoiled if he goes on with this nonsense. It mustn't be spoiled—I won't let it. Oh, *why* can't boys be just sensible!"

Anne had an uneasy doubt that it was not strictly "sensible" that she should still feel on her hand the warm pressure of Gilbert's, as distinctly as she had felt it for the swift second his had rested there; and still less sensible that the sensation was far from being an unpleasant one—very different from that which had attended a similar demonstration on Charlie Sloane's part, when she had been sitting out a dance with him at a White Sands party three nights before. Anne shivered over the disagreeable recollection. But all problems connected with infatuated swains vanished from her mind when she entered the homely, unsentimental atmosphere of the Green Gables kitchen where an eight-year-old boy was crying grievously on the sofa.

"What is the matter, Davy?" asked Anne, taking him up in her arms. "Where are Marilla and Dora?"

"Marilla's putting Dora to bed," sobbed Davy, "and I'm crying 'cause Dora fell down the outside cellar steps, heels over head, and scraped all the skin off her nose, and—"

"Oh, well, don't cry about it, dear. Of course, you are sorry for her, but crying won't help her any. She'll be all right tomorrow. Crying never helps any one, Davy-boy, and—"

"I ain't crying 'cause Dora fell down the cellar," said Davy, cutting short Anne's well-meant preachment with increasing bitterness. "I'm crying 'cause I wasn't there to see her fall. I'm always missing some fun or other, seems to me."

The Shadow of Change

"Oh, Davy!" Anne choked back an unholy shriek of laughter. "Would you call it fun to see poor little Dora fall down the steps and get hurt?"

"She wasn't *much* hurt," said Davy defiantly.

"'Course, if she'd been killed I'd have been real sorry, Anne. But the Keiths ain't so easy killed. They're like the Blewetts, I guess. Herb Blewett fell off the hayloft last Wednesday, and rolled right down through the turnip chute into the box stall, where they had a fearful wild, cross horse, and rolled right under his heels. And still he got out alive, with only three bones broke. Mrs. Lynde says there are some folks you can't kill with a meat-axe. Is Mrs. Lynde coming here tomorrow, Anne?"

"Yes, Davy, and I hope you'll be always very nice and good to her."

"I'll be nice and good. But will she ever put me to bed at nights, Anne?"

"Perhaps. Why?"

"'Cause," said Davy very decidedly, "if she does I won't say my prayers before her like I do before you, Anne."

"Why not?"

"'Cause I don't think it would be nice to talk to God before strangers, Anne. Dora can say hers to Mrs. Lynde if she likes, but *I* won't. I'll wait till she's gone and then say 'em. Won't that be all right, Anne?"

"Yes, if you are sure you won't forget to say them, Davy-boy."

"Oh, I won't forget, you bet. I think saying my prayers is great fun. But it won't be as good fun saying them alone as saying them to you. I wish you'd stay home, Anne. I don't see what you want to go away and leave us for."

"I don't exactly *want* to, Davy, but I feel I ought to go."

"If you don't want to go you needn't. You're grown up. When I'm grown up I'm not going to do one single thing I don't want to do, Anne."

"All your life, Davy, you'll find yourself doing things you don't want to do."

"I won't," said Davy flatly. "Catch me! I have to do things I don't want to now, 'cause you and Marilla'll send me to bed if I don't. But when I grow up you can't do that, and there'll be nobody to tell me not to do things. Won't I have the time! Say, Anne, Milty Boulter says his mother says you're going to college to see if you can catch a man. Are you, Anne? I want to know."

For a second Anne burned with resentment. Then she laughed, reminding herself that Mrs. Boulter's crude vulgarity of thought and speech could not harm her.

"No, Davy, I'm not. I'm going to study and grow and learn about many things."

"What things?"

"*'Shoes and ships and sealing wax
And cabbages and kings,'*"

quoted Anne.

"But if you *did* want to catch a man how would you go about it? I want to know," persisted Davy, for whom the subject evidently possessed a certain fascination.

"You'd better ask Mrs. Boulter," said Anne thoughtlessly. "I think it's likely she knows more about the process than I do."

"I will, the next time I see her," said Davy gravely.

"Davy! If you do!" cried Anne, realizing her mistake.

"But you just told me to," protested Davy aggrieved.

"It's time you went to bed," decreed Anne, by way of getting out of the scrape.

After Davy had gone to bed Anne wandered down to Victoria Island and sat there alone, curtained with fine-spun, moonlit gloom, while the water laughed around her in a duet of brook and wind. Anne had always loved that brook. Many a dream had she spun over its sparkling water in days gone by. She forgot lovelorn youths, and the cayenne speeches of malicious neighbors, and all the problems of her girlish existence. In imagination she sailed over storied seas that wash the distant shining shores of "faëry lands forlorn," where lost Atlantis and Elysium lie, with the evening star for pilot, to the land of Heart's Desire. And she was richer in those dreams than in realities; for things seen pass away, but the things that are unseen are eternal.

2

Garlands of Autumn

The following week sped swiftly, crowded with innumerable "last things," as Anne called them. Goodbye calls had to be made and received, being pleasant or otherwise, according to whether callers and called-upon were heartily in sympathy with Anne's hopes, or thought she was too much puffed-up over going to college and that it was their duty to "take her down a peg or two."

The A.V.I.S. gave a farewell party in honor of Anne and Gilbert one evening at the home of Josie Pye, choosing that place, partly because Mr. Pye's house was large and convenient, partly because it was strongly suspected that the Pye girls would have nothing to do with the affair if their offer of the house for the party was not accepted. It was a very pleasant little time, for the Pye girls were gracious, and said and did nothing to mar the harmony of the occasion—which was not according to their wont. Josie was unusually amiable—so much so that she even remarked condescendingly to Anne,

"Your new dress is rather becoming to you, Anne. Really, you look *almost pretty* in it."

"How kind of you to say so," responded Anne, with dancing eyes. Her sense of humor was developing, and the speeches that would have hurt her at fourteen were becoming merely food for amusement now. Josie suspected that Anne was laughing at her behind those wicked eyes; but she contented herself with whispering to Gertie, as they went downstairs, that Anne Shirley would put on more airs than ever now that she was going to college—you'd see!

All the "old crowd" was there, full of mirth and zest and youthful light-heartedness. Diana Barry, rosy and dimpled, shadowed by the faithful Fred; Jane Andrews, neat and sensible and plain; Ruby Gillis, looking her handsomest and brightest in a cream silk blouse, with red geraniums in her golden hair; Gilbert Blythe and Charlie Sloane, both trying to keep as near the elusive Anne as possible; Carrie Sloane, looking pale and melancholy because, so it was reported, her father would not allow Oliver Kimball to come near the place; Moody Spurgeon MacPherson, whose round face and objectionable ears were as round and objectionable as ever; and Billy Andrews, who sat in a corner all the evening, chuckled when any one spoke to him, and watched Anne Shirley with a grin of pleasure on his broad, freckled countenance.

Anne had known beforehand of the party, but she had not known that she and Gilbert were, as the founders of the Society, to be presented with a very complimentary "address" and "tokens of respect"—in her case a volume of Shakespeare's plays, in Gilbert's a fountain pen. She was so taken by surprise and pleased by the nice things said in the address, read in Moody Spurgeon's most solemn and ministerial tones, that the tears quite drowned the sparkle of her big gray eyes. She had worked hard and faithfully for the A.V.I.S., and it warmed the cockles of her heart that the members appreciated her efforts so sincerely.

Garlands of Autumn

And they were all so nice and friendly and jolly—even the Pye girls had their merits; at that moment Anne loved all the world.

She enjoyed the evening tremendously, but the end of it rather spoiled all. Gilbert again made the mistake of saying something sentimental to her as they ate their supper on the moonlit verandah; and Anne, to punish him, was gracious to Charlie Sloane and allowed the latter to walk home with her. She found, however, that revenge hurts nobody quite so much as the one who tries to inflict it. Gilbert walked airily off with Ruby Gillis, and Anne could hear them laughing and talking gaily as they loitered along in the still, crisp autumn air. They were evidently having the best of good times, while she was horribly bored by Charlie Sloane, who talked unbrokenly on, and never, even by accident, said one thing that was worth listening to. Anne gave an occasional absent "yes" or "no," and thought how beautiful Ruby had looked that night, how very goggly Charlie's eyes were in the moonlight—worse even than by daylight—and that the world, somehow, wasn't quite such a nice place as she had believed it to be earlier in the evening.

"I'm just tired out—that is what is the matter with me," she said, when she thankfully found herself alone in her own room. And she honestly believed it was. But a certain little gush of joy, as from some secret, unknown spring, bubbled up in her heart the next evening, when she saw Gilbert striding down through the Haunted Wood and crossing the old log bridge with that firm, quick step of his. So Gilbert was not going to spend this last evening with Ruby Gillis after all!

"You look tired, Anne," he said.

"I am tired, and, worse than that, I'm disgruntled. I'm tired because I've been packing my trunk and sewing all day. But I'm disgruntled because six women have been here to say good-bye to *me,* and every one of the six managed to say something that seemed to take the color right out of life and leave it as gray and dismal and cheerless as a November morning."

"Spiteful old cats!" was Gilbert's elegant comment. "Oh, no, they weren't," said Anne seriously. "That is just the trouble. If they had been spiteful cats I wouldn't have minded them. But they are all nice, kind, motherly souls, who like me and whom I like, and that is why what they said, or hinted, had such undue weight with me. They let me see they thought I was crazy going to Redmond and trying to take a B.A., and ever since I've been wondering if I am. Mrs. Peter Sloane sighed and said she hoped my strength would hold out till I got through; and at once I saw myself a hopeless victim of nervous prostration at the end of my third year; Mrs. Eben Wright said it must cost an awful lot to put in four years at Redmond; and I felt all over me that it was unpardonable in *me* to squander Marilla's money and my own on such a folly; Mrs. Jasper Bell said she hoped I wouldn't let college spoil me, as it did some people; and I felt in my bones that the end of my four Redmond years would see me a most insufferable creature, thinking I knew it all, and looking down on everything and everybody in Avonlea; Mrs. Elisha Wright said she understood that Redmond girls, especially those who belonged to Kingsport, were 'dreadful dressy and stuck-up,' and she guessed I wouldn't feel much at home among them; and I saw myself, a snubbed, dowdy, humiliated country girl, shuffling through Redmond's classic halls in copper-toned boots."

Anne ended with a laugh and a sigh commingled.

With her sensitive nature all disapproval had weight, even the disapproval of those for whose opinions she had scant respect. For the time being life was savorless, and ambition had gone out like a snuffed candle.

"You surely don't care for what they said," protested Gilbert. "You know exactly how narrow their outlook on life is, excellent creatures though they are. To do anything *they* have never done is anathema maranatha. You are the first Avonlea girl who has ever gone to college; and you know that all pioneers are considered to be afflicted with moonstruck madness."

Garlands of Autumn

"Oh, I know. But *feeling* is so different from *knowing*. My common sense tells me all you can say, but there are times when common sense has no power over me. Common nonsense takes possession of my soul. Really, after Mrs. Elisha went away I hardly had the heart to finish packing."

"You're just tired, Anne. Come, forget it all and take a walk with me—a ramble back through the woods beyond the marsh. There should be something there I want to show you."

"Should be! Don't you know if it is there?"

"No. I only know it should be, from something I saw there in spring. Come on. We'll pretend we are two children again and we'll go the way of the wind."

They started gaily off. Anne, remembering the unpleasantness of the preceding evening, was very nice to Gilbert; and Gilbert, who was learning wisdom, took care to be nothing save the schoolboy comrade again.

Mrs. Lynde and Marilla watched them from the kitchen window.

"That'll be a match some day," Mrs. Lynde said approvingly.

Marilla winced slightly. In her heart she hoped it would, but it went against her grain to hear the matter spoken of in Mrs. Lynde's gossipy matter-of-fact way.

"They're only children yet," she said shortly. Mrs. Lynde laughed good-naturedly.

"Anne is eighteen; I was married when I was that age. We old folks, Marilla, are too much given to thinking children never grow up, that's what. Anne is a young woman and Gilbert's a man, and he worships the ground she walks on, as any one can see. He's a fine fellow, and Anne can't do better. I hope she won't get any romantic nonsense into her head at Redmond. I don't approve of them coeducational places and never did, that's what. I don't believe," concluded Mrs. Lynde solemnly, "that the students at such colleges ever do much else than flirt."

"They must study a little," said Marilla, with a smile.

"Precious little," sniffed Mrs. Rachel. "However, I think Anne will. She never was flirtatious. But she doesn't appreciate Gilbert at his full value, that's what. Oh, I know girls! Charlie Sloane is wild about her, too, but I'd never advise her to marry a Sloane. The Sloanes are good, honest, respectable people, of course. But when all's said and done, they're *Sloanes.*"

Marilla nodded. To an outsider, the statement that Sloanes were Sloanes might not be very illuminating, but she understood. Every village has such a family; good, honest, respectable people they may be, but *Sloanes* they are and must ever remain, though they speak with the tongues of men and angels.

Gilbert and Anne, happily unconscious that their future was thus being settled by Mrs. Rachel, were sauntering through the shadows of the Haunted Wood. Beyond, the harvest hills were basking in an amber sunset radiance, under a pale, aerial sky of rose and blue. The distant spruce groves were burnished bronze, and their long shadows barred the upland meadows. But around them a little wind sang among the fir tassels, and in it there was the note of autumn.

"This wood really is haunted now—by old memories," said Anne, stooping to gather a spray of ferns, bleached to waxen whiteness by frost. "It seems to me that the little girls Diana and I used to be play here still, and sit by the Dryad's Bubble in the twilights, trysting with the ghosts. Do you know, I can never go up this path in the dusk without feeling a bit of the old fright and shiver? There was one especially horrifying phantom which we created—the ghost of the murdered child that crept up behind you and laid cold fingers on yours. I confess that, to this day, I cannot help fancying its little, furtive footsteps behind me when I come here after nightfall. I'm not afraid of the White Lady or the headless man or the skeletons, but I wish I had never imagined that baby's ghost into existence. How angry Marilla and Mrs. Barry were over that affair," concluded Anne, with reminiscent laughter.

Garlands of Autumn

The woods around the head of the marsh were full of purple vistas, threaded with gossamers. Past a dour plantation of gnarled spruces and a maple-fringed, sun-warm valley they found the "something" Gilbert was looking for.

"Ah, here it is," he said with satisfaction.

"An apple tree—and away back here!" exclaimed Anne delightedly.

"Yes, a veritable apple-bearing apple tree, too, here in the very midst of pines and beeches, a mile away from any orchard. I was here one day last spring and found it, all white with blossom. So I resolved I'd come again in the fall and see if it had been apples. See, it's loaded. They look good, too—tawny as russets but with a dusky red cheek. Most wild seedlings are green and uninviting."

"I suppose it sprang years ago from some chance-sown seed," said Anne dreamily. "And how it has grown and flourished and held its own here all alone among aliens, the brave determined thing!"

"Here's a fallen tree with a cushion of moss. Sit down, Anne—it will serve for a woodland throne. I'll climb for some apples. They all grow high—the tree had to reach up to the sunlight."

The apples proved to be delicious. Under the tawny skin was a white, white flesh, faintly veined with, red; and, besides their own proper apple taste, they had a certain wild, delightful tang no orchard-grown apple ever possessed.

"The fatal apple of Eden couldn't have had a rarer flavor," commented Anne. "But it's time we were going home. See, it was twilight three minutes ago and now it's moonlight. What a pity we couldn't have caught the moment of transformation. But such moments never are caught, I suppose."

"Let's go back around the marsh and home by way of Lover's Lane. Do you feel as disgruntled now as when you started out, Anne?"

"Not I. Those apples have been as manna to a hungry soul. I feel that I shall love Redmond and have a splendid four years there."

"And after those four years—what?"

"Oh, there's another bend in the road at their end," answered Anne lightly. "I've no idea what may be around it—I don't want to have. It's nicer not to know."

Lover's Lane was a dear place that night, still and mysteriously dim in the pale radiance of the moonlight. They loitered through it in a pleasant chummy silence, neither caring to talk.

"If Gilbert were always as he has been this evening how nice and simple everything would be," reflected Anne.

Gilbert was looking at Anne, as she walked along. In her light dress, with her slender delicacy, she made him think of a white iris.

"I wonder if I can ever make her care for me, he thought, with a pang of self-distrust.

3

Greeting and Farewell

Charlie Sloane, Gilbert Blythe and Anne Shirley left Avonlea the following Monday morning. Anne had hoped for a fine day. Diana was to drive her to the station and they wanted this, their last drive together for some time, to be a pleasant one. But when Anne went to bed Sunday night the east wind was moaning around Green Gables with an ominous prophecy which was fulfilled in the morning. Anne awoke to find raindrops pattering against her window and shadowing the pond's gray surface with

Greeting and Farewell 17

widening rings; hills and sea were hidden in mist, and the whole world seemed dim and dreary. Anne dressed in the cheerless gray dawn, for an early start was necessary to catch the boat train; she struggled against the tears that *would* well up in her eyes in spite of herself. She was leaving the home that was so dear to her, and something told her that she was leaving it forever, save as a holiday refuge. Things would never be the same again; coming back for vacations would not be living there. And oh, how dear and beloved everything was—that little white porch room, sacred to the dreams of girlhood, the old Snow Queen at the window, the brook in the hollow, the Dryad's Bubble, the Haunted Wood, and Lover's Lane—all the thousand and one dear spots where memories of the old years bided. Could she ever be really happy anywhere else?

Breakfast at Green Gables that morning was a rather doleful meal. Davy, for the first time in his life probably, could not eat, but blubbered shamelessly over his porridge. Nobody else seemed to have much appetite, save Dora, who tucked away her rations comfortably. Dora, like the immortal and most prudent Charlotte, who "went on cutting bread and butter" when her frenzied lover's body had been carried past on a shutter, was one of those fortunate creatures who are seldom disturbed by anything. Even at eight it took a great deal to ruffle Dora's placidity. She was sorry Anne was going away, of course, but was that any reason why she should fail to appreciate a poached egg on toast? Not at all. And, seeing that Davy could not eat his, Dora ate it for him.

Promptly on time Diana appeared with horse and buggy, her rosy face glowing above her raincoat. The good-byes had to be said then somehow. Mrs. Lynde came in from her quarters to give Anne a hearty embrace and warn her to be careful of her health, whatever she did. Marilla, brusque and tearless, pecked Anne's cheek and said she supposed they'd hear from her when she got settled. A casual observer might have concluded that

Anne's going mattered very little to her—unless said observer had happened to get a good look in her eyes. Dora kissed Anne primly and squeezed out two decorous little tears; but Davy, who had been crying on the back porch step ever since they rose from the table, refused to say good-bye at all. When he saw Anne coming towards him he sprang to his feet, bolted up the back stairs and hid in a clothes closet, out of which he would not come. His muffled howls were the last sounds Anne heard as she left Green Gables.

It rained heavily all the way to Bright River, to which station they had to go, since the branch line train from Carmody did not connect with the boat train. Charlie and Gilbert were on the station platform when they reached it, and the train was whistling. Anne had just time to get her ticket and trunk check, say a hurried farewell to Diana, and hasten on board. She wished she were going back with Diana to Avonlea; she knew she was going to die of homesickness. And oh, if only that dismal rain would stop pouring down as if the whole world were weeping over summer vanished and joys departed! Even Gilbert's presence brought her no comfort, for Charlie Sloane was there, too, and Sloanishness could be tolerated only in fine weather. It was absolutely insufferable in rain.

But when the boat steamed out of Charlottetown harbor things took a turn for the better. The rain ceased and the sun began to burst out goldenly now and again between the rents in the clouds, burnishing the gray seas with copper-hued radiance, and lighting up the mists that curtained the Island's red shores with gleams of gold foretokening a fine day after all. Besides, Charlie Sloane promptly became so seasick that he had to go below, and Anne and Gilbert were left alone on deck.

"I am very glad that all the Sloanes get seasick as soon as they go on water," thought Anne mercilessly. "I am sure I couldn't take my farewell look at the 'ould sod' with Charlie standing there pretending to look sentimentally at it, too."

Greeting and Farewell

"Well, we're off," remarked Gilbert unsentimentally.

"Yes, I feel like Byron's 'Childe Harold'—only it isn't really my 'native shore' that I'm watching," said Anne, winking her gray eyes vigorously. "Nova Scotia is that, I suppose. But one's native shore is the land one loves the best, and that's good old P.E.I. for me. I can't believe I didn't always live here. Those eleven years before I came seem like a bad dream. It's seven years since I crossed on this boat—the evening Mrs. Spencer brought me over from Hopetown. I can see myself, in that dreadful old wincey dress and faded sailor hat, exploring decks and cabins with enraptured curiosity. It was a fine evening; and how those red Island shores did gleam in the sunshine. Now I'm crossing the strait again. Oh, Gilbert, I do hope I'll like Redmond and Kingsport, but I'm sure I won't!"

"Where's all your philosophy gone, Anne?"

"It's all submerged under a great, swamping wave of loneliness and homesickness. I've longed for three years to go to Redmond—and now I'm going—and I wish I weren't! Never mind! I shall be cheerful and philosophical again after I have just one good cry. I *must* have that, 'as a went'—and I'll have to wait until I get into my boardinghouse bed tonight, wherever it may be, before I can have it. Then Anne will be herself again. I wonder if Davy has come out of the closet yet."

It was nine that night when their train reached Kingsport, and they found themselves in the blue-white glare of the crowded station. Anne felt horribly bewildered, but a moment later she was seized by Priscilla Grant, who had come to Kingsport on Saturday.

"Here you are, beloved! And I suppose you're as tired as I was when I got here Saturday night."

"Tired! Priscilla, don't talk of it. I'm tired, and green, and provincial, and only about ten years old. For pity's sake take your poor, broken-down chum to some place where she can hear herself think."

"I'll take you right up to our boardinghouse. I've a cab ready outside."

"It's such a blessing you're here, Prissy. If you weren't I think I should just sit down on my suitcase, here and now, and weep bitter tears. What a comfort one familiar face is in a howling wilderness of strangers!"

"Is that Gilbert Blythe over there, Anne? How he has grown up this past year! He was only a schoolboy when I taught in Carmody. And of course that's Charlie Sloane. *He* hasn't changed—couldn't! He looked just like that when he was born, and he'll look like that when he's eighty. This way, dear. We'll be home in twenty minutes."

"Home!" groaned Anne. "You mean we'll be in some horrible boardinghouse, in a still more horrible hall bedroom, looking out on a dingy back yard."

"It isn't a horrible boardinghouse, Anne-girl. Here's our cab. Hop in—the driver will get your trunk. Oh, yes, the boardinghouse—it's really a very nice place of its kind, as you'll admit tomorrow morning when a good night's sleep has turned your blues rosy pink. It's a big, old-fashioned, gray stone house on St. John Street, just a nice little constitutional from Redmond. It used to be the 'residence' of great folk, but fashion has deserted St. John Street and its houses only dream now of better days. They're so big that the people living in them have to take boarders just to fill up. At least, that is the reason our landladies are very anxious to impress on us. They're delicious, Anne—our landladies, I mean."

"How many are there?"

"Two. Miss Hannah Harvey and Miss Ada Harvey. They were born twins about fifty years ago."

"I can't get away from twins, it seems," smiled Anne. "Wherever I go they confront me."

"Oh, they're not twins now, dear. After they reached the age of thirty they never were twins again. Miss Hannah has grown

Greeting and Farewell 21

old, not too gracefully, and Miss Ada has stayed thirty, less gracefully still. I don't know whether Miss Hannah can smile or not; I've never caught her at it so far, but Miss Ada smiles all the time and that's worse. However, they're nice, kind souls, and they take two boarders every year because Miss Hannah's economical soul cannot bear to 'waste room space'—not because they need to or have to, as Miss Ada has told me seven times since Saturday night. As for our rooms, I admit they are hall bedrooms, and mine does look out on the back yard. Your room is a front one and looks out on Old St. John's graveyard, which is just across the street."

"That sounds gruesome," shivered Anne. "I think I'd rather have the back yard view."

"Oh, no, you wouldn't. Wait and see. Old St. John's is a darling place. It's been a graveyard so long that it's ceased to be one and has become one of the sights of Kingsport. I was all through it yesterday for a pleasure exertion. There's a big stone wall and a row of enormous trees all around it, and rows of trees all through it, and the queerest old tombstones, with the queerest and quaintest inscriptions. You'll go there to study, Anne, see if you don't. Of course, nobody is ever buried there now. But a few years ago they put up a beautiful monument to the memory of Nova Scotian soldiers who fell in the Crimean War. It is just opposite the entrance gates and there's 'scope for imagination' in it, as you used to say. Here's your trunk at last— and the boys coming to say good night. Must I really shake hands with Charlie Sloane, Anne? His hands are always so cold and fishy-feeling. We must ask them to call occasionally. Miss Hannah gravely told me we could have 'young gentlemen callers' two evenings in the week, if they went away at a reasonable hour; and Miss Ada asked me, smiling, please to be sure they didn't sit on her beautiful cushions. I promised to see to it; but goodness knows where else they *can* sit, unless they sit on the floor, for there are cushions on *everything*. Miss Ada even has an elaborate Battenburg one on top of the piano."

Anne was laughing by this time. Priscilla's gay chatter had the intended effect of cheering her up; homesickness vanished for the time being, and did not even return in full force when she finally found herself alone in her little bedroom. She went to her window and looked out. The street below was dim and quiet. Across it the moon was shining above the trees in Old St. John's, just behind the great dark head of the lion on the monument. Anne wondered if it could have been only that morning that she had left Green Gables. She had the sense of a long passage of time which one day of change and travel gives.

"I suppose that very moon is looking down on Green Gables now," she mused. "But I won't think about it—that way homesickness lies. I'm not even going to have my good cry. I'll put that off to a more convenient season, and just now I'll go calmly and sensibly to bed and to sleep."

4
April's Lady

Kingsport is a quaint old town, hearking back to early Colonial days, and wrapped in its ancient atmosphere, as some fine old dame in garments fashioned like those of her youth. Here and there it sprouts out into modernity, but at heart it is still unspoiled; it is full of curious relics, and haloed by the romance of many legends of the past. Once it was a mere frontier station on the fringe of the wilderness, and those were the days when

April's Lady

Indians kept life from being monotonous to the settlers. Then it grew to be a bone of contention between the British and the French, being occupied now by the one and now by the other, emerging from each occupation with some fresh scar of battling nations branded on it.

It has in its park a martello tower, autographed all over by tourists, a dismantled old French fort on the hills beyond the town, and several antiquated cannon in its public squares. It has other historic spots also, which may be hunted out by the curious, and none is more quaint and delightful than Old St. John's Cemetery at the very core of the town, with streets of quiet, old-time houses on two sides, and busy, bustling, modern thoroughfares on the others. Every citizen of Kingsport feels a thrill of possessive pride in Old St. John's, for, if he be of any pretensions at all, he has an ancestor buried there, with a queer, crooked slab at his head, or else sprawling protectively over the grave, on which all the main facts of his history are recorded. For the most part no great art or skill was lavished on those old tombstones. The larger number are of roughly chiselled brown or gray native stone, and only in a few cases is there any attempt at ornamentation. Some are adorned with skull and crossbones, and this grizzly decoration is frequently coupled with a cherub's head. Many are prostrate and in ruins. Into almost all Time's tooth has been gnawing, until some inscriptions have been completely effaced, and others can only be deciphered with difficulty. The graveyard is very full and very bowery, for it is surrounded and intersected by rows of elms and willows, beneath whose shade the sleepers must lie very dreamlessly, forever crooned to by the winds and leaves over them, and quite undisturbed by the clamor of traffic just beyond.

Anne took the first of many rambles in Old St. John's the next afternoon. She and Priscilla had gone to Redmond in the forenoon and registered as students, after which there was nothing more to do that day. The girls gladly made their escape, for it was not exhilarating to be surrounded by crowds of strangers, most of whom had a rather alien appearance, as if not quite sure where they belonged.

The "freshettes" stood about in detached groups of two or three, looking askance at each other; the "freshies," wiser in their day and generation, had banded themselves together on the big staircase of the entrance hall, where they were shouting out glees with all the vigor of youthful lungs, as a species of defiance to their traditional enemies, the Sophomores, a few of whom were prowling loftily about, looking properly disdainful of the "unlicked cubs" on the stairs. Gilbert and Charlie were nowhere to be seen.

"Little did I think the day would ever come when I'd be glad of the sight of a Sloane," said Priscilla, as they crossed the campus, "but I'd welcome Charlie's goggle eyes almost ecstatically. At least, they'd be familiar eyes."

"Oh," sighed Anne. "I can't describe how I felt when I was standing there, waiting my turn to be registered—as insignificant as the teeniest drop in a most enormous bucket. It's bad enough to feel insignificant, but it's unbearable to have it grained into your soul that you will never, *can* never, be anything but insignificant, and that is how I did feel—as if I were invisible to the naked eye and some of those Sophs might step on me. I knew I would go down to my grave unwept, unhonored and unsung."

"Wait till next year," comforted Priscilla. "Then we'll be able to look as bored and sophisticated as any Sophomore of them all. No doubt it is rather dreadful to feel insignificant; but I think it's better then to feel as big and awkward as I did—as if I were sprawled all over Redmond. That's how I felt—I suppose because I was a good two inches taller than any one else in the crowd. *I* wasn't afraid a Soph might walk over me; I was afraid they'd take me for an elephant, or an overgrown sample of a potato-fed Islander."

"I suppose the trouble is we can't forgive big Redmond for not being little Queen's," said Anne, gathering about her the shreds of her old cheerful philosophy to cover her nakedness of spirit. "When we left Queen's we knew everybody and had a place of our own. I suppose we have been unconsciously expecting to take life up at Redmond just where we left off at Queen's, and now we feel as if the ground had slipped from under our feet. I'm thankful that neither Mrs. Lynde nor Mrs. Elisha Wright know, or ever will know, my state of mind at present. They would exult in saying 'I told you so,' and be convinced it was the beginning of the end. Whereas it is just the end of the beginning."

"Exactly. That sounds more Anneish. In a little while we'll be acclimated and acquainted, and all will be well. Anne, did you notice the girl who stood alone just outside the door of the coeds' dressing room all the morning—the pretty one with the brown eyes and crooked mouth?"

"Yes, I did. I noticed her particularly because she seemed the only creature there who *looked* as lonely and friendless as I *felt.* I had *you,* but she had no one."

"I think she felt pretty all-by-herselfish, too. Several times I saw her make a motion as if to cross over to us, but she never did it—too shy, I suppose. I wished she would come. If I hadn't felt so much like the aforesaid elephant I'd have gone to her. But I couldn't lumber across that big hall with all those boys howling on the stairs. She was the prettiest freshette I saw today, but probably favor is deceitful and even beauty is vain on your first day at Redmond," concluded Priscilla with a laugh.

"I'm going across to Old St. John's after lunch," said Anne. "I don't know that a graveyard is a very good place to go to get cheered up, but it seems the only get-at-able place where there are trees, and trees I must have. I'll sit on one of those old slabs and shut my eyes and imagine I'm in the Avonlea woods."

Anne did not do that, however, for she found enough of interest in Old St. John's to keep her eyes wide open. They went in by the entrance gates, past the simple, massive, stone arch surmounted by the great lion of England.

*"'And on Inkerman yet the wild bramble is gory,
And those bleak heights henceforth shall be famous in story,'"*

quoted Anne, looking at it with a thrill. They found themselves in a dim, cool, green place where winds were fond of purring. Up and down the long grassy aisles they wandered, reading the quaint, voluminous epitaphs, carved in an age that had more leisure than our own.

"'Here lieth the body of Albert Crawford, Esq.,'" read Anne from a worn, gray slab, "'for many years Keeper of His Majesty's Ordnance at Kingsport. He served in the army till the peace of 1763, when he retired from bad health. He was a brave officer, the best of husbands, the best of fathers, the best of friends. He died October 29th, 1792, aged 84 years.' There's an epitaph for you, Prissy. There is certainly some 'scope for imagination' in it. How full such a life must have been of adventure! And as for his personal qualities, I'm sure human eulogy couldn't go further. I wonder if they told him he was all those best things while he was alive."

"Here's another," said Priscilla. "Listen—'To the memory of Alexander Ross, who died on the 22nd of September, 1840, aged 43 years. This is raised as a tribute of affection by one whom he served so faithfully for 27 years that he was regarded as a friend, deserving the fullest confidence and attachment.'"

"A very good epitaph," commented Anne thoughtfully. "I wouldn't wish a better. We are all servants of some sort, and if

April's Lady

the fact that we are faithful can be truthfully inscribed on our tombstones nothing more need be added. Here's a sorrowful little gray stone, Prissy—'to the memory of a favorite child.' And here is another 'erected to the memory of one who is buried elsewhere.' I wonder where that unknown grave is. Really, Pris, the graveyards of today will never be as interesting as this. You were right—I shall come here often. I love it already. I see we're not alone here—there's a girl down at the end of this avenue."

"Yes, and I believe it's the very girl we saw at Redmond this morning. I've been watching her for five minutes. She has started to come up the avenue exactly half a dozen times, and half a dozen times has she turned and gone back. Either she's dreadfully shy or she has got something on her conscience. Let's go and meet her. It's easier to get acquainted in a graveyard than at Redmond, I believe."

They walked down the long grassy arcade towards the stranger, who was sitting on a gray slab under an enormous willow. She was certainly very pretty, with a vivid, irregular, bewitching type of prettiness. There was a gloss as of brown nuts on her satin-smooth hair and a soft, ripe glow on her round cheeks. Her eyes were big and brown and velvety, under oddly-pointed black brows, and her crooked mouth was rose-red. She wore a smart brown suit, with two very modish little shoes peeping from beneath it; and her hat of dull pink straw, wreathed with golden-brown poppies, had the indefinable, unmistakable air which pertains to the "creation" of an artist in millinery. Priscilla had a sudden stinging consciousness that her own hat had been trimmed by her village store milliner, and Anne wondered uncomfortably if the blouse she had made herself, and which Mrs. Lynde had fitted, looked *very* countrified and home-made besides the stranger's smart attire. For a moment both girls felt like turning back.

But they had already stopped and turned towards the gray slab. It was too late to retreat, for the brown-eyed girl had evidently concluded that they were coming to speak to her. Instantly she sprang up and came forward with outstretched hand and a gay, friendly smile in which there seemed not a shadow of either shyness or burdened conscience.

"Oh, I want to know who you two girls are," she exclaimed eagerly. "I've been *dying* to know. I saw you at Redmond this morning. Say, wasn't it *awful* there? For the time I wished I had stayed home and got married."

Anne and Priscilla both broke into unconstrained laughter at this unexpected conclusion. The brown-eyed girl laughed, too.

"I really did. I *could* have, you know. Come, let's all sit down on this gravestone and get acquainted. It won't be hard. I know we're going to adore each other—I knew it as soon as I saw you at Redmond this morning. I wanted so much to go right over and hug you both."

"Why didn't you?" asked Priscilla.

"Because I simply couldn't make up my mind to do it. I never can make up my mind about anything myself—I'm always afflicted with indecision. Just as soon as I decide to do something I feel in my bones that another course would be the correct one. It's a dreadful misfortune, but I was born that way, and there is no use in blaming me for it, as some people do. So I couldn't make up my mind to go and speak to you, much as I wanted to."

" We thought you were too shy," said Anne.

"No, no, dear. Shyness isn't among the many failings—or virtues—of Philippa Gordon—Phil for short. Do call me Phil right off. Now, what are your handles?"

"She's Priscilla Grant," said Anne, pointing.

"And *she's* Anne Shirley," said Priscilla, pointing in turn.

April's Lady

"And we're from the Island," said both together.

"I hail from Bolingbroke, Nova Scotia," said Philippa.

"Bolingbroke!" exclaimed Anne. "Why, that is where I was born."

"Do you really mean it? Why, that makes you a Bluenose after all."

"No, it doesn't," retorted Anne. "Wasn't it Dan O'Connell who said that if a man was born in a stable it didn't make him a horse? I'm Island to the core."

"Well, I'm glad you were born in Bolingbroke anyway. It makes us kind of neighbors, doesn't it? And I like that, because when I tell you secrets it won't be as if I were telling them to a stranger. I *have* to tell them. I can't keep secrets—it's no use to try. That's my worst failing—that, and indecision, as aforesaid. Would you believe it?—it took me half an hour to decide what hat to wear when I was coming here—*here,* to a graveyard! At first I inclined to my brown one with the feather; but as soon as I put it on I thought this pink one with the floppy brim would be more becoming. When I got *it* pinned in place I liked the brown one better. At last I put them close together on the bed, shut my eyes, and jabbed with a hat pin. The pin speared the pink one, so I put it on. It is becoming, isn't it? Tell me, what do you think of my looks?"

At this naïve demand, made in a perfectly serious tone, Priscilla laughed again. But Anne said, impulsively squeezing Philippa's hand,

"We thought this morning that you were the prettiest girl we saw at Redmond."

Philippa's crooked mouth flashed into a bewitching, crooked smile over very white little teeth.

"I thought that myself," was her next astounding statement, "but I wanted some one else's opinion to bolster mine up. I can't decide even on my own appearance. Just as soon as I've decided that I'm pretty I begin to feel miserably that I'm not. Besides, I have a horrible old great-aunt who is always saying to me, with a mournful sigh, 'You were such a pretty baby. It's strange how children change when they grow up.' I adore aunts, but I detest great-aunts. Please tell me quite often that I am pretty, if you don't mind. I feel so much more comfortable when I can believe I'm pretty. And I'll be just as obliging to you if you want me to—I *can* be, with a clear conscience."

"Thanks," laughed Anne, "but Priscilla and I are so firmly convinced of our own good looks that we don't need any assurance about them, so you needn't trouble."

"Oh, you're laughing at me. I know you think I'm abominably vain, but I'm not. There really isn't one spark of vanity in me. And I'm never a bit grudging about paying compliments to other girls when they deserve them. I'm so glad I know you folks. I came up on Saturday and I've nearly died of homesickness ever since. It's a horrible feeling, isn't it? In Bolingbroke I'm an important personage, and in Kingsport I'm just nobody! There were times when I could feel my soul turning a delicate blue. Where do you hang out?"

"Thirty-eight St. John's Street."

"Better and better. Why, I'm just around the corner on Wallace Street. I don't like my boardinghouse, though. It's bleak and lonesome, and my room looks out on such an unholy back yard. It's the ugliest place in the world. As for cats—well, surely *all* the Kingsport cats can't congregate there at night, but half of them must. I adore cats on hearth rugs, snoozing before nice, friendly fires, but cats in back yards at midnight are totally different animals. The first night I was here I cried all night, and so did the cats. You should have seen my nose in the morning. How I wished I had never left home!"

"I don't know how you managed to make up your mind to come to Redmond at all, if you are really such an undecided person," said amused Priscilla.

April's Lady

"Bless your heart, honey, I didn't. It was father who wanted me to come here. His heart was set on it—why, I don't know. It seems perfectly ridiculous to think of *me* studying for a B.A. degree, doesn't it? Not but what I can do it, all right. I have heaps of brains."

"Oh!" said Priscilla vaguely.

"Yes. But it's such hard work to use them. And B.A.'s are such learned, dignified, wise, solemn creatures—they must be. No, *I* didn't want to come to Redmond. I did it just to oblige father. He *is* such a duck. Besides, I knew if I stayed home I'd have to get married. Mother wanted that—wanted it decidedly. Mother has plenty of decision. But I really hated the thought of being married for a few years yet. I want to have heaps of fun before I settle down. And, ridiculous as the idea of my being a B.A. is, the idea of my being an old married woman is still more absurd, isn't it? I'm only eighteen. No, I concluded I would rather come to Redmond than be married. Besides, how could I ever have made up my mind which man to marry?"

"Were there so many?" laughed Anne.

"Heaps. The boys like me awfully—they really do. But there were only two that mattered. The rest were all too young and too poor. I must marry a rich man, you know."

"Why must you?"

"Honey, you couldn't imagine *me* being a poor man's wife, could you? I can't do a single useful thing, and I am *very* extravagant. Oh, no, my husband must have heaps of money. So that narrowed them down to two. But I couldn't decide between two any easier than between two hundred. I knew perfectly well that whichever one I chose I'd regret all my life that I hadn't married the other."

"Didn't you—love—either of them?" asked Anne, a little hesitatingly. It was not easy for her to speak to a stranger of the great mystery and transformation of life.

"Goodness, no. *I* couldn't love anybody. It isn't in me. Besides I wouldn't want to. Being in love makes you a perfect slave, *I* think. And it would give a man such power to hurt you. I'd be afraid. No, no, Alec and Alonzo are two dear boys, and I like them both so much that I really don't know which I like the better. That is the trouble. Alec is the best looking, of course, and I simply couldn't marry a man who wasn't handsome. He is good-tempered, too, and has lovely, curly, black hair. He's rather too perfect—I don't believe I'd like a perfect husband—somebody I could never find fault with."

"Then why not marry Alonzo?" asked Priscilla gravely.

"Think of marrying a name like Alonzo!" said Phil dolefully. "I don't believe I could endure it. But he has a classic nose, and it *would* be a comfort to have a nose in the family that could be depended on. I can't depend on mine. So far, it takes after the Gordon pattern, but I'm so afraid it will develop Byrne tendencies as I grow older. I examine it every day anxiously to make sure it's still Gordon. Mother was a Byrne and has the Byrne nose in the Byrnest degree. Wait till you see it. I adore nice noses. Your nose is awfully nice, Anne Shirley. Alonzo's nose nearly turned the balance in his favor. But *Alonzo!* No, I couldn't decide. If I could have done as I did with the hats—stood them both up together, shut my eyes, and jabbed with a hatpin—it would have been quite easy."

"What did Alec and Alonzo feel like when you came away?" queried Priscilla.

"Oh, they still have hope. I told them they'd have to wait till I could make up my mind. They're quite willing to wait. They both worship me, you know. Meanwhile, I intend to have a good time. I expect I shall have heaps of beaux at Redmond. I can't be happy unless I have, you know. But don't you think the freshmen are fearfully homely? I saw only one really handsome fellow among them. He went away before you came. I heard his chum call him Gilbert. His chum had eyes that stuck out *that far*. But you're not going yet, girls? Don't go yet."

"I think we must," said Anne, rather coldly. "It's getting late, and I've some work to do."

"But you'll both come to see me, won't you?" asked Philippa, getting up and putting an arm around each. "And let me come to see you. I want to be chummy with you. I've taken such a fancy to you both. And I haven't quite disgusted you with my frivolity, have I?"

"Not quite," laughed Anne, responding to Phil's squeeze, with a return of cordiality.

"Because I'm not half so silly as I seem on the surface, you know. You just accept Philippa Gordon, as the Lord made her, with all her faults, and I believe you'll come to like her. Isn't this graveyard a sweet place? I'd love to be buried here. Here's a grave I didn't see before—this one in the iron railing—oh, girls, look, see—the stone says it's the grave of a middy who was killed in the fight between the *Shannon* and the *Chesapeake*. Just fancy!"

Anne paused by the railing and looked at the worn stone, her pulses thrilling with sudden excitement. The old graveyard, with its over-arching trees and long aisles of shadows, faded from her sight. Instead, she saw the Kingsport Harbor of nearly a century agone. Out of the mist came slowly a great frigate, brilliant with "the meteor flag of England." Behind her was another, with a still, heroic form, wrapped in his own starry flag, lying on the quarter deck—the gallant *Lawrence*. Time's finger had turned back his pages, and that was the *Shannon* sailing triumphant up the bay with the *Chesapeake* as her prize.

"Come back, Anne Shirley—come back," laughed Philippa, pulling her arm. "You're a hundred years away from us. Come back."

Anne came back with a sigh; her eyes were shining softly.

'I've always loved that old story," she said, "and although the English won that victory, I think it was because of the brave, defeated commander I love it. This grave seems to bring it so near and make it so real. This poor little middy was only eighteen. He 'died of desperate wounds received in gallant action'—so reads his epitaph. It is such as a soldier might wish for."

Before she turned away, Anne unpinned the little cluster of purple pansies she wore and dropped it softly on the grave of the boy who had perished in the great sea-duel.

"Well, what do you think of our new friend?" asked Priscilla, when Phil had left them.

"I like her. There is something very lovable about her, in spite of all her nonsense. I believe, as she says herself, that she isn't half as silly as she sounds. She's a dear, kissable baby—and I don't know that she'll ever really grow up."

"I like her, too," said Priscilla decidedly. "She talks as much about boys as Ruby Gillis does. But it always enrages or sickens me to hear Ruby, whereas I just wanted to laugh good-naturedly at Phil. Now, what is the why of that?"

"There is a difference," said Anne meditatively. "I think it's because Ruby is really so *conscious* of boys. She plays at love and love-making. Besides, you feel, when she is boasting of her beaux that she is doing it to rub it well into you that you haven't half so many. Now, when Phil talks of her beaux it sounds as if she was just speaking of chums. She really looks upon boys as good comrades, and she is pleased when she has dozens of them tagging round, simply because she likes to be popular and to be thought popular. Even Alec and Alonzo—I'll never be able to think of those two names separately after this—are to her just two playfellows who want her to play with them all their lives. I'm glad we met her, and I'm glad we went to Old St. John's. I believe I've put forth a tiny soul-root into Kingsport soil this afternoon. I hope so. I hate to feel transplanted."

5

Letters from Home

For the next three weeks Anne and Priscilla continued to feel as strangers in a strange land. Then, suddenly, everything seemed to fall into focus—Redmond, professors, classes, students, studies, social doings. Life became homogeneous again, instead of being made up of detached fragments. The Freshmen, instead of being a collection of unrelated individuals, found themselves a class, with a class spirit, a class yell, class interests, class antipathies, and class ambitions. They won the day in the annual "Arts Rush" against the Sophomores, and thereby gained the respect of all the classes, and an enormous, confidence-giving opinion of themselves. For three years the Sophomores had won in the "rush"; that the victory of this year perched upon the Freshmen's banner was attributed to the strategic generalship of Gilbert Blythe, who marshalled the campaign and originated certain new tactics, which demoralized the Sophs and swept the Freshmen to triumph. As a reward of merit he was elected president of the Freshman Class, a position of honor and responsibility—from a Fresh point of view, at least—coveted by many. He was also invited to join the "Lambs"—Redmondese for Lamba Theta—a compliment rarely paid to a Freshman. As a preparatory initiation ordeal he had to parade the principal business streets of Kingsport for a whole day wearing a sunbonnet and a voluminous kitchen apron of gaudily flowered calico. This he did cheerfully, doffing his sunbonnet with courtly grace when he met ladies of his acquaintance. Charlie Sloane, who had not been asked to join the Lambs, told Anne he did not see how Blythe could do it, and *he,* for his part, could never humiliate himself so.

"Fancy Charlie Sloane in a 'caliker' apron and a 'sunbunnit,'" giggled Priscilla. "He'd look exactly like his old Grandmother

Sloane. Gilbert, now, looked as much like a man in them as in his own proper habiliments."

Anne and Priscilla found themselves in the thick of the social life of Redmond. That this came about so speedily was due in great measure to Philippa Gordon. Philippa was the daughter of a rich and well-known man, and belonged to an old and exclusive "Bluenose" family. This, combined with her beauty and charm—a charm acknowledged by all who met her— promptly opened the gates of all cliques, clubs, and classes in Redmond to her; and where she went Anne and Priscilla went, too. Phil "adored" Anne and Priscilla, especially Anne. She was a loyal little soul, crystal-free from any form of snobbishness. "Love me, love my friends" seemed to be her unconscious motto. Without effort, she took them with her into her ever widening circle of acquaintanceship, and the two Avonlea girls found their social pathway at Redmond made very easy and pleasant for them, to the envy and wonderment of the other freshettes, who, lacking Philippa's sponsorship, were doomed to remain rather on the fringe of things during their first college year.

To Anne and Priscilla, with their more serious views of life, Phil remained the amusing, lovable baby she had seemed on their first meeting. Yet, as she said herself, she had "heaps" of brains. When or where she found time to study was a mystery, for she seemed always in demand for some kind of "fun," and her home evenings were crowded with callers. She had all the "beaux" that heart could desire, for nine-tenths of the Freshmen and a big fraction of all the other classes were rivals for her smiles. She was naively delighted over this, and gleefully recounted each new conquest to Anne and Priscilla, with comments that might have made the unlucky lover's ears burn fiercely.

"Alec and Alonzo don't seem to have any serious rival yet," remarked Anne, teasingly.

Letters from Home

"Not one," agreed Philippa. "I write them both every week and tell them all about my young men here. I'm sure it must amuse them. But, of course, the one I like best I can't get. Gilbert Blythe won't take any notice of me, except to look at me as if I were a nice little kitten he'd like to pat. Too well I know the reason. I owe you a grudge, Queen Anne. I really ought to hate you and instead I love you madly, and I'm miserable if I don't see you every day. You're different from any girl I ever knew before. When you look at me in a certain way I feel what an insignificant, frivolous little beast I am, and I long to be better and wiser and stronger. And then I make good resolutions; but the first nice-looking mannie who comes my way knocks them all out of my head. Isn't college life magnificent? It's so funny to think I hated it that first day. But if I hadn't I might never got really acquainted with you. Anne, please tell me over again that you like me a little bit. I yearn to hear it."

"I like you a big bit—and I think you're a dear, sweet, adorable, velvety, clawless, little—kitten," laughed Anne, "but I don't see when you ever get time to learn your lessons."

Phil must have found time for she held her own in every class of her year. Even the grumpy old professor of Mathematics, who detested coeds, and had bitterly opposed their admission to Redmond, couldn't floor her. She led the freshettes everywhere, except in English, where Anne Shirley left her far behind. Anne herself found the studies of her Freshman year very easy, thanks in great part to the steady work she and Gilbert had put in during those two past years in Avonlea. This left her more time for a social life which she thoroughly enjoyed. But never for a moment did she forget Avonlea and the friends there. To her, the happiest moments in each week were those in which letters came from home. It was not until she had got her first letters that she began to think she could ever like Kingsport or feel at home there. Before they came, Avonlea had seemed thousands of miles away; those letters brought it near and linked the old life to the new so closely that they began to seem one and the same, instead of two hopelessly segregated existences. The first batch contained six letters, from Jane Andrews, Ruby Gillis, Diana Barry, Marilla, Mrs. Lynde, and Davy. Jane's was a copper-plate production, with every "t" nicely crossed and every "i" precisely dotted, and not an interesting sentence in it. She never mentioned the school, concerning which Anne was avid to hear; she never answered one of the questions Anne had asked in her letter. But she told Anne how many yards of lace she had recently crocheted, and the kind of weather they were having in Avonlea, and how she intended to have her new dress made, and the way she felt when her head ached. Ruby Gillis wrote a gushing epistle deploring Anne's absence, assuring her she was horribly missed in everything, asking what the Redmond "fellows" were like, and filling the rest with accounts of her own harrowing experiences with her numerous admirers. It was a silly, harmless letter, and Anne would have laughed over it had it not been for the postscript. "Gilbert seems to be enjoying Redmond, judging from his letters," wrote Ruby. "I don't think Charlie is so stuck on it."

So Gilbert was writing to Ruby! Very well. He had a perfect right to, of course. Only—!! Anne did not know that Ruby had written the first letter and that Gilbert had answered it from mere courtesy. She tossed Ruby's letter aside contemptuously. But it took all Diana's breezy, newsy, delightful epistle to banish the sting of Ruby's postscript. Diana's letter contained a little too much Fred, but was otherwise crowded and crossed with items of interest, and Anne almost felt herself back in Avonlea while reading it. Marilla's was a rather prim and colorless epistle, severely innocent of gossip or emotion. Yet somehow it conveyed to Anne a whiff of the wholesome, simple life at Green Gables, with its savor of ancient peace, and the steadfast

Letters from Home 39

abiding love that was there for her. Mrs. Lynde's letter was full of church news. Having broken up housekeeping, Mrs. Lynde had more time than ever to devote to church affairs and had flung herself into them heart and soul. She was at present much worked up over the poor "supplies" they were having in the vacant Avonlea pulpit.

"I don't believe any but fools enter the ministry nowadays," she wrote bitterly. "Such candidates as they have sent us, and such stuff as they preach! Half of it ain't true, and, what's worse, it ain't sound doctrine. The one we have now is the worst of the lot. He mostly takes a text and preaches about something else. And he says he doesn't believe all the heathen will be eternally lost. The idea! If they won't all the money we've been giving to Foreign Missions will be clean wasted, that's what! Last Sunday night he announced that next Sunday he'd preach on the axe-head that swam. I think he'd better confine himself to the Bible and leave sensational subjects alone. Things have come to a pretty pass if a minister can't find enough in Holy Writ to preach about, that's what. What church do you attend, Anne? I hope you go regularly. People are apt to get so careless about church-going away from home, and I understand college students are great sinners in this respect. I'm told many of them actually study their lessons on Sunday. I hope you'll never sink that low, Anne. Remember how you were brought up. And be very careful what friends you make. You never know what sort of creatures are in them colleges. Outwardly they may be as whited sepulchers and inwardly as ravening wolves, that's what. You'd better not have anything to say to any young man who isn't from the Island.

"I forgot to tell you what happened the day the minister called here. It was the funniest thing I ever saw. I said to Marilla, 'If Anne had been here wouldn't she have had a laugh?' Even Marilla laughed. You know he's a very short, fat little man with bow legs. Well, that old pig of Mr. Harrison's—the big, tall one—had wandered over here that day again and broke into the yard, and it got into the back porch, unbeknowns to us, and it was there when the minister appeared in the doorway. It made one wild bolt to get out, but there was nowhere to bolt to except between them bow legs. So there it went, and, being as it was so big and the minister so little, it took him clean off his feet and carried him away. His hat went one way and his cane another, just as Marilla and I got to the door. I'll never forget the look of him. And that poor pig was near scared to death. I'll never be able to read that account in the Bible of the swine that rushed madly down the steep place into the sea without seeing Mr. Harrison's pig careering down the hill with that minister. I guess the pig thought he had the Old Boy on his back instead of inside of him. I was thankful the twins weren't about. It wouldn't have been the right thing for them to have seen a minister in such an undignified predicament. Just before they got to the brook the minister jumped off or fell off. The pig rushed through the brook like mad and up through the woods. Marilla and I run down and helped the minister get up and brush his coat. He wasn't hurt, but he was mad. He seemed to hold Marilla and me responsible for it all, though we told him the pig didn't belong to us, and had been pestering us all summer. Besides, what did he come to the back door for? You'd never have caught Mr. Allan doing that. It'll be a long time before we get a man like Mr. Allan. But it's an ill wind that blows no good. We've never seen hoof or hair of that pig since, and it's my belief we never will.

"Things is pretty quiet in Avonlea. I don't find Green Gables as lonesome as I expected. I think I'll start another cotton warp quilt this winter. Mrs. Silas Sloane has a handsome new apple-leaf pattern.

"When I feel that I must have some excitement I read the murder trials in that Boston paper my niece sends me. I never used to do it, but they're real interesting. The States must be an awful place. I hope you'll never go there, Anne. But the way girls roam over the earth now is something terrible. It always makes me think of Satan in the Book of Job, going to and fro and walking up and down. I don't believe the Lord ever intended it, that's what.

"Davy has been pretty good since you went away. One day he was bad and Marilla punished him by making him wear Dora's apron all day, and then he went and cut all Dora's aprons up. I spanked him for that and then he went and chased my rooster to death.

"The MacPhersons have moved down to my place. She's a great housekeeper and very particular. She's rooted all my June lilies up because she says they make a garden look so untidy. Thomas set them lilies out when we were married. Her husband seems a nice sort of a man, but she can't get over being an old maid, that's what.

"Don't study too hard, and be sure and put your winter underclothes on as soon as the weather gets cool. Marilla worries a lot about you, but I tell her you've got a lot more sense than I ever thought you would have at one time, and that you'll be all right."

Davy's letter plunged into a grievance at the start.

"Dear anne, please write and tell marilla not to tie me to the rale of the bridge when I go fishing the boys make fun of me when she does. Its awful lonesome here without you but grate fun in school. Jane andrews is crosser than you. I scared mrs. lynde with a jacky lantern last nite. She was offel mad and she was mad cause I chased her old rooster round the yard till he fell down ded. I didn't mean to make him fall down ded. What made him die, anne, I want to know.

Mrs. lynde threw him into the pig pen she mite of sold him to mr. blair. mr. blair is giving 50 sense apeace for good ded roosters now. I herd mrs. lynde asking the minister to pray for her. What did she do that was so bad, anne, I want to know. I've got a kite with a magnificent tail, anne. Milty bolter told me a grate story in school yesterday. it is troo. old Joe Mosey and Leon were playing cards one nite last week in the woods. The cards were on a stump and a big black man bigger than the trees come along and grabbed the cards and the stump and disapered with a nays like thunder. Ill bet they were skared. Milty says the black man was the old harry. was he, anne, I want to know. Mr. kimball over at spenservale is very sick and will have to go to the hospitable. please excuse me while I ask marilla if thats spelled rite. Marilla says its the silem he has to go to not the other place. He thinks he has a snake inside of him. whats it like to have a snake inside of you, anne. I want to know. mrs. lawrence bell is sick to. mrs. lynde says that all that is the matter with her is that she thinks too much about her insides."

"I wonder," said Anne, as she folded up her letters, "what Mrs. Lynde would think of Philippa."

6

In the Park

"What are you going to do with yourselves today, girls?" asked Philippa, popping into Anne's room one Saturday afternoon.

"We are going for a walk in the park," answered Anne. "I

In the Park

ought to stay in and finish my blouse. But I couldn't sew on a day like this. There's something in the air that gets into my blood and makes a sort of glory in my soul. My fingers would twitch and I'd sew a crooked seam. So it's ho for the park and the pines."

"Does 'we' include any one but yourself and Priscilla?"

"Yes, it includes Gilbert and Charlie, and we'll be very glad if it will include you, also."

"But," said Philippa dolefully, "if I go I'll have to be gooseberry, and that will be a new experience for Philippa Gordon."

"Well, new experiences are broadening. Come along, and you'll be able to sympathize with all poor souls who have to play gooseberry often. But where are all the victims?"

"Oh, I was tired of them all and simply couldn't be bothered with any of them today. Besides, I've been feeling a little blue—just a pale, elusive azure. It isn't serious enough for anything darker. I wrote Alec and Alonzo last week. I put the letters into envelopes and addressed them, but I didn't seal them up. That evening something funny happened. That is, Alec would think it funny, but Alonzo wouldn't be likely to. I was in a hurry, so I snatched Alec's letter—as I thought—out of the envelope and scribbled down a postscript. Then I mailed both letters. I got Alonzo's reply this morning. Girls, I had put that postscript to *his* letter and he was furious. Of course he'll get over it—and I don't care if he doesn't—but it spoiled my day. So I thought I'd come to you darlings to get cheered up. After the football season opens I won't have any spare Saturday afternoons. I adore football. I've got the most gorgeous cap and sweater striped in Redmond colors to wear to the games. To be sure, a little way off I'll look like a walking barber's pole. Do you know that that Gilbert of yours has been elected Captain of the Freshman football team?"

"Yes, he told us so last evening," said Priscilla, seeing that outraged Anne would not answer. "He and Charlie were down. We knew they were coming, so we painstakingly put out of sight or out of reach all Miss Ada's cushions. That very elaborate one with the raised embroidery I dropped on the floor in the corner behind the chair it was on. I thought it would be safe there. But would you believe it? Charlie Sloane made for that chair, noticed the cushion behind it, solemnly fished it up, and sat on it the whole evening. Such a wreck of a cushion as it was! Poor Miss Ada asked me today, still smiling, but oh, so reproachfully, why I had allowed it to be sat upon. I told her I hadn't—that it was a matter of predestination coupled with inveterate Sloanishness and I wasn't a match for both combined."

"Miss Ada's cushions are really getting on my nerves," said Anne. "She finished two new ones last week, stuffed and embroidered within an inch of their lives. There being absolutely no other cushionless place to put them she stood them up against the wall on the stair landing. They topple over half the time and if we come up or clown the stairs in the dark we fall over them. Last Sunday, when Dr. Davis prayed for all those exposed to the perils of the sea, I added in thought 'and for all those who live in houses where cushions are loved not wisely but too well!' There! we're ready, and I see the boys coming through Old St. John's. Do you cast in your lot with us, Phil?"

"I'll go, if I can walk with Priscilla and Charlie. That will be a bearable degree of gooseberry. That Gilbert of yours is a darling, Anne, but why *does* he go around so much with Goggle-eyes?"

Anne stiffened. She had no great liking for Charlie Sloane; but he was of Avonlea, so no outsider had any business to laugh at him.

"Charlie and Gilbert have always been friends," she said coldly. "Charlie is a nice boy. He's not to blame for his eyes."

"Don't tell me that! He is! He must have done something dreadful in a previous existence to be punished with such eyes.

In the Park 45

Pris and I are going to have such sport with him this afternoon. We'll make fun of him to his face and he'll never know it."

Doubtless; "the abandoned P's," as Anne called them, did carry out their amiable intentions. But Sloane was blissfully ignorant; he thought he was quite a fine fellow to be walking with two such coeds, especially Philippa Gordon, the class beauty and belle. It must surely impress Anne. She would see that some people appreciated him at his real value.

Gilbert and Anne loitered a little behind the others, enjoying the calm, still beauty of the autumn afternoon under the pines of the park, on the road that climbed and twisted around the harbor shore.

"The silence here is like a prayer, isn't it?" said Anne, her face upturned to the shining sky. "How I love the pines! They seem to strike their roots deep into the romance of all the ages. It is so comforting to creep away now and then for a good talk with them. I always feel so happy out here."

*"'And so in mountain solitudes o'ertaken
As by some spell divine,
Their cares drop from them like the needles shaken
From out the gusty pine,'"*

quoted Gilbert.

"They make our little ambitions seem rather petty, don't they, Anne?"

"I think, if ever any great sorrow came to me, I would come to the pines for comfort," said Anne dreamily.

"I hope no great sorrow ever will come to you, Anne," said Gilbert, who could not connect the idea of sorrow with the vivid, joyous creature beside him, unwitting that those who can soar to the highest heights can also plunge to the deepest depths, and that the natures which enjoy most keenly are those which also suffer most sharply.

"But there must—sometime," mused Anne. "Life seems like a cup of glory held to my lips just now. But there must be some bitterness in it—there is in every cup. I shall taste mine some day. Well, I hope I shall be strong and brave to meet it. And I hope it won't be through my own fault that it will come. Do you remember what Dr. Davis said last Sunday evening—that the sorrows God sent us brought comfort and strength with them, while the sorrows we brought on ourselves, through folly or wickedness, were by far the hardest to bear? But we mustn't talk of sorrow on an afternoon like this. It's meant for the sheer joy of living, isn't it?"

"If I had my way I'd shut everything out of your life but happiness and pleasure, Anne," said Gilbert in the tone that meant "danger ahead."

"Then you would be very unwise," rejoined Anne hastily. "I'm sure no life can be properly developed and rounded out without some trial and sorrow—though I suppose it is only when we are pretty comfortable that we admit it. Come—the others have got to the pavilion and are beckoning to us."

They all sat clown in the little pavilion to watch an autumn sunset of deep red fire and pallid gold. To their left lay Kingsport, its roofs and spires dim in their shroud of violet smoke. To their right lay the harbor, taking on tints of rose and copper as it stretched out into the sunset. Before them the water shimmered, satin smooth and silver gray, and beyond, clean shaven William's Island loomed out of the mist, guarding the town like a sturdy bulldog. Its lighthouse beacon flared through the mist like a baleful star, and was answered by another in the far horizon.

"Did you ever see such a strong-looking place?" asked Philippa. "I don't want William's Island especially, but I'm sure I couldn't get it if I did. Look at that sentry on the summit of the fort, right beside the flag. Doesn't he look as if he had stepped out of a romance?"

"Speaking of romance," said Priscilla, "we've been looking

In the Park

for heather—but, of course, we couldn't find any. It's too late in the season, I suppose."

"Heather!" exclaimed Anne. "Heather doesn't grow in America, does it?"

"There are just two patches of it in the whole continent," said Phil, "one right here in the park, and one somewhere else in Nova Scotia, I forget where. The famous Highland Regiment, the Black Watch, camped here one year, and, when the men shook out the straw of their beds in the spring, some seeds of heather took root."

"Oh, how delightful!" said enchanted Anne.

"Let's go home around by Spofford Avenue," suggested Gilbert. "We can see all 'the handsome houses where the wealthy nobles dwell.' Spofford Avenue is the finest residential street in Kingsport. Nobody can build on it unless he's a millionaire."

"Oh, do," said Phil. "There's a perfectly killing little place I want to show you, Anne. *It* wasn't built by a millionaire. It's the first place after you leave the park, and must have grown while Spofford Avenue was still a country road. It *did* grow—it wasn't built! I don't care for the houses on the Avenue. They're too brand new and plate-glassy. But this little spot is a dream—and its name—but wait till you see it."

They saw it as they walked up the pine-fringed hill from the park. Just on the crest, where Spofford Avenue petered out into a plain road, was a little white frame house with groups of pines on either side of it, stretching their arms protectingly over its low roof. It was covered with red and gold vines, through which its green-shuttered windows peeped. Before it was a tiny garden, surrounded by a low stone wall. October though it was, the garden was still very sweet with dear, old-fashioned, unworldly flowers and shrubs—sweet may, southern-wood, lemon verbena, alyssum, petunias, marigolds, and chrysanthemums. A tiny brick wall, in herring-bone pattern, led from the gate to the front porch. The whole place might have been transplanted from some remote country village; yet there was something about it that made its nearest neighbor, the big lawn-encircled palace of a tobacco king, look exceedingly crude and showy and ill-bred by contrast. As Phil said, it was the difference between being born and being made.

"It's the dearest place I ever saw," said Anne delightedly. "It gives me one of my old, delightful, funny aches. It's dearer and quainter than even Miss Lavendar's stone house."

"It's the name I want you to notice especially," said Phil. "Look—in white letters, around the archway over the gate. 'Patty's Place.' Isn't that killing? Especially on this Avenue of Pinehursts and Elmwolds and Cedarcrofts? 'Patty's Place,' if you please! I adore it."

"Have you any idea who Patty is?" asked Priscilla.

"Patty Spofford is the name of the old lady who owns it, I've discovered. She lives there with her niece, and they've lived there for hundreds of years, more or less—maybe a little less, Anne. Exaggeration is merely a flight of poetic fancy. I understand that wealthy folk have tried to buy the lot time and again—it's really worth a small fortune now, you know—but 'Patty' won't sell upon any consideration. And there's an apple orchard behind the house in place of a back yard—you'll see it when we get a little past—a real apple orchard on Spofford Avenue!"

"I'm going to dream about 'Patty's Place' tonight," said Anne. "Why, I feel as if I belonged to it. I wonder if, by any chance, we'll ever see the inside of it."

"It isn't likely," said Priscilla. Anne smiled mysteriously.

"No, it isn't likely. But I believe it will happen. I have a queer, creepy, crawly feeling—you can call it a presentiment, if you like—that 'Patty's Place' and I are going to be better acquainted yet."

7

Home Again

Those first three weeks at Redmond had seemed long; but the rest of the term flew by on wings of wind. Before they realized it the Redmond students found themselves in the grind of Christmas examinations, emerging therefrom more or less triumphantly. The honor of leading in the Freshman classes fluctuated between Anne, Gilbert, and Philippa; Priscilla did very well; Charlie Sloane scraped through respectably, and comported himself as complacently as if he had led in everything.

"I can't really believe that this time tomorrow I'll be in Green Gables," said Anne on the night before departure. "But I shall be. And you, Phil, will be in Bolingbroke with Alec and Alonzo."

"I'm longing to see them," admitted Phil, between the chocolate she was nibbling. "They really are such dear boys, you know. Oh, I'm going to have a splendid time in the holidays. There's to be no end of dances and drives and general jamborees. I shall never forgive you, Queen Anne, for not coming home with me for the holidays."

"'Never' means three days with you, Phil. It was dear of you to ask me—and I'd love to go to Bolingbroke some day. But I can't go this year—I *must* go home. You don't know how my heart longs for it."

"You won't have much of a time," said Phil scornfully. "There'll be one or two quilting parties, I suppose; and all the old gossips will talk you over to your face and behind your back. You'll die of lonesomeness, child."

"In Avonlea?" said Anne, highly amused.

"Now, if you'd come with me you'd have a perfectly gorgeous time. Bolingbroke would go wild over you, Queen Anne—your hair and your style and, oh, everything! You're so *different.* You'd be such a success—and I would bask in reflected glory—'not the rose but near the rose.' *Do* come, after all, Anne."

"Your picture of social triumphs is quite fascinating, Phil, but I'll paint one to offset it. I'm going home to an old country farmhouse, once green, rather faded now, set among leafless apple orchards. There is a brook below and a December fir wood beyond, where I've heard harps swept by the fingers of rain and wind. There is a pond nearby that will be gray and brooding now. There will be two oldish ladies in the house, one tall and thin, one short and fat; and there will be two twins, one a perfect model, the other what Mrs. Lynde calls a 'holy terror.' There will be a little room upstairs over the porch, where old dreams hang thick, and a big, fat, glorious feather bed which will almost seem the height of luxury after a boardinghouse mattress. How do you like my picture, Phil?"

"It seems a very dull one," said Phil, with a grimace.

"Oh, but I've left out the transforming thing," said Anne softly. "There'll be love there, Phil—faithful, tender love, such as I'll never find anywhere else in the world—love that's waiting for *me.* That makes my picture a masterpiece, doesn't it, even if the colors are not very brilliant?"

Phil silently got up, tossed her box of chocolates away, went up to Anne, and put her arms about her.

"Anne, I wish I was like you," she said soberly.

Diana met Anne at the Carmody station the next night, and they drove home together under silent, star-sown depths of sky. Green Gables had a very festal appearance as they drove up the lane. There was a light in every window, the glow breaking out through the darkness like flame-red blossoms swung against the dark background of the Haunted Wood. And in the yard was a brave bonfire with two gay little figures dancing around it, one of which gave an unearthly yell as the buggy turned in under the poplars.

Home Again

"Davy means that for an Indian war-whoop," said Diana. "Mr. Harrison's hired boy taught it to him, and he's been practicing it up to welcome you with. Mrs. Lynde says it has worn her nerves to a frazzle. He creeps up behind her, you know, and then lets go. He was determined to have a bonfire for you, too. He's been piling up dry branches for a fortnight and pestering Marilla to be let pour some kerosene oil over it before setting it on fire. I guess she did, by the smell, though Mrs. Lynde said up to the last that Davy would blow himself and everybody else up if he was let."

Anne was out of the buggy by this time, and Davy was rapturously hugging her knees, while even Dora was clinging to her hand.

"Isn't that a bully bonfire, Anne? Just let me show you how to poke it—see the sparks? I did it for you, Anne, 'cause I was so glad you were coming home.

The kitchen door opened and Marilla's spare form darkened against the inner light. She preferred to meet Anne in the shadows, for she was horribly afraid that she was going to cry with joy—she, stern, repressed Marilla, who thought all display of deep emotion unseemly. Mrs. Lynde was behind her, sonsy, kindly, matronly, as of yore. The love that Anne had told Phil was waiting for her surrounded her and enfolded her with its blessing and its sweetness. Nothing, after all, could compare with old ties, old friends, and old Green Gables! How starry Anne's eyes were as they sat down to the loaded supper table, her pink her cheeks, how silver-clear her laughter! And Diana was going to stay all night, too. How like the dear old times it was! And the rose-bud tea-set graced the table! With Marilla the force of nature could no further go.

"I suppose you and Diana will now proceed to talk all night," said Marilla sarcastically, as the girls went upstairs. Marilla was always sarcastic after any self-betrayal.

"Yes," agreed Anne gaily, "but I'm going to put Davy to bed first. He insists on that."

"You bet," said Davy, as they went along the hall. "I want somebody to say my prayers to again. It's no fun saying them alone."

"You don't say them alone, Davy. God is always with you to hear you."

"Well, I can't see Him," objected Davy. "I want to pray to somebody I can see, but I *won't* say them to Mrs. Lynde or Marilla, there now!"

Nevertheless, when Davy was garbed in his gray flannel nighty, he did not seem in a hurry to begin. He stood before Anne, shuffling one bare foot over the other, and looked undecided.

"Come, dear, kneel down," said Anne.

Davy came and buried his head in Anne's lap, but he did not kneel down.

"Anne," he said in a muffled voice, "I don't feel like praying after all. I haven't felt like it for a week now. I—I *didn't* pray last night nor the night before."

"Why not, Davy?" asked Anne gently.

"You—you won't be mad if I tell you?" implored Davy.

Anne lifted the little gray-flannelled body on her knee and cuddled his head on her arm.

"Do I ever get 'mad' when you tell me things, Davy?"

"No-o-o, you never do. But you get sorry, and that's worse. You'll be awful sorry when I tell you this, Anne—and you'll be 'shamed of me, I s'pose."

"Have you done something naughty, Davy, and is that why you can't say your prayers?"

"No, I haven't done anything naughty—yet. But I want to do it."

"What is it, Davy?"

Home Again 53

"I—I want to say a bad word, Anne," blurted out Davy, with a desperate effort. "I heard Mr. Harrison's hired boy say it one day last week, and ever since I've been wanting to say it *all* the time—even when I'm saying my prayers."

"Say it then, Davy."

Davy lifted his flushed face in amazement. "But, Anne, it's an *awful* bad word."

"Say it!"

Davy gave her another incredulous look, then in a low voice he said the dreadful word. The next minute his face was burrowing against her.

"Oh, Anne, I'll never say it again—never. I'll never *want* to say it again. I knew it was bad, but I didn't s'pose it was so—so—I didn't s'pose it was like *that.*"

"No, I don't think you'll ever want to say it again, Davy—or think it, either. And I wouldn't go about much with Mr. Harrison's hired boy if I were you."

"He can make bully war-whoops," said Davy a little regretfully.

"But you don't want your mind filled with bad words, do you, Davy—words that will poison it and drive out all that is good and manly?"

"No," said Davy, owl-eyed with introspection.

"Then don't go with those people who use them. And now do you feel as if you could say your prayers, Davy?"

"Oh, yes," said Davy, eagerly wriggling down on his knees, "I can say them now all right. I ain't scared now to say 'if I should die before I wake,' like I was when I was wanting to say that word."

Probably Anne and Diana did empty out their souls to each other that night, but no record of their confidences has been preserved. They both looked as fresh and bright-eyed at breakfast as only youth can look after unlawful hours of revelry and confession. There had been no snow up to this time, but as Diana crossed the old log bridge on her homeward way the white flakes were beginning to flutter down over the fields and woods, russet and gray in their dreamless sleep. Soon the faraway slopes and hills were dim and wraith-like through their gauzy scarfing, as if pale autumn had flung a misty bridal veil over her hair and was waiting for her wintry bridegroom. So they had a white Christmas after all, and a very pleasant day it was. In the forenoon letters and gifts came from Miss Lavendar and Paul; Anne opened them in the cheerful Green Gables kitchen, which was filled with what Davy, sniffing in ecstasy, called "pretty smells."

"Miss Lavendar and Mr. Irving are settled in their new home now," reported Anne. "I am sure Miss Lavendar is perfectly happy—I know it by the general tone of her letter—but there's a note from Charlotta the Fourth. She doesn't like Boston at all, and she is fearfully homesick. Miss Lavendar wants me to go through to Echo Lodge some day while I'm home and light a fire to air it, and see that the cushions aren't getting moldy. I think I'll get Diana to go over with me next week, and we can spend the evening with Theodora Dix. I want to see Theodora. By the way, is Ludovic Speed still going to see her?"

"They say so," said Marilla, "and he's likely to continue it. Folks have given up expecting that that courtship will ever arrive anywhere."

"I'd hurry him up a bit, if I was Theodora, that's what," said Mrs. Lynde. And there is not the slightest doubt but that she would.

There was also a characteristic scrawl from Philippa, full of Alec and Alonzo, what they said and what they did, and how they looked when they saw her.

"But I can't make up my mind yet which to marry," wrote Phil. "I do wish you had come with me to decide for me. Some one will have to. When I saw Alec my heart gave a great thump and I thought, 'He must be the right one.' And then, when Alonzo came, thump went my heart again. So that's no guide, though it should be, according to all the novels I've ever read. Now, Anne, *your* heart wouldn't thump for anybody but the genuine Prince Charming, would it? There must be something radically wrong with mine. But I'm having a perfectly gorgeous time. How I wish you were here! It's snowing today, and I'm rapturous. I was so afraid we'd have a green Christmas and I loathe them. You know, when Christmas is a dirty grayey-browney affair, looking as if it had been left over a hundred years ago and had been in soak ever since, it is called a *green* Christmas! Don't ask me why. As Lord Dundreary says 'there are thome thingth no fellow can underthtand.'

"Anne, did you ever get on a street car and then discover that you hadn't any money with you to pay your fare? I did, the other day. It's quite awful. I had a nickel with me when I got on the car. I thought it was in the left pocket of my coat. When I got settled down comfortably I felt for it. It wasn't there. I had a cold chill. I felt in the other pocket. Not there. I had another chill. Then I felt in a little inside pocket. All in vain. I had two chills at once.

"I took off my gloves, laid them on the seat, and went over all my pockets again. It was not there. I stood up and shook myself, and then looked on the floor. The car was full of people, who were going home from the opera, and they all stared at me, but I was past caring for a little thing like that.

"But I could not find my fare. I concluded I must have put it in my mouth and swallowed it inadvertently.

"I didn't know what to do. Would the conductor, I wondered, stop the car and put me off in ignominy and shame? Was it possible that I could convince him that I was merely the victim of my own absent-mindedness, and not an unprincipled creature trying to obtain a ride upon false pretenses? How I wished that Alec or Alonzo were there. But they weren't because I wanted them. If I *hadn't* wanted them they would have been there by the dozen. And I couldn't decide what to say to the conductor when he came around. As soon as I got one sentence of explanation mapped out in my mind I felt nobody could believe it and I must compose another. It seemed there was nothing to do but trust in Providence, and for all the comfort that gave me I might as well have been the old lady who, when told by the captain during a storm that she must put her trust in the Almighty exclaimed, 'Oh, Captain, is it as bad as that?'

"Just at the conventional moment, when all hope had fled, and the conductor was holding out his box to the passenger next to me, I suddenly remembered where I had put that wretched coin of the realm. I hadn't swallowed it after all. I meekly fished it out of the index finger of my glove and poked it in the box. I smiled at everybody and felt that it was a beautiful world."

The visit to Echo Lodge was not the least pleasant of many pleasant holiday outings. Anne and Diana went back to it by the old way of the beech woods, carrying a lunch basket with them. Echo Lodge, which had been closed ever since Miss Lavendar's wedding, was briefly thrown open to wind and sunshine once more, and firelight glimmered again in the little rooms.

The perfume of Miss Lavendar's rose bowl still filled the air. It was hardly possible to believe that Miss Lavendar would not come tripping in presently, with her brown eyes a-star with welcome, and that Charlotta the Fourth, blue of bow and wide of smile, would not pop through the door. Paul, too, seemed hovering around, with his fairy fancies.

"It really makes me feel a little bit like a ghost revisiting the old time glimpses of the moon," laughed Anne. "Let's go out and see if the echoes are at home. Bring the old horn. It is still behind the kitchen door.

The echoes were at home, over the white river, as silver-clear and multitudinous as ever; and when they had ceased to answer the girls locked up Echo Lodge again and went away in the perfect half hour that follows the rose and saffron of a winter sunset.

8

Anne's First Proposal

The old year did not slip away in a green twilight, with a pinky-yellow sunset. Instead, it went out with a wild, white bluster and blow. It was one of the nights when the storm-wind hurtles over the frozen meadows and black hollows, and moans around the eaves like a lost creature, and drives the snow sharply against the shaking panes.

"Just the sort of night people like to cuddle down between their blankets and count their mercies," said Anne to Jane Andrews, who had come up to spend the afternoon and stay all night. But when they were cuddled between their blankets, in Anne's little porch room, it was not her mercies of which Jane was thinking.

"Anne," she said very solemnly, "I want to tell you something. May I?"

Anne was feeling rather sleepy after the party Ruby Gillis had given the night before. She would much rather have gone to sleep than listen to Jane's confidences, which she was sure would bore her. She had no prophetic inkling of what was coming. Probably Jane was engaged, too; rumor averred that Ruby Gillis was engaged to the Spencervale schoolteacher, about whom all the girls were said to be quite wild.

"I'll soon be the only fancy-free maiden of our old quartet," thought Anne, drowsily. Aloud she said, "Of course."

"Anne," said Jane, still more solemnly, "what do you think of my brother Billy?"

Anne gasped over this unexpected question, and floundered helplessly in her thoughts. Goodness, what *did* she think of Billy Andrews? She had never thought *anything* about him—round-faced, stupid, perpetually smiling, good-natured Billy Andrews. Did *anybody* ever think about Billy Andrews?

"I—I don't understand, Jane," she stammered. "What do you mean—exactly?"

"Do you like Billy?" asked Jane bluntly.

"Why—why—yes, I like him, of course," gasped Anne, wondering if she were telling the literal truth. Certainly she did not *dis*like Billy. But could the indifferent tolerance with which she regarded him, when he happened to be in her range of vision, be considered positive enough for liking? *What* was Jane trying to elucidate?

"Would you like him for a husband?" asked Jane calmly.

"A husband!" Anne had been sitting up in bed, the better to wrestle with the problem of her exact opinion of Billy Andrews. Now she fell flatly back on her pillows, the very breath gone out of her. "*Whose* husband?"

"Yours, of course," answered Jane. "Billy wants to marry you. He's always been crazy about you—and now father has given him the upper farm in his own name and there's nothing to prevent him from getting married. But he's so shy he couldn't ask you himself if you'd have him, so he got me to do it. I'd rather not have, but he gave me no peace till I said I would, if I got a good chance. What do you think about it, Anne?"

Was it a dream? Was it one of those nightmare things in which you find yourself engaged or married to some one you hate or don't know, without the slightest idea how it ever came

Anne's First Proposal

about? No, she, Anne Shirley, was lying there, wide awake, in her own bed, and Jane Andrews was beside her, calmly proposing for her brother Billy. Anne did not know whether she wanted to writhe or laugh; but she could do neither, for Jane's feelings must not be hurt.

"I—I couldn't marry Billy, you know, Jane," she managed to gasp. "Why, such an idea never occurred to me—never!

"I don't suppose it did," agreed Jane. "Billy has always been far too shy to think of courting. But you might think it over, Anne. Billy is a good fellow. I must say that, if he *is* my brother. He has no bad habits and he's a great worker, and you can depend on him. 'A bird in the hand is worth two in the bush.' He told me to tell you he'd be quite willing to wait till you got through college, if you insisted, though he'd *rather* get married this spring before the planting begins. He'd always be very good to you, I'm sure, and you know, Anne, I'd love to have you for a sister."

"I can't marry Billy," said Anne decidedly. She had recovered her wits, and was even feeling a little angry. It was all so ridiculous. "There is no use thinking of it, Jane. I don't care anything for him in that way, and you must tell him so."

"Well, I didn't suppose you would," said Jane with a resigned sigh, feeling that she had done her best. "I told Billy I didn't believe it was a bit of use to ask you, but he insisted. Well, you've made your decision, Anne, and I hope you won't regret it."

Jane spoke rather coldly. She had been perfectly sure that the enamored Billy had no chance at all of inducing Anne to marry him. Nevertheless, she felt a little resentment that Anne Shirley, who was, after all, merely an adopted orphan, without kith or kin, should refuse *her* brother—one of the Avonlea Andrews. Well, pride sometimes goes before a fall, Jane reflected ominously.

Anne permitted herself to smile in the darkness over the idea that she might ever regret not marrying Billy Andrews.

"I hope Billy won't feel very badly over it," she said nicely.

Jane made a movement as if she were tossing her head on her pillow.

"Oh, he won't break his heart. Billy has too much good sense for that. He likes Nettie Blewett pretty well, too, and mother would rather he married her than any one. She's such a good manager and saver. I think, when Billy is once sure you won't have him, he'll take Nettie. Please don't mention this to any one, will you, Anne?"

"Certainly not," said Anne, who had no desire whatever to publish abroad the fact that Billy Andrews wanted to marry her, preferring her, when all was said and done, to Nettie Blewett. Nettie Blewett!

"And now I suppose we'd better go to sleep," suggested Jane.

To sleep went Jane easily and speedily; but, though very unlike MacBeth in most respects, she had certainly contrived to murder sleep for Anne. That proposed-to damsel lay on a wakeful pillow until the wee sma's, but her meditations were far from being romantic. It was not, however, until the next morning that she had an opportunity to indulge in a good laugh over the whole affair. When Jane had gone home—still with a hint of frost in voice and manner because Anne had declined so ungratefully and decidedly the honor of an alliance with the House of Andrews—Anne retreated to the porch room, shut the door, and had her laugh out at last.

"If I could only share the joke with some one!" she thought. "But I can't. Diana is the only one I'd want to tell, and, even if I hadn't sworn secrecy to Jane, I can't tell Diana things now. She tells everything to Fred—I know she does. Well, I've had my first proposal. I supposed it would come some day—but I certainly never thought it would be by proxy. It's awfully funny—and yet there's a sting in it, too, somehow."

Anne knew quite well wherein the sting consisted, though she did not put it into words. She had had her secret dreams of the first time some one should ask her the great question. And it had, in those dreams, always been very romantic and beautiful: and the "some one" was to be very handsome and dark-eyed and distinguished-looking and eloquent, whether he were Prince Charming to be enraptured with "yes," or one to whom a regretful, beautifully worded, but hopeless refusal must be given. If the latter, the refusal was to be expressed so delicately that it would be next best thing to acceptance, and he would go away, after kissing her hand, assuring her of his unalterable, life-long devotion. And it would always be a beautiful memory, to be proud of and a little sad about, also.

And now, this thrilling experience had turned out to be merely grotesque. Billy Andrews had got his sister to propose for him because his father had given him the upper farm; and if Anne wouldn't "have him" Nettie Blewett would. There was romance for you, with a vengeance! Anne laughed—and then sighed.

The bloom had been brushed from one little maiden dream. Would the painful process go on until everything became prosaic and hum-drum?

9

An Unwelcome Lover and a Welcome Friend

The second term at Redmond sped as quickly as had the first—"actually whizzed away," Philippa said. Anne enjoyed it thoroughly in all its phases—the stimulating class rivalry, the making and deepening of new and helpful friendships, the gay little social stunts, the doings of the various societies of which she was a member, the widening of horizons and interests. She studied hard, for she had made up her mind to win the Thorburn Scholarship in English. This being won, meant that she could come back to Redmond the next year without trenching on Marilla's small savings—something Anne was determined she would not do.

Gilbert, too, was in full chase after a scholarship, but found plenty of time for frequent calls at Thirty-eight, St. John's. He was Anne's escort at nearly all the college affairs, and she knew that their names were coupled in Redmond gossip. Anne raged over this but was helpless; she could not cast an old friend like Gilbert aside, especially when he had grown suddenly wise and wary, as behooved him in the dangerous proximity of more than one Redmond youth who would gladly have taken his place by the side of the slender, red-haired coed, whose gray eyes were as alluring as stars of evening. Anne was never attended by the crowd of willing victims who hovered around Philippa's conquering march through her Freshman year; but there was a lanky, brainy Freshie, a jolly, little, round Sophomore, and a tall, learned Junior who all liked to call at Thirty-eight, St. John's, and talk over 'ologies and 'isms, as well as lighter subjects, with Anne, in the be-cushioned parlor of that domicile. Gilbert did not love any of them, and he was exceedingly careful to give none of them the advantage over him by any untimely display of his real feelings Anne-ward. To her he had become again the boy-comrade of Avonlea days, and as such could hold his own against any smitten swain who had so far entered the lists against him. As a companion, Anne honestly acknowledged nobody could be so satisfactory as Gilbert; she was very glad, so she told herself, that he had evidently dropped all nonsensical ideas—though she spent considerable time secretly wondering why.

An Unwelcome Lover and a Welcome Friend 63

Only one disagreeable incident marred that winter. Charlie Sloane, sitting bolt upright on Miss Ada's most dearly beloved cushion, asked Anne one night if she would promise "to become Mrs. Charlie Sloane some day." Coming after Billy Andrews' proxy effort, this was not quite the shock to Anne's romantic sensibilities that it would otherwise have been; but it was certainly another heart-rending disillusion. She was angry, too, for she felt that she had never given Charlie the slightest encouragement to suppose such a thing possible. But what could you expect of a Sloane, as Mrs. Rachel Lynde would ask scornfully? Charlie's whole attitude, tone, air, words, fairly reeked with Sloanishness. He was conferring a great honor—no doubt whatever about that. And when Anne, utterly insensible to the honor, refused him, as delicately and considerately as she could—for even a Sloane had feelings which ought not to be unduly lacerated—Sloanishness still further betrayed itself. Charlie certainly did not take his dismissal as Anne's imaginary rejected suitors did. Instead, he became angry, and showed it; he said two or three quite nasty things; Anne's temper flashed up mutinously and she retorted with a cutting little speech whose keenness pierced even Charlie's protective Sloanishness and reached the quick; he caught up his hat and flung himself out of the house with a very red face; Anne rushed upstairs, falling twice over Miss Ada's cushions on the way, and threw herself on her bed, in tears of humiliation and rage. Had she actually stooped to quarrel with a Sloane? Was it possible anything Charlie Sloane could say had power to make her angry? Oh, this was degradation, indeed—worse even than being the rival of Nettie Blewett!

"I wish I need never see the horrible creature again," she sobbed vindictively into her pillows.

She could not avoid seeing him again, but the outraged Charlie took care that it should not be at very close quarters.

Miss Ada's cushions were henceforth safe from his depredations, and when he met Anne on the street, or in Redmond's halls, his bow was icy in the extreme. Relations between these two old schoolmates continued to be thus strained for nearly a year! Then Charlie transferred his blighted affections to a round, rosy, snub-nosed, blue-eyed, little Sophomore who appreciated them as they deserved, whereupon he forgave Anne and condescended to be civil to her again; in a patronizing manner intended to show her just what she had lost.

One day Anne scurried excitedly into Priscilla's room.

"Read that," she cried, tossing Priscilla a letter. "It's from Stella—and she's coming to Redmond next year—and what do you think of her idea? I think it's a perfectly splendid one, if we can only carry it out. Do you suppose we can, Pris?"

"I'll be better able to tell you when I find out what it is," said Priscilla, casting aside a Greek lexicon and taking up Stella's letter. Stella Maynard had been one of their chums at Queen's Academy and had been teaching school ever since.

"But I'm going to give it up, Anne dear," she wrote, "and go to college next year. As I took the third year at Queen's I can enter the Sophomore year. I'm tired of teaching in a back country school. Some day I'm going to write a treatise on 'The Trials of a Country Schoolmarm.' It will be a harrowing bit of realism. It seems to be the prevailing impression that we live in clover, and have nothing to do but draw our quarter's salary. My treatise shall tell the truth about us. Why, if a week should pass without some one telling me that I am doing easy work for big pay I would conclude that I might as well order my ascension robe 'immediately and to onct.' 'Well, you get your money easy,' some rate-payer will tell me, condescendingly. 'All you have to do is to sit there and hear lessons.' I used to argue the matter at first, but I'm wiser now. Facts are stubborn things, but, as some one has wisely said, not half so stubborn as fallacies. So I only

An Unwelcome Lover and a Welcome Friend   65

smile loftily now in eloquent silence. Why, I have nine grades in my school and I have to teach a little of everything, from investigating the interiors of earthworms to the study of the solar system. My youngest pupil is four—his mother sends him to school to 'get him out of the way'—and my oldest twenty—it 'suddenly struck him' that it would be easier to go to school and get an education than follow the plough any longer. In the wild effort to cram all sorts of research into six hours a day I don't wonder if the children feel like the little boy who was taken to see the biograph. 'I have to look for what's coming next before I know what went last,' he complained. I feel like that myself.

"And the letters I get, Anne! Tommy's mother writes me that Tommy is not coming on in arithmetic as fast as she would like. He is only in simple reduction yet, and Johnny Johnson is in fractions, and Johnny isn't half as smart as her Tommy, and she can't understand it. And Susy's father wants to know why Susy can't write a letter without misspelling half the words, and Dick's aunt wants me to change his seat, because that bad Brown boy he is sitting with is teaching him to say naughty words.

"As to the financial part—but I'll not begin on *that*. Those whom the gods wish to destroy they first make country schoolmarms!

"There, I feel better, after that growl. After all, I've enjoyed these past two years. But I'm coming to Redmond.

"And now, Anne, I've a little plan. You know how I loathe boarding. I've boarded for four years and I'm so tired of it. I don't feel like enduring three years more of it. Now, why can't you and Priscilla and I club together, rent a little house somewhere in Kingsport, and board ourselves? It would be cheaper than any other way. Of course, we would have to have a housekeeper and I have one ready on the spot. You've heard me speak of Aunt Jamesina? She's the sweetest aunt that ever lived, in spite of her name. She can't help that! She was called Jamesina because her father, whose name was James, was drowned at sea a month before she was born. I always call her Aunt Jimsie. Well, her only daughter has recently married and gone to the foreign mission field. Aunt Jamesina is left alone in a great big house, and she is horribly lonesome. She will come to Kingsport and keep house for us if we want her, and I know you'll both love her. The more I think of the plan the more I like it. We could have such good, independent times.

"Now, if you and Priscilla agree to it, wouldn't it be a good idea for you, who are on the spot, to look around and see if you can find a suitable house this spring? That would be better than leaving it till the fall. If you could get a furnished one so much the better, but if not, we can scare up a few sticks of furniture between us and old family friends with attics. Anyhow, decide as soon as you can and write me, so that Aunt Jamesina will know what plans to make for next year."

"I think it's a good idea," said Priscilla.

"So do I," agreed Anne delightedly. "Of course, we have a nice boardinghouse here, but, when all's said and done, a boardinghouse isn't home. So let's go house-hunting at once, before exams come on."

"I'm afraid it will be hard enough to get a really suitable house," warned Priscilla. "Don't expect too much, Anne. Nice houses in nice localities will probably be away beyond our means. We'll likely have to content ourselves with a shabby little place on some street whereon live people whom to know is to be unknown, and make life inside compensate for the outside."

Accordingly they went house-hunting, but to find just what they wanted proved even harder than Priscilla had feared. Houses there were galore, furnished and unfurnished; but one was too big, another too small; this one too expensive, that one too far from Redmond. Exams were on and over; the last week of the term came and still their "house o' dreams," as Anne called it, remained a castle in the air.

"We shall have to give up and wait till the fall, I suppose," said Priscilla wearily, as they rambled through the park on one of April's darling days of breeze and blue, when the harbor was creaming and shimmering beneath the pearl-hued mists floating over it. "We may find some shack to shelter us then; and if not, boardinghouses we shall have always with us."

"I'm not going to worry about it just now, anyway, and spoil this lovely afternoon," said Anne, gazing around her with delight. The fresh chill air was faintly charged with the aroma of pine balsam, and the sky above was crystal clear and blue—a great inverted cup of blessing. "Spring is singing in my blood today, and the lure of April is abroad on the air. I'm seeing visions and dreaming dreams, Pris. That's because the wind is from the west. I do love the west wind. It sings of hope and gladness, doesn't it? When the east wind blows I always think of sorrowful rain on the eaves and sad waves on a gray shore. When I get old I shall have rheumatism when the wind is east."

"And isn't it jolly when you discard furs and winter garments for the first time and sally forth, like this, in spring attire?" laughed Priscilla. "Don't you feel as if you had been made over new?"

"Everything is new in the spring," said Anne. "Springs themselves are always so new, too. No spring is ever just like any other spring. It always has something of its own to be its own peculiar sweetness. See how green the grass is around that little pond, and how the willow buds are bursting."

"And exams are over and gone—the time of Convocation will soon come—next Wednesday. This day week we'll be home."

"I'm glad," said Anne dreamily. "There are so many things I want to do. I want to sit on the back porch steps and feel the breeze blowing down over Mr. Harrison's fields. I want to hunt ferns in the Haunted Wood and gather violets in Violet Vale. Do you remember the day of our golden picnic, Priscilla? I want to hear the frogs singing and the poplars whispering. But I've learned to love Kingsport, too, and I'm glad I'm coming back next fall. If I hadn't won the Thorburn I don't believe I could have. I *couldn't* take any of Marilla's little hoard."

"If we could only find a house!" sighed Priscilla.

"Look over there at Kingsport, Anne—houses, houses everywhere, and not one for us."

"Stop it, Pris. 'The best is yet to be.' Like the old Roman, we'll find a house or build one. On a day like this there's no such word as fail in my bright lexicon."

They lingered in the park until sunset, living in the amazing miracle and glory and wonder of the springtide; and they went home as usual, by way of Spofford Avenue, that they might have the delight of looking at Patty's Place.

"I feel as if something mysterious were going to happen right away—'by the pricking of my thumbs,'" said Anne, as they went up the slope. "It's a nice story-bookish feeling. Why—why—why! Priscilla Grant, look over there and tell me if it's true, or am I seein' things?"

Priscilla looked. Anne's thumbs and eyes had not deceived her. Over the arched gateway of Patty's Place dangled a little, modest sign. It said "To Let, Furnished. Inquire Within."

"Priscilla," said Anne, in a whisper, "do you suppose it's possible that we could rent Patty's Place?"

"No, I don't," averred Priscilla. "It would be too good to be true. Fairy tales don't happen nowadays. I *won't* hope, Anne. The disappointment would be too awful to bear. They're sure to want more for it than we can afford. Remember, it's on Spofford Avenue."

"We must find out anyhow," said Anne resolutely. "It's too late to call this evening, but we'll come tomorrow. Oh, Pris, if we can get this darling spot! I've always felt that my fortunes were linked with Patty's Place, ever since I saw it first."

10
Patty's Place

The next evening found them treading resolutely the herringbone walk through the tiny garden. The April wind was filling the pine trees with its roundelay, and the grove was alive with robins—great, plump, saucy fellows, strutting along the paths. The girls rang rather timidly, and were admitted by a grim and ancient handmaiden. The door opened directly into a large living-room, where by a cheery little fire sat two other ladies, both of whom were also grim and ancient. Except that one looked to be about seventy and the other fifty, there seemed little difference between them. Each had amazingly big, light-blue eyes behind steel-rimmed spectacles; each wore a cap and a gray shawl; each was knitting without haste and without rest; each rocked placidly and looked at the girls without speaking; and just behind each sat a large white china dog, with round green spots all over it, a green nose and green ears. Those dogs captured Anne's fancy on the spot; they seemed like the twin guardian deities of Patty's Place.

For a few minutes nobody spoke. The girls were too nervous to find words, and neither the ancient ladies nor the china dogs seemed conversationally inclined. Anne glanced about the room. What a dear place it was! Another door opened out of it directly into the pine grove and the robins came boldly up on the very step. The floor was spotted with round, braided mats, such as Marilla made at Green Gables, but which were considered out of date everywhere else, even in Avonlea. And yet here they were on Spofford Avenue! A big, polished grandfather's clock ticked loudly and solemnly in a corner. There were delightful little cupboards over the mantelpiece, behind whose glass doors gleamed quaint bits of china. The walls were hung with old prints and silhouettes. In one corner the stairs went up, and at the first low turn was a long window with an inviting seat. It was all just as Anne had known it must be.

By this time the silence had grown too dreadful, and Priscilla nudged Anne to intimate that she *must* speak.

"We—we—saw by your sign that this house is to let," said Anne faintly, addressing the older lady, who was evidently Miss Patty Spofford.

"Oh, yes," said Miss Patty. "I intended to take that sign down today."

"Then then we are too late," said Anne sorrowfully. "You've let it to some one else?"

"No, but we have decided not to let it at all."

"Oh, I'm so sorry," exclaimed Anne impulsively. "I love this place so. I did hope we could have got it."

Then did Miss Patty lay down her knitting, take off her specs, rub them, put them on again, and for the first time look at Anne as at a human being. The other lady followed her example so perfectly that she might as well have been a reflection in a mirror.

"You *love* it," said Miss Patty with emphasis. "Does that mean that you really *love* it? Or that you merely like the looks of it? The girls nowadays indulge in such exaggerated statements that one never can tell what they *do* mean. It wasn't so in my young days. *Then* a girl did not say she *loved* turnips, in just the same tone as she might have said she loved her mother or her Savior."

Anne's conscience bore her up.

Patty's Place

"I really do love it," she said gently. "I've loved it ever since I saw it last fall. My two college chums and I want to keep house next year instead of boarding, so we are looking for a little place to rent; and when I saw that this house was to let I was so happy."

"If you love it, you can have it," said Miss Patty. "Maria and I decided today that we would not let it after all, because we did not like any of the people who have wanted it. We don't *have* to let it. We can afford to go to Europe even if we don't let it. It would help us out, but not for gold will I let my home pass into the possession of such people as have come here and looked at it. *You* are different. I believe you do love it and will be good to it. You can have it."

"If—if we can afford to pay what you ask for it," hesitated Anne.

Miss Patty named the amount required. Anne and Priscilla looked at each other. Priscilla shook her head.

"I'm afraid we can't afford quite so much," said Anne, choking back her disappointment. "You see, we are only college girls and we are poor."

"What were you thinking you could afford?" demanded Miss Patty, ceasing not to knit.

Anne named her amount. Miss Patty nodded gravely.

"That will do. As I told you, it is not strictly necessary that we should let it at all. We are not rich, but we have enough to go to Europe on. I have never been in Europe in my life, and never expected or wanted to go. But my niece there, Maria Spofford, has taken a fancy to go. Now, you know a young person like Maria can't go globe-trotting alone."

"No—I—I suppose not," murmured Anne, seeing that Miss Patty was quite solemnly in earnest.

"Of course not. So I have to go along to look after her. I expect to enjoy it, too; I'm seventy years old, but I'm not tired of living yet. I daresay I'd have gone to Europe before if the idea had occurred to me. We shall be away for two years, perhaps three. We sail in June and we shall send you the key, and leave all in order for you to take possession when you choose. We shall pack away a few things we prize especially, but all the rest will be left."

"Will you leave the china dogs?" asked Anne timidly.

"Would you like me to?"

"Oh, indeed, yes. They are delightful."

A pleased expression came into Miss Patty's face.

"I think a great deal of those dogs," she said proudly. "They are over a hundred years old, and they have sat on either side of this fireplace ever since my brother Aaron brought them from London fifty years ago. Spofford Avenue was called after my brother Aaron."

"A fine man he was," said Miss Maria, speaking for the first time. "Ah, you don't see the like of him nowadays.

"He was a good uncle to you, Maria," said Miss Patty, with evident emotion. "You do well to remember him."

"I shall always remember him," said Miss Maria solemnly. "I can see him, this minute, standing there before that fire, with his hands under his coat-tails, beaming on us."

Miss Maria took out her handkerchief and wiped her eyes; but Miss Patty came resolutely back from the regions of sentiment to those of business.

"I shall leave the dogs where they are, if you will promise to be very careful of them," she said. "Their names are Gog and Magog. Gog looks to the right and Magog to the left. And there's just one thing more. You don't object, I hope, to this house being called Patty's Place?"

"No, indeed. We think that is one of the nicest things about it."

"You have sense, I see," said Miss Patty in a tone of great satisfaction. "Would you believe it? All the people who came here to rent the house wanted to know if they couldn't take the name off the gate during their occupation of it. I told them roundly that the name went with the house. This has been Patty's Place ever since my brother Aaron left it to me in his will, and Patty's Place it shall remain until I die and Maria dies. After that happens the next possessor can call it any fool name he likes," concluded Miss Patty, much as she might have said, "After that—the deluge."

"And now, wouldn't you like to go over the house and see it all before we consider the bargain made?"

Further exploration still further delighted the girls. Besides the big living-room, there was a kitchen and a small bedroom downstairs. Upstairs were three rooms, one large and two small. Anne took an especial fancy to one of the small ones, looking out into the big pines, and hoped it would be hers. It was papered in pale blue and had a little, old-timey toilet table with sconces for candles. There was a diamond-paned window with a seat under the blue muslin frills that would be a satisfying spot for studying or dreaming.

"It's all so delicious that I know we are going to wake up and find it a fleeting vision of the night," said Priscilla as they went away.

"Miss Patty and Miss Maria are hardly such stuff as dreams are made of," laughed Anne. "Can you fancy them 'globe-trotting'—especially in those shawls and caps?"

"I suppose they'll take them off when they really begin to trot," said Priscilla, "but I know they'll take their knitting with them everywhere. They simply couldn't be parted from it. They will walk about Westminster Abbey and knit, I feel sure. Meanwhile, Anne, we shall be living in Patty's Place—*and* on Spofford Avenue. I feel like a millionairess even now."

"I feel like one of the morning stars that sang for joy," said Anne.

Phil Gordon crept into Thirty-eight, St. John's, that night and flung herself on Anne's bed.

"Girls, dear, I'm tired to death. I feel like the man without a country—or was it without a shadow? I forget which. Anyway, I've been packing up."

"And I suppose you are worn out because you couldn't decide which things to pack first, or where to put them," laughed Priscilla.

"E-zackly. And when I had got everything jammed in somehow, and my landlady and her maid had both sat on it while I locked it, I discovered I had packed a whole lot of things I wanted for Convocation at the very bottom. I had to unlock the old thing and poke and dive into it for an hour before I fished out what I wanted. I would get hold of something that felt like what I was looking for, and I'd yank it up, and it would be something else. No, Anne, I did NOT swear."

"I didn't say you did."

"Well, you looked it. But I admit my thoughts verged on the profane. And I have such a cold in the head—I can do nothing but sniffle, sigh, and sneeze. Isn't that alliterative agony for you? Queen Anne, do say something to cheer me up."

"Remember that next Thursday night you'll be back in the land of Alec and Alonzo," suggested Anne.

Phil shook her head dolefully.

"More alliteration. No, I don't want Alec and Alonzo when I have a cold in the head. But what has happened you two? Now that I look at you closely you seem all lighted up with an internal iridescence. Why, you're actually *shining*! What's up?"

"We are going to live in Patty's Place next winter," said Anne triumphantly. "*Live*, mark you, not board! We've rented it, and Stella Maynard is coming, and her aunt is going to keep house for us."

Phil bounced up, wiped her nose, and fell on her knees before Anne.

"Girls—girls—let me come, too. Oh, I'll be so good. If there's no room for me I'll sleep in the little doghouse in the orchard—I've seen it. Only let me come."

"Get up, you goose."

"I won't stir off my marrow bones till you tell me I can live with you next winter."

Anne and Priscilla looked at each other. Then Anne said slowly, "Phil dear, we'd love to have you. But we may as well speak plainly. I'm poor—Pris is poor—Stella Maynard is poor—our housekeeping will have to be very simple and our table plain. You'd have to live as we would. Now, you are rich and your boardinghouse fare attests the fact."

"Oh, what do I care for that?" demanded Phil tragically. "Better a dinner of herbs where your chums are than a stalled ox in a lonely boardinghouse. Don't think I'm *all* stomach, girls. I'll be willing to live on bread and water—with just a *leetle* jam—if you'll let me come."

"And then," continued Anne, "there will be a good deal of work to be done. Stella's aunt can't do it all. We all expect to have our chores to do. Now, you—"

"Toil not, neither do I spin," finished Philippa. "But I'll learn to do things. You'll only have to show me once. I *can* make my own bed to begin with. And remember that, though I can't cook, I *can* keep my temper. That's something. And I *never* growl about the weather. That's more. Oh, please, please! I never wanted anything so much in my life—and this floor is awfully hard."

"There's just one more thing," said Priscilla resolutely. "You, Phil, as all Redmond knows, entertain callers almost every evening. Now, at Patty's Place we can't do that. We have decided that we shall be at home to our friends on Friday evenings only. If you come with us you'll have to abide by that rule."

"Well, you don't think I'll mind that, do you? Why, I'm glad of it. I knew I should have had some such rule myself, but I hadn't enough decision to make it or stick to it. When I can shuffle off the responsibility on you it will be a real relief. If you won't let me cast in my lot with you I'll die of the disappointment and then I'll come back and haunt you. I'll camp on the very doorstep of Patty's Place and you won't be able to go out or come in without falling over my spook."

Again Anne and Priscilla exchanged eloquent looks.

"Well," said Anne, "of course we can't promise to take you until we've consulted with Stella; but I don't think she'll object, and, as far as we are concerned, you may come and glad welcome."

"If you get tired of our simple life you can leave us, and no questions asked," added Priscilla.

Phil sprang up, hugged them both jubilantly, and went on her way rejoicing.

"I hope things will go right," said Priscilla soberly.

"We must *make* them go right," avowed Anne. "I think Phil will fit into our 'appy little 'ome very well."

"Oh, Phil's a dear to rattle round with and be chums. And, of course, the more there are of us the easier it will be on our slim purses. But how will she be to live with? You have to summer and winter with any one before you know if she's *livable* or not."

"Oh, well, we'll all be put to the test, as far as that goes. And we must quit us like sensible folk, living and let live. Phil isn't selfish, though she's a little thoughtless, and I believe we will all get on beautifully in Patty's Place."

11

The Round of Life

Anne was back in Avonlea with the luster of the Thorburn Scholarship on her brow. People told her she hadn't changed much, in a tone which hinted they were surprised and a little disappointed she hadn't. Avonlea had not changed, either. At least, so it seemed at first. But as Anne sat in the Green Gables pew, on the first Sunday after her return, and looked over the congregation, she saw several little changes which, all coming home to her at once, made her realize that time did not quite stand still, even in Avonlea. A new minister was in the pulpit. In the pews more than one familiar face was missing forever. Old "Uncle Abe," his prophesying over and done with, Mrs. Peter Sloane, who had sighed, it was to be hoped, for the last time, Timothy Cotton, who, as Mrs. Rachel Lynde said "had actually managed to die at last after practicing at it for twenty years," and old Josiah Sloane, whom nobody knew in his coffin because he had his whiskers neatly trimmed, were all sleeping in the little graveyard behind the church. And Billy Andrews was married to Nettie Blewett! They "appeared out" that Sunday. When Billy, beaming with pride and happiness, showed his be-plumed and be-silked bride into the Hannon Andrews' pew, Anne dropped her lids to hide her dancing eyes. She recalled the stormy winter night of the Christmas holidays when Jane had proposed for Billy. He certainly had not broken his heart over his rejection. Anne wondered if Jane had also proposed to Nettie for him, or if he had mustered enough spunk to ask the fateful question himself. All the Andrews family seemed to share in his pride and pleasure, from Mrs. Harmon in the pew to Jane in the choir. Jane had resigned from the Avonlea school and intended to go West in the fall.

"Can't get a beau in Avonlea, that's what," said Mrs. Rachel Lynde scornfully. "*Says* she thinks she'll have better health out West. I never heard her health was poor before."

"Jane is a nice girl," Anne had said loyally. "She never tried to attract attention, as some did."

"Oh, she never chased the boys, if that's what you mean," said Mrs. Rachel. "But she'd like to be married, just as much as anybody, that's what. What else would take her out West to some forsaken place whose only recommendation is that men are plenty and women scarce? Don't you tell me!"

But it was not at Jane Anne gazed that day in dismay and surprise. It was at Ruby Gillis, who sat beside her in the choir. What had happened to Ruby? She was even handsomer than ever; but her blue eyes were too bright and lustrous, and the color of her cheeks was hectically brilliant; besides, she was very thin; the hands that held her hymn—book were almost transparent in their delicacy.

"Is Ruby Gillis ill?" Anne asked of Mrs. Lynde, as they went home from church.

"Ruby Gillis is dying of galloping consumption," said Mrs. Lynde bluntly. "Everybody knows it except herself and her family. *They* won't give in. If you ask *them*, she's perfectly well. She hasn't been able to teach since she had that attack of congestion in the winter, but she says she's going to teach again in the fall, and she's after the White Sands school. She'll be in her grave, poor girl, when White Sands school opens, that's what."

Anne listened in shocked silence. Ruby Gillis, her old school-chum, dying? Could it be possible? Of late years they had grown apart; but the old tie of schoolgirl intimacy was there, and made itself felt sharply in the tug the news gave at Anne's heartstrings. Ruby, the brilliant, the merry, the coquettish! It was impossible to associate the thought of her with anything like death. She had greeted Anne with gay cordiality after church, and urged her to come up the next evening.

"I'll be away Tuesday and Wednesday evenings," she had whispered triumphantly. "There's a concert at Carmody and a party at White Sands. Herb Spencer's going to take me. He's my *latest*. Be sure to come up tomorrow. I'm dying for a good talk with you. I want to hear all about your doings at Redmond."

Anne knew that Ruby meant that she wanted to tell Anne all about her own recent flirtations, but she promised to go, and Diana offered to go with her.

"I've been wanting to go to see Ruby for a long while," she told Anne, when they left Green Gables the next evening, "but I really couldn't go alone. It's so awful to hear Ruby rattling on as she does, and pretending there is nothing the matter with her, even when she can hardly speak for coughing. She's fighting so hard for her life, and yet she hasn't any chance at all, they say."

The girls walked silently down the red, twilit road. The robins were singing vespers in the high treetops, filling the golden air with their jubilant voices. The silver fluting of the frogs came from marshes and ponds, over fields where seeds were beginning to stir with life and thrill to the sunshine and rain that had drifted over them. The air was fragrant with the wild, sweet, wholesome smell of young raspberry copses. White mists were hovering in the silent hollows and violet stars were shining bluely on the brooklands.

"What a beautiful sunset," said Diana. "Look, Anne, it's just like a land in itself, isn't it? That long, low bank of purple cloud is the shore, and the clear sky further on is like a golden sea."

"If we could sail to it in the moonshine boat Paul wrote of in his old composition—you remember?—how nice it would be," said Anne, rousing from her reverie. "Do you think we could find all our yesterdays there, Diana—all our old springs and blossoms? The beds of flowers that Paul saw there are the roses that have bloomed for us in the past?"

"Don't!" said Diana. "You make me feel as if we were old women with everything in life behind us."

"I think I've almost felt as if we were since I heard about poor Ruby," said Anne. "If it is true that she is dying any other sad thing might be true, too."

"You don't mind calling in at Elisha Wright's for a moment, do you?" asked Diana. "Mother asked me to leave this little dish of jelly for Aunt Atossa."

"Who is Aunt Atossa?"

"Oh, haven't you heard? She's Mrs. Samson Coates of Spencervale—Mrs. Elisha Wright's aunt. She's father's aunt, too. Her husband died last winter and she was left very poor and lonely, so the Wrights took her to live with them. Mother thought we ought to take her, but father put his foot down. Live with Aunt Atossa he would not."

"Is she so terrible?" asked Anne absently.

"You'll probably see what she's like before we can get away," said Diana significantly. "Father says she has a face like a hatchet—it cuts the air. But her tongue is sharper still."

Late as it was Aunt Atossa was cutting potato sets in the Wright kitchen. She wore a faded old wrapper, and her gray hair was decidedly untidy. Aunt Atossa did not like being "caught in a kilter," so she went out of her way to be disagreeable.

"Oh, so you're Anne Shirley?" she said, when Diana introduced Anne. "I've heard of you." Her tone implied that she had heard nothing good. "Mrs. Andrews was telling me you were home. She said you had improved a good deal."

There was no doubt Aunt Atossa thought there was plenty of room for further improvement. She ceased not from cutting sets with much energy.

"Is it any use to ask you to sit down?" she inquired sarcastically. "Of course, there's nothing very entertaining here for you. The rest are all away."

The Round of Life   81

"Mother sent you this little pot of rhubarb jelly," said Diana pleasantly. "She made it today and thought you might like some."

"Oh, thanks," said Aunt Atossa sourly. "I never fancy your mother's jelly—she always makes it too sweet. However, I'll try to worry some down. My appetite's been dreadful poor this spring. I'm far from well," continued Aunt Atossa solemnly, "but still I keep a-doing. People who can't work aren't wanted *here*. If it isn't too much trouble will you be condescending enough to set the jelly in the pantry? I'm in a hurry to get these spuds done tonight. I suppose you two *ladies* never do anything like this. You'd be afraid of spoiling your hands."

"I used to cut potato sets before we rented the farm," smiled Anne.

"I do it yet," laughed Diana. "I cut sets three days last week. Of course," she added teasingly, "I did my hands up in lemon juice and kid gloves every night after it."

Aunt Atossa sniffed.

"I suppose you got that notion out of some of those silly magazines you read so many of. I wonder your mother allows you. But she always spoiled you. We all thought when George married her she wouldn't be a suitable wife for him."

Aunt Atossa sighed heavily, as if all forebodings upon the occasion of George Barry's marriage had been amply and darkly fulfilled.

"Going, are you?" she inquired, as the girls rose. "Well, I suppose you can't find much amusement talking to an old woman like me. It's such a pity the boys ain't home."

"We want to run in and see Ruby Gillis a little while," explained Diana.

"Oh, anything does for an excuse, of course," said Aunt Atossa, amiably. "Just whip in and whip out before you have time to say how-do decently. It's college airs, I s'pose. You'd be wiser to keep away from Ruby Gillis. The doctors say consumption's catching. I always knew Ruby'd get something, gadding off to Boston last fall for a visit. People who ain't content to stay home always catch something."

"People who don't go visiting catch things, too. Sometimes they even die," said Diana solemnly.

"Then they don't have themselves to blame for it," retorted Aunt Atossa triumphantly. "I hear you are to be married in June, Diana."

"There is no truth in that report," said Diana, blushing.

"Well, don't put it off too long," said Aunt Atossa significantly. "You'll fade soon—you're all complexion and hair. And the Wrights are terrible fickle. You ought to wear a hat, *Miss Shirley*. Your nose is freckling scandalous. My, but you *are* redheaded! Well, I s'pose we're all as the Lord made us! Give Marilla Cuthbert my respects. She's never been to see me since I come to Avonlea, but I s'pose I oughtn't to complain. The Cuthberts always did think themselves a cut higher than any one else round here."

"Oh, isn't she dreadful?" gasped Diana, as they escaped down the lane.

"She's worse than Miss Eliza Andrews," said Anne. "But then think of living all your life with a name like Atossa! Wouldn't it sour almost any one? She should have tried to imagine her name was Cordelia. It might have helped her a great deal. It certainly helped me in the days when I didn't like *Anne.*"

"Josie Pye will be just like her when she grows up," said Diana. "Josie's mother and Aunt Atossa are cousins, you know. Oh, dear, I'm glad that's over. She's so malicious—she seems to put a bad flavor in everything. Father tells such a funny story about her. One time they had a minister in Spencervale who was a very good, spiritual man but very deaf. He couldn't hear any ordinary conversation at all. Well, they used to have a prayer

The Round of Life 83

meeting on Sunday evenings, and all the church members present would get up and pray in turn, or say a few words on some Bible verse. But one evening Aunt Atossa bounced up. She didn't either pray or preach. Instead, she lit into everybody else in the church and gave them a fearful raking down, calling them right out by name and telling them how they all had behaved, and casting up all the quarrels and scandals of the past ten years. Finally she wound up by saying that she was disgusted with Spencervale church and she never meant to darken its door again, and she hoped a fearful judgment would come upon it. Then she sat down out of breath, and the minister, who hadn't heard a word she said, immediately remarked, in a very devout voice, 'Amen! The Lord grant our dear sister's prayer!' You ought to hear father tell the story."

"Speaking of stories, Diana," remarked Anne, in a significant, confidential tone, "do you know that lately I have been wondering if I could write a short story—a story that would be good enough to be published?"

"Why, of course you could," said Diana, after she has grasped the amazing suggestion. "You used to write perfectly thrilling stories years ago in our old Story Club."

"Well, I hardly meant one of that kind of stories," smiled Anne. "I've been thinking about it a little of late, but I'm almost afraid to try, for, if I should fail, it would be too humiliating."

"I heard Priscilla say once that all Mrs. Morgan's first stories were rejected. But I'm sure yours wouldn't be, Anne, for it's likely editors have more sense nowadays."

"Margaret Burton, one of the Junior girls at Redmond, wrote a story last winter and it was published in the *Canadian Woman*. I really do think I could write one at least as good."

"And will you have it published in the *Canadian Woman*?"

"I might try one of the bigger magazines first. It all depends on what kind of a story I write."

"What is it to be about?"

"I don't know yet. I want to get hold of a good plot. I believe that is very necessary from an editor's point of view. The only thing I've settled on is the heroine's name. It is to be *Averil Lester*. Rather pretty, don't you think? Don't mention this to any one, Diana. I haven't told anybody but you and Mr. Harrison. *He* wasn't very encouraging—he said there was far too much trash written nowadays as it was, and he'd expected something better of me, after a year at college."

"What does Mr. Harrison know about it?" demanded Diana scornfully.

They found the Gillis home gay with lights and callers. Leonard Kimball, of Spencervale, and Morgan Bell, of Carmody, were glaring at each other across the parlor. Several merry girls had dropped in. Ruby was dressed in white and her eyes and cheeks were very brilliant. She laughed and chattered incessantly, and after the other girls had gone she took Anne upstairs to display her new summer dresses.

"I've a blue silk to make up yet, but it's a little heavy for summer wear. I think I'll leave it until the fall. I'm going to teach in White Sands, you know. How do you like my hat? That one you had on in church yesterday was real dinky. But I like something brighter for myself. Did you notice those two ridiculous boys downstairs? They've both come determined to sit each other out. I don't care a single bit about either of them, you know. Herb Spencer is the one I like. Sometimes I really do think's he's *Mr. Right*. At Christmas I thought the Spencervale schoolmaster was that. But I found out something about him that turned me against him. He nearly went insane when I turned him down. I wish those two boys hadn't come tonight. I wanted to have a nice good talk with you, Anne, and tell you such heaps of things. You and I were always good chums, weren't we?"

Ruby slipped her arm about Anne's waist with a shallow little laugh. But just for a moment their eyes met, and, behind all the luster of Ruby's, Anne saw something that made her heart ache.

"Come up often, won't you, Anne?" whispered Ruby. "Come alone—I want you."

"Are you feeling quite well, Ruby?"

"Me! Why, I'm perfectly well. I never felt better in my life. Of course, that congestion last winter pulled me down a little. But just see my color. I don't look much like an invalid, I'm sure."

Ruby's voice was almost sharp. She pulled her arm away from Anne, as if in resentment, and ran downstairs, where she was gayer than ever, apparently so much absorbed in bantering her two swains that Diana and Anne felt rather out of it and soon went away.

12

"Averil's Atonement"

"What are you dreaming of Anne?"

The two girls were loitering one evening in a fairy hollow of the brook. Ferns nodded in it, and little grasses were green, and wild pears hung finely-scented, white curtains around it.

Anne roused herself from her reverie with a happy sigh.

"I was thinking out my story, Diana."

"Oh, have you really begun it?" cried Diana, all alight with eager interest in a moment.

"Yes, I have only a few pages written, but I have it all pretty well thought out. I've had such a time to get a suitable plot. None of the plots that suggested themselves suited a girl named *Averil*."

"Couldn't you have changed her name?"

"No, the thing was impossible. I tried to, but I couldn't do it, any more than I could change yours. *Averil* was so real to me that no matter what other name I tried to give her I just thought of her as *Averil* behind it all. But finally I got a plot that matched her. Then came the excitement of choosing names for all my characters. You have no idea how fascinating that is. I've lain awake for hours thinking over those names. The hero's name is *Perceval Dalrymple*."

"Have you named *all* the characters?" asked Diana wistfully. "If you hadn't I was going to ask you to let me name *one*—just some unimportant person. I'd feel as if I had a share in the story then."

"You may name the little hired boy who lived with the *Lesters,*" conceded Anne. "He is not very important, but he is the only one left unnamed."

"Call him *Raymond Fitzosborne,*" suggested Diana, who had a store of such names laid away in her memory, relics of the old "Story Club," which she and Anne and Jane Andrews and Ruby Gillis had had in their schooldays.

Anne shook her head doubtfully.

"I'm afraid that is too aristocratic a name for a chore boy, Diana. I couldn't imagine a Fitzosborne feeding pigs and picking up chips, could you?"

Diana didn't see why, if you had an imagination at all, you couldn't stretch it to that extent; but probably Anne knew best, and the chore boy was finally christened *Robert Ray,* to be called *Bobby* should occasion require.

"How much do you suppose you'll get for it?" asked Diana.

But Anne had not thought about this at all. She was in pursuit of fame, not filthy lucre, and her literary dreams were as yet untainted by mercenary considerations.

"You'll let me read it, won't you?" pleaded Diana. "When it is finished I'll read it to you and Mr. Harrison, and I shall want you to criticize it *severely*. No one else shall see it until it is published."

"How are you going to end it—happily or unhappily?"

"I'm not sure. I'd like it to end unhappily, because that would be so much more romantic. But I understand editors have a prejudice against sad endings. I heard Professor Hamilton say once that nobody but a genius should try to write an unhappy ending. And," concluded Anne modestly, "I'm anything but a genius."

"Oh, I like happy endings best. You'd better let him marry her," said Diana, who, especially since her engagement to Fred, thought this was how every story should end.

"But you like to cry over stories?"

"Oh, yes, in the middle of them. But I like everything to come right at last."

"I must have *one* pathetic scene in it," said Anne thoughtfully. "I might let *Robert Ray* be injured in an accident and have a death scene."

"No, you mustn't kill *Bobby* off," declared Diana, laughing. "He belongs to me and I want him to live and flourish. Kill somebody else if you have to."

For the next fortnight Anne writhed or reveled, according to mood, in her literary pursuits. Now she would be jubilant over a brilliant idea, now despairing because some contrary character would *not* behave properly. Diana could not understand this.

"*Make* them do as you want them to," she said.

"I can't," mourned Anne. "Averil is such an unmanageable heroine. She *will* do and say things I never meant her to. Then that spoils everything that went before and I have to write it all over again."

Finally, however, the story was finished, and Anne read it to Diana in the seclusion of the porch gable. She had achieved her "pathetic scene" without sacrificing *Robert Ray,* and she kept a watchful eye on Diana as she read it. Diana rose to the occasion and cried properly; but, when the end came, she looked a little disappointed.

"Why did you kill *Maurice Lennox?*" she asked reproachfully.

"He was the villain," protested Anne. "He had to be punished."

"I like him best of them all," said unreasonable Diana.

"Well, he's dead, and he'll have to stay dead," said Anne, rather resentfully. "If I had let him live he'd have gone on persecuting *Averil* and *Perceval.*"

"Yes—unless you had reformed him."

"That wouldn't have been romantic, and, besides, it would have made the story too long."

"Well, anyway, it's a perfectly elegant story, Anne, and will make you famous, of that I'm sure. Have you got a title for it?"

"Oh, I decided on the title long ago. I call it *Averil's Atonement.* Doesn't that sound nice and alliterative? Now, Diana, tell me candidly, do you see any faults in my story?"

"Well," hesitated Diana, "that part where *Averil* makes the cake doesn't seem to me quite romantic enough to match the rest. It's just what anybody might do. Heroines shouldn't do cooking, *I* think."

"Why, that is where the humor comes in, and it's one of the best parts of the whole story," said Anne. And it may be stated that in this she was quite right. Diana prudently refrained from any further criticism, but Mr. Harrison was much harder to please. First he told her there was entirely too much description in the story.

"Cut out all those flowery passages," he said unfeelingly.

Anne had an uncomfortable conviction that Mr. Harrison was right, and she forced herself to expunge most of her beloved descriptions, though it took three re-writings before the story could be pruned down to please the fastidious Mr. Harrison.

"I've left out *all* the descriptions but the sunset," she said at last. "I simply *couldn't* let it go. It was the best of them all."

"It hasn't anything to do with the story," said Mr. Harrison, "and you shouldn't have laid the scene among rich city people. What do you know of them? Why didn't you lay it right here in Avonlea—changing the name, of course, or else Mrs. Rachel Lynde would probably think she was the heroine."

"Oh, that would never have done," protested Anne. "Avonlea is the dearest place in the world, but it isn't quite romantic enough for the scene of a story."

"I daresay there's been many a romance in Avonlea—and many a tragedy, too," said Mr. Harrison drily. "But your folks ain't like real folks anywhere. They talk too much and use too high-flown language. There's one place where that *Dalrymple* chap talks even on for two pages, and never lets the girl get a word in edgewise. If he'd done that in real life she'd have pitched him."

"I don't believe it," said Anne flatly. In her secret soul she thought that the beautiful, poetical things said to *Averil* would win any girl's heart completely. Besides, it was gruesome to hear of *Averil,* the stately, queen-like *Averil,* "pitching" any one. *Averil* "declined her suitors."

"Anyhow," resumed the merciless Mr. Harrison, "I don't see why *Maurice Lennox* didn't get her. He was twice the man the other is. He did bad things, but he *did* them. *Perceval* hadn't time for anything but mooning."

"Mooning." That was even worse than "pitching!"

"Maurice Lennox was the villain," said Anne indignantly. "I don't see why every one likes him better than *Perceval.*"

"Perceval is too good. He's aggravating. Next time you write about a hero put a little spice of human nature in him."

"*Averil* couldn't have married *Maurice*. He was bad."

"She'd have reformed him. You *can* reform a man; you can't reform a jelly-fish, of course. Your story isn't bad—it's kind of interesting, I'll admit. But you're too young to write a story that would be worthwhile. Wait ten years."

Anne made up her mind that the next time she wrote a story she wouldn't ask anybody to criticize it. It was too discouraging. She would not read the story to Gilbert, although she told him about it.

"If it is a success you'll see it when it is published, Gilbert, but if it is a failure nobody shall ever see it."

Marilla knew nothing about the venture. In imagination Anne saw herself reading a story out of a magazine to Marilla, entrapping her into praise of it—for in imagination all things are possible—and then triumphantly announcing herself the author.

One day Anne took to the Post Office a long, bulky envelope, addressed, with the delightful confidence of youth and inexperience, to the very biggest of the "big" magazines. Diana was as excited over it as Anne herself.

"How long do you suppose it will be before you hear from it?" she asked.

"It shouldn't be longer than a fortnight. Oh, how happy and proud I shall be if it is accepted!"

"Of course it will be accepted, and they will likely ask you to send them more. You may be as famous as Mrs. Morgan some day, Anne, and then how proud I'll be of knowing you," said Diana, who possessed, at least, the striking merit of an unselfish admiration of the gifts and graces of her friends.

A week of delightful dreaming followed, and then came a bitter awakening. One evening Diana found Anne in the porch gable, with suspicious-looking eyes. On the table lay a long envelope and a crumpled manuscript.

"Averil's Atonement"

"Anne, your story hasn't come back?" cried Diana incredulously.

"Yes, it has," said Anne shortly.

"Well, that editor must be crazy. What reason did he give?"

"No reason at all. There is just a printed slip saying that it wasn't found acceptable."

"I never thought much of that magazine, anyway," said Diana hotly. "The stories in it are not half as interesting as those in the *Canadian Woman,* although it costs so much more. I suppose the editor is prejudiced against any one who isn't a Yankee. Don't be discouraged, Anne. Remember how Mrs. Morgan's stories came back. Send yours to the *Canadian Woman.*"

"I believe I will," said Anne, plucking up heart. "And if it is published I'll send that American editor a marked copy. But I'll cut the sunset out. I believe Mr. Harrison was right."

Out came the sunset; but in spite of this heroic mutilation the editor of the *Canadian Woman* sent *Averil's Atonement* back so promptly that the indignant Diana declared that it couldn't have been read at all, and vowed she was going to stop her subscription immediately. Anne took this second rejection with the calmness of despair. She locked the story away in the garret trunk where the old Story Club tales reposed; but first she yielded to Diana's entreaties and gave her a copy.

"This is the end of my literary ambitions," she said bitterly.

She never mentioned the matter to Mr. Harrison, but one evening he asked her bluntly if her story had been accepted.

"No, the editor wouldn't take it," she answered briefly.

Mr. Harrison looked sidewise at the flushed, delicate profile.

"Well, I suppose you'll keep on writing them," he said encouragingly.

"No, I shall never try to write a story again," declared Anne, with the hopeless finality of nineteen when a door is shut in its face.

"I wouldn't give up altogether," said Mr. Harrison reflectively. "I'd write a story once in a while, but I wouldn't pester editors with it. I'd write of people and places like I knew, and I'd make my characters talk everyday English; and I'd let the sun rise and set in the usual quiet way without much fuss over the fact. If I had to have villains at all, I'd give them a chance, Anne—I'd give them a chance. There *are* some terrible bad men in the world, I suppose, but you'd have to go a long piece to find them—though Mrs. Lynde believes we're all bad. But most of us have got a little decency somewhere in us. Keep on writing, Anne."

"No. It was very foolish of me to attempt it. When I'm through Redmond I'll stick to teaching. I *can* teach. I can't write stories."

"It'll be time for you to be getting a husband when you're through Redmond," said Mr. Harrison. "I don't believe in putting marrying off too long—like I did."

Anne got up and marched home. There were times when Mr. Harrison was really intolerable. "Pitching,"

"mooning," and "getting a husband." Ow!!

13

The Way of Transgressors

Davy and Dora were ready for Sunday School. They were going alone, which did not often happen, for Mrs. Lynde always attended Sunday School. But Mrs. Lynde had twisted her ankle and was lame, so she was staying home this morning. The twins were also to represent the family at church, for Anne had

The Way of Transgressors

gone away the evening before to spend Sunday with friends in Carmody, and Marilla had one of her headaches.

Davy came downstairs slowly. Dora was waiting in the hall for him, having been made ready by Mrs. Lynde. Davy had attended to his own preparations. He had a cent in his pocket for the Sunday School collection, and a five-cent piece for the church collection; he carried his Bible in one hand and his Sunday School quarterly in the other; he knew his lesson and his Golden Text and his catechism question perfectly. Had he not studied them—perforce—in Mrs. Lynde's kitchen, all last Sunday afternoon? Davy, therefore, should have been in a placid frame of mind. As a matter of fact, despite text and catechism, he was inwardly as a ravening wolf.

Mrs. Lynde limped out of her kitchen as he joined Dora.

"Are you clean?" she demanded severely.

"Yes—all of me that shows," Davy answered with a defiant scowl.

Mrs. Rachel sighed. She had her suspicions about Davy's neck and ears. But she knew that if she attempted to make a personal examination Davy would likely take to his heels and she could not pursue him today.

"Well, be sure you behave yourselves," she warned them. "Don't walk in the dust. Don't stop in the porch to talk to the other children. Don't squirm or wriggle in your places. Don't forget the Golden Text. Don't lose your collection or forget to put it in. Don't whisper at prayer time, and don't forget to pay attention to the sermon."

Davy deigned no response. He marched away down the lane, followed by the meek Dora. But his soul seethed within him. Davy had suffered, or thought he had suffered, many things at the hands and tongue of Mrs. Rachel Lynde since she had come to Green Gables, for Mrs. Lynde could not live with anybody, whether they were nine or ninety, without trying to bring them up properly. And it was only the preceding afternoon that she had interfered to influence Marilla against allowing Davy to go fishing with the Timothy Cottons. Davy was still boiling over this.

As soon as he was out of the lane Davy stopped and twisted his countenance into such an unearthly and terrific contortion that Dora, although she knew his gifts in that respect, was honestly alarmed lest he should never in the world be able to get it straightened out again.

"Darn her," exploded Davy.

"Oh, Davy, don't swear," gasped Dora in dismay.

"'Darn' isn't swearing—not real swearing. And I don't care if it is," retorted Davy recklessly.

"Well, if you *must* say dreadful words don't say them on Sunday," pleaded Dora.

Davy was as yet far from repentance, but in his secret soul he felt that, perhaps, he had gone a little too far.

"I'm going to invent a swear word of my own," he declared.

"God will punish you if you do," said Dora solemnly.

"Then I think God is a mean old scamp," retorted Davy. "Doesn't He know a fellow must have some way of 'spressing his feelings?"

"Davy!!!" said Dora. She expected that Davy would be struck down dead on the spot. But nothing happened.

"Anyway, I ain't going to stand any more of Mrs. Lynde's bossing," spluttered Davy. "Anne and Marilla may have the right to boss me, but *she* hasn't. I'm going to do every single thing she told me not to do. You watch me."

In grim, deliberate silence, while Dora watched him with the fascination of horror, Davy stepped off the green grass of the roadside, ankle deep into the fine dust which four weeks of rainless weather had made on the road, and marched along in it, shuffling his feet viciously until he was enveloped in a hazy cloud.

"That's the beginning," he announced triumphantly. "And I'm going to stop in the porch and talk as long as there's anybody there to talk to. I'm going to squirm and wriggle and whisper, and I'm going to say I don't know the Golden Text. And I'm going to throw away both of my collections *right now.*"

And Davy hurled cent and nickel over Mr. Barry's fence with fierce delight.

"Satan made you do that," said Dora reproachfully.

"He didn't," cried Davy indignantly. "I just thought it out for myself. And I've thought of something else. I'm not going to Sunday School or church at all. I'm going up to play with the Cottons. They told me yesterday they weren't going to Sunday School today, 'cause their mother was away and there was nobody to make them. Come along, Dora, we'll have a great time."

"I don't want to go," protested Dora.

"You've got to," said Davy. "If you don't come I'll tell Marilla that Frank Bell kissed you in school last Monday."

"I couldn't help it. I didn't know he was going to," cried Dora, blushing scarlet.

"Well, you didn't slap him or seem a bit cross," retorted Davy. "I'll tell her *that,* too, if you don't come. We'll take the short cut up this field."

"I'm afraid of those cows," protested poor Dora, seeing a prospect of escape.

"The very idea of your being scared of those cows" scoffed Davy. "Why, they're both younger than you.

"They're bigger," said Dora.

"They won't hurt you. Come along, now. This is great. When I grow up I ain't going to bother going to church at all. I believe I can get to heaven by myself."

"You'll go to the other place if you break the Sabbath day," said unhappy Dora, following him sorely against her will.

But Davy was not scared—yet. Hell was very far off, and the delights of a fishing expedition with the Cottons were very near. He wished Dora had more spunk. She kept looking back as if she were going to cry every minute, and that spoiled a fellow's fun. Hang girls, anyway. Davy did not say "darn" this time, even in thought. He was not sorry—yet—that he had said it once, but it might be as well not to tempt the Unknown Powers too far on one day.

The small Cottons were playing in their back yard, and hailed Davy's appearance with whoops of delight. Pete, Tommy, Adolphus, and Mirabel Cotton were all alone. Their mother and older sisters were away. Dora was thankful Mirabel was there, at least. She had been afraid she would be alone in a crowd of boys. Mirabel was almost as bad as a boy—she was so noisy and sunburned and reckless. But at least she wore dresses.

"We've come to go fishing," announced Davy.

"Whoop," yelled the Cottons. They rushed away to dig worms at once, Mirabel leading the van with a tin can. Dora could have sat down and cried. Oh, if only that hateful Frank Bell had never kissed her! Then she could have defied Davy, and gone to her beloved Sunday School.

They dared not, of course, go fishing on the pond, where they would be seen by people going to church. They had to resort to the brook in the woods behind the Cotton house. But it was full of trout, and they had a glorious time that morning— at least the Cottons certainly had, and Davy seemed to have it. Not being entirely bereft of prudence, he had discarded boots and stockings and borrowed Tommy Cotton's overalls. Thus accoutered, bog and marsh and undergrowth had no terrors for him. Dora was frankly and manifestly miserable. She followed the others in their peregrinations from pool to pool, clasping her Bible and quarterly tightly and thinking with bitterness of soul of her beloved class where she should be sitting that very moment, before a teacher she adored. Instead, here she was roaming the woods with those half-wild Cottons, trying to keep her boots clean and her pretty white dress free from rents and stains. Mirabel had offered the loan of an apron but Dora had scornfully refused.

The trout bit as they always do on Sundays. In an hour the transgressors had all the fish they wanted, so they returned to the house, much to Dora's relief. She sat primly on a hencoop in the yard while the others played an uproarious game of tag; and then they all climbed to the top of the pig-house roof and cut their initials on the saddle-board. The flat-roofed henhouse and a pile of straw beneath gave Davy another inspiration. They spent a splendid half hour climbing on the roof and diving off into the straw with whoops and yells.

But even unlawful pleasures must come to an end. When the rumble of wheels over the pond bridge told that people were going home from church Davy knew they must go. He discarded Tommy's overalls, resumed his own rightful attire, and turned away from his string of trout with a sigh. No use to think of taking them home.

"Well, hadn't we a splendid time?" he demanded defiantly, as they went down the hill field.

"I hadn't," said Dora flatly. "And I don't believe you had—really—either," she added, with a flash of insight that was not to be expected of her.

"I had so," cried Davy, but in the voice of one who doth protest too much. "No wonder *you* hadn't—just sitting there like a—like a mule."

"I ain't going to 'sociate with the Cottons," said Dora loftily.

"The Cottons are all right," retorted Davy. "And they have far better times than we have. They do just as they please and say just what they like before everybody. *I'm* going to do that, too, after this."

"There are lots of things you wouldn't dare say before everybody," averred Dora.

"No, there isn't."

"There is, too. Would you," demanded Dora gravely, "would you say 'tomcat' before the minister?"

This was a staggerer. Davy was not prepared for such a concrete example of the freedom of speech. But one did not have to be consistent with Dora.

"Of course not," he admitted sulkily. "'Tomcat' isn't a holy word. I wouldn't mention such an animal before a minister at all."

"But if you had to?" persisted Dora.

"I'd call it a Thomas pussy," said Davy.

"*I* think 'gentleman cat' would he more polite," reflected Dora.

"*You* thinking!" retorted Davy with withering scorn.

Davy was not feeling comfortable, though he would have died before he admitted it to Dora. Now that the exhilaration of truant delights had died away, his conscience was beginning to give him salutary twinges. After all, perhaps it would have been better to have gone to Sunday School and church. Mrs. Lynde might be bossy; but there was always a box of cookies in her kitchen cupboard and she was not stingy. At this inconvenient moment Davy remembered that when he had torn his new school pants the week before, Mrs. Lynde had mended them beautifully and never said a word to Marilla about them.

But Davy's cup of iniquity was not yet full. He was to discover that one sin demands another to cover it. They had dinner with Mrs. Lynde that day, and the first thing she asked Davy was,

"Were all your class in Sunday School today?"

"Yes'm," said Davy with a gulp. "All were there—'cept one."

"Did you say your Golden Text and catechism?"

"Yes'm."

The Way of Transgressors

"Did you put your collection in?"

"Yes'm."

"Was Mrs. Malcolm MacPherson in church?"

"I don't know." This, at least, was the truth, thought wretched Davy.

"Was the Ladies' Aid announced for next week?"

"Yes'm"—quakingly.

"Was prayer-meeting?"

"I—I don't know."

"You *should* know. You should listen more attentively to the announcements. What was Mr. Harvey's text?"

Davy took a frantic gulp of water and swallowed it and the last protest of conscience together. He glibly recited an old Golden Text learned several weeks ago. Fortunately Mrs. Lynde now stopped questioning him; hut Davy did not enjoy his dinner. He could only eat one helping of pudding.

"What's the matter with you?" demanded justly astonished Mrs. Lynde. "Are you sick?"

"No," muttered Davy.

"You look pale. You'd better keep out of the sun this afternoon," admonished Mrs. Lynde.

"Do you know how many lies you told Mrs. Lynde?" asked Dora reproachfully, as soon as they were alone after dinner.

Davy, goaded to desperation, turned fiercely.

"I don't know and I don't care," he said. "You just shut up, Dora Keith."

Then poor Davy betook himself to a secluded retreat behind the woodpile to think over the way of transgressors.

Green Gables was wrapped in darkness and silence when Anne reached home. She lost no time going to bed, for she was very tired and sleepy. There had been several Avonlea jollifications the preceding week, involving rather late hours. Anne's head was hardly on her pillow before she was half asleep;

hut just then her door was softly opened and a pleading voice said, "Anne."

Anne sat up drowsily.

"Davy, is that you? What is the matter?"

A white-clad figure flung itself across the floor and on to the bed.

"Anne," sobbed Davy, getting his arms about her neck. "I'm awful glad you're home. I couldn't go to sleep till I'd told somebody."

"Told somebody what?"

"How mis'rubul I am."

"Why are you miserable, dear?"

"'Cause I was so bad today, Anne. Oh, I was awful bad—badder'n I've ever been yet."

"What did you do?"

"Oh, I'm afraid to tell you. You'll never like me again, Anne. I couldn't say my prayers tonight. I couldn't tell God what I'd done. I was 'shamed to have Him know."

"But He knew anyway, Davy."

"That's what Dora said. But I thought p'raps He mightn't have noticed just at the time. Anyway, I'd rather tell you first."

"*What* is it you did?"

Out it all came in a rush.

"I run away from Sunday School—and went fishing with the Cottons—and I told ever so many whoppers to Mrs. Lynde—oh! 'most half a dozen—and—and—I—I said a swear word, Anne—a pretty near swear word, anyhow—and I called God names."

There was a silence. Davy didn't know what to make of it. Was Anne so shocked that she never would speak to him again?

"Anne, what are you going to do to me?" he whispered.

"Nothing, dear. You've been punished already, I think."

"No, I haven't. Nothing's been done to me."

The Way of Transgressors 101

"You've been very unhappy ever since you did wrong, haven't you?"

"You bet!" said Davy emphatically.

"That was your conscience punishing you, Davy."

"What's my conscience? I want to know."

"It's something in you, Davy, that always tells you when you are doing wrong and makes you unhappy if you persist in doing it. Haven't you noticed that?"

"Yes, but I didn't know what it was. I wish I didn't have it. I'd have lots more fun. Where is my conscience, Anne? I want to know. Is it in my stomach?"

"No, it's in your soul," answered Anne, thankful for the darkness, since gravity must be preserved in serious matters.

"I s'pose I can't get clear of it then," said Davy with a sigh. "Are you going to tell Marilla and Mrs. Lynde on me, Anne?"

"No, dear, I'm not going to tell any one. You are sorry you were naughty, aren't you?"

"You bet!"

"And you'll never be bad like that again."

"No, but—" added Davy cautiously, "I might be bad some other way."

"You won't say naughty words, or run away on Sundays, or tell falsehoods to cover up your sins?"

"No. It doesn't pay," said Davy.

"Well, Davy, just tell God you are sorry and ask Him to forgive you."

"Have *you* forgive me, Anne?"

"Yes, dear."

"Then," said Davy joyously, "I don't care much whether God does or not."

"Davy!"

"Oh—I'll ask Him—I'll ask Him," said Davy quickly, scrambling off the bed, convinced by Anne's tone that he must have said something dreadful. "I don't mind asking him, Anne.

—Please, God, I'm awful sorry I behaved bad today and I'll try to be good on Sundays always and please forgive me.—There now, Anne.

"Well, now, run off to bed like a good boy."

"All right. Say, I don't feel mis'rubul any more. I feel fine. Good night."

"Good night."

Anne slipped down on her pillows with a sigh of relief. Oh—how sleepy—she was! In another second—

"Anne!"

Davy was back again by her bed. Anne dragged her eyes open.

"What is it now, dear?" she asked, trying to keep a note of impatience out of her voice.

"Anne, have you ever noticed how Mr. Harrison spits? Do you s'pose, if I practice hard, I can learn to spit just like him?"

Anne sat up.

"Davy Keith," she said, "go straight to your bed and don't let me catch you out of it again tonight! Go, now!"

Davy went, and stood not upon the order of his going.

14

The Summons

Anne was sitting with Ruby Gillis in the Gillis' garden after the day had crept lingeringly through it and was gone. It had been a warm, smoky summer afternoon. The world was in a splendor of out-flowering. The idle valleys were full of hazes. The woodways were pranked with shadows and the fields with the purple of the asters.

The Summons

Anne had given up a moonlight drive to the White Sands beach that she might spend the evening with Ruby. She had so spent many evenings that summer, although she often wondered what good it did any one, and sometimes went home deciding that she could not go again.

Ruby grew paler as the summer waned; the White Sands school was given up—"her father thought it better that she shouldn't teach till New Year's"—and the fancy work she loved oftener and oftener fell from hands grown too weary for it. But she was always gay, always hopeful, always chattering and whispering of her beaux, and their rivalries and despairs. It was this that made Anne's visits hard for her. What had once been silly or amusing was gruesome now; it was death peering through a wilful mask of life. Yet Ruby seemed to cling to her, and never let her go until she had promised to come again soon. Mrs. Lynde grumbled about Anne's frequent visits, and declared she would catch consumption; even Marilla was dubious.

"Every time you go to see Ruby you come home looking tired out," she said.

"It's so very sad and dreadful," said Anne in a low tone. "Ruby doesn't seem to realize her condition in the least. And yet I somehow feel she needs help—craves it—and I want to give it to her and can't. All the time I'm with her I feel as if I were watching her struggle with an invisible foe—trying to push it back with such feeble resistance as she has. That is why I come home tired."

But tonight Anne did not feel this so keenly. Ruby was strangely quiet. She said not a word about parties and drives and dresses and "fellows." She lay in the hammock, with her untouched work beside her, and a white shawl wrapped about her thin shoulders. Her long yellow braids of hair—how Anne had envied those beautiful braids in old schooldays!—lay on either side of her. She had taken the pins out—they made her head ache, she said. The hectic flush was gone for the time, leaving her pale and childlike.

The moon rose in the silvery sky, empearling the clouds around her. Below, the pond shimmered in its hazy radiance. Just beyond the Gillis homestead was the church, with the old graveyard beside it. The moonlight shone on the white stones, bringing them out in clear-cut relief against the dark trees behind.

"How strange the graveyard looks by moonlight!" said Ruby suddenly. "How ghostly!" she shuddered. "Anne, it won't be long now before I'll be lying over there. You and Diana and all the rest will be going about, full of life—and I'll be there—in the old graveyard—dead!"

The surprise of it bewildered Anne. For a few moments she could not speak.

"You know it's so, don't you?" said Ruby insistently.

"Yes, I know," answered Anne in a low tone. "Dear Ruby, I know."

"Everybody knows it," said Ruby bitterly. "I know it—I've known it all summer, though I wouldn't give in. And, oh, Anne"—she reached out and caught Anne's hand pleadingly, impulsively—"I don't want to die. I'm *afraid* to die."

"Why should you be afraid, Ruby?" asked Anne quietly.

"Because—because—oh, I'm not afraid but that I'll go to heaven, Anne. I'm a church member. But—it'll be all so different. I think—and think—and I get so frightened—and—and—homesick. Heaven must be very beautiful, of course, the Bible says so—but, Anne, *it won't be what I've been used to.*"

Through Anne's mind drifted an intrusive recollection of a funny story she had heard Philippa Gordon tell—the story of some old man who had said very much the same thing about the world to come. It *had* sounded funny then—she remembered how she and Priscilla had laughed over it. But it did not seem in the least humorous now, coming from Ruby's pale, trembling

The Summons

lips. It was sad, tragic—and *true!* Heaven could not be what Ruby had been used to. There had been nothing in her gay, frivolous life, her shallow ideals and aspirations, to fit her for that great change, or make the life to come seem to her anything but alien and unreal and undesirable. Anne wondered helplessly what she could say that would help her. Could she say anything? "I think, Ruby," she began hesitatingly—for it was difficult for Anne to speak to any one of the deepest thoughts of her heart, or the new ideas that had vaguely begun to shape themselves in her mind, concerning the great mysteries of life here and hereafter, superseding her old childish conceptions, and it was hardest of all to speak of them to such as Ruby Gillis—"I think, perhaps, we have very mistaken ideas about heaven—what it is and what it holds for us. I don't think it can be so very different from life here as most people seem to think. I believe we'll just go on living, a good deal as we live here—and be *ourselves* just the same—only it will be easier to be good and to—follow the highest. All the hindrances and perplexities will be taken away, and we shall see clearly. Don't be afraid, Ruby."

"I can't help it," said Ruby pitifully. "Even if what you say about heaven is true—and you can't be sure—it may be only that imagination of yours—it won't be *just* the same. It *can't* be. I want to go on living *here.* I'm so young, Anne. I haven't had my life. I've fought so hard to live—and it isn't any use—I have to die—and leave *everything* I care for."

Anne sat in a pain that was almost intolerable. She could not tell comforting falsehoods; and all that Ruby said was so horribly true. She *was* leaving everything she cared for. She had laid up her treasures on earth only; she had lived solely for the little things of life—the things that pass—forgetting the great things that go onward into eternity, bridging the gulf between the two lives and making of death a mere passing from one dwelling to the other—from twilight to unclouded day. God would take care of her there—Anne believed—she would learn—but now it was no wonder her soul clung, in blind helplessness, to the only things she knew and loved.

Ruby raised herself on her arm and lifted up her bright, beautiful blue eyes to the moonlit skies.

"I want to live," she said, in a trembling voice. "I want to live like other girls. I—I want to be married, Anne—and—and—have little children. You know I always loved babies, Anne. I couldn't say this to any one but you. I know you understand. And then poor Herb—he—he loves me and I love him, Anne. The others meant nothing to me, but *he* does—and if I could live I would be his wife and be so happy. Oh, Anne, it's hard."

Ruby sank back on her pillows and sobbed convulsively. Anne pressed her hand in an agony of sympathy—silent sympathy, which perhaps helped Ruby more than broken, imperfect words could have done; for presently she grew calmer and her sobs ceased.

"I'm glad I've told you this, Anne," she whispered. "It has helped me just to say it all out. I've wanted to all summer—every time you came I wanted to talk it over with you—but I *couldn't*. It seemed as if it would make death so *sure* if I *said* I was going to die, or if any one else said it or hinted it. I wouldn't say it, or even think it. In the daytime, when people were around me and everything was cheerful, it wasn't so hard to keep from thinking of it. But in the night, when I couldn't sleep—it was so dreadful, Anne. I couldn't get away from it then. Death just came and stared me in the face, until I got so frightened I could have screamed."

"But you won't be frightened any more, Ruby, will you? You'll be brave, and believe that all is going to be well with you."

"I'll try. I'll think over what you have said, and try to believe it. And you'll come up as often as you can, won't you, Anne?"

"Yes, dear."

The Summons

"It—it won't be very long now, Anne. I feel sure of that. And I'd rather have you than any one else. I always liked you best of all the girls I went to school with. You were never jealous, or mean, like some of them were. Poor Em White was up to see me yesterday. You remember Em and I were such chums for three years when we went to school? And then we quarrelled the time of the school concert. We've never spoken to each other since. Wasn't it silly? Anything like that seems silly *now.* But Em and I made up the old quarrel yesterday. She said she'd have spoken years ago, only she thought I wouldn't. And I never spoke to her because I was sure she wouldn't speak to me. Isn't it strange how people misunderstand each other, Anne?"

"Most of the trouble in life comes from misunderstanding, I think," said Anne. "I must go now, Ruby. It's getting late—and you shouldn't be out in the damp."

"You'll come up soon again."

"Yes, very soon. And if there's anything I can do to help you I'll be so glad."

"I know. You *have* helped me already. Nothing seems quite so dreadful now. Good night, Anne."

"Good night, dear."

Anne walked home very slowly in the moonlight. The evening had changed something for her. Life held a different meaning, a deeper purpose. On the surface it would go on just the same; but the deeps had been stirred. It must not be with her as with poor butterfly Ruby. When she came to the end of one life it must not be to face the next with the shrinking terror of something wholly different—something for which accustomed thought and ideal and aspiration had unfitted her. The little things of life, sweet and excellent in their place, must not be the things lived for; the highest must be sought and followed; the life of heaven must be begun here on earth.

That good night in the garden was for all time. Anne never saw Ruby in life again. The next night the A.V.I.S. gave a farewell party to Jane Andrews before her departure for the West. And, while light feet danced and bright eyes laughed and merry tongues chattered, there came a summons to a soul in Avonlea that might not be disregarded or evaded. The next morning the word went from house to house that Ruby Gillis was dead. She had died in her sleep, painlessly and calmly, and on her face was a smile—as if, after all, death had come as a kindly friend to lead her over the threshold, instead of the grisly phantom she had dreaded.

Mrs. Rachel Lynde said emphatically after the funeral that Ruby Gillis was the handsomest corpse she ever laid eyes on. Her loveliness, as she lay, white-clad, among the delicate flowers that Anne had placed about her, was remembered and talked of for years in Avonlea. Ruby had always been beautiful; but her beauty had been of the earth, earthy; it had had a certain insolent quality in it, as if it flaunted itself in the beholder's eye; spirit had never shone through it, intellect had never refined it. But death had touched it and consecrated it, bringing out delicate modelings and purity of outline never seen before—doing what life and love and great sorrow and deep womanhood joys might have done for Ruby. Anne, looking down through a mist of tears, at her old playfellow, thought she saw the face God had meant Ruby to have, and remembered it so always.

Mrs. Gillis called Anne aside into a vacant room before the funeral procession left the house, and gave her a small packet.

"I want you to have this," she sobbed. "Ruby would have liked you to have it. It's the embroidered centerpiece she was working at. It isn't quite finished—the needle is sticking in it just where her poor little fingers put it the last time she laid it down, the afternoon before she died."

"There's always a piece of unfinished work left," said Mrs. Lynde, with tears in her eyes. "But I suppose there's always some one to finish it."

The Summons

"How difficult it is to realize that one we have always known can really be dead," said Anne, as she and Diana walked home. "Ruby is the first of our schoolmates to go. One by one, sooner or later, all the rest of us must follow."

"Yes, I suppose so," said Diana uncomfortably. She did not want to talk of that. She would have preferred to have discussed the details of the funeral—the splendid white velvet casket Mr. Gillis had insisted on having for Ruby—"the Gillises must always make a splurge, even at funerals," quoth Mrs. Rachel Lynde—Herb Spencer's sad face, the uncontrolled, hysteric grief of one of Ruby's sisters—but Anne would not talk of these things. She seemed wrapped in a reverie in which Diana felt lonesomely that she had neither lot nor part.

"Ruby Gillis was a great girl to laugh," said Davy suddenly. "Will she laugh as much in heaven as she did in Avonlea, Anne? I want to know."

"Yes, I think she will," said Anne.

"Oh, Anne," protested Diana, with a rather shocked smile.

"Well, why not, Diana?" asked Anne seriously. "Do you think we'll never laugh in heaven?"

"Oh—I—I don't know," floundered Diana. "It doesn't seem just right, somehow. You know it's rather dreadful to laugh in church."

"But heaven won't be like church—all the time," said Anne.

"I hope it ain't," said Davy emphatically. "If it is *I* don't want to go. Church is awful dull. Anyway, I don't mean to go for ever so long. I mean to live to be a hundred years old, like Mr. Thomas Blewett of White Sands. He says he's lived so long 'cause he always smoked tobacco and it killed all the germs. Can I smoke tobacco pretty soon, Anne?"

"No, Davy, I hope you'll never use tobacco," said Anne absently.

"What'll you feel like if the germs kill me then?" demanded Davy.

15

A Dream Turned Upside Down

"Just one more week and we go back to Redmond," said Anne. She was happy at the thought of returning to work, classes, and Redmond friends. Pleasing visions were also being woven around Patty's Place. There was a warm pleasant sense of home in the thought of it, even though she had never lived there.

But the summer had been a very happy one, too—a time of glad living with summer suns and skies, a time of keen delight in wholesome things; a time of renewing and deepening of old friendships; a time in which she had learned to live more nobly, to work more patiently, to play more heartily.

"All life lessons are not learned at college," she thought. "Life teaches them everywhere."

But alas, the final week of that pleasant vacation was spoiled for Anne, by one of those impish happenings which are like a dream turned upside down.

"Been writing any more stories lately?" inquired Mr. Harrison genially one evening when Anne was taking tea with him and Mrs. Harrison.

"No," answered Anne, rather crisply.

"Well, no offense meant. Mrs. Hiram Sloane told me the other day that a big envelope addressed to the Rollings Reliable Baking Powder Company of Montreal had been dropped into the post office box a month ago, and she suspicioned that somebody was trying for the prize they'd offered for the best story that introduced the name of their baking powder. She said it wasn't addressed in your writing, but I thought maybe it was you."

"Indeed, no! I saw the prize offer, but I'd never dream of competing for it. I think it would be perfectly disgraceful to

A Dream Turned Upside Down 111

write a story to advertise a baking powder. It would be almost as bad as Judson Parker's patent medicine fence."

So spake Anne loftily, little dreaming of the valley of humiliation awaiting her. That very evening Diana popped into the porch gable, bright-eyed and rosy cheeked, carrying a letter.

"Oh, Anne, here's a letter for you. I was at the office, so I thought I'd bring it along. Do open it quick. If it is what I believe it is I shall just be wild with delight."

Anne, puzzled, opened the letter and glanced over the typewritten contents.

> "Miss Anne Shirley,
> "Green Gables,
> "Avonlea, P.E. Island.
>
> "DEAR MADAM:
> We have much pleasure in informing you that your charming story *'Averil's Atonement'* has won the prize of twenty-five dollars offered in our recent competition. We enclose the check herewith. We are arranging for the publication of the story in several prominent Canadian newspapers, and we also intend to have it printed in pamphlet form for distribution among our patrons. Thanking you for the interest you have shown in our enterprise, we remain,
> "Yours very truly,
> "THE ROLLINGS RELIABLE BAKING POWDER CO."

"I don't understand," said Anne, blankly. Diana clapped her hands.

"Oh, I *knew* it would win the prize—I was sure of it. *I* sent your story into the competition, Anne."

"Diana—Barry!"

"Yes, I did," said Diana gleefully, perching herself on the bed. "When I saw the offer I thought of your story in a minute, and at first I thought I'd ask you to send it in. But then I was afraid you wouldn't—you had so little faith left in it. So I just decided I'd send the copy you gave me, and say nothing about it. Then, if it didn't win the prize, you'd never know and you wouldn't feel badly over it, because the stories that failed were not to be returned, and if it did you'd have such a delightful surprise."

Diana was not the most discerning of mortals, but just at this moment it struck her that Anne was not looking exactly overjoyed. The surprise was there, beyond doubt—but where was the delight?

"Why, Anne, you don't seem a bit pleased!" she exclaimed.

Anne instantly manufactured a smile and put it on.

"Of course I couldn't be anything but pleased over your unselfish wish to give me pleasure," she said slowly. "But you know—I'm so amazed—I can't realize it—and I don't understand. There wasn't a word in my story about—about—" Anne choked a little over the word—"baking powder."

"Oh, *I* put that in," said Diana, reassured. "It was as easy as wink—and of course my experience in our old Story Club helped me. You know the scene where Averil makes the cake? Well, I just stated that she used the Rollings Reliable in it, and that was why it turned out so well; and then, in the last paragraph, where *Perceval* clasps *Averil* in his arms and says, 'Sweetheart, the beautiful coming years will bring us the fulfilment of our home of dreams,' I added, 'in which we will never use any baking powder except Rollings Reliable.'"

"Oh," gasped poor Anne, as if some one had dashed cold water on her.

"And you've won the twenty-five dollars," continued Diana jubilantly. "Why, I heard Priscilla say once that the *Canadian Woman* only pays five dollars for a story!"

A Dream Turned Upside Down

Anne held out the hateful pink slip in shaking fingers.

"I can't take it—it's yours by right, Diana. You sent the story in and made the alterations. I—I would certainly never have sent it. So you must take the check."

"I'd like to see myself," said Diana scornfully. "Why, what I did wasn't any trouble. The honor of being a friend of the prize-winner is enough for me. Well, I must go. I should have gone straight home from the post office for we have company. But I simply had to come and hear the news. I'm *so* glad for your sake, Anne."

Anne suddenly bent forward, put her arms about Diana, and kissed her cheek.

"I think you are the sweetest and truest friend in the world, Diana," she said, with a little tremble in her voice, "and I assure you I appreciate the motive of what you've done."

Diana, pleased and embarrassed, got herself away, and poor Anne, after flinging the innocent check into her bureau drawer as if it were blood-money, cast herself on her bed and wept tears of shame and outraged sensibility. Oh, she could never live this down—never!

Gilbert arrived at dusk, brimming over with congratulations, for he had called at Orchard Slope and heard the news. But his congratulations died on his lips at sight of Anne's face.

"Why, Anne, what is the matter? I expected to find you radiant over winning Rollings Reliable prize. Good for you!"

"Oh, Gilbert, not you," implored Anne, in an *et-tu Brute* tone. "I thought *you* would understand. Can't you see how awful it is?"

"I must confess I can't. *What* is wrong?"

"Everything," moaned Anne. "I feel as if I were disgraced forever. What do you think a mother would feel like if she found her child tattooed over with a baking powder advertisement? I feel just the same. I loved my poor little story, and I wrote it out of the best that was in me. And it is *sacrilege* to have it degraded to the level of a baking powder advertisement. Don't you remember what Professor Hamilton used to tell us in the literature class at Queen's? He said we were never to write a word for a low or unworthy motive, but always to cling to the very highest ideals. What will he think when he hears I've written a story to advertise Rollings Reliable? And, oh, when it gets out at Redmond! Think how I'll be teased and laughed at.

"That you won't," said Gilbert, wondering uneasily if it were that confounded Junior's opinion in particular over which Anne was worried. "The Reds will think just as I thought—that you, being like nine out of ten of us, not overburdened with worldly wealth, had taken this way of earning an honest penny to help yourself through the year. I don't see that there's anything low or unworthy about that, or anything ridiculous either. One would rather write masterpieces of literature no doubt—but meanwhile board and tuition fees have to be paid."

This commonsense, matter-of-fact view of the case cheered Anne a little. At least it removed her dread of being laughed at, though the deeper hurt of an outraged ideal remained.

16
Adjusted Relationships

"It's the homiest spot I ever saw—it's homier than home," avowed Philippa Gordon, looking about her with delighted eyes. They were all assembled at twilight in the big living-room at Patty's Place—Anne and Priscilla, Phil and Stella, Aunt Jamesina, Rusty, Joseph, the Sarah-Cat, and Gog and Magog.

Adjusted Relationships

The firelight shadows were dancing over the walls; the cats were purring; and a huge bowl of hothouse chrysanthemums, sent to Phil by one of the victims, shone through the golden gloom like creamy moons.

It was three weeks since they had considered themselves settled, and already all believed the experiment would be a success. The first fortnight after their return had been a pleasantly exciting one; they had been busy setting up their household goods, organizing their little establishment, and adjusting different opinions.

Anne was not over-sorry to leave Avonlea when the time came to return to college. The last few days of her vacation had not been pleasant. Her prize story had been published in the Island papers; and Mr. William Blair had, upon the counter of his store, a huge pile of pink, green, and yellow pamphlets, containing it, one of which he gave to every customer. He sent a complimentary bundle to Anne, who promptly dropped them all in the kitchen stove. Her humiliation was the consequence of her own ideals only, for Avonlea folks thought it quite splendid that she should have won the prize. Her many friends regarded her with honest admiration; her few foes with scornful envy. Josie Pye said she believed Anne Shirley had just copied the story; she was sure she remembered reading it in a paper years before. The Sloanes, who had found out or guessed that Charlie had been "turned down," said they didn't think it was much to be proud of; almost any one could have done it, if she tried. Aunt Atossa told Anne she was very sorry to hear she had taken to writing novels; nobody born and bred in Avonlea would do it; that was what came of adopting orphans from goodness knew where, with goodness knew what kind of parents. Even Mrs. Rachel Lynde was darkly dubious about the propriety of writing fiction, though she was almost reconciled to it by that twenty-five-dollar check.

"It is perfectly amazing, the price they pay for such lies, that's what," she said, half-proudly, half-severely.

All things considered, it was a relief when going-away time came. And it was very jolly to be back at Redmond, a wise, experienced Soph with hosts of friends to greet on the merry opening day. Pris and Stella and Gilbert were there, Charlie Sloane, looking more important than ever Sophomore looked before, Phil, with the Alec-and-Alonzo question still unsettled, and Moody Spurgeon MacPherson. Moody Spurgeon had been teaching school ever since leaving Queen's, but his mother had concluded it was high time he gave it up and turned his attention to learning how to be a minister. Poor Moody Spurgeon fell on hard luck at the very beginning of his college career. Half a dozen ruthless Sophs, who were among his fellow-boarders, swooped down upon him one night and shaved half of his head. In this guise the luckless Moody Spurgeon had to go about until his hair grew again. He told Anne bitterly that there were times when he had his doubts as to whether he was really called to be a minister.

Aunt Jamesina did not come until the girls had Patty's Place ready for her. Miss Patty had sent the key to Anne, with a letter in which she said Gog and Magog were packed in a box under the spare-room bed, but might be taken out when wanted; in a postscript she added that she hoped the girls would be careful about putting up pictures. The living room had been newly papered five years before and she and Miss Maria did not want any more holes made in that new paper than was absolutely necessary. For the rest she trusted everything to Anne.

How those girls enjoyed putting their nest in order! As Phil said, it was almost as good as getting married. You had the fun of homemaking without the bother of a husband. All brought something with them to adorn or make comfortable the little house. Pris and Phil and Stella had knick-knacks and pictures

Adjusted Relationships 117

galore, which latter they proceeded to hang according to taste, in reckless disregard of Miss Patty's new paper.

"We'll putty the holes up when we leave, dear—she'll never know," they said to protesting Anne.

Diana had given Anne a pine needle cushion and Miss Ada had given both her and Priscilla a fearfully and wonderfully embroidered one. Marilla had sent a big box of preserves, and darkly hinted at a hamper for Thanksgiving, and Mrs. Lynde gave Anne a patchwork quilt and loaned her five more.

"You take them," she said authoritatively. "They might as well be in use as packed away in that trunk in the garret for moths to gnaw."

No moths would ever have ventured near those quilts, for they reeked of mothballs to such an extent that they had to be hung in the orchard of Patty's Place a full fortnight before they could be endured indoors. Verily, aristocratic Spofford Avenue had rarely beheld such a display. The gruff old millionaire who lived "next door" came over and wanted to buy the gorgeous red and yellow "tulip-pattern" one which Mrs. Rachel had given Anne. He said his mother used to make quilts like that, and by Jove, he wanted one to remind him of her. Anne would not sell it, much to his disappointment, but she wrote all about it to Mrs. Lynde. That highly-gratified lady sent word back that she had one just like it to spare, so the tobacco king got his quilt after all, and insisted on having it spread on his bed, to the disgust of his fashionable wife.

Mrs. Lynde's quilts served a very useful purpose that winter. Patty's Place for all its many virtues, had its faults also. It was really a rather cold house; and when the frosty nights came the girls were very glad to snuggle down under Mrs. Lynde's quilts, and hoped that the loan of them might be accounted unto her for righteousness. Anne had the blue room she had coveted at sight. Priscilla and Stella had the large one. Phil was blissfully content with the little one over the kitchen; and Aunt Jamesina was to have the downstairs one off the living-room. Rusty at first slept on the doorstep.

Anne, walking home from Redmond a few days after her return, became aware that the people that she met surveyed her with a covert, indulgent smile. Anne wondered uneasily what was the matter with her. Was her hat crooked? Was her belt loose? Craning her head to investigate, Anne, for the first time, saw Rusty.

Trotting along behind her, close to her heels, was quite the most forlorn specimen of the cat tribe she had ever beheld. The animal was well past kittenhood, lank, thin, disreputable-looking. Pieces of both ears were lacking, one eye was temporarily out of repair, and one jowl ludicrously swollen. As for color, if a once black cat had been well and thoroughly singed the result would have resembled the hue of this waifs thin, draggled, unsightly fur.

Anne "shooed," but the cat would not "shoo." As long as she stood he sat back on his haunches and gazed at her reproachfully out of his one good eye; when she resumed her walk he followed. Anne resigned herself to his company until she reached the gate of Patty's Place, which she coldly shut in his face, fondly supposing she had seen the last of him. But when, fifteen minutes later, Phil opened the door, there sat the rusty-brown cat on the step. More, he promptly darted in and sprang upon Anne's lap with a half-pleading, half-triumphant "miaow."

"Anne," said Stella severely, "do you own that animal?"

"No, I do *not*," protested disgusted Anne. "The creature followed me home from somewhere. I couldn't get rid of him. Ugh, get down. I like decent cats reasonably well; but I don't like beasties of your complexion."

Pussy, however, refused to get down. He coolly curled up in Anne's lap and began to purr.

Adjusted Relationships

"He has evidently adopted you," laughed Priscilla.

"I won't *be* adopted," said Anne stubbornly.

"The poor creature is starving," said Phil pityingly. "Why, his bones are almost coming through his skin."

"Well, I'll give him a square meal and then he must return to whence he came," said Anne resolutely.

The cat was fed and put out. In the morning he was still on the doorstep. On the doorstep he continued to sit, bolting in whenever the door was opened. No coolness of welcome had the least effect on him; of nobody save Anne did he take the least notice. Out of compassion the girls fed him; but when a week had passed they decided that something must be done.

The cat's appearance had improved. His eye and cheek had resumed their normal appearance; he was not quite so thin; and he had been seen washing his face.

"But for all that we can't keep him," said Stella. "Aunt Jimsie is coming next week and she will bring the Sarah-cat with her. We can't keep two cats; and if we did this Rusty Coat would fight all the time with the Sarah-cat. He's a fighter by nature. He had a pitched battle last evening with the tobacco-king's cat and routed him, horse, foot and artillery."

"We must get rid of him," agreed Anne, looking darkly at the subject of their discussion, who was purring on the hearth rug with an air of lamb-like meekness. "But the question is—how? How can four unprotected females get rid of a cat who *won't* be got rid of?"

"We must chloroform him," said Phil briskly. "That is the most humane way."

"Who of us knows anything about chloroforming a cat?" demanded Anne gloomily.

"I do, honey. It's one of my few—sadly few—useful accomplishments. I've disposed of several at home. You take the cat in the morning and give him a good breakfast. Then you take an old burlap bag—there's one in the back porch—put the cat on it and turn over him a wooden box. Then take a two-ounce bottle of chloroform, uncork it, and slip it under the edge of the box. Put a heavy weight on top of the box and leave it till evening. The cat will be dead, curled up peacefully as if he were asleep. No pain—no struggle."

"It sounds easy," said Anne dubiously.

"It *is* easy. Just leave it to me. I'll see to it," said Phil reassuringly.

Accordingly the chloroform was procured, and the next morning Rusty was lured to his doom. He ate his breakfast, licked his chops, and climbed into Anne's lap. Anne's heart misgave her. This poor creature loved her—trusted her. How could she be a party to his destruction?

"Here, take him," she said hastily to Phil. "I feel like a murderess."

"He won't suffer, you know," comforted Phil, but Anne had fled.

The fatal deed was done in the back porch. Nobody went near it that day. But at dusk Phil declared that Rusty must be buried.

"Pris and Stella must dig his grave in the orchard," decreed Phil, "and Anne must come with me to lift the box off. That's the part I always hate."

The two conspirators tip-toed reluctantly to the back porch. Phil gingerly lifted the stone she had put on the box. Suddenly, faint but distinct, sounded an unmistakable mew under the box.

"He—he isn't dead," gasped Anne, sitting blankly down on the kitchen doorstep.

"He must be," said Phil incredulously.

Another tiny mew proved that he wasn't. The two girls stared at each other.

"What will we do?" questioned Anne.

Adjusted Relationships 121

"Why in the world don't you come?" demanded Stella, appearing in the doorway. "We've got the grave ready. 'What, silent still and silent all?'" she quoted teasingly.

"'Oh, no, the voices of the dead
Sound like the distant torrent's fall,'"
promptly counter-quoted Anne, pointing solemnly to the box.

A burst of laughter broke the tension.

"We must leave him here till morning," said Phil, replacing the stone. "He hasn't mewed for five minutes. Perhaps the mews we heard were his dying groan. Or perhaps we merely imagined them, under the strain of our guilty consciences."

But, when the box was lifted in the morning, Rusty bounded at one gay leap to Anne's shoulder where he began to lick her face affectionately. Never was there a cat more decidedly alive.

"Here's a knot hole in the box," groaned Phil. "I never saw it. That's why he didn't die. Now, we've got to do it all over again."

"No, we haven't," declared Anne suddenly. "Rusty isn't going to be killed again. He's my cat—and you've just got to make the best of it."

"Oh, well, if you'll settle with Aunt Jimsie and the Sarah-cat," said Stella, with the air of one washing her hands of the whole affair.

From that time Rusty was one of the family. He slept o' nights on the scrubbing cushion in the back porch and lived on the fat of the land. By the time Aunt Jamesina came he was plump and glossy and tolerably respectable. But, like Kipling's cat, he "walked by himself." His paw was against every cat, and every cat's paw against him. One by one he vanquished the aristocratic felines of Spofford Avenue. As for human beings, he loved Anne and Anne alone. Nobody else even dared stroke him. An angry spit and something that sounded much like very improper language greeted any one who did.

"The airs that cat puts on are perfectly intolerable," declared Stella.

"Him was a nice old pussens, him was," vowed Anne, cuddling her pet defiantly.

"Well, I don't know how he and the Sarah-cat will ever make out to live together," said Stella pessimistically. "Cat-fights in the orchard o' nights are bad enough. But cat-fights here in the living-room are unthinkable."

In due time Aunt Jamesina arrived. Anne and Priscilla and Phil had awaited her advent rather dubiously; but when Aunt Jamesina was enthroned in the rocking chair before the open fire they figuratively bowed down and worshipped her.

Aunt Jamesina was a tiny old woman with a little, softly-triangular face, and large, soft blue eyes that were alight with unquenchable youth, and as full of hopes as a girl's. She had pink cheeks and snow-white hair which she wore in quaint little puffs over her ears.

"It's a very old-fashioned way," she said, knitting industriously at something as dainty and pink as a sunset cloud. "But *I* am old-fashioned. My clothes are, and it stands to reason my opinions are, too. I don't say they're any the better of that, mind you. In fact, I daresay they're a good deal the worse. But they've worn nice and easy. New shoes are smarter than old ones, but the old ones are more comfortable. I'm old enough to indulge myself in the matter of shoes and opinions. I mean to take it real easy here. I know you expect me to look after you and keep you proper, but I'm not going to do it. You're old enough to know how to behave if you're ever going to be. So, as far as I am concerned," concluded Aunt Jamesina, with a twinkle in her young eyes, "you can all go to destruction in your own way."

"Oh, will somebody separate those cats?" pleaded Stella, shudderingly.

Aunt Jamesina had brought with her not only the Sarah-cat but Joseph. Joseph, she explained, had belonged to a dear friend of hers who had gone to live in Vancouver.

Adjusted Relationships 123

"She couldn't take Joseph with her so she begged me to take him. I really couldn't refuse. He's a beautiful cat—that is, his disposition is beautiful. She called him Joseph because his coat is of many colors."

It certainly was. Joseph, as the disgusted Stella said, looked like a walking rag-bag. It was impossible to say what his ground color was. His legs were white with black spots on them. His back was gray with a huge patch of yellow on one side and a black patch on the other. His tail was yellow with a gray tip. One ear was black and one yellow. A black patch over one eye gave him a fearfully rakish look. In reality he was meek and inoffensive, of a sociable disposition. In one respect, if in no other, Joseph was like a lily of the field. He toiled not neither did he spin or catch mice. Yet Solomon in all his glory slept not on softer cushions, or feasted more fully on fat things.

Joseph and the Sarah-cat arrived by express in separate boxes. After they had been released and fed, Joseph selected the cushion and corner which appealed to him, and the Sarah-cat gravely sat her down before the fire and proceeded to wash her face. She was a large, sleek, gray-and-white cat, with an enormous dignity which was not at all impaired by any consciousness of her plebeian origin. She had been given to Aunt Jamesina by her washerwoman.

"Her name was Sarah, so my husband always called puss the Sarah-cat," explained Aunt Jamesina. "She is eight years old, and a remarkable mouser. Don't worry, Stella. The Sarah-cat *never* fights and Joseph rarely."

"They'll have to fight here in self-defense," said Stella.

At this juncture Rusty arrived on the scene. He bounded joyously half way across the room before he saw the intruders. Then he stopped short; his tail expanded until it was as big as three tails. The fur on his back rose up in a defiant arch; Rusty lowered his head, uttered a fearful shriek of hatred and defiance, and launched himself at the Sarah-cat.

That stately animal had stopped washing her face and was looking at him curiously. She met his onslaught with one contemptuous sweep of her capable paw. Rusty went rolling helplessly over on the rug; he picked himself up dazedly. What sort of a cat was this who had boxed his ears? He looked dubiously at the Sarah-cat. Would he or would he not? The Sarah-cat deliberately turned her back on him and resumed her toilet operations. Rusty decided that he would not. He never did. From that time on the Sarah-cat ruled the roost. Rusty never again interfered with her.

But Joseph rashly sat up and yawned. Rusty, burning to avenge his disgrace, swooped down upon him. Joseph, pacific by nature, could fight upon occasion and fight well. The result was a series of drawn battles. Every day Rusty and Joseph fought at sight. Anne took Rusty's part and detested Joseph. Stella was in despair. But Aunt Jamesina only laughed.

"Let them fight it out," she said tolerantly. "They'll make friends after a bit. Joseph needs some exercise—he was getting too fat. And Rusty has to learn he isn't the only cat in the world."

Eventually Joseph and Rusty accepted the situation and from sworn enemies became sworn friends. They slept on the same cushion with their paws about each other, and gravely washed each other's faces.

"We've all got used to each other," said Phil. "And I've learned how to wash dishes and sweep a floor."

"But you needn't try to make us believe you can chloroform a cat," laughed Anne.

"It was all the fault of the knothole," protested Phil.

"It was a good thing the knothole was there," said Aunt Jamesina rather severely. "Kittens *have* to be drowned, I admit, or the world would be overrun. But no decent, grown-up cat should be done to death—unless he sucks eggs."

"You wouldn't have thought Rusty very decent if you'd seen him when he came here," said Stella. "He positively looked like the Old Nick."

"I don't believe Old Nick can be so very ugly," said Aunt Jamesina reflectively. "He wouldn't do so much harm if he was. *I* always think of him as a rather handsome gentleman."

17

A Letter from Davy

"It's beginning to snow, girls," said Phil, coming in one November evening, "and there are the loveliest little stars and crosses all over the garden walk. I never noticed before what exquisite things snowflakes really are. One has time to notice things like that in the simple life. Bless you all for permitting me to live it. It's really delightful to feel worried because butter has gone up five cents a pound."

"Has it?" demanded Stella, who kept the household accounts.

"It has—and here's your butter. I'm getting quite expert at marketing. It's better fun than flirting," concluded Phil gravely.

"Everything is going up scandalously," sighed Stella.

"Never mind. Thank goodness air and salvation are still free," said Aunt Jamesina.

"And so is laughter," added Anne. "There's no tax on it yet and that is well, because you're all going to laugh presently. I'm going to read you Davy's letter. His spelling has improved immensely this past year, though he is not strong on apostrophes, and he certainly possesses the gift of writing an interesting letter. Listen and laugh, before we settle down to the evening's study-grind."

***

"Dear Anne," ran Davy's letter, "I take my pen to tell you that we are all pretty well and hope this will find you the same. It's snowing some today and Marilla says the old woman in the sky is shaking her feather beds. Is the old woman in the sky God's wife, Anne? I want to know.

"Mrs. Lynde has been real sick but she is better now. She fell down the cellar stairs last week. When she fell she grabbed hold of the shelf with all the milk pails and stewpans on it, and it gave way and went down with her and made a splendid crash. Marilla thought it was an earthquake at first. One of the stewpans was all dinged up and Mrs. Lynde straned her ribs. The doctor come and gave her medicine to rub on her ribs but she didn't understand him and took it all inside instead. The doctor said it was a wonder it dident kill her but it dident and it cured her ribs and Mrs. Lynde says doctors dont know much anyhow. But we couldent fix up the stewpan. Marilla had to throw it out. Thanksgiving was last week. There was no school and we had a great dinner. I et mince pie and rost turkey and frut cake and donuts and cheese and jam and choklut cake. Marilla said I'd die but I dident. Dora had earake after it, only it wasent in her ears it was in her stummick. I dident have earake anywhere.

"Our new teacher is a man. He does things for jokes. Last week he made all us third-class boys write a composishun on what kind of a wife we'd like to have and the girls on what kind of a husband. He laughed fit to kill when he read them. This was mine. I thought you'd like to see it.

"'The kind of a wife I'd like to Have.

"'She must have good manners and get my meals on time and do what I tell her and always be very polite to me. She must be fifteen yers old. She must be good to the poor and keep her house tidy and be good tempered and go to church regularly. She must be very handsome and have curly hair. If I get a wife that is just what I like Ill be an awful good husband to her. I think a woman ought to be awful good to her husband. Some poor women havent any husbands. 'THE END.'

"I was at Mrs. Isaac Wrights funeral at White Sands last week. The husband of the corpse felt real sorry. Mrs. Lynde says Mrs. Wrights grandfather stole a sheep but Marilla says we mustent speak ill of the dead. Why mustent we, Anne? I want to know. It's pretty safe, ain't it?

"Mrs. Lynde was awful mad the other day because I asked her if she was alive in Noah's time. I dident mean to hurt her feelings. I just wanted to know. Was she, Anne?

"Mr. Harrison wanted to get rid of his dog. So he hunged him once but he come to life and scooted for the barn while Mr. Harrison was digging the grave, so he hunged him again and he stayed dead that time. Mr. Harrison has a new man working for him. He's awful okward. Mr. Harrison says he is left handed in both his feet. Mr. Barry's hired man is lazy. Mrs. Barry says that but Mr. Barry says he aint lazy exactly only he thinks it easier to pray for things than to work for them.

"Mrs. Harmon Andrews prize pig that she talked so much of died in a fit. Mrs. Lynde says it was a judgment on her for pride. But I think it was hard on the pig. Milty Boulter has been sick. The doctor gave him medicine and it tasted horrid. I offered to take it for him for a quarter but the Boulters are so mean. Milty says he'd rather take it himself and save his money. I asked Mrs. Boulter how a person would go about catching a man and she got awful mad and said she dident know, shed never chased men.

"The A.V.I.S. is going to paint the hall again. They're tired of having it blue.

"The new minister was here to tea last night. He took three pieces of pie. If I did that Mrs. Lynde would call me piggy. And he et fast and took big bites and Marilla is always telling me not to do that. Why can ministers do what boys can't? I want to know.

"I haven't any more news. Here are six kisses. xxxxxx. Dora sends one. Heres hers. x.

"Your loving friend
"DAVID KEITH"
"P.S. Anne, who was the devils father? I want to know."

18

Miss Josephine Remembers the Anne-Girl

When Christmas holidays came the girls of Patty's Place scattered to their respective homes, but Aunt Jamesina elected to stay where she was.

"I couldn't go to any of the places I've been invited and take those three cats," she said. "And I'm not going to leave the poor creatures here alone for nearly three weeks. If we had any decent neighbors who would feed them I might, but there's nothing except millionaires on this street. So I'll stay here and keep Patty's Place warm for you."

Anne went home with the usual joyous anticipations—which were not wholly fulfilled. She found Avonlea in the grip of such an early, cold, and stormy winter as even the "oldest inhabitant" could not recall. Green Gables was literally hemmed

Miss Josephine Remembers the Anne-Girl

in by huge drifts. Almost every day of that ill-starred vacation it stormed fiercely; and even on fine days it drifted unceasingly. No sooner were the roads broken than they filled in again. It was almost impossible to stir out. The A.V.I.S. tried, on three evenings, to have a party in honor of the college student, and on each evening the storm was so wild that nobody could go, so they gave up the attempt in despair. Anne, despite her love of and loyalty to Green Gables, could not help thinking longingly of Patty's Place, its cosy open fire, Aunt Jamesina's mirthful eyes, the three cats, the merry chatter of the girls, the pleasantness of Friday evenings when college friends dropped in to talk of grave and gay.

Anne was lonely; Diana, during the whole of the holidays, was imprisoned at home with a bad attack of bronchitis. She could not come to Green Gables and it was rarely Anne could get to Orchard Slope, for the old way through the Haunted Wood was impassable with drifts, and the long way over the frozen Lake of Shining Waters was almost as bad. Ruby Gillis was sleeping in the white-heaped graveyard; Jane Andrews was teaching a school on western prairies. Gilbert, to be sure, was still faithful, and waded up to Green Gables every possible evening. But Gilbert's visits were not what they once were. Anne almost dreaded them. It was very disconcerting to look up in the midst of a sudden silence and find Gilbert's hazel eyes fixed upon her with a quite unmistakable expression in their grave depths; and it was still more disconcerting to find herself blushing hotly and uncomfortably under his gaze, just as if—just as if—well, it was very embarrassing. Anne wished herself back at Patty's Place, where there was always somebody else about to take the edge off a delicate situation. At Green Gables Marilla went promptly to Mrs. Lynde's domain when Gilbert came and insisted on taking the twins with her. The significance of this was unmistakable and Anne was in a helpless fury over it.

Davy, however, was perfectly happy. He reveled in getting out in the morning and shoveling out the paths to the well and henhouse. He gloried in the Christmas-tide delicacies which Marilla and Mrs. Lynde vied with each other in preparing for Anne, and he was reading an enthralling tale, in a school library book, of a wonderful hero who seemed blessed with a miraculous faculty for getting into scrapes from which he was usually delivered by an earthquake or a volcanic explosion, which blew him high and dry out of his troubles, handed him in a fortune, and closed the story with proper *éclat*.

"I tell you it's a bully story, Anne," he said ecstatically. "I'd ever so much rather read it than the Bible."

"Would you?" smiled Anne.

Davy peered curiously at her.

"You don't seem a bit shocked, Anne. Mrs. Lynde was awful shocked when I said it to her."

"No, I'm not shocked, Davy. I think it's quite natural that a nine-year-old boy would sooner read an adventure story than the Bible. But when you are older I hope and think that you will realize what a wonderful hook the Bible is."

"Oh, I think some parts of it are fine," conceded Davy. "That story about Joseph now—it's bully. But if I'd been Joseph *I* wouldn't have forgive the brothers. No, siree, Anne. I'd have cut all their heads off. Mrs. Lynde was awful mad when I said that and shut the Bible up and said she'd never read me any more of it if I talked like that. So I don't talk now when she reads it Sunday afternoons; I just think things and say them to Milty Boulter next day in school. I told Milty the story about Elisha and the bears and it scared him so he's never made fun of Mr. Harrison's bald head since. Are there any bears on P.E. Island, Anne? I want to know."

"Not nowadays," said Anne, absently, as the wind blew a scud of snow against the window. "Oh, dear, will it ever stop storming."

"God knows," said Davy airily, preparing to resume his reading.

Anne *was* shocked this time.

"Davy!" she exclaimed reproachfully.

"Mrs. Lynde says that," protested Davy. "One night last week Marilla said 'Will Ludovic Speed and Theodora Dix *ever* get married,' and Mrs. Lynde said, 'God knows'—just like that."

"Well, it wasn't right for her to say it," said Anne, promptly deciding upon which horn of this dilemma to empale herself. "It isn't right for anybody to take that name in vain or speak it lightly, Davy. Don't ever do it again."

"Not if I say it slow and solemn, like the minister?" queried Davy gravely.

"No, not even then."

"Well, I won't. Ludovic Speed and Theodora Dix live in Middle Grafton and Mrs. Rachel says he has been courting her for a hundred years. Won't they soon be too old to get married, Anne? I hope Gilbert won't court *you* that long. When are you going to be married, Anne? Mrs. Lynde says it's a sure thing."

"Mrs. Lynde is a—" began Anne hotly; then stopped.

"Awful old gossip," completed Davy calmly. "That's what every one calls her. But *is* it a sure thing, Anne? I want to know."

"You're a very silly little boy, Davy," said Anne, stalking haughtily out of the room. The kitchen was deserted and she sat down by the window in the fast falling wintry twilight. The sun had set and the wind had died down. A pale chilly moon looked out behind a bank of purple clouds in the west. The sky faded out, but the strip of yellow along the western horizon grew brighter and fiercer, as if all the stray gleams of light were concentrating in one spot; the distant hills, rimmed with priestlike firs, stood out in dark distinctness against it. Anne looked across the still, white fields, cold and lifeless in the harsh light of that grim sunset, and sighed. She was very lonely; and she was sad at heart; for she was wondering if she would be able to return to Redmond next year. It did not seem likely. The only scholarship possible in the Sophomore year was a very small affair. She would not take Marilla's money; and there seemed little prospect of being able to earn enough in the summer vacation.

"I suppose I'll just have to drop out next year," she thought drearily, "and teach a district school again until I earn enough to finish my course. And by that time all my old class will have graduated and Patty's Place will be out of the question. But there! I'm not going to be a coward. I'm thankful I can earn my way through if necessary."

"Here's Mr. Harrison wading up the lane," announced Davy, running out. "I hope he's brought the mail. It's three days since we got it. I want to see what them pesky Grits are doing. I'm a Conservative, Anne. And I tell you, you have to keep your eye on them Grits."

Mr. Harrison had brought the mail, and merry letters from Stella and Priscilla and Phil soon dissipated Anne's blues. Aunt Jamesina, too, had written, saying that she was keeping the hearth-fire alight, and that the cats were all well, and the house plants doing fine.

"The weather has been real cold," she wrote, "so I let the cats sleep in the house—Rusty and Joseph on the sofa in the living-room, and the Sarah-cat on the foot of my bed. It's real company to hear her purring when I wake up in the night and think of my poor daughter in the foreign field. If it was anywhere but in India I wouldn't worry, but they say the snakes out there are terrible. It takes all the Sarah-cats's purring to drive away the thought of those snakes. I have enough faith for everything but the snakes. I can't think why Providence ever made them. Sometimes I don't think He did. I'm inclined to believe the Old Harry had a hand in making *them*."

Miss Josephine Remembers the Anne-Girl   133

Anne had left a thin, typewritten communication till the last, thinking it unimportant. When she had read it she sat very still, with tears in her eyes.

"What is the matter, Anne?" asked Marilla.

"Miss Josephine Barry is dead," said Anne, in a low tone.

"So she has gone at last," said Marilla. "Well, she has been sick for over a year, and the Barrys have been expecting to hear of her death any time. It is well she is at rest for she has suffered dreadfully, Anne. She was always kind to you."

"She has been kind to the last, Marilla. This letter is from her lawyer. She has left me a thousand dollars in her will."

"Gracious, ain't that an awful lot of money," exclaimed Davy. "She's the woman you and Diane lit on when you jumped into the spare room bed, ain't she? Diana told me that story. Is that why she left you so much?"

"Hush, Davy," said Anne gently. She slipped away to the porch gable with a full heart, leaving Marilla and Mrs. Lynde to talk over the news to their hearts' content.

"Do you s'pose Anne will ever get married now?" speculated Davy anxiously. "When Dorcas Sloane got married last summer she said if she'd had enough money to live on she'd never have been bothered with a man, but even a widower with eight children was better'n living with a sister-in-law."

"Davy Keith, do hold your tongue," said Mrs. Rachel severely. "The way you talk is scandalous for a small boy, that's what."

19

An Interlude

"To think that this is my twentieth birthday, and that I've left my teens behind me forever," said Anne, who was curled up on the hearth-rug with Rusty in her lap, to Aunt Jamesina who was reading in her pet chair. They were alone in the living room. Stella and Priscilla had gone to a committee meeting and Phil was upstairs adorning herself for a party.

"I suppose you feel kind of sorry," said Aunt Jamesina. "The teens are such a nice part of life. I'm glad I've never gone out of them myself."

Anne laughed.

"You never will, Aunty. You'll be eighteen when you should be a hundred. Yes, I'm sorry, and a little dissatisfied as well. Miss Stacy told me long ago that by the time I was twenty my character would be formed, for good or evil. I don't feel that it's what it should be. It's full of flaws."

"So's everybody's," said Aunt Jamesina cheerfully. "Mine's cracked in a hundred places. Your Miss Stacy likely meant that when you are twenty your character would have got its permanent bent in one direction or 'tother, and would go on developing in that line. Don't worry over it, Anne. Do your duty by God and your neighbor and yourself, and have a good time. That's my philosophy and it's always worked pretty well. Where's Phil off to tonight?"

"She's going to a dance, and she's got the sweetest dress for it—creamy yellow silk and cobwebby lace. It just suits those brown tints of hers."

'There's magic in the words 'silk' and 'lace,' isn't there?" said Aunt Jamesina. "The very sound of them makes me feel like skipping off to a dance. And *yellow* silk. It makes one think of a dress of sunshine. I always wanted a yellow silk dress, but first my mother and then my husband wouldn't hear of it. The very first thing I'm going to do when I get to heaven is to get a yellow silk dress."

Amid Anne's peal of laughter Phil came downstairs, trailing clouds of glory, and surveyed herself in the long oval mirror on the wall.

"A flattering looking glass is a promoter of amiability," she said. "The one in my room does certainly make me green. Do I look pretty nice, Anne?"

"Do you really know how pretty you are, Phil?" asked Anne, in honest admiration.

"Of course I do. What are looking glasses and men for? That wasn't what I meant. Are all my ends tucked in? Is my skirt straight? And would this rose look better lower down? I'm afraid it's too high—it will make me look lop-sided. But I hate things tickling my ears."

"Everything is just right, and that southwest dimple of yours is lovely."

"Anne, there's one thing in particular I like about you—you're so ungrudging. There isn't a particle of envy in you."

"Why should she be envious?" demanded Aunt Jamesina. "She's not quite as good-looking as you, maybe, but she's got a far handsomer nose."

"I know it," conceded Phil.

"My nose always has been a great comfort to me," confessed Anne.

"And I love the way your hair grows on your forehead, Anne. And that one wee curl, always looking as if it were going to drop, but never dropping, is delicious. But as for noses, mine is a dreadful worry to me. I know by the time I'm forty it will be Byrney. What do you think I'll look like when I'm forty, Anne?"

"Like an old, matronly, married woman," teased Anne.

"I won't," said Phil, sitting down comfortably to wait for her escort. "Joseph, you calico beastie, don't you dare jump on my lap. I won't go to a dance all over cat hairs. No, Anne, I *won't* look matronly. But no doubt I'll be married."

"To Alec or Alonzo?" asked Anne.

"To one of them, I suppose," sighed Phil, "if I can ever decide which."

"It shouldn't be hard to decide," scolded Aunt Jamesina.

"I was born a see-saw, Aunty, and nothing can ever prevent me from teetering."

"You ought to be more levelheaded, Philippa."

"It's best to be levelheaded, of course," agreed Philippa, "but you miss lots of fun. As for Alec and Alonzo, if you knew them you'd understand why it's difficult to choose between them. They're equally nice."

"Then take somebody who is nicer," suggested Aunt Jamesina. "There's that Senior who is so devoted to you—Will Leslie. He has such nice, large, mild eyes."

"They're a little bit too large and too mild—like a cow's," said Phil cruelly.

"What do you say about George Parker?"

"There's nothing to say about him except that he always looks as if he had just been starched and ironed."

"Marr Holworthy then. You can't find a fault with him."

"No, he would do if he wasn't poor. I must marry a rich man, Aunt Jamesina. That—and good looks—is an indispensable qualification. I'd marry Gilbert Blythe if he were rich."

"Oh, would you?" said Anne, rather viciously.

"We don't like that idea a little bit, although we don't want Gilbert ourselves, oh, no," mocked Phil. "But don't let's talk of disagreeable subjects. I'll have to marry sometime, I suppose, but I shall put off the evil day as long as I can."

"You mustn't marry anybody you don't love, Phil, when all's said and done," said Aunt Jamesina.

*"'Oh, hearts that loved in the good old way,
Have been out o' the fashion this many a day,'"*

trilled Phil mockingly. "There's the carriage. I fly—Bi-bi, you two old-fashioned darlings."

When Phil had gone Aunt Jamesina looked solemnly at Anne.

"That girl is pretty and sweet and good-hearted, but do you think she is quite right in her mind, by spells, Anne?"

"Oh, I don't think there's anything the matter with Phil's mind," said Anne, hiding a smile. "It's just her way of talking."

Aunt Jamesina shook her head.

"Well, I hope so, Anne. I do hope so, because I love her. But *I* can't understand her—she beats me. She isn't like any of the girls I ever knew, or any of the girls I was myself."

"How many girls were you, Aunt Jimsie?"

"About half a dozen, my dear."

20

Gilbert Speaks

"This has been a dull, prosy day," yawned Phil, stretching herself idly on the sofa, having previously dispossessed two exceedingly indignant cats.

Anne looked up from *Pickwick Papers*. Now that spring examinations were over she was treating herself to Dickens.

"It has been a prosy day for us," she said thoughtfully, "but to some people it has been a wonderful day. Some one has been rapturously happy in it. Perhaps a great deed has been done somewhere today—or a great poem written—or a great man born. And some heart has been broken, Phil."

"Why did you spoil your pretty thought by tagging that last sentence on, honey?" grumbled Phil. "I don't like to think of broken hearts—or anything unpleasant."

"Do you think you'll be able to shirk unpleasant things all your life, Phil?"

"Dear me, no. Am I not up against them now? You don't call Alec and Alonzo pleasant things, do you, when they simply plague my life out?"

"You never take anything seriously, Phil."

"Why should I? There are enough folks who do. The world needs people like me, Anne, just to amuse it. It would be a terrible place if *everybody* were intellectual and serious and in deep, deadly earnest. *My* mission is, as *Josiah Allen* says, 'to charm and allure.' Confess now. Hasn't life at Patty's Place been really much brighter and pleasanter this past winter because I've been here to leaven you?"

"Yes, it has," owned Anne.

"And you all love me—even Aunt Jamesina, who thinks I'm stark mad. So why should I try to be different? Oh, dear, I'm so sleepy. I was awake until one last night, reading a harrowing ghost story. I read it in bed, and after I had finished it do you suppose I could get out of bed to put the light out? No! And if Stella had not fortunately come in late that lamp would have burned good and bright till morning. When I heard Stella I called her in, explained my predicament, and got her to put out the light. If I had got out myself to do it I knew something would grab me by the feet when I was getting in again. By the way, Anne, has Aunt Jamesina decided what to do this summer?"

"Yes, she's going to stay here. I know she's doing it for the sake of those blessed cats, although she says it's too much trouble to open her own house, and she hates visiting."

"What are you reading?"

Gilbert Speaks

"*Pickwick.*"

"That's a book that always makes me hungry," said Phil. "There's so much good eating in it. The characters seem always to be reveling on ham and eggs and milk punch. I generally go on a cupboard rummage after reading *Pickwick*. The mere thought reminds me that I'm starving. Is there any tidbit in the pantry, Queen Anne?"

"I made a lemon pie this morning. You may have a piece of it."

Phil dashed out to the pantry and Anne betook herself to the orchard in company with Rusty. It was a moist, pleasantly-odorous night in early spring. The snow was not quite all gone from the park; a little dingy bank of it yet lay under the pines of the harbor road, screened from the influence of April suns. It kept the harbor road muddy, and chilled the evening air. But grass was growing green in sheltered spots and Gilbert had found some pale, sweet arbutus in a hidden corner. He came up from the park, his hands full of it.

Anne was sitting on the big gray boulder in the orchard looking at the poem of a bare, birchen bough hanging against the pale red sunset with the very perfection of grace. She was building a castle in air—a wondrous mansion whose sunlit courts and stately halls were steeped in Araby's perfume, and where she reigned queen and chatelaine. She frowned as she saw Gilbert coming through the orchard. Of late she had managed not to be left alone with Gilbert. But he had caught her fairly now; and even Rusty had deserted her.

Gilbert sat down beside her on the boulder and held out his Mayflowers.

"Don't these remind you of home and our old schoolday picnics, Anne?"

Anne took them and buried her face in them.

"I'm in Mr. Silas Sloane's barrens this very minute," she said rapturously.

"I suppose you will be there in reality in a few days?"

"No, not for a fortnight. I'm going to visit with Phil in Bolingbroke before I go home. You'll be in Avonlea before I will."

"No, I shall not be in Avonlea at all this summer, Anne. I've been offered a job in the *Daily News* office and I'm going to take it."

"Oh," said Anne vaguely. She wondered what a whole Avonlea summer would be like without Gilbert. Somehow she did not like the prospect. "Well," she concluded flatly, "it is a good thing for you, of course."

"Yes, I've been hoping I would get it. It will help me out next year."

"You mustn't work *too* hard," said Anne, without any very clear idea of what she was saying. She wished desperately that Phil would come out. "You've studied very constantly this winter. Isn't this a delightful evening? Do you know, I found a cluster of white violets under that old twisted tree over there today? I felt as if I had discovered a gold mine."

"You are always discovering gold mines," said Gilbert—also absently.

"Let us go and see if we can find some more," suggested Anne eagerly. "I'll call Phil and—"

"Never mind Phil and the violets just now, Anne," said Gilbert quietly, taking her hand in a clasp from which she could not free it. "There is something I want to say to you."

"Oh, don't say it," cried Anne, pleadingly. "Don't—*please*, Gilbert."

"I must. Things can't go on like this any longer. Anne, I love you. You know I do. I—I can't tell you how much. Will you promise me that some day you'll be my wife?"

"I—I can't," said Anne miserably. "Oh, Gilbert—you—you've spoiled everything."

Gilbert Speaks

"Don't you care for me at all?" Gilbert asked after a very dreadful pause, during which Anne had not dared to look up.

"Not—not in that way. I do care a great deal for you as a friend. But I don't love you, Gilbert."

"But can't you give me some hope that you will—yet?"

"No, I can't," exclaimed Anne desperately. "I never, never can love you—in that way—Gilbert. You must never speak of this to me again."

There was another pause—so long and so dreadful that Anne was driven at last to look up. Gilbert's face was white to the lips. And his eyes—but Anne shuddered and looked away. There was nothing romantic about this. Must proposals be either grotesque or—horrible? Could she ever forget Gilbert's face?

"Is there anybody else?" he asked at last in a low voice.

"No—no," said Anne eagerly. "I don't care for any one like *that*—and I *like* you better than anybody else in the world, Gilbert. And we must—we *must* go on being friends, Gilbert."

Gilbert gave a bitter little laugh.

"Friends! Your friendship can't satisfy me, Anne. I want your love—and you tell me I can never have that."

"I'm sorry. Forgive me, Gilbert," was all Anne could say. Where, oh, where were all the gracious and graceful speeches wherewith, in imagination, she had been wont to dismiss rejected suitors?

Gilbert released her hand gently.

"There isn't anything to forgive. There have been times when I thought you did care. I've deceived myself, that's all. Good-bye, Anne."

Anne got herself to her room, sat down on her window seat behind the pines, and cried bitterly. She felt as if something incalculably precious had gone out of her life. It was Gilbert's friendship, of course. Oh, why must she lose it after this fashion?

"What is the matter, honey?" asked Phil, coming in through the moonlit gloom.

Anne did not answer. At that moment she wished Phil were a thousand miles away.

"I suppose you've gone and refused Gilbert Blythe. You are an idiot, Anne Shirley!"

"Do you call it idiotic to refuse to marry a man I don't love?" said Anne coldly, goaded to reply.

"You don't know love when you see it. You've tricked something out with your imagination that you think love, and you expect the real thing to look like that. There, that's the first sensible thing I've ever said in my life. I wonder how I managed it?"

"Phil," pleaded Anne, "please go away and leave me alone for a little while. My world has tumbled into pieces. I want to reconstruct it."

"Without any Gilbert in it?" said Phil, going.

A world without any Gilbert in it! Anne repeated the words drearily. Would it not be a very lonely, forlorn place? Well, it was all Gilbert's fault. He had spoiled their beautiful comradeship. She must just learn to live without it.

21

Roses of Yesterday

The fortnight Anne spent in Bolingbroke was a very pleasant one, with a little undercurrent of vague pain and dissatisfaction running through it whenever she thought about Gilbert. There was not, however, much time to think about him. "Mount

Holly," the beautiful old Gordon homestead, was a very gay place, overrun by Phil's friends of both sexes. There was quite a bewildering succession of drives, dances, picnics, and boating parties, all expressively lumped together by Phil under the head of "jamborees"; Alec and Alonzo were so constantly on hand that Anne wondered if they ever did anything but dance attendance on that will-o'-the-wisp of a Phil. They were both nice, fellows, but Anne would not be drawn into any opinion as to which was the nicer.

"And I depended so on you to help me make up my mind which of them I should promise to many," mourned Phil.

"You must do that for yourself. You are quite expert at making up your mind as to whom other people should marry," retorted Anne, rather caustically.

"Oh, that's a very different thing," said Phil, truly. But the sweetest incident of Anne's sojourn in Bolingbroke was the visit to her birthplace—the little shabby yellow house in an out-of-the-way street she had so often dreamed about. She looked at it with delighted eyes, as she and Phil turned in at the gate. "It's almost exactly as I've pictured it," she said.

"There is no honeysuckle over the windows, but there *is* a lilac tree by the gate, and—yes, there are the muslin curtains in the windows. How glad I am it is still painted yellow."

A very tall, very thin woman opened the door.

"Yes, the Shirleys lived here twenty years ago," she said, in answer to Anne's question. "They had it rented. I remember 'em. They both died of fever at once. It was turrible sad. They left a baby. I guess it's dead long ago. It was a sickly thing. Old Thomas and his wife took it—as if they hadn't enough of their own."

"It didn't die," said Anne, smiling. "I was that baby."

"You don't say so! Why, you *have* grown," exclaimed the woman, as if she were much surprised that Anne was not still a baby. "Come to look at you, I see the resemblance. You're complected like your pa. He had red hair. But you favor your ma in your eyes and mouth. She was a nice little thing. My darter went to school to her and was nigh crazy about her. They was buried in the one grave and the School Board put up a tombstone to them as a reward for faithful service. Will you come in?"

"Will you let me go all over the house?" asked Anne eagerly.

"Laws, yes, you can if you like. 'Twon't take you long—there ain't much of it. I keep at my man to build a new kitchen, but he ain't one of your hustlers. The parlor's in there and there's two rooms upstairs. Just prowl about yourselves. I've got to see to the baby. The east room was the one you were born in. I remember your ma saying she loved to see the sunrise; and I mind hearing that you was born just as the sun was rising and its light on your face was the first thing your ma saw."

Anne went up the narrow stairs and into that little east room with a full heart. It was as a shrine to her. Here her mother had dreamed the exquisite, happy dreams of anticipated motherhood; here that red sunrise light had fallen over them both in the sacred hour of birth; here her mother had died. Anne looked about her reverently, her eyes dim with tears. It was for her one of the jeweled hours of life that gleam out radiantly forever in memory.

"Just to think of it—mother was younger than I am now when I was born," she whispered.

When Anne went downstairs the lady of the house met her in the hall. She held out a dusty little packet tied with faded blue ribbon.

"Here's a bundle of old letters I found in that closet upstairs when I came here," she said. "I dunno what they are—I never bothered to look in 'em, but the address on the top one is 'Miss Bertha Willis,' and that was your ma's maiden name. You can take 'em if you'd keer to have 'em."

"Oh, thank you—thank you," cried Anne, clasping the packet rapturously.

"That was all that was in the house," said her hostess. "The furniture was all sold to pay the doctor bills, and Mrs. Thomas got your ma's clothes and little things. I reckon they didn't last long among that drove of Thomas youngsters. They was destructive young animals, as I mind 'em."

"I haven't one thing that belonged to my mother," said Anne, chokily. "I—I can never thank you enough for these letters."

"You're quite welcome. Laws, but your eyes is like your ma's. She could just about talk with hers. Your father was sorter homely but awful nice. I mind hearing folks say when they was married that there never was two people more in love with each other—Pore creetures, they didn't live much longer; but they was awful happy while they was alive, and I s'pose that counts for a good deal."

Anne longed to get home to read her precious letters; but she made one little pilgrimage first. She went alone to the green corner of the "old" Bolingbroke cemetery where her father and mother were buried, and left on their grave the white flowers she carried. Then she hastened back to Mount Holly, shut herself up in her room, and read the letters: Some were written by her father, some by her mother. There were not many—only a dozen in all—for Walter and Bertha Shirley had not been often separated during their courtship. The letters were yellow and faded and dim, blurred with the touch of passing years. No profound words of wisdom were traced on the stained and wrinkled pages, but only lines of love and trust. The sweetness of forgotten things clung to them—the far-off, fond imaginings of those long-dead lovers. Bertha Shirley had possessed the gift of writing letters which embodied the charming personality of the writer in words and thoughts that retained their beauty and fragrance after the lapse of time. The letters were tender, intimate, sacred. To Anne, the sweetest of all was the one written after her birth to the father on a brief absence. It was full of a proud young mother's accounts of "baby"—her cleverness, her brightness, her thousand sweetnesses.

"I love her best when she is asleep and better still when she is awake," Bertha Shirley had written in the postscript. Probably it was the last sentence she had ever penned. The end was very near for her.

"This has been the most beautiful day of my life," Anne said to Phil that night. "I've *found* my father and mother. Those letters have made them *real* to me. I'm not an orphan any longer. I feel as if I had opened a book and found roses of yesterday, sweet and beloved, between its leaves."

22

Spring and Anne Return to Green Gables

The firelight shadows were dancing over the kitchen walls at Green Gables, for the spring evening was chilly; through the open east window drifted in the subtly sweet voices of the night. Marilla was sitting by the fire—at least, in body. In spirit she was roaming olden ways, with feet grown young. Of late Marilla had thus spent many an hour, when she thought she should have been knitting for the twins.

"I suppose I'm growing old," she said.

Yet Marilla had changed but little in the past nine years, save to grow something thinner, and even more angular; there was a little more gray in the hair that was still twisted up in the same hard knot, with two hairpins—*were* they the same hairpins?—

Spring and Anne Return to Green Gables

still stuck through it. But her expression was very different; the something about the mouth which had hinted at a sense of humor had developed wonderfully; her eyes were gentler and milder, her smile more frequent and tender.

Marilla was thinking of her whole past life, her cramped but not unhappy childhood, the jealously hidden dreams and the blighted hopes of her girlhood, the long, gray, narrow, monotonous years of dull middle life that followed. And the coming of Anne—the vivid, imaginative, impetuous child with her heart of love, and her world of fancy, bringing with her color and warmth and radiance, until the wilderness of existence had blossomed like the rose. Marilla felt that out of her sixty years she had *lived* only the nine that had followed the advent of Anne. And Anne would be home tomorrow night.

The kitchen door opened. Marilla looked up expecting to see Mrs. Lynde. Anne stood before her, tall and starry-eyed, with her hands full of Mayflowers and violets.

"Anne Shirley!" exclaimed Marilla. For once in her life she was surprised out of her reserve; she caught her girl in her arms and crushed her and her flowers against her heart, kissing the bright hair and sweet face warmly. "I never looked for you till tomorrow night. How did you get from Carmody?"

"Walked, dearest of Marillas. Haven't I done it a score of times in the Queen's days? The mailman is to bring my trunk tomorrow; I just got homesick all at once, and came a day earlier. And oh! I've had such a lovely walk in the May twilight; I stopped by the barrens and picked these Mayflowers; I came through Violet-Vale; it's just a big bowlful of violets now—the dear, sky-tinted things. Smell them, Marilla—drink them in."

Marilla sniffed obligingly, but she was more interested in Anne than in drinking violets.

"Sit down, child. You must be real tired. I'm going to get you some supper."

"There's a darling moonrise behind the hills tonight, Marilla, and oh, how the frogs sang me home from Carmody! I do love the music of the frogs. It seems bound up with all my happiest recollections of old spring evenings. And it always reminds me of the night I came here first. Do you remember it, Marilla?"

"Well, yes," said Marilla with emphasis. "I'm not likely to forget it ever."

"They used to sing so madly in the marsh and brook that year. I would listen to them at my window in the dusk, and wonder how they could seem so glad and so sad at the same time. Oh, but it's good to be home again! Redmond was splendid and Bolingbroke delightful—but Green Gables is *home.*"

"Gilbert isn't coming home this summer, I hear," said Marilla.

"No." Something in Anne's tone made Marilla glance at her sharply, but Anne was apparently absorbed in arranging her violets in a bowl. "See, aren't they sweet?" she went on hurriedly. "The year is a book, isn't it, Marilla? Spring's pages are written in Mayflowers and violets, summer's in roses, autumn's in red maple leaves, and winter in holly and evergreen."

"Did Gilbert do well in his examinations?" persisted Marilla.

"Excellently well. He led his class. But where are the twins and Mrs. Lynde?"

"Rachel and Dora are over at Mr. Harrison's. Davy is down at Boulters'. I think I hear him coming now."

Davy burst in, saw Anne, stopped, and then hurled himself upon her with a joyful yell.

"Oh, Anne, ain't I glad to see you! Say, Anne, I've grown two inches since last fall. Mrs. Lynde measured me with her tape today, and say, Anne, see my front tooth. It's gone. Mrs. Lynde tied one end of a string to it and the other end to the door, and then shut the door. I sold it to Milty for two cents. Milty's collecting teeth."

"What in the world does he want teeth for?" asked Marilla.

"To make a necklace for playing Indian Chief," explained Davy, climbing upon Anne's lap. "He's got fifteen already, and everybody's else's promised, so there's no use in the rest of us starting to collect, too. I tell you the Boulters are great business people."

"Were you a good boy at Mrs. Boulter's?" asked Marilla severely.

"Yes; but say, Marilla, I'm tired of being good."

"You'd get tired of being bad much sooner, Davy-boy," said Anne.

"Well, it'd be fun while it lasted, wouldn't it?" persisted Davy. "I could be sorry for it afterwards, couldn't I?"

"Being sorry wouldn't do away with the consequences of being bad, Davy. Don't you remember the Sunday last summer when you ran away from Sunday School? You told me then that being bad wasn't worth while. What were you and Milty doing today?"

"Oh, we fished and chased the cat, and hunted for eggs, and yelled at the echo. There's a great echo in the bush behind the Boulter barn. Say, what is echo, Anne; I want to know."

"Echo is a beautiful nymph, Davy, living far away in the woods, and laughing at the world from among the hills."

"What does she look like?"

"Her hair and eyes are dark, but her neck and arms are white as snow. No mortal can ever see how fair she is. She is fleeter than a deer, and that mocking voice of hers is all we can know of her. You can hear her calling at night; you can hear her laughing under the stars. But you can never see her. She flies afar if you follow her, and laughs at you always just over the next hill."

"Is that all true, Anne? Or is it a whopper?" demanded Davy staring.

"Davy," said Anne despairingly, "haven't you sense enough to distinguish between a fairytale and a falsehood?"

"Then *what* is it that sasses back from the Boulter bush? I want to know," insisted Davy.

"When you are a little older, Davy, I'll explain it all to you."

The mention of age evidently gave a new turn to Davy's thoughts for after a few moments of reflection, he whispered solemnly:

"Anne, I'm going to be married."

"When?" asked Anne with equal solemnity.

"Oh, not until I'm grown-up, of course."

"Well, that's a relief, Davy. Who is the lady?"

"Stella Fletcher; she's in my class at school. And say, Anne, she's the prettiest girl you ever saw. If I die before I grow up you'll keep an eye on her, won't you?"

"Davy Keith, do stop talking such nonsense," said Marilla severely.

"'Tisn't nonsense," protested Davy in an injured tone. "She's my promised wife, and if I was to die she'd be my promised widow, wouldn't she? And she hasn't got a soul to look after her except her old grandmother."

"Come and have your supper, Anne," said Marilla, "and don't encourage that child in his absurd talk."

23

Paul Cannot Find the Rock People

Life was very pleasant in Avonlea that summer, although Anne, amid all her vacation joys, was haunted by a sense of "something gone which should be there." She would not admit, even in her inmost reflections, that this was caused by Gilbert's absence. But

Paul Cannot Find the Rock People

when she had to walk home alone from prayer meetings and A.V.I.S. pow-wows, while Diana and Fred, and many other gay couples, loitered along the dusky, starlit country roads, there was a queer, lonely ache in her heart which she could not explain away. Gilbert did not even write to her, as she thought he might have done. She knew he wrote to Diana occasionally, but she would not inquire about him; and Diana, supposing that Anne heard from him, volunteered no information. Gilbert's mother, who was a gay, frank, light-hearted lady, but not overburdened with tact, had a very embarrassing habit of asking Anne, always in a painfully distinct voice and always in the presence of a crowd, if she had heard from Gilbert lately. Poor Anne could only blush horribly and murmur, "not very lately," which was taken by all, Mrs. Blythe included, to be merely a maidenly evasion.

Apart from this, Anne enjoyed her summer. Priscilla came for a merry visit in June; and, when she had gone, Mr. and Mrs. Irving, Paul and Charlotta the Fourth came "home" for July and August.

Echo Lodge was the scene of gaieties once more, and the echoes over the river were kept busy mimicking the laughter that rang in the old garden behind the spruces.

"Miss Lavendar" had not changed, except to grow even sweeter and prettier. Paul adored her, and the companionship between them was beautiful to see.

"But I don't call her 'mother' just by itself," he explained to Anne. "You see, *that* name belongs just to my own little mother, and I can't give it to any one else. *You* know, teacher. But I call her 'Mother Lavendar' and I love her next best to father. I—I even love her a *little* better than you, teacher."

"Which is just as it ought to be," answered Anne. Paul was thirteen now and very tall for his years.

His face and eyes were as beautiful as ever, and his fancy was still like a prism, separating everything that fell upon it into rainbows. He and Anne had delightful rambles to wood and field and shore. Never were there two more thoroughly "kindred spirits."

Charlotta the Fourth had blossomed out into young ladyhood. She wore her hair now in an enormous pompadour and had discarded the blue ribbon bows of auld lang syne, but her face was as freckled, her nose as snubbed, and her mouth and smiles as wide as ever.

"You don't think I talk with a Yankee accent, do you, Miss Shirley, ma'am?" she demanded anxiously.

"I don't notice it, Charlotta."

"I'm real glad of that. They said I did at home, but I thought likely they just wanted to aggravate me. I don't want no Yankee accent. Not that I've a word to say against the Yankees, Miss Shirley, ma'am. They're real civilized. But give me old P.E. Island every time."

Paul spent his first fortnight with his grandmother Irving in Avonlea. Anne was there to meet him when he came, and found him wild with eagerness to get to the shore—Nora and the Golden Lady and the Twin Sailors would be there. He could hardly wait to eat his supper. Could he not see Nora's elfin face peering around the point, watching for him wistfully? But it was a very sober Paul who came back from the shore in the twilight.

"Didn't you find your Rock People?" asked Anne. Paul shook his chestnut curls sorrowfully.

"The Twin Sailors and the Golden Lady never came at all," he said. "Nora was there—but Nora is not the same, teacher. She is changed."

"Oh, Paul, it is you who are changed," said Anne. "You have grown too old for the Rock People. They like only children for playfellows. I am afraid the Twin Sailors will never again come to you in the pearly, enchanted boat with the sail of moonshine;

and the Golden Lady will play no more for you on her golden harp. Even Nora will not meet you much longer. You must pay the penalty of growing-up, Paul. You must leave fairyland behind you."

"You two talk as much foolishness as ever you did," said old Mrs. Irving, half-indulgently, half-reprovingly.

"Oh, no, we don't," said Anne, shaking her head gravely. "We are getting very, very wise, and it is such a pity. We are never half so interesting when we have learned that language is given us to enable us to conceal our thoughts."

"But it isn't—it is given us to exchange our thoughts," said Mrs. Irving seriously. She had never heard of Tallyrand and did not understand epigrams.

Anne spent a fortnight of halcyon days at Echo Lodge in the golden prime of August. While there she incidentally contrived to hurry Ludovic Speed in his leisurely courting of Theodora Dix, as related duly in another chronicle of her history.[1] Arnold Sherman, an elderly friend of the Irvings, was there at the same time, and added not a little to the general pleasantness of life.

"What a nice play-time this has been," said Anne. "I feel like a giant refreshed. And it's only a fortnight more till I go back to Kingsport, and Redmond and Patty's Place. Patty's Place is the dearest spot, Miss Lavendar. I feel as if I had two homes—one at Green Gables and one at Patty's Place. But where has the summer gone? It doesn't seem a day since I came home that spring evening with the Mayflowers. When I was little I couldn't see from one end of the summer to the other. It stretched before me like an unending season. Now 'tis a handbreadth, 'tis a tale.'"

"Anne, are you and Gilbert Blythe as good friends as you used to be?" asked Miss Lavendar quietly.

"I am just as much Gilbert's friend as ever I was, Miss Lavendar."

---

[1] *Chronicles of Avonlea.*

Miss Lavendar shook her head.

"I see something's gone wrong, Anne. I'm going to be impertinent and ask what. Have you quarrelled?"

"No; it's only that Gilbert wants more than friendship and I can't give him more."

"Are you sure of that, Anne?"

"Perfectly sure."

"I'm very, very sorry."

"I wonder why everybody seems to think I ought to marry Gilbert Blythe," said Anne petulantly.

"Because you were made and meant for each other, Anne—that is why. You needn't toss that young head of yours. It's a fact."

24

Enter Jonas

"PROSPECT POINT,
"August 20th.

"Dear Anne—spelled—with—an—E," wrote Phil, "I must prop my eyelids open long enough to write you. I've neglected you shamefully this summer, honey, but all my other corespondents have been neglected, too. I have a huge pile of letters to answer, so I must gird up the loins of my mind and hoe in. Excuse my mixed metaphors. I'm fearfully sleepy. Last night Cousin Emily and I were calling at a neighbor's. There were several other callers there, and as soon as those unfortunate creatures left, our hostess and her three daughters picked them all to pieces. I knew they would begin on Cousin Emily and me as soon as the door shut behind us. When we came home Mrs. Lilly informed us that the aforesaid neighbor's hired boy was supposed to be down with scarlet fever. You can always trust Mrs. Lilly to tell you cheerful things like that. I have a horror of scarlet fever. I couldn't sleep when I went to bed for thinking of it. I tossed and tumbled about, dreaming fearful dreams when I did snooze for a minute; and at three I wakened up with a high fever, a sore throat, and a raging headache. I knew I had scarlet fever; I got up in a panic and hunted up Cousin Emily's 'doctor book' to read up the symptoms. Anne, I had them all. So I went back to bed, and knowing the worst, slept like a top the rest of the night. Though why a top should sleep sounder than anything else I never could understand. But this morning I was quite well, so it couldn't have been the fever. I suppose if I did catch it last night it couldn't have developed so soon. I can remember that in daytime, but at three o'clock at night I never can be logical.

"I suppose you wonder what I'm doing at Prospect Point. Well, I always like to spend a month of summer at the shore, and father insists that I come to his second-cousin Emily's 'select boardinghouse' at Prospect Point. So a fortnight ago I came as usual. And as usual old 'Uncle Mark Miller' brought me from the station with his ancient buggy and what he calls his 'generous purpose' horse. He is a nice old man and gave me a handful of pink peppermints. Peppermints always seem to me such a religious sort of candy—I suppose because when I was a little girl Grandmother Gordon always gave them to me in church. Once I asked, referring to the smell of peppermints, 'Is that the odor of sanctity?' I didn't like to eat Uncle Mark's peppermints because he just fished them loose out of his pocket, and had to pick some rusty nails and other things from among them before he gave them to me. But I wouldn't hurt his dear old feelings for anything, so I carefully sowed them along the road at intervals. When the last one was gone, Uncle Mark said, a little rebukingly, 'Ye shouldn't a'et all them candies to onct, Miss Phil. You'll likely have the stummick-ache.'

"Cousin Emily has only five boarders besides myself—four old ladies and one young man. My right-hand neighbor is Mrs. Lilly. She is one of those people who seem to take a gruesome pleasure in detailing all their many aches and pains and sicknesses. You cannot mention any ailment but she says, shaking her head, 'Ah, I know too well what that is'—and then you get all the details. Jonas declares he once spoke of locomotor ataxia in hearing and she said she knew too well what that was. She suffered from it for ten years and was finally cured by a traveling doctor.

"Who is Jonas? Just wait, Anne Shirley. You'll hear all about Jonas in the proper time and place. He is not to be mixed up with estimable old ladies.

'My left-hand neighbor at the table is Mrs. Phinney. She always speaks with a wailing, dolorous voice—you are nervously expecting her to burst into tears every moment. She gives you the impression that life to her is indeed a vale of tears, and that a smile, never to speak of a laugh, is a frivolity truly reprehensible. She has a worse opinion of me than Aunt Jamesina, and she doesn't love me hard to atone for it, as Aunty J. does, either.

"Miss Maria Grimsby sits cati-corner from me. The first day I came I remarked to Miss Maria that it looked a little like rain—and Miss Maria laughed. I said the road from the station was very pretty—and Miss Maria laughed. I said there seemed to be a few mosquitoes left yet—and

Enter Jonas 157

Miss Maria laughed. I said that Prospect Point was as beautiful as ever—and Miss Maria laughed. If I were to say to Miss Maria, 'My father has hanged himself, my mother has taken poison, my brother is in the penitentiary, and I am in the last stages of consumption,' Miss Maria would laugh. She can't help it—she was born so; but is very sad and awful.

"The fifth old lady is Mrs. Grant. She is a sweet old thing; but she never says anything but good of anybody and so she is a very uninteresting conversationalist.

"And now for Jonas, Anne.

"That first day I came I saw a young man sitting opposite me at the table, smiling at me as if he had known me from my cradle. I knew, for Uncle Mark had told me, that his name was Jonas Blake, that he was a Theological Student from St. Columbia, and that he had taken charge of the Point Prospect Mission Church for the summer.

"He is a very ugly young man—really, the ugliest young man I've ever seen. He has a big, loose-jointed figure with absurdly long legs. His hair is tow-color and lank, his eyes are green, and his mouth is big, and his ears—but I never think about his ears if I can help it.

"He has a lovely voice—if you shut your eyes he is adorable—and he certainly has a beautiful soul and disposition.

"We were good chums right way. Of course he is a graduate of Redmond, and that is a link between us. We fished and boated together; and we walked on the sands by moonlight. He didn't look so homely by moonlight and oh, he was nice. Niceness fairly exhaled from him. The old ladies—except Mrs. Grant—don't approve of Jonas, because he laughs and jokes—and because he evidently likes the society of frivolous me better than theirs.

"Somehow, Anne, I don't want him to think me

frivolous. This is ridiculous. Why should I care what a tow-haired person called Jonas, whom I never saw before thinks of me?

"Last Sunday Jonas preached in the village church. I went, of course, but I couldn't realize that Jonas was going to preach. The fact that he was a minister—or going to be one—persisted in seeming a huge joke to me.

"Well, Jonas preached. And, by the time he had preached ten minutes, I felt so small and insignificant that I thought I must be invisible to the naked eye. Jonah never said a word about women and he never looked at me. But I realized then and there what a pitiful, frivolous, small-souled little butterfly I was, and how horribly different I must be from Jonas' ideal woman. *She* would be grand and strong and noble. He was so earnest and tender and true. He was everything a minister ought to be. I wondered how I could ever have thought him ugly—but he really is!—with those inspired eyes and that intellectual brow which the roughly-falling hair hid on week days.

"It was a splendid sermon and I could have listened to it forever, and it made me feel utterly wretched. Oh, I wish I was like *you,* Anne.

"He caught up with me on the road home, and grinned as cheerfully as usual. But his grin could never deceive me again. I had seen the *real* Jonas. I wondered if he could ever see the *real* Phil—whom *nobody,* not even you, Anne, has ever seen yet.

"'Jonas,' I said—I forgot to call him Mr. Blake. Wasn't it dreadful? But there are times when things like that don't matter—'Jonas, you were born to be a minister. You *couldn't* be anything else.'

"'No, I couldn't,' he said soberly. 'I tried to be something else for a long time—I didn't want to be a minister. But I came to see at last that it was the work given me to do—and God helping me, I shall try to do it.'

"His voice was low and reverent. I thought that he would do his work and do it well and nobly; and happy the woman fitted by nature and training to help him do it. *She* would be no feather, blown about by every fickle wind of fancy. *She* would always know what hat to put on. Probably she would have only one. Ministers never have much money. But she wouldn't mind having one hat or none at all, because she would have Jonas.

"Anne Shirley, don't you dare to say or hint or think that I've fallen in love with Mr. Blake. Could I care for a lank, poor, ugly theologue—named Jonas? As Uncle Mark says, 'It's impossible, and what's more it's improbable.'

"Good night,
"PHIL."

"P.S. It is impossible—but I am horribly afraid it's true. I'm happy and wretched and scared. *He* can *never* care for me, I know. Do you think I could ever develop into a passable minister's wife, Anne? And *would* they expect me to lead in prayer? P.G."

25

Enter Prince Charming

"I'm contrasting the claims of indoors and out," said Anne, looking from the window of Patty's Place to the distant pines of the park.

"I've an afternoon to spend in sweet doing nothing, Aunt Jimsie. Shall I spend it here where there is a cosy fire, a plateful of delicious russets, three purring and harmonious cats, and two impeccable china dogs with green noses? Or shall I go to the park, where there is the lure of gray woods and of gray water lapping on the harbor rocks?"

"If I was as young as you, I'd decide in favor of the park," said Aunt Jamesina, tickling Joseph's yellow ear with a knitting needle.

"I thought that you claimed to be as young as any of us, Aunty," teased Anne.

"Yes, in my soul. But I'll admit my legs aren't as young as yours. You go and get some fresh air, Anne. You look pale lately."

"I think I will go to the park," said Anne restlessly. "I don't feel like tame domestic joys today. I want to feel alone and free and wild. The park will be empty, for every one will be at the football match."

"Why didn't you go to it?"

"'Nobody axed me, sir, she said,'—at least, nobody but that horrid little Dan Ranger. I wouldn't go anywhere with him; but rather than hurt his poor little tender feelings I said I wasn't going to the game at all. I don't mind. I'm not in the mood for football today somehow."

"You go and get some fresh air," repeated Aunt Jamesina, "but take your umbrella, for I believe it's going to rain. I've rheumatism in my leg."

Enter Prince Charming

"Only old people should have rheumatism, Aunty."

"Anybody is liable to rheumatism in her legs. Anne. It's only old people who should have rheumatism in their souls, though. Thank goodness, I never have. When you get rheumatism in your soul you might as well go and pick out your coffin."

It was November—the month of crimson sunsets, parting birds, deep, sad hymns of the sea, passionate wind-songs in the pines. Anne roamed through the pineland alleys in the park and, as she said, let that great sweeping wind blow the fogs out of her soul. Anne was not wont to be troubled with soul fog. But, somehow, since her return to Redmond for this third year, life had not mirrored her spirit back to her with its old, perfect, sparkling clearness.

Outwardly, existence at Patty's Place was the same pleasant round of work and study and recreation that it had always been. On Friday evenings the big, fire-lighted living-room was crowded by callers and echoed to endless jest and laughter, while Aunt Jamesina smiled beamingly on them all. The "Jonas" of Phil's letter came often, running up from St. Columba on the early train and departing on the late. He was a general favorite at Patty's Place, though Aunt Jamesina shook her head and opined that divinity students were not what they used to be.

"He's *very* nice, my dear," she told Phil, "but ministers ought to be graver and more dignified."

"Can't a man laugh and laugh and be a Christian still?" demanded Phil.

"Oh, men—*yes*. But I was speaking of *ministers*, my dear," said Aunt Jamesina rebukingly. "And you shouldn't flirt so with Mr. Blake—you really shouldn't."

"I'm not flirting with him," protested Phil.

Nobody believed her, except Anne. The others thought she was amusing herself as usual, and told her roundly that she was behaving very badly.

"Mr. Blake isn't of the Alec-and-Alonzo type, Phil," said Stella severely. "He takes things seriously. You may break his heart."

"Do you really think I could?" asked Phil. "I'd love to think so."

"Philippa Gordon! I never thought you were utterly unfeeling. The idea of you saying you'd love to break a man's heart!"

"I didn't say so, honey. Quote me correctly. I said I'd like to think I *could* break it. I would like to know I had the *power* to do it."

"I don't understand you, Phil. You are leading that man on deliberately—and you know you don't mean anything by it."

"I mean to make him ask me to marry him if I can," said Phil calmly.

"I give you up," said Stella hopelessly.

Gilbert came occasionally on Friday evenings. He seemed always in good spirits, and held his own in the jests and repartee that flew about. He neither sought nor avoided Anne. When circumstances brought them in contact he talked to her pleasantly and courteously, as to any newly-made acquaintance. The old camaraderie was gone entirely. Anne felt it keenly; but she told herself she was very glad and thankful that Gilbert had got so completely over his disappointment in regard to her. She had really been afraid, that April evening in the orchard, that she had hurt him terribly and that the wound would be long in healing. Now she saw that she need not have worried. Men have died and the worms have eaten them but not for love. Gilbert evidently was in no danger of immediate dissolution. He was enjoying life, and he was full of ambition and zest. For him there was to be no wasting in despair because a woman was fair and cold. Anne, as she listened to the ceaseless badinage that went on between him and Phil, wondered if she had only imagined that look in his eyes when she had told him she could never care for him.

Enter Prince Charming

There were not lacking those who would gladly have stepped into Gilbert's vacant place. But Anne snubbed them without fear and without reproach. If the real Prince Charming was never to come she would none of a substitute. So she sternly told herself that gray day in the windy park.

Suddenly the rain of Aunt Jamesina's prophecy came with a swish and rush. Anne put up her umbrella and hurried down the slope. As she turned out on the harbor road a savage gust of wind tore along it. Instantly her umbrella turned wrong side out. Anne clutched at it in despair. And then—there came a voice close to her:

"Pardon me—may I offer you the shelter of my umbrella?"

Anne looked up. Tall and handsome and distinguished-looking—dark, melancholy, inscrutable eyes-melting, musical, sympathetic voice—yes, the very hero of her dreams stood before her in the flesh. He could not have more closely resembled her ideal if he had been made to order.

"Thank you," she said confusedly.

"We'd better hurry over to that little pavilion on the point," suggested the unknown. "We can wait there until this shower is over. It is not likely to rain so heavily very long."

The words were very commonplace, but oh, the tone! And the smile which accompanied them! Anne felt her heart beating strangely.

Together they scurried to the pavilion and sat breathlessly down under its friendly roof. Anne laughingly held up her false umbrella.

"It is when my umbrella turns inside out that I am convinced of the total depravity of inanimate things," she said gaily.

The raindrops sparkled on her shining hair; its loosened rings curled around her neck and forehead. Her cheeks were flushed, her eyes big and starry. Her companion looked down at her admiringly. She felt herself blushing under his gaze. Who could he be? Why, there was a bit of the Redmond white and scarlet pinned to his coat lapel. Yet she had thought she knew, by sight at least, all the Redmond students except the Freshmen. And this courtly youth surely was no Freshman.

"We are schoolmates, I see," he said, smiling at Anne's colors. "That ought to be sufficient introduction. My name is Royal Gardner. And you are the Miss Shirley who read the Tennyson paper at the Philomathic the other evening, aren't you?"

"Yes; but I cannot place you at all," said Anne, frankly. "Please, where *do* you belong?"

"I feel as if I didn't belong anywhere yet. I put in my Freshman and Sophomore years at Redmond two years ago. I've been in Europe ever since. Now I've come back to finish my Arts course."

'This is my Junior year, too," said Anne.

"So we are classmates as well as college-mates. I am reconciled to the loss of the years that the locust has eaten," said her companion, with a world of meaning in those wonderful eyes of his.

The rain came steadily down for the best part of an hour. But the time seemed really very short. When the clouds parted and a burst of pale November sunshine fell athwart the harbor and the pines Anne and her companion walked home together. By the time they had reached the gate of Patty's Place he had asked permission to call, and had received it. Anne went in with cheeks of flame and her heart beating to her fingertips. Rusty, who climbed into her lap and tried to kiss her, found a very absent welcome. Anne, with her soul full of romantic thrills, had no attention to spare just then for a crop-eared pussy cat.

That evening a parcel was left at Patty's Place for Miss Shirley. It was a box containing a dozen magnificent roses. Phil pounced impertinently on the card that fell from it, read the name and the poetical quotation written on the back.

"Royal Gardner!" she exclaimed. "Why, Anne, I didn't know you were acquainted with Roy Gardner!"

"I met him in the park this afternoon in the rain," explained Anne hurriedly. "My umbrella turned inside out and he came to my rescue with his."

"Oh!" Phil peered curiously at Anne. "And is that exceedingly commonplace incident any reason why he should send us long-stemmed roses by the dozen, with a very sentimental rhyme? Or why we should blush divinest rosy-red when we look at his card? Anne, thy face betrayeth thee."

"Don't talk nonsense, Phil. Do you know Mr. Gardner?"

"I've met his two sisters, and I know of him. So does everybody worthwhile in Kingsport. The Gardners are among the richest, bluest, of Bluenose. Roy is adorably handsome and clever. Two years ago his mother's health failed and he had to leave college and go abroad with her—his father is dead. He must have been greatly disappointed to have to give up his class, but they say he was perfectly sweet about it. Fee-fi-fo-fum, Anne. I smell romance. Almost do I envy you, but not quite. After all, Roy Gardner isn't Jonas."

"You goose!" said Anne loftily. But she lay long awake that night, nor did she wish for sleep. Her waking fancies were more alluring than any vision of dreamland. Had the real Prince come at last? Recalling those glorious dark eyes which had gazed so deeply into her own, Anne was very strongly inclined to think he had.

26

Enter Christine

The girls at Patty's Place were dressing for the reception which the Juniors were giving for the Seniors in February. Anne surveyed herself in the mirror of the blue room with girlish satisfaction. She had a particularly pretty gown on. Originally it had been only a simple little slip of cream silk with a chiffon overdress. But Phil had insisted on taking it home with her in the Christmas holidays and embroidering tiny rosebuds all over the chiffon. Phil's fingers were deft, and the result was a dress which was the envy of every Redmond girl. Even Allie Boone, whose frocks came from Paris, was wont to look with longing eyes on that rosebud concoction as Anne trailed up the main staircase at Redmond in it.

Anne was trying the effect of a white orchid in her hair. Roy Gardner had sent her white orchids for the reception, and she knew no other Redmond girl would have them that night—when Phil came in with admiring gaze.

"Anne, this is certainly your night for looking handsome. Nine nights out of ten I can easily outshine you. The tenth you blossom out suddenly into something that eclipses me altogether. How do you manage it?"

"It's the dress, dear. Fine feathers."

"'Tisn't. The last evening you flamed out into beauty you wore your old blue flannel shirtwaist that Mrs. Lynde made you. If Roy hadn't already lost head and heart about you he certainly would tonight. But I don't like orchids on you, Anne. No; it isn't jealousy. Orchids don't seem to *belong* to you. They're too exotic—too tropical—too insolent. Don't put them in your hair, anyway."

Enter Christine 167

"Well, I won't. I admit I'm not fond of orchids myself. I don't think they're related to me. Roy doesn't often send them—he knows I like flowers I can live with. Orchids are only things you can visit with."

"Jonas sent me some dear pink rosebuds for the evening—but—he isn't coming himself. He said he had to lead a prayer-meeting in the slums! I don't believe he wanted to come. Anne, I'm horribly afraid Jonas doesn't really care anything about me. And I'm trying to decide whether I'll pine away and die, or go on and get my B.A. and be sensible and useful."

"You couldn't possibly be sensible and useful, Phil, so you'd better pine away and die," said Anne cruelly.

"Heartless Anne!"

"Silly Phil! You know quite well that Jonas loves you."

"But—he won't *tell* me so. And I can't *make* him. He *looks* it, I'll admit. But speak-to-me-only-with-thine-eyes isn't a really reliable reason for embroidering doilies and hemstitching tablecloths. I don't want to begin such work until I'm really engaged. It would be tempting Fate."

"Mr. Blake is afraid to ask you to marry him, Phil. He is poor and can't offer you a home such as you've always had. You know that is the only reason he hasn't spoken long ago."

"I suppose so," agreed Phil dolefully. "Well"—brightening up—"if he *won't* ask me to marry him I'll ask him, that's all. So it's bound to come right. I won't worry. By the way, Gilbert Blythe is going about constantly with Christine Stuart. Did you know?"

Anne was trying to fasten a little gold chain about her throat. She suddenly found the clasp difficult to manage. *What* was the matter with it—or with her fingers?

"No," she said carelessly. "Who is Christine Stuart?"

"Ronald Stuart's sister. She's in Kingsport this winter studying music. I haven't seen her, but they say she's very pretty and that Gilbert is quite crazy over her. How angry I was when you refused Gilbert, Anne. But Roy Gardner was foreordained for you. I can see that now. You were right, after all."

Anne did not blush, as she usually did when the girls assumed that her eventual marriage to Roy Gardner was a settled thing. All at once she felt rather dull. Phil's chatter seemed trivial and the reception a bore. She boxed poor Rusty's ears.

"Get off that cushion instantly, you cat, you! Why don't you stay down where you belong?"

Anne picked up her orchids and went downstairs, where Aunt Jamesina was presiding over a row of coats hung before the fire to warm. Roy Gardner was waiting for Anne and teasing the Sarah-cat while he waited. The Sarah-cat did not approve of him. She always turned her back on him. But everybody else at Patty's Place liked him very much. Aunt Jamesina, carried away by his unfailing and deferential courtesy, and the pleading tones of his delightful voice, declared he was the nicest young man she ever knew, and that Anne was a very fortunate girl. Such remarks made Anne restive. Roy's wooing had certainly been as romantic as girlish heart could desire, but—she wished Aunt Jamesina and the girls would not take things so for granted. When Roy murmured a poetical compliment as he helped her on with her coat, she did not blush and thrill as usual; and he found her rather silent in their brief walk to Redmond. He thought she looked a little pale when she came out of the coeds' dressing room; but as they entered the reception room her color and sparkle suddenly returned to her. She turned to Roy with her gayest expression. He smiled back at her with what Phil called "his deep, black, velvety smile." Yet she really did not see Roy at all. She was acutely conscious that Gilbert was standing under the palms just across the room talking to a girl who must be Christine Stuart.

She was very handsome, in the stately style destined to become rather massive in middle life. A tall girl, with large dark-blue eyes, ivory outlines, and a gloss of darkness on her smooth hair.

"She looks just as I've always wanted to look," thought Anne miserably. "Rose-leaf complexion—starry violet eyes—raven hair—yes, she has them all. It's a wonder her name isn't Cordelia Fitzgerald into the bargain! But I don't believe her figure is as good as mine, and her nose certainly isn't."

Anne felt a little comforted by this conclusion.

27

Mutual Confidences

March came in that winter like the meekest and mildest of lambs, bringing days that were crisp and golden and tingling, each followed by a frosty pink twilight which gradually lost itself in an elfland of moonshine.

Over the girls at Patty's Place was falling the shadow of April examinations. They were studying hard; even Phil had settled down to text and notebooks with a doggedness not to be expected of her.

"I'm going to take the Johnson Scholarship in Mathematics," she announced calmly. "I could take the one in Greek easily, but I'd rather take the mathematical one because I want to prove to Jonas that I'm really enormously clever."

"Jonas likes you better for your big brown eyes and your crooked smile than for all the brains you carry under your curls," said Anne.

"When I was a girl it wasn't considered lady-like to know anything about Mathematics," said Aunt Jamesina. "But times have changed. I don't know that it's all for the better. Can you cook, Phil?"

"No, I never cooked anything in my life except a gingerbread and it was a failure—flat in the middle and hilly round the edges. You know the kind. But, Aunty, when I begin in good earnest to learn to cook don't you think the brains that enable me to win a mathematical scholarship will also enable me to learn cooking just as well?"

"Maybe," said Aunt Jamesina cautiously. "I am not decrying the higher education of women. My daughter is an M.A. She can cook, too. But I taught her to cook *before* I let a college professor teach her Mathematics."

In mid-March came a letter from Miss Patty Spofford, saying that she and Miss Maria had decided to remain abroad for another year.

"So you may have Patty's Place next winter, too," she wrote. "Maria and I are going to run over Egypt. I want to see the Sphinx once before I die."

"Fancy those two dames 'running over Egypt'! I wonder if they'll look up at the Sphinx and knit," laughed Priscilla.

"I'm so glad we can keep Patty's Place for another year," said Stella. "I was afraid they'd come back. And then our jolly little nest here would be broken up—and we poor callow nestlings thrown out on the cruel world of boardinghouses again."

"I'm off for a tramp in the park," announced Phil, tossing her book aside. "I think when I am eighty I'll be glad I went for a walk in the park tonight."

"What do you mean?" asked Anne.

"Come with me and I'll tell you, honey."

They captured in their ramble all the mysteries and magics of a March evening. Very still and mild it was, wrapped in a great, white, brooding silence—a silence which was yet threaded through with many little silvery sounds which you could hear if you hearkened as much with your soul as your ears. The girls wandered down a long pineland aisle that seemed to lead right out into the heart of a deep-red, overflowing winter sunset.

Mutual Confidences

"I'd go home and write a poem this blessed minute if I only knew how," declared Phil, pausing in an open space where a rosy light was staining the green tips of the pines. "It's all so wonderful here—this great, white stillness, and those dark trees that always seem to be thinking."

"'The woods were God's first temples,'" quoted Anne softly. "One can't help feeling reverent and adoring in such a place. I always feel so near Him when I walk among the pines."

"Anne, I'm the happiest girl in the world," confessed Phil suddenly.

"So Mr. Blake has asked you to marry him at last?" said Anne calmly.

"Yes. And I sneezed three times while he was asking me. Wasn't that horrid? But I said 'yes' almost before he finished—I was so afraid he might change his mind and stop. I'm besottedly happy. I couldn't really believe before that Jonas would ever care for frivolous me."

"Phil, you're not really frivolous," said Anne gravely. "'Way down underneath that frivolous exterior of yours you've got a dear, loyal, womanly little soul. Why do you hide it so?"

"I can't help it, Queen Anne. You are right—I'm not frivolous at heart. But there's a sort of frivolous skin over my soul and I can't take it off. As *Mrs. Poyser* says, I'd have to be hatched over again and hatched different before I could change it. But Jonas knows the real me and loves me, frivolity and all. And I love him. I never was so surprised in my life as I was when I found out I loved him. I'd never thought it possible to fall in love with an ugly man. Fancy me coming down to one solitary beau. And one named Jonas! But I mean to call him Jo. That's such a nice, crisp little name. I couldn't nickname Alonzo."

"What about Alec and Alonzo?"

"Oh, I told them at Christmas that I never could marry either of them. It seems so funny now to remember that I ever thought it possible that I might. They felt so badly I just cried over both of them—howled. But I knew there was only one man in the world I could ever marry. I had made up my own mind for once and it was real easy, too. It's very delightful to feel so sure, and know it's your own sureness and not somebody else's."

"Do you suppose you'll be able to keep it up?"

"Making up my mind, you mean? I don't know, but Jo has given me a splendid rule. He says, when I'm perplexed, just to do what I would wish I had done when I shall be eighty. Anyhow, Jo can make up his mind quickly enough, and it would be uncomfortable to have too much mind in the same house."

"What will your father and mother say?"

"Father won't say much. He thinks everything I do right. But mother *will* talk. Oh, her tongue will be as Byrney as her nose. But in the end it will be all right."

"You'll have to give up a good many things you've always had, when you marry Mr. Blake, Phil."

"But I'll have *him*. I won't miss the other things. We're to be married a year from next June. Jo graduates from St. Columba this spring, you know. Then he's going to take a little mission church down on Patterson Street in the slums. Fancy me in the slums! But I'd go there or to Greenland's icy mountains with him."

"And this is the girl who would *never* marry a man who wasn't rich," commented Anne to a young pine tree.

"Oh, don't cast up the follies of my youth to me. I shall be poor as gaily as I've been rich. You'll see. I'm going to learn how to cook and make over dresses. I've learned how to market since I've lived at Patty's Place; and once I taught a Sunday School class for a whole summer. Aunt Jamesina says I'll ruin Jo's career if I marry him. But I won't. I know I haven't much sense or sobriety, but I've got what is ever so much better—the knack of making people like me. There is a man in Bolingbroke who lisps and always testifies in prayer-meeting. He says, 'If you can't thine like an electric thtar thine like a candlethtick.' I'll be Jo's little candlestick."

"Phil, you're incorrigible. Well, I love you so much that I can't make nice, light, congratulatory little speeches. But I'm heart-glad of your happiness."

"I know. Those big gray eyes of yours are brimming over with real friendship, Anne. Some day I'll look the same way at you. You're going to marry Roy, aren't you, Anne?"

"My dear Philippa, did you ever hear of the famous Betty Baxter, who 'refused a man before he'd axed her'? I am not going to emulate that celebrated lady by either refusing or accepting any one before he 'axes' me."

"All Redmond knows that Roy is crazy about you," said Phil candidly. "And you *do* love him, don't you, Anne?"

"I—I suppose so," said Anne reluctantly. She felt that she ought to be blushing while making such a confession; but she was not; on the other hand, she always blushed hotly when any one said anything about Gilbert Blythe or Christine Stuart in her hearing. Gilbert Blythe and Christine Stuart were nothing to her—absolutely nothing. But Anne had given up trying to analyze the reason of her blushes. As for Roy, of course she was in love with him—madly so. How could she help it? Was he not her ideal? Who could resist those glorious dark eyes, and that pleading voice? Were not half the Redmond girls wildly envious? And what a charming sonnet he had sent her, with a box of violets, on her birthday! Anne knew every word of it by heart. It was very good stuff of its kind, too. Not exactly up to the level of Keats or Shakespeare—even Anne was not so deeply in love as to think that. But it was very tolerable magazine verse. And it was addressed to *her*—not to Laura or Beatrice or the Maid of Athens, but to her, Anne Shirley. To be told in rhythmical cadences that her eyes were stars of the morning—that her cheek had the flush it stole from the sunrise—that her lips were redder than the roses of Paradise, was thrillingly romantic. Gilbert would never have dreamed of writing a sonnet to her eyebrows. But then, Gilbert could see a joke. She had once told Roy a funny story—and he had not seen the point of it. She recalled the chummy laugh she and Gilbert had had together over it, and wondered uneasily if life with a man who had no sense of humor might not be somewhat uninteresting in the long run. But who could expect a melancholy, inscrutable hero to see the humorous side of things? It would be flatly unreasonable.

28

A June Evening

"I wonder what it would be like to live in a world where it was always June," said Anne, as she came through the spice and bloom of the twilit orchard to the front door steps, where Marilla and Mrs. Rachel were sitting, talking over Mrs. Samson Coates' funeral, which they had attended that day. Dora sat between them, diligently studying her lessons; but Davy was sitting tailor-fashion on the grass, looking as gloomy and depressed as his single dimple would let him.

"You'd get tired of it," said Marilla, with a sigh. "I daresay; but just now I feel that it would take me a long time to get tired of it, if it were all as charming as today. Everything loves June. Davy-boy, why this melancholy November face in blossomtime?"

"I'm just sick and tired of living," said the youthful pessimist.

"At ten years? Dear me, how sad!"

"I'm not making fun," said Davy with dignity. "I'm dis— dis—discouraged"—bringing out the big word with a valiant effort.

"Why and wherefore?" asked Anne, sitting down beside him.

"'Cause the new teacher that come when Mr. Holmes got sick give me ten sums to do for Monday. It'll take me all day tomorrow to do them. It isn't fair to have to work Saturdays. Milty Boulter said he wouldn't do them, but Marilla says I've got to. I don't like Miss Carson a bit."

"Don't talk like that about your teacher, Davy Keith," said Mrs. Rachel severely. "Miss Carson is a very fine girl. There is no nonsense about her."

"That doesn't sound very attractive," laughed Anne. "I like people to have a little nonsense about them. But I'm inclined to have a better opinion of Miss Carson than you have. I saw her in prayer-meeting last night, and she has a pair of eyes that can't always look sensible. Now, Davy-boy, take heart of grace. 'Tomorrow will bring another day' and I'll help you with the sums as far as in me lies. Don't waste this lovely hour 'twixt light and dark worrying over arithmetic."

"Well, I won't," said Davy, brightening up. "If you help me with the sums I'll have 'em done in time to go fishing with Milty. I wish old Aunt Atossa's funeral was tomorrow instead of today. I wanted to go to it 'cause Milty said his mother said Aunt Atossa would be sure to rise up in her coffin and say sarcastic things to the folks that come to see her buried. But Marilla said she didn't."

"Poor Atossa laid in her coffin peaceful enough," said Mrs. Lynde solemnly. "I never saw her look so pleasant before, that's what. Well, there weren't many tears shed over her, poor old soul. The Elisha Wrights are thankful to be rid of her, and I can't say I blame them a mite."

"It seems to me a most dreadful thing to go out of the world and not leave one person behind you who is sorry you are gone," said Anne, shuddering.

"Nobody except her parents ever loved poor Atossa, that's certain, not even her husband," averred Mrs. Lynde. "She was his fourth wife. He'd sort of got into the habit of marrying. He only lived a few years after he married her. The doctor said he died of dyspepsia, but I shall always maintain that he died of Atossa's tongue, that's what. Poor soul, she always knew everything about her neighbors, but she never was very well acquainted with herself. Well, she's gone anyhow; and I suppose the next excitement will be Diana's wedding."

"It seems so funny and horrible to think of Diana's being married," sighed Anne, hugging her knees and looking through the gap in the Haunted Wood to the light that was shining in Diana's room.

"I don't see what's horrible about it, when she's doing so well," said Mrs. Lynde emphatically. "Fred Wright has a fine farm and he is a model young man."

"He certainly isn't the wild, dashing, wicked, young man Diana once wanted to marry," smiled Anne. "Fred is extremely good."

"That's just what he ought to be. Would you want Diana to marry a wicked man? Or marry one yourself?"

"Oh, no. I wouldn't want to marry anybody who was wicked, but I think I'd like it if he *could* be wicked and *wouldn't*. Now, Fred is *hopelessly* good."

"You'll have more sense some day, I hope," said Marilla.

Marilla spoke rather bitterly. She was grievously disappointed. She knew Anne had refused Gilbert Blythe. Avonlea gossip buzzed over the fact, which had leaked out, nobody knew how. Perhaps Charlie Sloane had guessed and told his guesses for truth. Perhaps Diana had betrayed it to Fred and Fred had been

A June Evening   177

indiscreet. At all events it was known; Mrs. Blythe no longer asked Anne, in public or private, if she had heard lately from Gilbert, but passed her by with a frosty bow. Anne, who had always liked Gilbert's merry, young-hearted mother, was grieved in secret over this. Marilla said nothing; but Mrs. Lynde gave Anne many exasperated digs about it, until fresh gossip reached that worthy lady, through the medium of Moody Spurgeon MacPherson's mother, that Anne had another "beau" at college, who was rich and handsome and good all in one. After that Mrs. Rachel held her tongue, though she still wished in her inmost heart that Anne had accepted Gilbert. Riches were all very well; but even Mrs. Rachel, practical soul though she was, did not consider them the one essential. If Anne "liked" the Handsome Unknown better than Gilbert there was nothing more to be said; but Mrs. Rachel was dreadfully afraid that Anne was going to make the mistake of marrying for money. Marilla knew Anne too well to fear this; but she felt that something in the universal scheme of things had gone sadly awry.

"What is to be, will be," said Mrs. Rachel gloomily, "and what isn't to be happens sometimes. I can't help believing it's going to happen in Anne's case, if Providence doesn't interfere, that's what."

Mrs. Rachel sighed. She was afraid Providence wouldn't interfere; and she didn't dare to.

Anne had wandered down to the Dryad's Bubble and was curled up among the ferns at the root of the big white birch where she and Gilbert had so often sat in summers gone by. He had gone into the newspaper office again when college closed, and Avonlea seemed very dull without him. He never wrote to her, and Anne missed the letters that never came. To be sure, Roy wrote twice a week; his letters were exquisite compositions which would have read beautifully in a memoir or biography. Anne felt herself more deeply in love with him than ever when she read them; but her heart never gave the queer, quick, painful bound at sight of his letters which it had given one day when Mrs. Hiram Sloane had handed her out an envelope addressed in Gilbert's black, upright handwriting. Anne had hurried home to the east gable and opened it eagerly—to find a typewritten copy of some college society report—"only that and nothing more." Anne flung the harmless screed across her room and sat down to write an especially nice epistle to Roy.

Diana was to be married in five more days. The gray house at Orchard Slope was in a turmoil of baking and brewing and boiling and stewing, for there was to be a big, old-timey wedding. Anne, of course, was to be bridesmaid, as had been arranged when they were twelve years old, and Gilbert was coming from Kingsport to be best man. Anne was enjoying the excitement of the various preparations, but under it all she carried a little heartache. She was, in a sense, losing her dear old chum; Diana's new home would be two miles from Green Gables, and the old constant companionship could never be theirs again. Anne looked up at Diana's light and thought how it had beaconed to her for many years; but soon it would shine through the summer twilights no more. Two big, painful tears welled up in her gray eyes.

"Oh," she thought, "how horrible it is that people have to grow up—and marry—and *change!*"

29

Diana's Wedding

"After all, the only real roses are the pink ones, said Anne, as she tied white ribbon around Diana's bouquet in the westward-looking gable at Orchard Slope. "They are the flowers of love and faith."

Diana was standing nervously in the middle of the room, arrayed in her bridal white, her black curls frosted over with the film of her wedding veil. Anne had draped that veil, in accordance with the sentimental compact of years before.

"It's all pretty much as I used to imagine it long ago, when I wept over your inevitable marriage and our consequent parting," she laughed. "You are the bride of my dreams, Diana, with the 'lovely misty veil'; and I am your bridesmaid. But, alas! I haven't the puffed sleeves—though these short lace ones are even prettier. Neither is my heart wholly breaking nor do I exactly hate Fred."

"We are not really parting, Anne," protested Diana. "I'm not going far away. We'll love each other just as much as ever. We've always kept that 'oath' of friendship we swore long ago, haven't we?"

"Yes. We've kept it faithfully. We've had a beautiful friendship, Diana. We've never marred it by one quarrel or coolness or unkind word; and I hope it will always be so. But things can't be quite the same after this. You'll have other interests. I'll just be on the outside. But 'such is life' as Mrs. Rachel says. Mrs. Rachel has given you one of her beloved knitted quilts of the 'tobacco stripe' pattern, and she says when I am married she'll give me one, too."

"The mean thing about your getting married is that I won't be able to be *your* bridesmaid," lamented Diana.

"I'm to be Phil's bridesmaid next June, when she marries Mr. Blake, and then I must stop, for you know the proverb 'three times a bridesmaid, never a bride,'" said Anne, peeping through the window over the pink and snow of the blossoming orchard beneath. "Here comes the minister, Diana."

"Oh, Anne," gasped Diana, suddenly turning very pale and beginning to tremble. "Oh, Anne—I'm so nervous—I can't go through with it—Anne, I know I'm going to faint."

"If you do I'll drag you down to the rain-water hogshed and drop you in," said Anne unsympathetically. "Cheer up, dearest. Getting married can't be so very terrible when so many people survive the ceremony. See how cool and composed *I* am, and take courage."

"Wait till your turn comes, Miss Anne. Oh, Anne, I hear father coming upstairs. Give me my bouquet. Is my veil right? Am I very pale?"

"You look just lovely. Di, darling, kiss me goodbye for the last time. Diana Barry will never kiss me again."

"Diana Wright will, though. There, mother's calling. Come."

Following the simple, old-fashioned way in vogue then, Anne went down to the parlor on Gilbert's arm. They met at the top of the stairs for the first time since they had left Kingsport, for Gilbert had arrived only that day. Gilbert shook hands courteously. He was looking very well, though, as Anne instantly noted, rather thin. He was not pale; there was a flush on his cheek that had burned into it as Anne came along the dim hall towards him, in her soft, white dress with lilies-of-the-valley in the shining masses of her hair. As they entered the crowded parlor together a little murmur of admiration ran around the room. "What a fine-looking pair they are," whispered the impressible Mrs. Rachel to Marilla.

Fred ambled in alone, with a very red face, and then Diana swept in on her father's arm. She did not faint, and nothing

Diana's Wedding

untoward occurred to interrupt the ceremony. Feasting and merry-making followed; then, as the evening waned, Fred and Diana drove away through the moonlight to their new home, and Gilbert walked with Anne to Green Gables.

Something of their old comradeship had returned during the informal mirth of the evening. Oh, it was nice to be walking over that well-known road with Gilbert again!

The night was so very still that one should have been able to hear the whisper of roses in blossom—the laughter of daisies—the piping of grasses—many sweet sounds, all tangled up together. The beauty of moonlight on familiar fields irradiated the world.

"Can't we take a ramble up Lovers' Lane before you go in?" asked Gilbert as they crossed the bridge over the Lake of Shining Waters, in which the moon lay like a great, drowned blossom of gold.

Anne assented readily. Lovers' Lane was a veritable path in a fairyland that night—a shimmering, mysterious place, full of wizardry in the white-woven enchantment of moonlight. There had been a time when such a walk with Gilbert through Lovers' Lane would have been far too dangerous. But Roy and Christine had made it very safe now. Anne found herself thinking a good deal about Christine as she chatted lightly to Gilbert. She had met her several times before leaving Kingsport, and had been charmingly sweet to her. Christine had also been charmingly sweet. Indeed, they were a most cordial pair. But for all that, their acquaintance had not ripened into friendship. Evidently Christine was not a kindred spirit.

"Are you going to be in Avonlea all summer?" asked Gilbert.

"No. I'm going down east to Valley Road next week. Esther Haythorne wants me to teach for her through July and August. They have a summer term in that school, and Esther isn't feeling well. So I'm going to substitute for her. In one way I don't mind.

Do you know, I'm beginning to feel a little bit like a stranger in Avonlea now? It makes me sorry—but it's true. It's quite appalling to see the number of children who have shot up into big boys and girls—really young men and women—these past two years. Half of my pupils are grown up. It makes me feel awfully old to see them in the places you and I and our mates used to fill."

Anne laughed and sighed. She felt very old and mature and wise—which showed how young she was. She told herself that she longed greatly to go back to those dear merry days when life was seen through a rosy mist of hope and illusion, and possessed an indefinable something that had passed away forever. Where was it now—the glory and the dream?

"'So wags the world away,'" quoted Gilbert practically, and a trifle absently. Anne wondered if he were thinking of Christine. Oh, Avonlea was going to be so lonely now—with Diana gone!

30

Mrs. Skinner's Romance

Anne stepped off the train at Valley Road station and looked about to see if anyone had come to meet her. She was to board with a certain Miss Janet Sweet, but she saw no one who answered in the least to her preconception of that lady, as formed from Esther's letter. The only person in sight was an elderly woman, sitting in a wagon with mail bags piled around her. Two hundred would have been a charitable guess at her weight; her face was as round and red as a harvest-moon and almost as featureless. She wore a tight, black, cashmere dress, made in the fashion of ten years ago, a little dusty black straw hat trimmed with bows of yellow ribbon, and faded black lace mits.

"Here, you," she called, waving her whip at Anne. "Are you the new Valley Road schoolma'am?"

"Yes."

"Well, I thought so. Valley Road is noted for its good-looking schoolma'ams, just as Millersville is noted for its humly ones. Janet Sweet asked me this morning if I could bring you out. I said, 'Sartin I kin, if she don't mind being scrunched up some. This rig of mine's kinder small for the mail bags and I'm some heftier than Thomas!' Just wait, miss, till I shift these bags a bit and I'll tuck you in somehow. It's only two miles to Janet's. Her next-door neighbor's hired boy is coming for your trunk tonight. My name is Skinner—Amelia Skinner."

Anne was eventually tucked in, exchanging amused smiles with herself during the process.

"Jog along, black mare," commanded Mrs. Skinner, gathering up the reins in her pudgy hands. "This is my first trip on the mail rowte. Thomas wanted to hoe his turnips today so he asked me to come. So I jest sot down and took a standing-up snack and started. I sorter like it. O' course it's rather tejus. Part of the time I sits and thinks and the rest I jest sits. Jog along, black mare. I want to git home airly. Thomas is terrible lonesome when I'm away. You see, we haven't been married very long."

"Oh!" said Anne politely.

"Just a month. Thomas courted me for quite a spell, though. It was real romantic."

Anne tried to picture Mrs. Skinner on speaking terms with romance and failed.

"Oh?" she said again.

"Yes. Y'see, there was another man after me. Jog along, black mare. I'd been a widder so long folks had given up expecting me to marry again. But when my darter—she's a schoolma'am like you—went out West to teach I felt real lonesome and wasn't nowise sot against the idea. Bime-by Thomas began to come up and so did the other feller—William Obadiah Seaman, *his* name was. For a long time I couldn't make up my mind which of them to take, and they kep' coming and coming, and I kep' worrying. Y'see, W.O. was rich—he had a fine place and carried considerable style. He was by far the best match. Jog along, black mare."

"Why didn't you marry him?" asked Anne.

"Well, y'see, he didn't love me," answered Mrs. Skinner, solemnly.

Anne opened her eyes widely and looked at Mrs. Skinner. But there was not a glint of humor on that lady's face. Evidently Mrs. Skinner saw nothing amusing in her own case.

"He'd been a widder-man for three yers, and his sister kept house for him. Then she got married and he just wanted some one to look after his house. It was worth looking after, too, mind you that. It's a handsome house. Jog along, black mare. As for Thomas, he was poor, and if his house didn't leak in dry weather it was about all that could be said for it, though it looks kind of pictureaskew. But, y'see, I loved Thomas, and I didn't care one red cent for W.O. So I argued it out with myself. 'Sarah Crowe,' say I—my first was a Crowe—'you can marry your rich man if you like but you won't be happy. Folks can't get along together in this world without a little bit of love. You'd just better tie up to Thomas, for he loves you and you love him and nothing else ain't going to do you.' Jog along, black mare. So I told Thomas I'd take him. All the time I was getting ready I never dared drive past W. O.'s place for fear the sight of that fine house of his would put me in the swithers again. But now I never think of it at all, and I'm just that comfortable and happy with Thomas. Jog along, black mare."

"How did William Obadiah take it?" queried Anne.

Mrs. Skinner's Romance

"Oh, he rumpussed a bit. But he's going to see a skinny old maid in Millersville now, and I guess she'll take him fast enough. She'll make him a better wife than his first did. W.O. never wanted to marry *her*. He just asked her to marry him 'cause his father wanted him to, never dreaming but that she'd say 'no.' But mind you, she said 'yes.' There was a predicament for you. Jog along, black mare. She was a great house-keeper, but most awful mean. She wore the same bonnet for eighteen years. Then she got a new one and W.O. met her on the road and didn't know her. Jog along, black mare. I feel that I'd a narrer escape. I might have married him and been most awful miserable, like my poor cousin, Jane Ann. Jane Ann married a rich man she didn't care anything about, and she hasn't the life of a dog. She come to see me last week and says, says she, 'Sarah Skinner, I envy you. I'd rather live in a little hut on the side of the road with a man I was fond of than in my big house with the one I've got.' Jane Ann's man ain't such a bad sort, nuther, though he's so contrary that he wears his fur coat when the thermometer's at ninety. The only way to git him to do anything is to coax him to do the opposite. But there ain't any love to smooth things down and it's a poor way of living. Jog along, black mare. There's Janet's place in the hollow—'Wayside,' she calls it. Quite pictureaskew, ain't it? I guess you'll be glad to git out of this, with all them mail bags jam ming round you."

"Yes, but I have enjoyed my drive with you very much," said Anne sincerely.

"Git away now!" said Mrs. Skinner, highly flattered. "Wait till I tell Thomas that. He always feels dretful tickled when I git a compliment. Jog along, black mare. Well, here we are. I hope you'll git on well in the school, miss. There's a short cut to it through the ma'sh back of Janet's. If you take that way be awful keerful. If you once got stuck in that black mud you'd be sucked right down and never seen or heard tell of again till the day of judgment, like Adam Palmer's cow. Jog along, black mare."

31

Anne to Philippa

"Anne Shirley to Philippa Gordon, greeting.

"Well-beloved, it's high time I was writing you. Here am I, installed once more as a country 'schoolma'am' at Valley Road, boarding at 'Wayside,' the home of Miss Janet Sweet. Janet is a dear soul and very nice-looking; tall, but not over-tall; stoutish, yet with a certain restraint of outline suggestive of a thrifty soul who is not going to be over-lavish even in the matter of avoirdupois. She has a knot of soft, crimpy, brown hair with a thread of gray in it, a sunny face with rosy cheeks, and big, kind eyes as blue as forget-me-nots. Moreover, she is one of those delightful, old-fashioned cooks who don't care a bit if they ruin your digestion as long as they can give you feasts of fat things.

"I like her; and she likes me—principally, it seems, because she had a sister named Anne who died young.

"'I'm real glad to see you,' she said briskly, when I landed in her yard. 'My, you don't look a mite like I expected. I was sure you'd be dark—my sister Anne was dark. And here you're redheaded!'

"For a few minutes I thought I wasn't going to like Janet as much as I had expected at first sight. Then I reminded myself that I really must be more sensible than to be prejudiced against any one simply because she called my hair red. Probably the word 'auburn' was not in Janet's vocabulary at all.

"'Wayside' is a dear sort of little spot. The house is small and white, set down in a delightful little hollow that drops away from the road. Between road and house is an orchard and flower-garden all mixed up together. The front door walk is bordered with quahog clam-shells—'cow-hawks,' Janet calls them; there is Virginia Creeper over the porch and moss on the roof. My room is a neat little spot 'off the parlor'—just big enough for the bed and me. Over the head of my bed there is a picture of Robby Burns standing at Highland Mary's grave, shadowed by an enormous weeping willow tree. Robby's face is so lugubrious that it is no wonder I have bad dreams. Why, the first night I was here I dreamed I *couldn't laugh.*

"The parlor is tiny and neat. Its one window is so shaded by a huge willow that the room has a grotto-like effect of emerald gloom. There are wonderful tidies on the chairs, and gay mats on the floor, and books and cards carefully arranged on a round table, and vases of dried grass on the mantel-piece. Between the vases is a cheerful decoration of preserved coffin plates—five in all, pertaining respectively to Janet's father and mother, a brother, her sister Anne, and a hired man who died here once! If I go suddenly insane some of these days 'know all men by these presents' that those coffin-plates have caused it.

"But it's all delightful and I said so. Janet loved me for it, just as she detested poor Esther because Esther had said so much shade was unhygienic and had objected to sleeping on a feather bed. Now, I glory in feather-beds, and the more unhygienic and feathery they are the more I glory. Janet says it is such a comfort to see me eat; she had been so afraid I would be like Miss Haythorne, who wouldn't eat anything but fruit and hot water for breakfast and tried to make Janet give up frying things. Esther is really a dear girl, but she is rather given to fads. The trouble is that she hasn't enough imagination and *has* a tendency to indigestion.

"Janet told me I could have the use of the parlor when any young men called! I don't think there are many to call. I haven't seen a young man in Valley Road yet, except the next-door hired boy—Sam Tolliver, a very tall, lank, tow-haired youth. He came over one evening recently and sat for an hour on the garden fence, near the front porch where Janet and I were doing fancy-work. The only remarks he volunteered in all that time were, 'Hev a peppermint, miss! *Dew* now—fine thing for catarrh, peppermints,' and, 'Powerful lot o' jump-grasses round here ter-night. Yep.'

"But there *is* a love affair going on here. It seems to be my fortune to be mixed up, more or less actively, with elderly love affairs. Mr. and Mrs. Irving always say that I brought about their marriage. Mrs. Stephen Clark of Carmody persists in being most grateful to me for a suggestion which somebody else would probably have made if I hadn't. I do really think, though, that Ludovic Speed would never have got any further along than placid courtship if I had not helped him and Theodora Dix out.

"In the present affair I am only a passive spectator. I've tried once to help things along and made an awful mess of it. So I shall not meddle again. I'll tell you all about it when we meet."

32

Tea with Mrs. Douglas

On the first Thursday night of Anne's sojourn in Valley Road Janet asked her to go to prayer-meeting. Janet blossomed out like a rose to attend that prayer-meeting. She wore a pale-blue, pansy-sprinkled muslin dress with more ruffles than one would ever have supposed economical Janet could be guilty of, and a white leghorn hat with pink roses and three ostrich feathers on it. Anne felt quite amazed. Later on she found out Janet's motive in so arraying herself—a motive as old as Eden.

Valley Road prayer-meetings seemed to be essentially feminine. There were thirty-two women present, two half-grown boys, and one solitary man, beside the minister. Anne

Tea with Mrs. Douglas

found herself studying this man. He was not handsome or young or graceful; he had remarkably long legs—so long that he had to keep them coiled up under his chair to dispose of them—and he was stoop-shouldered. His hands were big, his hair wanted barbering, and his moustache was unkempt. But Anne thought she liked his face; it was kind and honest and tender; there was something else in it, too—just what, Anne found it hard to define. She finally concluded that this man had suffered and been strong, and it had been made manifest in his face. There was a sort of patient, humorous endurance in his expression which indicated that he would go to the stake if need be, but would keep on looking pleasant until he really had to begin squirming.

When prayer-meeting was over this man came up to Janet and said,

"May I see you home, Janet?"

Janet took his arm—"as primly and shyly as if she were no more than sixteen, having her first escort home," Anne told the girls at Patty's Place later on.

"Miss Shirley, permit me to introduce Mr. Douglas," she said stiffly.

Mr. Douglas nodded and said,

"I was looking at you in prayer-meeting, miss, and thinking what a nice little girl you were."

Such a speech from ninety-nine people out of a hundred would have annoyed Anne bitterly; but the way in which Mr. Douglas said it made her feel that she had received a very real and pleasing compliment. She smiled appreciatively at him and dropped obligingly behind on the moonlit road.

So Janet had a beau! Anne was delighted. Janet would make a paragon of a wife—cheery, economical, tolerant, and a very queen of cooks. It would be a flagrant waste on Nature's part to keep her a permanent old maid.

"John Douglas asked me to take you up to see his mother," said Janet the next day. "She's bed-rid a lot of the time and never goes out of the house. But she's powerful fond of company and always wants to see my boarders. Can you go up this evening?"

Anne assented; but later in the day Mr. Douglas called on his mother's behalf to invite them up to tea on Saturday evening.

"Oh, why didn't you put on your pretty pansy dress?" asked Anne, when they left home. It was a hot day, and poor Janet, between her excitement and her heavy black cashmere dress, looked as if she were being broiled alive.

"Old Mrs. Douglas would think it terrible frivolous and unsuitable, I'm afraid. John likes that dress, though," she added wistfully.

The old Douglas homestead was half a mile from "Wayside" cresting a windy hill. The house itself was large and comfortable, old enough to be dignified, and girdled with maple groves and orchards. There were big, trim barns behind it, and everything bespoke prosperity. Whatever the patient endurance in Mr. Douglas' face had meant it hadn't, so Anne reflected, meant debts and duns.

John Douglas met them at the door and took them into the sitting-room, where his mother was enthroned in an armchair.

Anne had expected old Mrs. Douglas to be tall and thin, because Mr. Douglas was. Instead, she was a tiny scrap of a woman, with soft pink cheeks, mild blue eyes, and a mouth like a baby's. Dressed in a beautiful, fashionably-made black silk dress, with a fluffy white shawl over her shoulders, and her snowy hair surmounted by a dainty lace cap, she might have posed as a grandmother doll.

"How do you do, Janet dear?" she said sweetly. "I am *so* glad to see you again, dear." She put up her pretty old face to be kissed. "And this is our new teacher. I'm delighted to meet you. My son has been singing your praises until I'm half jealous, and I'm sure Janet ought to be wholly so."

Tea with Mrs. Douglas 191

Poor Janet blushed, Anne said something polite and conventional, and then everybody sat down and made talk. It was hard work, even for Anne, for nobody seemed at ease except old Mrs. Douglas, who certainly did not find any difficulty in talking. She made Janet sit by her and stroked her hand occasionally. Janet sat and smiled, looking horribly uncomfortable in her hideous dress, and John Douglas sat without smiling.

At the tea table Mrs. Douglas gracefully asked Janet to pour the tea. Janet turned redder than ever but did it. Anne wrote a description of that meal to Stella.

"We had cold tongue and chicken and strawberry preserves, lemon pie and tarts and chocolate cake and raisin cookies and pound cake and fruit cake—and a few other things, including more pie—caramel pie, I think it was. After I had eaten twice as much as was good for me, Mrs. Douglas sighed and said she feared she had nothing to tempt my appetite.

"I'm afraid dear Janet's cooking has spoiled you for any other,' she said sweetly. 'Of course nobody in Valley Road aspires to rival *her*. *Won't* you have another piece of pie, Miss Shirley? You haven't eaten *anything*.'

"Stella, I had eaten a helping of tongue and one of chicken, three biscuits, a generous allowance of preserves, a piece of pie, a tart, and a square of chocolate cake!"

After tea Mrs. Douglas smiled benevolently and told John to take "dear Janet" out into the garden and get her some roses. "Miss Shirley will keep me company while you are out—won't you?" she said plaintively. She settled down in her armchair with a sigh.

"I am a very frail old woman, Miss Shirley. For over twenty years I've been a great sufferer. For twenty long, weary years I've been dying by inches."

"How painful!" said Anne, trying to be sympathetic and succeeding only in feeling idiotic.

"There have been scores of nights when they've thought I could never live to see the dawn," went on Mrs. Douglas solemnly. "Nobody knows what I've gone through—nobody can know but myself. Well, it can't last very much longer now. My weary pilgrimage will soon be over, Miss Shirley. It is a great comfort to me that John will have such a good wife to look after him when his mother is gone—a great comfort, Miss Shirley."

"Janet is a lovely woman," said Anne warmly.

"Lovely! A beautiful character," assented Mrs. Douglas. "And a perfect housekeeper—something *I* never was. My health would not permit it, Miss Shirley. I am indeed thankful that John has made such a wise choice. I hope and believe that he will be happy. He is my only son, Miss Shirley, and his happiness lies very near my heart."

"Of course," said Anne stupidly. For the first time in her life she was stupid. Yet she could not imagine why. She seemed to have absolutely nothing to say to this sweet, smiling, angelic old lady who was patting her hand so kindly.

"Come and see me soon again, dear Janet," said Mrs. Douglas lovingly, when they left. "You don't come half often enough. But then I suppose John will be bringing you here to stay all the time one of these days."

Anne, happening to glance at John Douglas, as his mother spoke, gave a positive start of dismay. He looked as a tortured man might look when his tormentors gave the rack the last turn of possible endurance. She felt sure he must be ill and hurried poor blushing Janet away.

"Isn't old Mrs. Douglas a sweet woman?" asked Janet, as they went down the road.

"M—m," answered Anne absently. She was wondering why John Douglas had looked so.

"She's been a terrible sufferer," said Janet feelingly. "She takes terrible spells. It keeps John all worried up. He's scared to leave home for fear his mother will take a spell and nobody there but the hired girl."

33

"He Just Kept Coming and Coming"

Three days later Anne came home from school and found Janet crying. Tears and Janet seemed so incongruous that Anne was honestly alarmed.

"Oh, what is the matter?" she cried anxiously.

"I'm—I'm forty today," sobbed Janet.

"Well, you were nearly that yesterday and it didn't hurt," comforted Anne, trying not to smile.

"But—but," went on Janet with a big gulp, "John Douglas won't ask me to marry him."

"Oh, but he will," said Anne lamely. "You must give him time, Janet."

"Time!" said Janet with indescribable scorn. "He has had twenty years. How much time does he want?"

"Do you mean that John Douglas has been coming to see you for twenty years?"

"He has. And he has never so much as mentioned marriage to me. And I don't believe he ever will now. I've never said a word to a mortal about it, but it seems to me I've just got to talk it out with some one at last or go crazy. John Douglas begun to go with me twenty years ago, before mother died. Well, he kept coming and coming, and after a spell I begun making quilts and things; but he never said anything about getting married, only just kept coming and coming. There wasn't anything I could do. Mother died when we'd been going together for eight years. I thought he maybe would speak out then, seeing as I was left alone in the world. He was real kind and feeling, and did everything he could for me, but he never said marry. And that's the way it has been going on ever since. People blame *me* for it. They say I won't marry him because his mother is so sickly and I don't want the bother of waiting on her. Why, I'd *love* to wait on John's mother! But I let them think so. I'd rather they'd blame me than pity me! It's so dreadful humiliating that John won't ask me. And *why* won't he? Seems to me if I only knew his reason I wouldn't mind it so much."

"Perhaps his mother doesn't want him to marry anybody," suggested Anne.

"Oh, she does. She's told me time and again that she'd love to see John settled before her time comes. She's always giving him hints—you heard her yourself the other day. I thought I'd ha' gone through the floor.

"It's beyond me," said Anne helplessly. She thought of Ludovic Speed. But the cases were not parallel. John Douglas was not a man of Ludovic's type.

"You should show more spirit, Janet," she went on resolutely. "Why didn't you send him about his business long ago?"

"I couldn't," said poor Janet pathetically. "You see, Anne, I've always been awful fond of John. He might just as well keep coming as not, for there was never anybody else I'd want, so it didn't matter."

"But it might have made him speak out like a man," urged Anne.

Janet shook her head.

"No, I guess not. I was afraid to try, anyway, for fear he'd think I meant it and just go. I suppose I'm a poor-spirited creature, but that is how I feel. And I can't help it."

"Oh, you *could* help it, Janet. It isn't too late yet. Take a firm stand. Let that man know you are not going to endure his shilly-shallying any longer. *I'll* back you up."

"I dunno," said Janet hopelessly. "I dunno if I could ever get up enough spunk. Things have drifted so long. But I'll think it over."

Anne felt that she was disappointed in John Douglas. She had liked him so well, and she had not thought him the sort

"He Just Kept Coming and Coming" 195

of man who would play fast and loose with a woman's feelings for twenty years. He certainly should be taught a lesson, and Anne felt vindictively that she would enjoy seeing the process. Therefore she was delighted when Janet told her, as they were going to prayer-meeting the next night, that she meant to show some "sperrit."

"I'll let John Douglas see I'm not going to be trodden on any longer."

"You are perfectly right," said Anne emphatically.

When prayer-meeting was over John Douglas came up with his usual request. Janet looked frightened but resolute.

"No, thank you," she said icily. "I know the road home pretty well alone. I ought to, seeing I've been traveling it for forty years. So you needn't trouble yourself, *Mr.* Douglas."

Anne was looking at John Douglas; and, in that brilliant moonlight, she saw the last twist of the rack again. Without a word he turned and strode down the road.

"Stop! Stop!" Anne called wildly after him, not caring in the least for the other dumbfounded onlookers. "Mr. Douglas, stop! Come back."

John Douglas stopped but he did not come back. Anne flew down the road, caught his arm and fairly dragged him back to Janet.

"You must come back," she said imploringly. "It's all a mistake, Mr. Douglas—all my fault. I made Janet do it. She didn't want to—but it's all right now, isn't it, Janet?"

Without a word Janet took his arm and walked away. Anne followed them meekly home and slipped in by the back door.

"Well, you are a nice person to back one up," said Janet sarcastically.

"I couldn't help it, Janet," said Anne repentantly. "I just felt as if I had stood by and seen murder done. I *had* to run after him."

"Oh, I'm just as glad you did. When I saw John Douglas making off down that road I just felt as if every little bit of joy and happiness that was left in my life was going with him. It was an awful feeling."

"Did he ask you why you did it?" asked Anne.

"No, he never said a word about it," replied Janet dully.

34

John Douglas Speaks at Last

Anne was not without a feeble hope that something might come of it after all. But nothing did. John Douglas came and took Janet driving, and walked home from prayer-meeting with her, as he had been doing for twenty years, and as he seemed likely to do for twenty years more. The summer waned. Anne taught her school and wrote letters and studied a little. Her walks to and from school were pleasant. She always went by way of the swamp; it was a lovely place—a boggy soil, green with the greenest of mossy hillocks; a silvery brook meandered through it and spruces stood erectly, their boughs a-trail with gray-green mosses, their roots overgrown with all sorts of woodland lovelinesses.

Nevertheless, Anne found life in Valley Road a little monotonous. To be sure, there was one diverting incident.

She had not seen the lank, tow-headed Samuel of the peppermints since the evening of his call, save for chance meetings on the road. But one warm August night he appeared, and solemnly seated himself on the rustic bench by the porch. He wore his usual working habiliments, consisting of vari-

John Douglas Speaks at Last 197

patched trousers, a blue jean shirt, out at the elbows, and a ragged straw hat. He was chewing a straw and he kept on chewing it while he looked solemnly at Anne. Anne laid her book aside with a sigh and took up her doily. Conversation with Sam was really out of the question.

After a long silence Sam suddenly spoke.

"I'm leaving over there," he said abruptly, waving his straw in the direction of the neighboring house.

"Oh, are you?" said Anne politely.

"Yep."

"And where are you going now?"

"Wall, I've been thinking some of gitting a place of my own. There's one that'd suit me over at Millersville. But ef I rents it I'll want a woman."

"I suppose so," said Anne vaguely.

"Yep."

There was another long silence. Finally Sam removed his straw again and said,

"Will yeh hev me?"

"Wh—a—t!" gasped Anne.

"Will yeh hev me?"

"Do you mean—*marry* you?" queried poor Anne feebly.

"Yep."

"Why, I'm hardly acquainted with you," cried Anne indignantly.

"But yeh'd git acquainted with me after we was married," said Sam.

Anne gathered up her poor dignity.

"Certainly I won't marry you," she said haughtily.

"Wall, yeh might do worse," expostulated Sam. "I'm a good worker and I've got some money in the bank."

"Don't speak of this to me again. Whatever put such an idea into your head?" said Anne, her sense of humor getting the better of her wrath. It was such an absurd situation.

"Yeh're a likely-looking girl and hev a right-smart way o' stepping," said Sam. "I don't want no lazy woman. Think it over. I won't change my mind yit awhile. Wall, I must be gitting. Gotter milk the cows."

Anne's illusions concerning proposals had suffered so much of late years that there were few of them left. So she could laugh wholeheartedly over this one, not feeling any secret sting. She mimicked poor Sam to Janet that night, and both of them laughed immoderately over his plunge into sentiment.

One afternoon, when Anne's sojourn in Valley Road was drawing to a close, Alec Ward came driving down to "Wayside" in hot haste for Janet.

"They want you at the Douglas place quick," he said. "I really believe old Mrs. Douglas is going to die at last, after pretending to do it for twenty years."

Janet ran to get her hat. Anne asked if Mrs. Douglas was worse than usual.

"She's not half as bad," said Alec solemnly, "and that's what makes me think it's serious. Other times she'd be screaming and throwing herself all over the place. This time she's lying still and mum. When Mrs. Douglas is mum she is pretty sick, you bet."

"You don't like old Mrs. Douglas?" said Anne curiously.

"I like cats as *is* cats. I don't like cats as is women," was Alec's cryptic reply.

Janet came home in the twilight.

"Mrs. Douglas is dead," she said wearily. "She died soon after I got there. She just spoke to me once—'I suppose you'll marry John now?' she said. It cut me to the heart, Anne. To think John's own mother thought I wouldn't marry him because of her! I couldn't say a word either—there were other women there. I was thankful John had gone out."

Janet began to cry drearily. But Anne brewed her a hot drink of ginger tea to her comforting. To be sure, Anne discovered

John Douglas Speaks at Last

later on that she had used white pepper instead of ginger; but Janet never knew the difference.

The evening after the funeral Janet and Anne were sitting on the front porch steps at sunset. The wind had fallen asleep in the pinelands and lurid sheets of heat-lightning flickered across the northern skies. Janet wore her ugly black dress and looked her very worst, her eyes and nose red from crying. They talked little, for Janet seemed faintly to resent Anne's efforts to cheer her up. She plainly preferred to be miserable.

Suddenly the gate-latch clicked and John Douglas strode into the garden. He walked towards them straight over the geranium bed. Janet stood up. So did Anne. Anne was a tall girl and wore a white dress; but John Douglas did not see her.

"Janet," he said, "will you marry me?"

The words burst out as if they had been wanting to be said for twenty years and *must* be uttered now, before anything else.

Janet's face was so red from crying that it couldn't turn any redder, so it turned a most unbecoming purple.

"Why didn't you ask me before?" she said slowly.

"I couldn't. She made me promise not to—mother made me promise not to. Nineteen years ago she took a terrible spell. We thought she couldn't live through it. She implored me to promise not to ask you to marry me while she was alive. I didn't want to promise such a thing, even though we all thought she couldn't live very long—the doctor only gave her six months. But she begged it on her knees, sick and suffering. I had to promise."

"What had your mother against me?" cried Janet.

"Nothing—nothing. She just didn't want another woman—*any* woman—there while she was living. She said if I didn't promise she'd die tight there and I'd have killed her. So I promised. And she's held me to that promise ever since, though I've gone on my knees to her in my turn to beg her to let me off"

"Why didn't you tell me this?" asked Janet chokingly. "If I'd only *known!* Why didn't you just tell me?"

"She made me promise I wouldn't tell a soul," said John hoarsely. "She swore me to it on the Bible; Janet, I'd never have done it if I'd dreamed it was to be for so long. Janet, you'll never know what I've suffered these nineteen years. I know I've made you suffer, too, but you'll marry me for all, won't you, Janet? Oh, Janet , won't you? I've come as soon as I could to ask you."

At this moment the stupefied Anne came to her senses and realized that she had no business to be there. She slipped away and did not see Janet until the next morning, when the latter told her the rest of the story.

"That cruel, relentless, deceitful old woman!" cried Anne.

"Hush—she's dead," said Janet solemnly. "If she wasn't—but she *is*. So we mustn't speak evil of her. But I'm happy at last, Anne. And I wouldn't have minded waiting so long a bit if I'd only known why."

"When are you to be married?"

"Next month. Of course it will be very quiet. I suppose people will talk terrible. They'll say I made enough haste to snap John up as soon as his poor mother was out of the way. John wanted to let them know the truth but I said, 'No, John; after all she was your mother, and we'll keep the secret between us, and not cast any shadow on her memory. I don't mind what people say, now that I know the truth myself. It don't matter a mite. Let it all be buried with the dead,' says I to him. So I coaxed him round to agree with me."

"You're much more forgiving than I could ever be," Anne said, rather crossly.

"You'll feel differently about a good many things when you get to be my age," said Janet tolerantly. "That's one of the things we learn as we grow older—how to forgive. It comes easier at forty than it did at twenty."

35

The Last Redmond Year Opens

"Here we are, all back again, nicely sunburned and rejoicing as a strong man to run a race," said Phil, sitting down on a suitcase with a sigh of pleasure. "Isn't it jolly to see this dear old Patty's Place again—and Aunty—and the cats? Rusty has lost another piece of ear, hasn't he?"

"Rusty would be the nicest cat in the world if he had no ears at all," declared Anne loyally from her trunk, while Rusty writhed about her lap in a frenzy of welcome.

"Aren't you glad to see us back, Aunty?" demanded Phil.

"Yes. But I wish you'd tidy things up," said Aunt Jamesina plaintively, looking at the wilderness of trunks and suitcases by which the four laughing, chattering girls were surrounded. "You can talk just as well later on. Work first and then play used to be my motto when I was a girl."

"Oh, we've just reversed that in this generation, Aunty. *Our* motto is play your play and then dig in. You can do your work so much better if you've had a good bout of play first."

"If you are going to marry a minister," said Aunt Jamesina, picking up Joseph and her knitting and resigning herself to the inevitable with the charming grace that made her the queen of housemothers, "you will have to give up such expressions as 'dig in.'"

"Why?" moaned Phil. "Oh, why must a minister's wife be supposed to utter only prunes and prisms? I shan't. Everybody on Patterson Street uses slang—that is to say, metaphorical language—and if I didn't they would think me insufferably proud and stuck up."

"Have you broken the news to your family?" asked Priscilla, feeding the Sarah-cat bits from her lunchbasket.

Phil nodded.

"How did they take it?"

"Oh, mother rampaged. But I stood rock-firm—even I, Philippa Gordon, who never before could hold fast to anything. Father was calmer. Father's own daddy was a minister, so you see he has a soft spot in his heart for the cloth. I had Jo up to Mount Holly, after mother grew calm, and they both loved him. But mother gave him some frightful hints in every conversation regarding what she had hoped for me. Oh, my vacation pathway hasn't been exactly strewn with roses, girls dear. But—I've won out and I've got Jo. Nothing else matters."

"To you," said Aunt Jamesina darkly.

"Nor to Jo, either," retorted Phil. "You keep on pitying him. Why, pray? *I* think he's to be envied. He's getting brains, beauty, and a heart of gold in *ME*."

"It's well we know how to take your speeches," said Aunt Jamesina patiently. "I hope you don't talk like that before strangers. What would they think?"

"Oh, I don't want to know what they think. *I* don't want to see myself as others see me. I'm sure it would be horribly uncomfortable most of the time. I don't believe Burns was really sincere in that prayer, either."

"Oh, I daresay we all pray for some things that we really don't want, if we were only honest enough to look into our hearts," owned Aunt Jamesina candidly. "I've a notion that such prayers don't rise very far. *I* used to pray that I might be enabled to forgive a certain person, but I know now I really didn't want to forgive her. When I finally got that I *did* want to I forgave her without having to pray about it."

"I can't picture you as being unforgiving for long," said Stella.

"Oh, I used to be. But holding spite doesn't seem worth while when you get along in years."

"That reminds me," said Anne, and told the tale of John and Janet.

"And now tell us about that romantic scene you hinted so darkly at in one of your letters," demanded Phil.

Anne acted out Samuel's proposal with great spirit. The girls shrieked with laughter and Aunt Jamesina smiled.

"It isn't in good taste to make fun of your beaux," she said severely; "but," she added calmly, "I always did it myself."

"Tell us about your beaux, Aunty," entreated Phil. "You must have had any number of them."

"They're not in the past tense," retorted Aunt Jamesina. "I've got them yet. There are three old widowers at home who have been casting sheep's eyes at me for some time. You children needn't think you own all the romance in the world."

"Widowers and sheep's eyes don't sound very romantic, Aunty."

"Well, no; but young folks aren't always romantic either. Some of my beaux certainly weren't. I used to laugh at them scandalous, poor boys. There was Jim Elwood—he was always in a sort of day-dream—never seemed to sense what was going on. He didn't wake up to the fact that I'd said 'no' till a year after I'd said it. When he did get married his wife fell out of the sleigh one night when they were driving home from church and he never missed her. Then there was Dan Winston. He knew too much. He knew everything in this world and most of what is in the next. He could give you an answer to any question, even if you asked him when the Judgment Day was to be. Milton Edwards was real nice and I liked him but I didn't marry him. For one thing, he took a week to get a joke through his head, and for another he never asked me. Horatio Reeve was the most interesting beau I ever had. But when he told a story he dressed it up so that you couldn't see it for frills. I never could decide whether he was lying or just letting his imagination run loose."

"And what about the others, Aunty?"

"Go away and unpack," said Aunt Jamesina, waving Joseph at them by mistake for a needle. "The others were too nice to make fun of. I shall respect their memory. There's a box of flowers in your room, Anne. They came about an hour ago."

After the first week the girls of Patty's Place settled down to a steady grind of study; for this was their last year at Redmond and graduation honors must be fought for persistently. Anne devoted herself to English, Priscilla pored over classics, and Philippa pounded away at Mathematics. Sometimes they grew tired, sometimes they felt discouraged, sometimes nothing seemed worth the struggle for it. In one such mood Stella wandered up to the blue room one rainy November evening. Anne sat on the floor in a little circle of light cast by the lamp beside her, amid a surrounding snow of crumpled manuscript.

"What in the world are you doing?"

"Just looking over some old Story Club yarns. I wanted something to cheer *and* inebriate. I'd studied until the world seemed azure. So I came up here and dug these out of my trunk. They are so drenched in tears and tragedy that they are excruciatingly funny."

"I'm blue and discouraged myself," said Stella, throwing herself on the couch. "Nothing seems worthwhile. My very thoughts are old. I've thought them all before. What is the use of living after all, Anne?"

"Honey, it's just brain fog that makes us feel that way, and the weather. A pouring rainy night like this, coming after a hard day's grind, would squelch any one but a *Mark Tapley*. You know it *is* worthwhile to live."

"Oh, I suppose so. But I can't prove it to myself just now."

"Just think of all the great and noble souls who have lived and worked in the world," said Anne dreamily. "Isn't it worthwhile to come after them and inherit what they won and taught? And think of all the great people in the world today!

Last Redmond Year Opens

Isn't it worthwhile to think we can share their inspiration? And then, all the great souls that will come in the future? Isn't it worthwhile to work a little and prepare the way for them—make just one step in their path easier?"

"Oh, my mind agrees with you, Anne. But my soul remains doleful and uninspired. I'm always grubby and dingy on rainy nights."

"Some nights I like the rain—I like to lie in bed and hear it pattering on the roof and drifting through the pines."

"I like it when it stays on the roof," said Stella. "It doesn't always. I spent a gruesome night in an old country farmhouse last summer. The roof leaked and the rain came pattering down on my bed. There was no poetry in *that*. I had to get up in the 'mirk midnight' and chivy round to pull the bedstead out of the drip—and it was one of those solid, old-fashioned beds that weigh a ton—more or less. And then that drip-drop, drip-drop kept up all night until my nerves just went to pieces. You've no idea what an eerie noise a great drop of rain falling with a mushy thud on a bare floor makes in the night. It sounds like ghostly footsteps and all that sort of thing. What are you laughing over, Anne?"

"These stories. As Phil would say they are killing—in more senses than one, for everybody died in them. What dazzlingly lovely heroines we had—and how we dressed them! Silks—satins—velvets—jewels—laces—they never wore anything else. Here is one of Jane Andrews' stories depicting her heroine as sleeping in a beautiful white satin nightdress trimmed with seed pearls."

"Go on," said Stella. "I begin to feel that life *is* worth living as long as there's a laugh in it."

"Here's one I wrote. My heroine is disporting herself at a ball 'glittering from head to foot with large diamonds of the first water.' But what booted beauty or rich attire? 'The paths of glory lead but to the grave.' They must either be murdered or die of a broken heart. There was no escape for them."

"Let me read some of your stories."

"Well, here's my masterpiece. Note its cheerful title—'*My Graves.*' I shed quarts of tears while writing it, and the other girls shed gallons while I read it. Jane Andrews' mother scolded her frightfully because she had so many handkerchiefs in the wash that week. It's a harrowing tale of the wanderings of a Methodist minister's wife. I made her a Methodist because it was necessary that she should wander. She buried a child every place she lived in. There were nine of them and their graves were severed far apart, ranging from Newfoundland to Vancouver. I described the children, pictured their several death beds, and detailed their tombstones and epitaphs. I had intended to bury the whole nine but when I had disposed of eight my invention of horrors gave out and I permitted the tenth to live as a hopeless cripple."

While Stella read *My Graves,* punctuating its tragic paragraphs with chuckles, and Rusty slept the sleep of a just cat who has been out all night curled up on a Jane Andrews tale of a beautiful maiden of fifteen who went to nurse in a leper colony—of course dying of the loathsome disease finally— Anne glanced over the other manuscripts and recalled the old days at Avonlea school when the members of the Story Club, sitting under the spruce trees or down among the ferns by the brook, had written them. What fun they had had! How the sunshine and mirth of those olden summers returned as she read. Not all the glory that was Greece or the grandeur that was Rome could weave such wizardry as those funny, tearful tales of the Story Club. Among the manuscripts Anne found one written on sheets of wrapping paper. A wave of laughter filled her gray eyes as she recalled the time and place of its genesis. It was the sketch she had written the day she fell through the roof of the Cobb duckhouse on the Tory Road.

Anne glanced over it, then fell to reading it intently. It was a little dialogue between asters and sweet-peas, wild canaries in the lilac bush, and the guardian spirit of the garden. After she had read it, she sat, staring into space; and when Stella had gone she smoothed out the crumpled manuscript.

"I believe I will," she said resolutely.

36

The Gardners' Call

"Here is a letter with an Indian stamp for you, Aunt Jimsie," said Phil. "Here are three for Stella, and two for Pris, and a glorious fat one for me from Joe. There's nothing for you, Anne, except a circular."

Nobody noticed Anne's flush as she took the thin letter Phil tossed her carelessly. But a few minutes later Phil looked up to see a transfigured Anne.

"Honey, what good thing has happened?"

"The *Youth's Friend* has accepted a little sketch I sent them a fortnight ago," said Anne, trying hard to speak as if she were accustomed to having sketches accepted every mail, but not quite succeeding.

"Anne Shirley! How glorious! What was it? When is it to be published? Did they pay you for it?"

"Yes; they've sent a check for ten dollars, and the editor writes that he would like to see more of my work Dear man, he shall. It was an old sketch I found in my box. I re-wrote it and sent it in—but I never really thought it could be accepted because it had no plot," said Anne, recalling the bitter experience of *Averil's Atonement*.

"What are you going to do with that ten dollars, Anne? Let's all go up town and get drunk," suggested Phil.

"I *am* going to squander it in a wild soulless revel of some sort," declared Anne gaily. "At all events it isn't tainted money—like the check I got for that horrible Reliable Baking Powder story. I spent *it* usefully for clothes and hated them every time I put them on."

"Think of having a real live author at Patty's Place," said Priscilla.

"It's a great responsibility," said Aunt Jamesina solemnly.

"Indeed it is," agreed Pris with equal solemnity. "Authors are kittle cattle. You never know when or how they will break out. Anne may make copy of *us*."

"I meant that the ability to write for the Press was a great responsibility," said Aunt Jamesina severely; "and I hope Anne realizes it. My daughter used to write stories before she went to the foreign field, but now she has turned her attention to higher things. She used to say her motto was 'Never write a line you would be ashamed to read at your own funeral.' You'd better take that for yours, Anne, if you are going to embark in literature. Though, to be sure," added Aunt Jamesina perplexedly, "Elizabeth always used to laugh when she said it. She always laughed so much that I don't know how she ever came to decide on being a missionary. I'm thankful she did—I prayed that she might—but—I wish she hadn't."

Then Aunt Jamesina wondered why those giddy girls all laughed.

Anne's eyes shone all that day; literary ambitions sprouted and budded in her brain; their exhilaration accompanied her to Jennie Cooper's walking party, and not even the sight of Gilbert and Christine, walking just ahead of her and Roy, could quite subdue the sparkle of her starry hopes. Nevertheless, she was not so rapt from things of earth as to be unable to notice that Christine's walk was decidedly ungraceful.

"But I suppose Gilbert looks only at her face. So like a man," thought Anne scornfully.

The Gardners' Call

"Shall you be home Saturday afternoon?" asked Roy.

"Yes."

"My mother and sisters are coming to call on you," said Roy quietly.

Something went over Anne which might be described as a thrill, but it was hardly a pleasant one. She had never met any of Roy's family; she realized the significance of his statement; and it had, somehow, an irrevocableness about it that chilled her.

"I shall be glad to see them," she said flatly; and then wondered if she really would be glad. She ought to be, of course. But would it not be something of an ordeal? Gossip had filtered to Anne regarding the light in which the Gardners viewed the "infatuation" of son and brother. Roy must have brought pressure to bear in the matter of this call. Anne knew she would be weighed in the balance. From the fact that they had consented to call she understood that, willingly or unwillingly, they regarded her as a possible member of their clan.

"I shall just be myself. I shall not *try* to make a good impression," thought Anne loftily. But she was wondering what dress she would better wear Saturday afternoon, and if the new style of high hair-dressing would suit her better than the old; and the walking party was rather spoiled for her. By night she had decided that she would wear her brown chiffon on Saturday, but would do her hair low.

Friday afternoon none of the girls had classes at Redmond. Stella took the opportunity to write a paper for the Philomathic Society, and was sitting at the table in the corner of the living-room with an untidy litter of notes and manuscript on the floor around her. Stella always vowed she never could write anything unless she threw each sheet down as she completed it. Anne, in her flannel blouse and serge skirt, with her hair rather blown from her windy walk home, was sitting squarely in the middle of the floor, teasing the Sarah-cat with a wishbone. Joseph and Rusty were both curled up in her lap. A warm plummy odor filled the whole house, for Priscilla was cooking in the kitchen. Presently she came in, enshrouded in a huge work-apron, with a smudge of flour on her nose, to show Aunt Jamesina the chocolate cake she had just iced.

At this auspicious moment the knocker sounded. Nobody paid any attention to it save Phil, who sprang up and opened it, expecting a boy with the hat she had bought that morning. On the doorstep stood Mrs. Gardner and her daughters.

Anne scrambled to her feet somehow, emptying two indignant cats out of her lap as she did so, and mechanically shifting her wishbone from her right hand to her left. Priscilla, who would have had to cross the room to reach the kitchen door, lost her head, wildly plunged the chocolate cake under a cushion on the inglenook sofa, and dashed upstairs. Stella began feverishly gathering up her manuscript. Only Aunt Jamesina and Phil remained normal. Thanks to them, everybody was soon sitting at ease, even Anne. Priscilla came down, apronless and smudgeless, Stella reduced her corner to decency, and Phil saved the situation by a stream of ready small talk.

Mrs. Gardner was tall and thin and handsome, exquisitely gowned, cordial with a cordiality that seemed a trifle forced. Aline Gardner was a younger edition of her mother, lacking the cordiality. She endeavored to be nice, but succeeded only in being haughty and patronizing. Dorothy Gardner was slim and jolly and rather tomboyish. Anne knew she was Roy's favorite sister and warmed to her. She would have looked very much like Roy if she had had dreamy dark eyes instead of roguish hazel ones. Thanks to her and Phil, the call really went off very well, except for a slight sense of strain in the atmosphere and two rather untoward incidents. Rusty and Joseph, left to themselves, began a game of chase, and sprang madly into Mrs. Gardner's silken lap and out of it in their wild career. Mrs. Gardner lifted her lorgnette and gazed after their flying forms as if she had never seen cats before, and Anne, choking back slightly nervous laughter, apologized as best she could.

"You are fond of cats?" said Mrs. Gardner, with a slight intonation of tolerant wonder.

Anne, despite her affection for Rusty, was *not* especially fond of cats, but Mrs. Gardner's tone annoyed her. Inconsequently she remembered that Mrs. John Blythe was so fond of cats that she kept as many as her husband would allow.

"They *are* adorable animals, aren't they?" she said wickedly.

"I have never liked cats," said Mrs. Gardner remotely.

"I love them," said Dorothy. "They are so nice and selfish. Dogs are *too* good and unselfish. They make me feel uncomfortable. But cats are gloriously human."

"You have two delightful old china dogs there. May I look at them closely?" said Aline, crossing the room towards the fireplace and thereby becoming the unconscious cause of the other accident. Picking up Magog, she sat down on the cushion under which was secreted Priscilla's chocolate cake. Priscilla and Anne exchanged agonized glances but could do nothing. The stately Aline continued to sit on the cushion and discuss china dogs until the time of departure.

Dorothy lingered behind a moment to squeeze Anne's hand and whisper impulsively.

"I *know* you and I are going to be chums. Oh, Roy has told me all about you. I'm the only one of the family he tells things to, poor boy—nobody *could* confide in mamma and Aline, you know. What glorious times you girls must have here! Won't you let me come often and have a share in them?"

"Come as often as you like," Anne responded heartily, thankful that one of Roy's sisters was likable. She would never like Aline, so much was certain; and Aline would never like her, though Mrs. Gardner might be won. Altogether, Anne sighed with relief when the ordeal was over.

> "*Of all sad words of tongue or pen
> The saddest are it might have been,*"

quoted Priscilla tragically, lifting the cushion. "This cake is now what you might call a flat failure. And the cushion is likewise ruined. Never tell me that Friday isn't unlucky."

"People who send word they are coming on Saturday shouldn't come on Friday," said Aunt Jamesina.

"I fancy it was Roy's mistake," said Phil. "That boy isn't really responsible for what he says when he talks to Anne. Where *is* Anne?"

Anne had gone upstairs. She felt oddly like crying. But she made herself laugh instead. Rusty and Joseph had been *too* awful! And Dorothy *was* a dear.

37

Full-fledged B.A.'s

"I wish I were dead, or that it were tomorrow night," groaned Phil.

"If you live long enough both wishes will come true," said Anne calmly.

"It's easy for you to be serene. You're at home in Philosophy. I'm not—and when I think of that horrible paper tomorrow I quail. If I should fail in it what would Jo say?"

"You won't fail. How did you get on in Greek today?"

"I don't know. Perhaps it was a good paper and perhaps it was bad enough to make Homer turn over in his grave. I've studied and mulled over notebooks until I'm incapable of forming an opinion of anything. How thankful little Phil will be when all this examinating is over."

"Examinating? I never heard such a word."

"Well, haven't I as good a right to make a word as any one else?" demanded Phil.

"Words aren't made—they grow," said Anne.

"Never mind—I begin faintly to discern clear water ahead where no examination breakers loom. Girls, do you—can you realize that our Redmond life is almost over?"

"I can't," said Anne, sorrowfully. "It seems just yesterday that Pris and I were alone in that crowd of Freshmen at Redmond. And now we are Seniors in our final examinations."

"'Potent, wise, and reverend Seniors,'" quoted Phil. "Do you suppose we really are any wiser than when we came to Redmond?"

"You don't act as if you were by times," said Aunt Jamesina severely.

"Oh, Aunt Jimsie, haven't we been pretty good girls, take us by and large, these three winters you've mothered us?" pleaded Phil.

"You've been four of the dearest, sweetest, goodest girls that ever went together through college," averred Aunt Jamesina, who never spoiled a compliment by misplaced economy. "But I mistrust you haven't any too much sense yet. It's not to be expected, of course. Experience teaches sense. You can't learn it in a college course. You've been to college four years and I never was, but I know heaps more than you do, young ladies."

> "'*There are lots of things that never go by rule,*
> *There's a powerful pile o' knowledge*
> *That you never get at college,*
> *There are heaps of things you never learn at school,*'"

quoted Stella.

"Have you learned anything at Redmond except dead languages and geometry and such trash?" queried Aunt Jamesina.

"Oh, yes. I think we have, Aunty," protested Anne.

"We've learned the truth of what Professor Woodleigh told us last Philomathic," said Phil. "He said, 'Humor is the spiciest condiment in the feast of existence. Laugh at your mistakes but learn from them, joke over your troubles but gather strength from them, make a jest of your difficulties but overcome them.' Isn't that worth learning, Aunt Jimsie?"

"Yes, it is, dearie. When you've learned to laugh at the things that should be laughed at, and *not* to laugh at those that shouldn't, you've got wisdom and understanding."

"What have you got out of your Redmond course, Anne?" murmured Priscilla aside.

"I think," said Anne slowly, "that I really have learned to look upon each little hindrance as a jest and each great one as the foreshadowing of victory. Summing up, I think that is what Redmond has given me."

"I shall have to fall back on another Professor Woodleigh quotation to express what it has done for me," said Priscilla. "You remember that he said in his address, 'There is so much in the world for us all if we only have the eyes to see it, and the heart to love it, and the hand to gather it to ourselves—so much in men and women, so much in art and literature, so much everywhere in which to delight, and for which to be thankful.' I think Redmond has taught me that in some measure, Anne."

"Judging from what you all say," remarked Aunt Jamesina, "the sum and substance is that you can learn—if you've got natural gumption enough—in four years at college what it would take about twenty years of living to teach you. Well, that justifies higher education in my opinion. It's a matter I was always dubious about before."

"But what about people who haven't natural gumption, Aunt Jimsie?"

Full-fledged B.A.'s

"People who haven't natural gumption *never* learn," retorted Aunt Jamesina, "neither in college nor life. If they live to be a hundred they really don't know anything more than when they were born. It's their misfortune not their fault, poor souls. But those of us who have some gumption should duly thank the Lord for it."

"Will you please define what gumption is, Aunt Jimsie?" asked Phil.

"No, I won't, young woman. Any one who has gumption knows what it is, and any one who hasn't can never know what it is. So there is no need of defining it."

The busy days flew by and examinations were over. Anne took High Honors in English. Priscilla took Honors in Classics, and Phil in Mathematics. Stella obtained a good all-round showing. Then came Convocation.

"This is what I would once have called an epoch in my life," said Anne, as she took Roy's violets out of their box and gazed at them thoughtfully. She meant to carry them, of course, but her eyes wandered to another box on her table. It was filled with lilies-of-the-valley, as fresh and fragrant as those which bloomed in the Green Gables yard when June came to Avonlea. Gilbert Blythe's card lay beside it.

Anne wondered why Gilbert should have sent her flowers for Convocation. She had seen very little of him during the past winter. He had come to Patty's Place only one Friday evening since the Christmas holidays, and they rarely met elsewhere. She knew he was studying very hard, aiming at High Honors and the Cooper Prize, and he took little part in the social doings of Redmond. Anne's own winter had been quite gay socially. She had seen a good deal of the Gardners; she and Dorothy were very intimate; college circles expected the announcement of her engagement to Roy any day. Anne expected it herself. Yet just before she left Patty's Place for Convocation she flung Roy's violets aside and put Gilbert's lilies-of-the-valley in their place. She could not have told why she did it. Somehow, old Avonlea days and dreams and friendships seemed very close to her in this attainment of her long-cherished ambitions. She and Gilbert had once pictured out merrily the day on which they should be capped and gowned graduates in Arts. The wonderful day had come and Roy's violets had no place in it. Only her old friend's flowers seemed to belong to this fruition of old-blossoming hopes which he had once shared.

For years this day had beckoned and allured to her; but when it came the one single, keen, abiding memory it left with her was not that of the breathless moment when the stately president of Redmond gave her cap and diploma and hailed her B.A.; it was not of the flash in Gilbert's eyes when he saw her lilies, nor the puzzled pained glance Roy gave her as he passed her on the platform. It was not of Aline Gardner's condescending congratulations, or Dorothy's ardent, impulsive good wishes. It was of one strange, unaccountable pang that spoiled this long-expected day for her and left in it a certain faint but enduring flavor of bitterness.

The Arts graduates gave a graduation dance that night. When Anne dressed for it she tossed aside the pearl beads she usually wore and took from her trunk the small box that had come to Green Gables on Christmas day. In it was a thread-like gold chain with a tiny pink enamel heart as a pendant. On the accompanying card was written, "With all good wishes from your old chum, Gilbert." Anne, laughing over the memory the enamel heart conjured up the fatal day when Gilbert had called her "Carrots" and vainly tried to make his peace with a pink candy heart, had written him a nice little note of thanks. But she had never worn the trinket. Tonight she fastened it about her white throat with a dreamy smile.

She and Phil walked to Redmond together. Anne walked in silence; Phil chattered of many things. Suddenly she said,

"I heard today that Gilbert Blythe's engagement to Christine Stuart was to be announced as soon as Convocation was over. Did you hear anything of it?"

"No," said Anne.

"I think it's true," said Phil lightly.

Anne did not speak. In the darkness she felt her face burning. She slipped her hand inside her collar and caught at the gold chain. One energetic twist and it gave way. Anne thrust the broken trinket into her pocket. Her hands were trembling and her eyes were smarting.

But she was the gayest of all the gay revellers that night, and told Gilbert unregretfully that her card was full when he came to ask her for a dance. Afterwards, when she sat with the girls before the dying embers at Patty's Place, removing the spring chilliness from their satin skins, none chatted more blithely than she of the day's events.

"Moody Spurgeon MacPherson called here tonight after you left," said Aunt Jamesina, who had sat up to keep the fire on. "He didn't know about the graduation dance. That boy ought to sleep with a rubber band around his head to train his ears not to stick out. I had a beau once who did that and it improved him immensely. It was I who suggested it to him and he took my advice, but he never forgave me for it."

"Moody Spurgeon is a very serious young man," yawned Priscilla. "He is concerned with graver matters than his ears. He is going to be a minister, you know.

"Well, I suppose the Lord doesn't regard the ears of a man," said Aunt Jamesina gravely, dropping all further criticism of Moody Spurgeon. Aunt Jamesina had a proper respect for the cloth even in the case of an unfledged parson.

38

False Dawn

"Just imagine—this night week I'll be in Avonlea—delightful thought!" said Anne, bending over the box in which she was packing Mrs. Rachel Lynde's quilts. "But just imagine—this night week I'll be gone forever from Patty's Place—horrible thought!"

"I wonder if the ghost of all our laughter will echo through the maiden dreams of Miss Patty and Miss Maria," speculated Phil.

Miss Patty and Miss Maria were coming home, after having trotted over most of the habitable globe.

"We'll be back the second week in May," wrote Miss Patty. "I expect Patty's Place will seem rather small after the Hall of the Kings at Karnak, but I never did like big places to live in. And I'll be glad enough to be home again. When you start traveling late in life you're apt to do too much of it because you know you haven't much time left, and it's a thing that grows on you. I'm afraid Maria will never be contented again."

"I shall leave here my fancies and dreams to bless the next comer," said Anne, looking around the blue room wistfully—her pretty blue room where she had spent three such happy years. She had knelt at its window to pray and had bent from it to watch the sunset behind the pines. She had heard the autumn raindrops beating against it and had welcomed the spring robins at its sill. She wondered if old dreams could haunt rooms—if, when one left forever the room where she had joyed and suffered and laughed and wept, something of her, intangible and invisible, yet nonetheless real, did not remain behind like a voiceful memory.

"I think," said Phil, "that a room where one dreams and grieves and rejoices and *lives* becomes inseparably connected with those processes and acquires a personality of its own. I am sure if I came into this room fifty years from now it would say 'Anne, Anne' to me. What nice times we've had here, honey! What chats and jokes and good chummy jamborees! Oh, dear me! I'm to marry Jo in June and I know I will be rapturously happy. But just now I feel as if I wanted this lovely Redmond life to go on forever."

"I'm unreasonable enough just now to wish that, too," admitted Anne. "No matter what deeper joys may come to us later on we'll never again have just the same delightful, irresponsible existence we've had here. It's over forever, Phil."

"What are you going to do with Rusty?" asked Phil, as that privileged pussy padded into the room.

"*I* am going to take him home with me and Joseph and the Sarah-cat," announced Aunt Jamesina, following Rusty. "It would be a shame to separate those cats now that they have learned to live together. It's a hard lesson for cats and humans to learn."

"I'm sorry to part with Rusty," said Anne regretfully, "but it would be no use to take him to Green Gables. Marilla detests cats, and Davy would tease his life out. Besides, I don't suppose I'll be home very long. I've been offered the principalship of the Summerside High School."

"Are you going to accept it?" asked Phil.

"I—I haven't decided yet," answered Anne, with a confused flush.

Phil nodded understandingly. Naturally Anne's plans could not be settled until Roy had spoken. He would soon—there was no doubt of that. And there was no doubt that Anne would say "yes" when he said "Will you, please?" Anne herself regarded the state of affairs with a seldom-ruffled complacency. She was deeply in love with Roy. True, it was not just what she had imagined love to be. But was anything in life, Anne asked herself wearily, like one's imagination of it? It was the old diamond disillusion of childhood repeated—the same disappointment she had felt when she had first seen the chill sparkle instead of the purple splendor she had anticipated. "That's not my idea of a diamond," she had said. But Roy was a dear fellow and they would be very happy together, even if some indefinable zest was missing out of life. When Roy came down that evening and asked Anne to walk in the park every one at Patty's Place knew what he had come to say; and every one knew, or thought they knew, what Anne's answer would be.

"Anne is a very fortunate girl," said Aunt Jamesina.

"I suppose so," said Stella, shrugging her shoulders. "Roy is a nice fellow and all that. But there's really nothing in him."

"That sounds very like a jealous remark, Stella Maynard," said Aunt Jamesina rebukingly.

"It does—but I am not jealous," said Stella calmly. "I love Anne and I like Roy. Everybody says she is making a brilliant match, and even Mrs. Gardner thinks her charming now. It all sounds as if it were made in heaven, but I have my doubts. Make the most of that, Aunt Jamesina."

Roy asked Anne to marry him in the little pavilion on the harbor shore where they had talked on the rainy day of their first meeting. Anne thought it very romantic that he should have chosen that spot. And his proposal was as beautifully worded as if he had copied it, as one of Ruby Gillis' lovers had done, out of a Deportment of Courtship and Marriage. The whole effect was quite flawless. And it was also sincere. There was no doubt that Roy meant what he said. There was no false note to jar the symphony.

Anne felt that she ought to be thrilling from head to foot. But she wasn't; she was horribly cool. When Roy paused for his answer she opened her lips to say her fateful yes.

And then—she found herself trembling as if she were reeling back from a precipice. To her came one of those moments when we realize, as by a blinding flash of illumination, more than all our previous years have taught us. She pulled her hand from Roy's.

"Oh, I can't marry you—I can't—I can't," she cried, wildly.

Roy turned pale—and also looked rather foolish.

He had—small blame to him—felt very sure.

"What do you mean?" he stammered.

"I mean that I can't marry you," repeated Anne desperately. "I thought I could—but I can't."

"Why can't you?" Roy asked more calmly.

"Because—I don't care enough for you."

A crimson streak came into Roy's face.

"So you've just been amusing yourself these two years?" he said slowly.

"No, no, I haven't," gasped poor Anne. Oh, how could she explain? She *couldn't* explain. There are some things that cannot be explained. "I did think I cared—truly I did—but I know now I don't."

"You have ruined my life," said Roy bitterly.

"Forgive me," pleaded Anne miserably, with hot cheeks and stinging eyes.

Roy turned away and stood for a few minutes looking out seaward. When he came back to Anne, he was very pale again.

"You can give me no hope?" he said.

Anne shook her head mutely.

"Then—good-bye," said Roy. "I can't understand it—I can't believe you are not the woman I've believed you to be. But reproaches are idle between us. You are the only woman I can ever love. I thank you for your friendship, at least. Good-bye, Anne."

"Good-bye," faltered Anne. When Roy had gone she sat for a long time in the pavilion, watching a white mist creeping subtly and remorselessly landward up the harbor. It was her hour of humiliation and self-contempt and shame. Their waves went over her. And yet, underneath it all, was a queer sense of recovered freedom.

She slipped into Patty's Place in the dusk and escaped to her room. But Phil was there on the window seat.

"Wait," said Anne, flushing to anticipate the scene. "Wait till you hear what I have to say. Phil, Roy asked me to marry him—and I refused."

"You—you *refused* him?" said Phil blankly.

"Yes."

"Anne Shirley, are you in your senses?"

"I think so," said Anne wearily. "Oh, Phil, don't scold me. You don't understand."

"I certainly don't understand. You've encouraged Roy Gardner in every way for two years—and now you tell me you've refused him. Then you've just been flirting scandalously with him. Anne, I couldn't have believed it of *you.*"

"I *wasn't* flirting with him—I honestly thought I cared up to the last minute—and then—well, I just knew I *never* could marry him."

"I suppose," said Phil cruelly, "that you intended to marry him for his money, and then your better self rose up and prevented you."

"I *didn't*. I never thought about his money. Oh, I can't explain it to you any more than I could to him."

"Well, I certainly think you have treated Roy shamefully," said Phil in exasperation. "He's handsome and clever and rich and good. What more do you want?"

"I want some one who *belongs* in my life. He doesn't. I was swept off my feet at first by his good looks and knack of paying romantic compliments; and later on I thought I *must* be in love because he was my dark-eyed ideal."

"I am bad enough for not knowing my own mind, but you are worse," said Phil.

"*I do* know my own mind," protested Anne. "The trouble is, my mind changes and then I have to get acquainted with it all over again."

"Well, I suppose there is no use in saying anything to you."

"There is no need, Phil. I'm in the dust. This has spoiled everything backwards. I can never think of Redmond days without recalling the humiliation of this evening. Roy despises me—and you despise me—and I despise myself."

"You poor darling," said Phil, melting. "Just come here and let me comfort you. I've no right to scold you. I'd have married Alec or Alonzo if I hadn't met Jo. Oh, Anne, things are so mixed-up in real life. They aren't clear-cut and trimmed off, as they are in novels."

"I hope that *no* one will ever again ask me to marry him as long as I live," sobbed poor Anne, devoutly believing that she meant it.

39

Deals with Weddings

Anne felt that life partook of the nature of an anticlimax during the first few weeks after her return to Green Gables. She missed the merry comradeship of Patty's Place. She had dreamed some brilliant dreams during the past winter and now they lay in the dust around her. In her present mood of self-disgust, she could not immediately begin dreaming again. And she discovered that, while solitude with dreams is glorious, solitude without them has few charms.

She had not seen Roy again after their painful parting in the park pavilion; but Dorothy came to see her before she left Kingsport.

"I'm awfully sorry you won't marry Roy," she said. "I did want you for a sister. But you are quite right. He would bore you to death. I love him, and he is a dear sweet boy, but really he isn't a bit interesting. He looks as if he ought to be, but he isn't."

"This won't spoil *our* friendship, will it, Dorothy?" Anne had asked wistfully.

"No, indeed. You're too good to lose. If I can't have you for a sister I mean to keep you as a chum anyway. And don't fret over Roy. He *is* feeling terribly just now—I have to listen to his outpourings every day—but he'll get over it. He always does."

"Oh—*always?*" said Anne with a slight change of voice. "So he has 'got over it' before?"

"Dear me, yes," said Dorothy frankly. "Twice before. And he raved to me just the same both times. Not that the others actually refused him—they simply announced their engagements to some one else. Of course, when he met you he vowed to me that he had never really loved before—that the previous affairs had been merely boyish fancies. But I don't think you need worry."

Anne decided not to worry. Her feelings were a mixture of relief and resentment. Roy had certainly told her she was the only one he had ever loved. No doubt he believed it. But it was a comfort to feel that she had not, in all likelihood, ruined his life. There were other goddesses, and Roy, according to Dorothy, must needs be worshipping at some shrine. Nevertheless, life was stripped of several more illusions, and Anne began to think drearily that it seemed rather bare.

She came down from the porch gable on the evening of her return with a sorrowful face.

"What has happened to the old Snow Queen, Marilla?"

"Oh, I knew you'd feel bad over that," said Marilla. "I felt bad myself. That tree was there ever since I was a young girl. It blew down in the big gale we had in March. It was rotten at the core."

"I'll miss it so," grieved Anne. "The porch gable doesn't seem the same room without it. I'll never look from its window again without a sense of loss. And oh, I never came home to Green Gables before that Diana wasn't here to welcome me."

"Diana has something else to think of just now," said Mrs. Lynde significantly.

"Well, tell me all the Avonlea news," said Anne, sitting down on the porch steps, where the evening sunshine fell over her hair in a fine golden rain.

"There isn't much news except what we've wrote you," said Mrs. Lynde. "I suppose you haven't heard that Simon Fletcher broke his leg last week. It's a great thing for his family. They're getting a hundred things done that they've always wanted to do but couldn't as long as he was about, the old crank."

"He came of an aggravating family," remarked Marilla.

"Aggravating? Well, rather! His mother used to get up in prayer-meeting and tell all her children's shortcomings and ask prayers for them. 'Course it made them mad, and worse than ever."

"You haven't told Anne the news about Jane," suggested Marilla.

"Oh, Jane," sniffed Mrs. Lynde. "Well," she conceded grudgingly, "Jane Andrews is home from the West—came last week—and she's going to be married to a Winnipeg millionaire. You may be sure Mrs. Harmon lost no time in telling it far and wide."

"Dear old Jane—I'm so glad," said Anne heartily. "She deserves the good things of life."

"Oh, I ain't saying anything against Jane. She's a nice enough girl. But she isn't in the millionaire class, and you'll find there's not much to recommend that man but his money, that's what. Mrs. Harmon says he's an Englishman who has made money in mines but *I* believe he'll turn out to be a Yankee. He certainly must have money, for he has just showered Jane with jewelry. Her engagement ring is a diamond cluster so big that it looks like a plaster on Jane's fat paw."

Mrs. Lynde could not keep some bitterness out of her tone. Here was Jane Andrews, that plain little plodder, engaged to a millionaire, while Anne, it seemed, was not yet bespoken by any one, rich or poor. And Mrs. Harmon Andrews did brag insufferably.

"What has Gilbert Blythe been doing to himself at college?" asked Marilla. "I saw him when he came home last week, and he is so pale and thin I hardly knew him."

"He studied very hard last winter," said Anne. "You know he took High Honors in Classics and the Cooper Prize. It hasn't been taken for five years! So I think he's rather run down. We're all a little tired."

"Anyhow, you're a B.A. and Jane Andrews isn't and never will be," said Mrs. Lynde, with gloomy satisfaction.

A few evening later Anne went down to see Jane, but the latter was away in Charlottetown—"getting sewing done," Mrs. Harmon informed Anne proudly. "Of course an Avonlea dressmaker wouldn't do for Jane under the circumstances."

"I've heard something very nice about Jane," said Anne.

"Yes, Jane has done pretty well, even if she isn't a B.A.," said Mrs. Harmon, with a slight toss of her head. "Mr. Inglis is worth millions, and they're going to Europe on their wedding tour. When they come back they'll live in a perfect mansion of marble in Winnipeg. Jane has only one trouble—she can cook so well and her husband won't let her cook. He is so rich he hires his cooking done. They're going to keep a cook and two other maids and a coachman and a man-of-all-work. But what about

Deals with Weddings

you, Anne? I don't hear anything of your being married, after all your college-going."

"Oh," laughed Anne, "I am going to be an old maid. I really can't find any one to suit me."

It was rather wicked of her. She deliberately meant to remind Mrs. Andrews that if she became an old maid it was not because she had not had at least one chance of marriage. But Mrs. Harmon took swift revenge.

"Well, the over-particular girls generally get left, I notice. And what's this I hear about Gilbert Blythe being engaged to a Miss Stuart? Charlie Sloane tells me she is perfectly beautiful. Is it true?"

"I don't know if it is true that he is engaged to Miss Stuart," replied Anne, with Spartan composure, "but it is certainly true that she is very lovely."

"I once thought you and Gilbert would have made a match of it," said Mrs. Harmon. "If you don't take care, Anne, all your beaux will slip through your fingers."

Anne decided not to continue her duel with Mrs. Harmon. You could not fence with an antagonist who met rapier thrust with blow of battle axe.

"Since Jane is away," she said, rising haughtily, "I don't think I can stay longer this morning. I'll come down when she comes home."

"Do," said Mrs. Harmon effusively. "Jane isn't a bit proud. She just means to associate with her old friends the same as ever. She'll be real glad to see you.

Jane's millionaire arrived the last of May and carried her off in a blaze of splendor. Mrs. Lynde was spitefully gratified to find that Mr. Inglis was every day of forty, and short and thin and grayish. Mrs. Lynde did not spare him in her enumeration of his shortcomings, you may be sure.

"It will take all his gold to gild a pill like him, that's what," said Mrs. Rachel solemnly.

"He looks kind and good-hearted," said Anne loyally, "and I'm sure he thinks the world of Jane."

"Humph!" said Mrs. Rachel.

Phil Gordon was married the next week and Anne went over to Bolingbroke to be her bridesmaid. Phil made a dainty fairy of a bride, and the Rev. Jo was so radiant in his happiness that nobody thought him plain.

"We're going for a lovers' saunter through the land of Evangeline," Phil, "and then we'll settle down on Patterson Street. Mother thinks it is terrible—she thinks Jo might at least take a church in a decent place. But the wilderness of the Patterson slums will blossom like the rose for me if Jo is there. Oh, Anne, I'm so happy my heart aches with it."

Anne was always glad in the happiness of her friends; but it is sometimes a little lonely to be surrounded everywhere by a happiness that is not your own. And it was just the same when she went back to Avonlea. This time it was Diana who was bathed in the wonderful glory that comes to a woman when her first-born is laid beside her. Anne looked at the white young mother with a certain awe that had never entered into her feelings for Diana before. Could this pale woman with the rapture in her eyes be the little black-curled, rosy-cheeked Diana she had played with in vanished schooldays? It gave her a queer desolate feeling that she herself somehow belonged only in those past years and had no business in the present at all.

"Isn't he perfectly beautiful?" said Diana proudly.

The little fat fellow was absurdly like Fred—just as round, just as red. Anne really could not say conscientiously that she thought him beautiful, but she vowed sincerely that he was sweet and kissable and altogether delightful.

"Before he came I wanted a girl, so that I could call her *Anne*," said Diana. "But now that little Fred is here I wouldn't exchange him for a million girls. He just *couldn't* have been anything but his own precious self."

Deals with Weddings

"'Every little baby is the sweetest and the best,'" quoted Mrs. Allan gaily. "If little Anne *had* come you'd have felt just the same about her."

Mrs. Allan was visiting in Avonlea, for the first time since leaving it. She was as gay and sweet and sympathetic as ever. Her old girl friends had welcomed her back rapturously. The reigning minister's wife was an estimable lady, but she was not exactly a kindred spirit.

"I can hardly wait till he gets old enough to talk," sighed Diana. "I just long to hear him say 'mother.' And oh, I'm determined that his first memory of me shall be a nice one. The first memory I have of my mother is of her slapping me for something I had done. I am sure I deserved it, and mother was always a good mother and I love her dearly. But I do wish my first memory of her was nicer."

"I have just one memory of my mother and it is the sweetest of all my memories," said Mrs. Allan. "I was five years old, and I had been allowed to go to school one day with my two older sisters. When school came out my sisters went home in different groups, each supposing I was with the other. Instead I had run off with a little girl I had played with at recess. We went to her home, which was near the school, and began making mud pies. We were having a glorious time when my older sister arrived, breathless and angry.

"'You naughty girl,' she cried, snatching my reluctant hand and dragging me along with her. 'Come home this minute. Oh, you're going to catch it! Mother is awful cross. She is going to give you a good whipping.'

"I had never been whipped. Dread and terror filled my poor little heart. I have never been so miserable in my life as I was on that walk home. I had not meant to be naughty. Phemy Cameron had asked me to go home with her and I had not known it was wrong to go. And now I was to be whipped for it.

When we got home my sister dragged me into the kitchen where mother was sitting by the fire in the twilight. My poor wee legs were trembling so that I could hardly stand. And mother—mother just took me up in her arms, without one word of rebuke or harshness, kissed me and held me close to her heart. 'I was so frightened you were lost, darling,' she said tenderly. I could see the love shining in her eyes as she looked down on me. She never scolded or reproached me for what I had done—only told me I must never go away again without asking permission. She died very soon afterwards. That is the only memory I have of her. Isn't it a beautiful one?"

Anne felt lonelier than ever as she walked home, going by way of the Birch Path and Willowmere. She had not walked that way for many moons. It was a darkly-purple bloomy night. The air was heavy with blossom fragrance—almost too heavy. The cloyed senses recoiled from it as from an overfull cup. The birches of the path had grown from the fairy saplings of old to big trees. Everything had changed. Anne felt that she would be glad when the summer was over and she was away at work again. Perhaps life would not seem so empty then.

"'I've tried the world—it wears no more
The coloring of romance it wore,'"

sighed Anne—and was straightway much comforted by the romance in the idea of the world being denuded of romance!

40

A Book of Revelation

The Irvings came back to Echo Lodge for the summer, and Anne spent a happy three weeks there in July. Miss Lavendar had not changed; Charlotta the Fourth was a very grown-up young lady now, but still adored Anne sincerely.

"When all's said and done, Miss Shirley, ma'am, I haven't seen any one in Boston that's equal to you," she said frankly.

Paul was almost grown-up, too. He was sixteen, his chestnut curls had given place to close-cropped brown locks, and he was more interested in football than fairies. But the bond between him and his old teacher still held. Kindred spirits alone do not change with changing years.

It was a wet, bleak, cruel evening in July when Anne came back to Green Gables. One of the fierce summer storms which sometimes sweep over the gulf was ravaging the sea. As Anne came in the first raindrops dashed against the panes.

"Was that Paul who brought you home?" asked Marilla. "Why didn't you make him stay all night. It's going to be a wild evening."

"He'll reach Echo Lodge before the rain gets very heavy, I think. Anyway, he wanted to go back tonight. Well, I've had a splendid visit, but I'm glad to see you dear folks again. 'East, west, hame's best.' Davy, have you been growing again lately?"

'I've growed a whole inch since you left," said Davy proudly. "I'm as tall as Milty Boulter now. Ain't I glad. He'll have to stop crowing about being bigger. Say, Anne, did you know that Gilbert Blythe is dying?"

Anne stood quite silent and motionless, looking at Davy. Her face had gone so white that Marilla thought she was going to faint.

"Davy, hold your tongue," said Mrs. Rachel angrily. "Anne, don't look like that—*don't look like that!* We didn't mean to tell you so suddenly."

"Is—it—true?" asked Anne in a voice that was not hers.

"Gilbert is very ill," said Mrs. Lynde gravely. "He took down with typhoid fever just after you left for Echo Lodge. Did you never hear of it?"

"No," said that unknown voice.

"It was a very bad case from the start. The doctor said he'd been terribly run down. They've a trained nurse and everything's been done. *Don't* look like that, Anne. While there's life there's hope."

"Mr. Harrison was here this evening and he said they had no hope of him," reiterated Davy.

Marilla, looking old and worn and tired, got up and marched Davy grimly out of the kitchen.

"Oh, *don't* look so, dear," said Mrs. Rachel, putting her kind old arms about the pallid girl. "I haven't given up hope, indeed I haven't. He's got the Blythe constitution in his favor, that's what."

Anne gently put Mrs. Lynde's arms away from her, walked blindly across the kitchen, through the hall, up the stairs to her old room. At its window she knelt down, staring out unseeingly. It was very dark. The rain was beating down over the shivering fields. The Haunted Wood was full of the groans of mighty trees wrung in the tempest, and the air throbbed with the thunderous crash of billows on the distant shore. And Gilbert was dying!

There is a book of Revelation in every one's life, as there is in the Bible. Anne read hers that bitter night, as she kept her agonized vigil through the hours of storm and darkness. She loved Gilbert—had always loved him! She knew that now. She knew that she could no more cast him out of her life without agony than she could have cut off her right hand and cast it from her. And the knowledge had come too late—too late even

A Book of Revelation

for the bitter solace of being with him at the last. If she had not been so blind—so foolish—she would have had the right to go to him now. But he would never know that she loved him—he would go away from this life thinking that she did not care. Oh, the black years of emptiness stretching before her! She could not live through them—she could not! She cowered down by her window and wished, for the first time in her gay young life, that she could die, too. If Gilbert went away from her, without one word or sign or message, she could not live. Nothing was of any value without him. She belonged to him and he to her. In her hour of supreme agony she had no doubt of that. He did not love Christine Stuart—never had loved Christine Stuart. Oh, what a fool she had been not to realize what the bond was that had held her to Gilbert—to think that the flattered fancy she had felt for Roy Gardner had been love. And now she must pay for her folly as for a crime.

Mrs. Lynde and Marilla crept to her door before they went to bed, shook their heads doubtfully at each other over the silence, and went away. The storm raged all night, but when the dawn earn it was spent. Anne saw a fairy fringe of light on the skirts of darkness. Soon the eastern hilltops had a fire-shot ruby rim. The clouds rolled themselves away into great, soft, white masses on the horizon; the sky gleamed blue and silvery. A hush fell over the world.

Anne rose from her knees and crept downstairs. The freshness of the rain—wind blew against her white face as she went out into the yard, and cooled her dry, burning eyes. A merry rollicking whistle was lilting up the lane. A moment later Pacifique Buote came in sight.

Anne's physical strength suddenly failed her. If she had not clutched at a low willow bough she would have fallen. Pacifique was George Fletcher's hired man, and George Fletcher lived next door to the Blythes. Mrs. Fletcher was Gilbert's aunt. Pacifique would know if—if—Pacifique would know what there was to be known.

Pacifique strode sturdily on along the red lane, whistling. He did not see Anne. She made three futile attempts to call him. He was almost past before she succeeded in making her quivering lips call, "Pacifique!"

Pacifique turned with a grin and a cheerful good morning.

"Pacifique," said Anne faintly, "did you come from George Fletcher's this morning?"

"Sure," said Pacifique amiably. "I got de word las' night dat my fader, he was seeck. It was so stormy dat I couldn't go den, so I start vair early dis mornin'. I'm goin' troo de woods for short cut."

"Did you hear how Gilbert Blythe was this morning?"

Anne's desperation drove her to the question. Even the worst would be more endurable than this hideous suspense.

"He's better," said Pacifique. "He got de turn las' night. De doctor say he'll be all right now dis soon while. Had close shave, dough! Dat boy, he jus' keel himself at colloge. Well, I mus' hurry. De old man, he'll be in hurry to see me."

Pacifique resumed his walk and his whistle. Anne gazed after him with eyes where joy was driving out the strained anguish of the night. He was a very lank, very ragged, very homely youth. But in her sight he was as beautiful as those who bring good tidings on the mountains. Never, as long as she lived, would Anne see Pacifique's brown, round, black-eyed face without a warm remembrance of the moment when he had given to her the oil of joy for mourning.

Long after Pacifique's gay whistle had faded into the phantom of music and then into silence far up under the maples of Lover's Lane Anne stood under the willows, tasting the poignant sweetness of life when some great dread has been removed from it. The morning was a cup filled with mist and glamor. In the corner near her was a rich surprise of new-blown, crystal-dewed roses. The trills and trickles of song from the birds in the big tree above her seemed in perfect accord with her mood. A sentence from a very old, very true, very wonderful Book came to her lips,

"Weeping may endure for a night but joy cometh in the morning."

41

Love Takes Up the Glass of Time

"I've come up to ask you to go for one of our old-time rambles through September woods and 'over hills where spices grow,' this afternoon," said Gilbert, coming suddenly around the porch corner. "Suppose we visit Hester Gray's garden."

Anne, sitting on the stone step with her lap full of a pale, filmy, green stuff, looked up rather blankly.

"Oh, I wish I could," she said slowly, "but I really can't, Gilbert. I'm going to Alice Penhallow's wedding this evening, you know. I've got to do something to this dress, and by the time it's finished I'll have to get ready. I'm so sorry. I'd love to go."

"Well, can you go tomorrow afternoon, then?" asked Gilbert, apparently not much disappointed.

"Yes, I think so."

"In that case I shall hie me home at once to do something I should otherwise have to do tomorrow. So Alice Penhallow is to be married tonight. Three weddings for you in one summer, Anne—Phil's, Alice's, and Jane's. I'll never forgive Jane for not inviting me to her wedding."

"You really can't blame her when you think of the tremendous

Andrews connection who had to be invited. The house could hardly hold them all. I was only bidden by grace of being Jane's old chum—at least on Jane's part. I think Mrs. Harmon's motive for inviting me was to let me see Jane's surpassing gorgeousness."

"Is it true that she wore so many diamonds that you couldn't tell where the diamonds left off and Jane began?"

Anne laughed.

"She certainly wore a good many. What with all the diamonds and white satin and tulle and lace and roses and orange blossoms, prim little Jane was almost lost to sight. But she was *very* happy, and so was Mr. Inglis—and so was Mrs. Harmon."

"Is that the dress you're going to wear tonight?" asked Gilbert, looking down at the fluffs and frills.

"Yes. Isn't it pretty? And I shall wear starflowers in my hair. The Haunted Wood is full of them this summer."

Gilbert had a sudden vision of Anne, arrayed in a frilly green gown, with the virginal curves of arms and throat slipping out of it, and white stars shining against the coils of her ruddy hair. The vision made him catch his breath. But he turned lightly away.

"Well, I'll be up tomorrow. Hope you'll have a nice time tonight."

Anne looked after him as he strode away, and sighed. Gilbert was friendly—very friendly—far too friendly. He had come quite often to Green Gables after his recovery, and something of their old comradeship had returned. But Anne no longer found it satisfying. The rose of love made the blossom of friendship pale and scentless by contrast. And Anne had again begun to doubt if Gilbert now felt anything for her but friendship. In the common light of common day her radiant certainty of that rapt morning had faded. She was haunted by a miserable fear that her mistake could never be rectified. It was quite likely that

Love Takes up the Glass of Time

it was Christine whom Gilbert loved after all. Perhaps he was even engaged to her. Anne tried to put all unsettling hopes out of her heart, and reconcile herself to a future where work and ambition must take the place of love. She could do good, if not noble, work as a teacher; and the success her little sketches were beginning to meet with in certain editorial sanctums augured well for her budding literary dreams. But—but—Anne picked up her green dress and sighed again.

When Gilbert came the next afternoon he found Anne waiting for him, fresh as the dawn and fair as a star, after all the gaiety of the preceding night. She wore a green dress—not the one she had worn to the wedding, but an old one which Gilbert had told her at a Redmond reception he liked especially. It was just the shade of green that brought out the rich tints of her hair, and the starry gray of her eyes and the iris-like delicacy of her skin. Gilbert, glancing at her sideways as they walked along a shadowy woodpath, thought she had never looked so lovely. Anne, glancing sideways at Gilbert, now and then, thought how much older he looked since his illness. It was as if he had put boyhood behind him forever.

The day was beautiful and the way was beautiful. Anne was almost sorry when they reached Hester Gray's garden, and sat down on the old bench. But it was beautiful there, too—as beautiful as it had been on the far-away day of the Golden Picnic, when Diana and Jane and Priscilla and she had found it. Then it had been lovely with narcissus and violets; now golden rod had kindled its fairy torches in the corners and asters clotted it bluely. The call of the brook came up through the woods from the valley of birches with all its old allurement; the mellow air was full of the purr of the sea; beyond were fields rimmed by fences bleached silvery gray in the suns of many summers, and long hills scarfed with the shadows of autumnal clouds; with the blowing of the west wind old dreams returned.

"I think," said Anne softly, "that 'the land where dreams come true' is in the blue haze yonder, over that little valley."

"Have you any unfulfilled dreams, Anne?" asked Gilbert.

Something in his tone—something she had not heard since that miserable evening in the orchard at Patty's Place—made Anne's heart beat wildly. But she made answer lightly.

"Of course. Everybody has. It wouldn't do for us to have all our dreams fulfilled. We would be as good as dead if we had nothing left to dream about. What a delicious aroma that low-descending sun is extracting from the asters and ferns. I wish we could *see* perfumes as well as smell them. I'm sure they would be very beautiful."

Gilbert was not to be thus sidetracked.

"I have a dream," he said slowly. "I persist in dreaming it, although it has often seemed to me that it could never come true. I dream of a home with a hearth-fire in it, a cat and dog, the footsteps of friends—and *you!*"

Anne wanted to speak but she could find no words. Happiness was breaking over her like a wave. It almost frightened her.

"I asked you a question over two years ago, Anne. If I ask it again today will you give me a different answer?"

Still Anne could not speak. But she lifted her eyes, shining with all the love-rapture of countless generations, and looked into his for a moment. He wanted no other answer.

They lingered in the old garden until twilight, sweet as dusk in Eden must have been, crept over it. There was so much to talk over and recall—things said and done and heard and thought and felt and misunderstood.

"I thought you loved Christine Stuart," Anne told him, as reproachfully as if she had not given him every reason to suppose that she loved Roy Gardner.

Gilbert laughed boyishly.

"Christine was engaged to somebody in her home town. I knew it and she knew I knew it. When her brother graduated he told me his sister was coming to Kingsport the next winter to take music, and asked me if I would look after her a bit, as she knew no one and would be very lonely. So I did. And then I liked Christine for her own sake. She is one of the nicest girls I've ever known. I knew college gossip credited us with being in love with each other. I didn't care. Nothing mattered much to me for a time there, after you told me you could never love me, Anne. There was nobody else—there never could be anybody else for me but you. I've loved you ever since that day you broke your slate over my head in school."

"I don't see how you could keep on loving me when I was such a little fool," said Anne.

"Well, I tried to stop," said Gilbert frankly, "not because I thought you what you call yourself, but because I felt sure there was no chance for me after Gardner came on the scene. But I couldn't—and I can't tell you, either, what it's meant to me these two years to believe you were going to marry him, and be told every week by some busybody that your engagement was on the point of being announced. I believed it until one blessed day when I was sitting up after the fever. I got a letter from Phil Gordon—Phil Blake, rather—in which she told me there was really nothing between you and Roy, and advised me to 'try again.' Well, the doctor was amazed at my rapid recovery after that."

Anne laughed—then shivered.

"I can never forget the night I thought you were dying, Gilbert. Oh, I knew—I *knew* then—and I thought it was too late."

"But it wasn't, sweetheart. Oh, Anne, this makes up for everything, doesn't it? Let's resolve to keep this day sacred to perfect beauty all our lives for the gift it has given us."

"It's the birthday of our happiness," said Anne softly. "I've always loved this old garden of Hester Gray's, and now it will be dearer than ever."

"But I'll have to ask you to wait a long time, Anne," said Gilbert sadly. "It will be three years before I'll finish my medical course. And even then there will be no diamond sunbursts and marble halls."

Anne laughed.

"I don't want sunbursts and marble halls. I just want *you*. You see I'm quite as shameless as Phil about it. Sunbursts and marble halls may be all very well, but there is more 'scope for imagination' without them. And as for the waiting, that doesn't matter. We'll just be happy, waiting and working for each other—and dreaming. Oh, dreams will be very sweet now."

Gilbert drew her close to him and kissed her. Then they walked home together in the dusk, crowned king and queen in the bridal realm of love, along winding paths fringed with the sweetest flowers that ever bloomed, and over haunted meadows where winds of hope and memory blew.

The First Year

1

(Letter from Anne Shirley, B.A., Principal of Summerside High School, to Gilbert Blythe, medical student at Redmond College, Kingsport.)

"Windy Poplars,
"Spook's Lane,
"S'side, P.E.I.,
"Monday, September 12th.

"DEAREST:
"Isn't that an address! Did you ever hear anything so delicious? Windy Poplars is the name of my new home and I love it. I also love Spook's Lane, which has no legal existence. It should be Trent Street but it is never called Trent Street except on the rare occasions when it is mentioned in the *Weekly Courier*...and then people look at each other and say, 'Where on earth is that?' Spook's Lane it is...although for what reason I cannot tell you. I have already asked Rebecca Dew about it, but all she can say is that it has always been Spook's Lane and there was some old yarn years ago of its being haunted. But *she* has never seen anything worse-looking than herself in it.

"However, I mustn't get ahead of my story. You don't know Rebecca Dew yet. But you will, oh, yes, you will. I foresee that Rebecca Dew will figure largely in my future correspondence.

"It's dusk, dearest. (In passing, isn't 'dusk' a lovely word? I like it better than twilight. It sounds so velvety and shadowy and...and...*dusky.*) In daylight I belong to the world...in the night to sleep and eternity. But in the dusk I'm free from both and belong only to myself...and *you*. So I'm going to keep this hour sacred to writing to you. Though *this* won't be a love-letter. I have a scratchy pen and I can't write love-letters with a scratchy pen...or a sharp pen...or a stub pen. So you'll only get *that* kind of letter from me when I have exactly the right kind of pen. Meanwhile, I'll tell you about my new domicile and its inhabitants. Gilbert, they're such *dears*.

"I came up yesterday to look for a boarding-house. Mrs. Rachel Lynde came with me, ostensibly to do some shopping but really, I know, to choose a boarding-house for me. In spite of my Arts course and my B.A., Mrs. Lynde still thinks I am an inexperienced young thing who must be guided and directed and overseen.

"We came by train and oh, Gilbert, I had the funniest adventure. You know I've always been one to whom adventures came unsought. I just seem to attract them, as it were.

"It happened just as the train was coming to a stop at the station. I got up and, stooping to pick up Mrs. Lynde's suitcase (she was planning to spend Sunday with a friend in Summerside), I leaned my knuckles heavily on what I thought was the shiny arm of a seat. In a second I received a violent crack across them that nearly made me howl. Gilbert, what I had taken for the arm of a seat was a man's bald head. He was glaring fiercely at me and had evidently just waked up. I apologized abjectly and got off the train as quickly as possible. The last I saw of him he was still glaring. Mrs. Lynde was horrified and my knuckles are sore yet!

"I did not expect to have much trouble in finding a boarding-house, for a certain Mrs. Tom Pringle has been boarding the various principals of the High School for the

The First Year

last fifteen years. But, for some unknown reason, she has grown suddenly tired of 'being bothered' and wouldn't take me. Several other desirable places had some polite excuse. Several other places *weren't* desirable. We wandered about the town the whole afternoon and got hot and tired and blue and headachy...at least *I* did. I was ready to give up in despair...and then, Spook's Lane just happened!

"We had dropped in to see Mrs. Braddock, an old crony of Mrs. Lynde's. And Mrs. Braddock said she thought 'the widows' might take me in.

"'I've heard they want a boarder to pay Rebecca Dew's wages. They can't afford to keep Rebecca any longer unless a little extra money comes in. And if Rebecca goes, *who* is to milk that old red cow?'

"Mrs. Braddock fixed me with a stern eye as if she thought *I* ought to milk the red cow but wouldn't believe me on oath if I claimed I could.

"'What widows are you talking about?' demanded Mrs. Lynde.

"'Why, Aunt Kate and Aunt Chatty,' said Mrs. Braddock, as if everybody, even an ignorant B.A., ought to know that. 'Aunt Kate is Mrs. Amasa MacComber (she's the Captain's widow) and Aunt Chatty is Mrs. Lincoln MacLean, just a plain widow. But every one calls them "aunt." They live at the end of Spook's Lane.'

"Spook's Lane! That settled it. I knew I just had to board with the widows.

"'Let's go and see them at once,' I implored Mrs. Lynde. It seemed to me if we lost a moment Spook's Lane would vanish back into fairyland.

"'You can see them, but it'll be Rebecca who'll really decide whether they'll take you or not. Rebecca Dew rules the roost at Windy Poplars, I can tell you.'

"Windy Poplars! It couldn't be true...no it couldn't. I must be dreaming. And Mrs. Rachel Lynde was actually saying it was a funny name for a place.

"'Oh, Captain MacComber called it that. It was his house, you know. He planted all the poplars round it and was mighty proud of it, though he was seldom home and never stayed long. Aunt Kate used to say that was inconvenient, but we never got it figured out whether she meant his staying such a little time or his coming back at all. Well, Miss Shirley, I hope you'll get there. Rebecca Dew's a good cook and a genius with cold potatoes. If she takes a notion to you you'll be in clover. If she doesn't... well, she won't, that's all. I hear there's a new banker in town looking for a boarding-house and she may prefer him. It's kind of funny Mrs. Tom Pringle wouldn't take you. Summerside is full of Pringles and half Pringles. They're called "The Royal Family" and you'll have to get on their good side, Miss Shirley, or you'll never get along in Summerside High. They've always ruled the roost hereabouts...there's a street called after old Captain Abraham Pringle. There's a regular clan of them, but the two old ladies at Maplehurst boss the tribe. I did hear they were down on you.'

"'Why should they be?' I exclaimed. 'I'm a total stranger to them.'

"'Well, a third cousin of theirs applied for the Principalship and they all think he should have got it. When your application was accepted the whole kit and boodle of them threw back their heads and howled. Well, people are like that. We have to take them as we find them, you know. They'll be as smooth as cream to you but they'll work against you every time. I'm not wanting to discourage you but forewarned is forearmed. I hope you'll make good

The First Year

just to spite them. If the widows take you, you won't mind eating with Rebecca Dew, will you? She isn't a *servant*, you know. She's a far-off cousin of the Captain's. She doesn't come to the table when there's company...she knows her place *then*...but if you were boarding there she wouldn't consider you company, of course.'

"I assured the anxious Mrs. Braddock that I'd love eating with Rebecca Dew and dragged Mrs. Lynde away. I *must* get ahead of the banker.

"Mrs. Braddock followed us to the door.

"'And don't hurt Aunt Chatty's feelings, will you? Her feelings are so easily hurt. She's so sensitive, poor thing. You see, she hasn't *quite* as much money as Aunt Kate... though Aunt Kate hasn't any too much either. And then Aunt Kate liked her husband real well...her own husband, I mean...but Aunt Chatty didn't...didn't like hers, I mean. Small wonder! Lincoln MacLean was an old crank...but she thinks people hold it against her. It's lucky this is Saturday. If it was Friday Aunt Chatty wouldn't even consider taking you. You'd think Aunt Kate would be the superstitious one, wouldn't you? Sailors are kind of like that. But it's Aunt Chatty...although *her* husband was a carpenter. She was very pretty in her day, poor thing.'

"I assured Mrs. Braddock that Aunt Chatty's feelings would be sacred to me, but she followed us down the walk.

"'Kate and Chatty won't explore your belongings when you're out. They're very conscientious. Rebecca Dew may, but she won't tell on you. And I wouldn't go to the front door if I was you. They only use it for something real important. I don't think it's been opened since Amasa's funeral. Try the side door. They keep the key under the flower-pot on the window-sill, so if nobody's home just unlock the door and go in and wait. And whatever you do, don't praise the cat, because Rebecca Dew doesn't like him.'

"I promised I wouldn't praise the cat and we actually got away. Erelong we found ourselves in Spook's Lane. It is a very short side street, leading out to open country, and far away a blue hill makes a beautiful back-drop for it. On one side there are no houses at all and the land slopes down to the harbor. On the other side there are only three. The first one is just a house...nothing more to be said of it. The next one is a big, imposing, gloomy mansion of stone-trimmed red brick, with a mansard roof warty with dormer-windows, an iron railing around the flat top and so many spruces and firs crowding about it that you can hardly see the house. It must be frightfully dark inside. And the third and last is Windy Poplars, right on the corner, with the grass-grown street on the front and a real country road, beautiful with tree shadows, on the other side.

"I fell in love with it at once. You know there are houses which impress themselves upon you at first sight for some reason you can hardly define. Windy Poplars is like that. I may describe it to you as a white frame house... very white...with green shutters...very green...with a 'tower' in the corner and a dormer-window on either side, a low stone wall dividing it from the street, with aspen poplars growing at intervals along it, and a big garden at the back where flowers and vegetables are delightfully jumbled up together...but all this can't convey its charm to you. In short, it is a house with a delightful personality and has something of the flavor of Green Gables about it.

"'This is the spot for me...it's been foreordained,' I said rapturously.

"Mrs. Lynde looked as if she didn't quite trust foreordination.

"'It'll be a long walk to school,' she said dubiously.

The First Year

"'I don't mind that. It will be a good exercise. Oh, look at that lovely birch and maple grove across the road.'

"Mrs. Lynde looked but all she said was,

"'I hope you won't be pestered with mosquitoes.'

"I hoped so, too. I detest mosquitoes. One mosquito can keep me 'awaker' than a bad conscience.

"I was glad we didn't have to go in by the front door. It looked so forbidding...a big, doubleleaved, grained-wood affair, flanked by panels of red, flowered glass. It doesn't seem to belong to the house at all. The little green side door, which we reached by a darling path of thin, flat sandstones sunk at intervals in the grass, was much more friendly and inviting. The path was edged by very prim, well-ordered beds of ribbon grass and bleeding-heart and tiger-lilies and sweet-William and southernwood and bride's bouquet and red-and-white daisies and what Mrs. Lynde calls 'pinies.' Of course they weren't all in bloom at this season, but you could see they had bloomed at the proper time and done it well. There was a rose plot in a far corner and between Windy Poplars and the gloomy house next a brick wall all overgrown with Virginia creeper, with an arched trellis above a faded green door in the middle of it. A vine ran right across it, so it was plain it hadn't been opened for some time. It was really only half a door, for its top half is merely an open oblong through which we could catch a glimpse of a jungly garden on the other side.

"Just as we entered the gate of the garden of Windy Poplars I noticed a little clump of clover right by the path. Some impulse led me to stoop down and look at it. Would you believe it, Gilbert? There, right before my eyes, were *three* four-leafed clovers! Talk about omens! Even the Pringles can't contend against that. And I felt sure the banker hadn't an earthly chance.

"The side door was open so it was evident somebody was at home and we didn't have to look under the flowerpot. We knocked and Rebecca Dew came to the door. We knew it was Rebecca Dew because it couldn't have been any one else in the whole wide world. And she couldn't have had any other name.

"Rebecca Dew is 'around forty' and if a tomato had black hair racing away from its forehead, little twinkling black eyes, a tiny nose with a knobby end and a slit of a mouth, it would look exactly like her. Everything about her is a little too short...arms and legs and neck and nose... everything but her smile. It is long enough to reach from ear to ear.

"But we didn't see her smile just then. She looked very grim when I asked if I could see Mrs. MacComber.

"'You mean Mrs. *Captain* MacComber?' she said rebukingly, as if there were at least a dozen Mrs. MacCombers in the house.

"'Yes,' I said meekly. And we were forthwith ushered into the parlor and left there. It was rather a nice little room, a bit cluttered up with antimacassars but with a quiet, friendly atmosphere about it that I liked. Every bit of furniture had its own particular place which it had occupied for years. How that furniture shone! No bought polish ever produced that mirror-like gloss. I knew it was Rebecca Dew's elbow grease. There was a full-rigged ship in a bottle on the mantelpiece which interested Mrs. Lynde greatly. She couldn't imagine how it ever got into the bottle...but she thought it gave the room 'a nautical air.'

"'The widows' came in. I liked them at once. Aunt Kate was tall and thin and gray, and a little austere...Manila's type exactly: and Aunt Chatty was short and thin and gray, and a little wistful. She may have been very pretty once but

The First Year

nothing is now left of her beauty except her eyes. *They* are lovely...soft and big and brown.

"I explained my errand and the widows looked at each other.

"'We must consult Rebecca Dew,' said Aunt Chatty.

"'Undoubtedly,' said Aunt Kate.

"Rebecca Dew was accordingly summoned from the kitchen. The cat came in with her...a big fluffy Maltese, with a white breast and a white collar. I should have liked to stroke him, but, remembering Mrs. Braddock's warning, I ignored him.

"Rebecca gazed at me without the glimmer of a smile.

"'Rebecca,' said Aunt Kate, who, I have discovered, does not waste words, 'Miss Shirley wishes to board here. I don't think we can take her.'

"'Why not?' said Rebecca Dew.

"'It would be too much trouble for you, I am afraid,' said Aunt Chatty.

"'I'm well used to trouble,' said Rebecca Dew. You *can't* separate those names, Gilbert. It's impossible...though the widows do it. They call her Rebecca when they speak to her. I don't know how they manage it.

"'We are rather old to have young people coming and going,' persisted Aunt Chatty.

"'Speak for yourself,' retorted Rebecca Dew. "I'm only forty-five and I still have the use of my faculties. And *I* think it would be nice to have a young person sleeping in the house. A girl would be better than a boy any time. *He'd* be smoking day *and* night...burn us in our beds. If you must take a boarder, *my* advice would be to take *her*. But of course it's *your* house.'

"She said and vanished...as Homer was so fond of remarking. I knew the whole thing was settled but Aunt

Chatty said I must go up and see if I was suited with my room.

"'We will give you the tower room, dear. It's not quite as large as the spare room, but it has a stovepipe hole for a stove in winter and a much nicer view. You can see the old graveyard from it.'

"I knew I would love the room...the very name, 'tower room,' thrilled me. I felt as if we were living in that old song we used to sing in Avonlea School about the maiden who 'dwelt in a high tower beside a gray sea.' It proved to be the dearest place. We ascended to it by a little flight of comer steps leading up from the stair-landing. It was rather small...but not nearly as small as that dreadful hall bedroom I had my first year at Redmond. It had two windows, a dormer one looking west and a gable one looking north, and in the comer formed by the tower another three-sided window with casements opening outward and shelves underneath for my books. The floor was covered with round, braided rugs, the big bed had a canopy top and a 'wild-goose' quilt and looked so perfectly smooth and level that it seemed a shame to spoil it by sleeping in it. And, Gilbert, it is so high that I have to climb into it by a funny little movable set of steps which in daytime are stowed away under it. It seems Captain MacComber bought the whole contraption in some 'foreign' place and brought it home.

"There was a dear little corner cupboard with shelves trimmed with white scalloped paper and bouquets painted on its door. There was a round blue cushion on the window-seat...a cushion with a button deep in the center, making it look like a fat blue doughnut. And there was a sweet washstand with two shelves...the top one just big enough for a basin and jug of robin's-egg blue and the under one for a soap dish and hot water pitcher. It had a little brass-handled drawer full of towels and on a shelf over it a white china lady sat, with pink shoes and gilt sash and a red china rose in her golden china hair.

"The whole place was engoldened by the light that came through the corn-colored curtains and there was the rarest tapestry on the whitewashed walls where the shadow patterns of the aspens outside fell...living tapestry, always changing and quivering. Somehow, it seemed such a *happy* room. I felt as if I were the richest girl in the world.

"'You'll be safe there, that's what,' said Mrs. Lynde, as we went away.

"'I expect I'll find some things a bit cramping after the freedom of Patty's Place,' I said, just to tease her.

"'Freedom!' Mrs. Lynde sniffed. 'Freedom! Don't talk like a Yankee, Anne.'

"I came up today, bag and baggage. Of course I hated to leave Green Gables. No matter how often and long I'm away from it, the minute a vacation comes I'm part of it again as if I had never been away, and my heart is torn over leaving it. But I know I'll like it here. And it likes me. I always know whether a house likes me or not.

"The views from my windows are lovely...even the old graveyard, which is surrounded by a row of dark fir trees and reached by a winding, dyke-bordered lane. From my west window I can see all over the harbor to distant, misty shores, with the dear little sailboats I love and the ships outward bound 'for ports unknown'...fascinating phrase! Such 'scope for imagination' in it! From the north window I can see into the grove of birch and maple across the road. You know I've always been a tree worshiper. When we studied Tennyson in our English course at Redmond I was always sorrowfully at one with poor Enone, mourning her ravished pines.

"Beyond the grove and the graveyard is a lovable valley with the glossy red ribbon of a road winding through it and white houses dotted along it. Some valleys *are* lovable... you can't tell why. Just to look at them gives you pleasure. And beyond it again is my blue hill. I'm naming it Storm King...the ruling passion, etc.

"I can be so *alone* up here when I want to be. You know it's lovely to be alone once in a while. The winds will be my friends. They'll wail and sigh and croon around my tower... the white winds of winter...the green winds of spring...the blue winds of summer...the crimson winds of autumn... and the wild winds of all seasons...'stormy wind fulfilling his word.' How I've always thrilled to that Bible verse...as if each and every wind had a message for me. I've always envied the boy who flew with the north wind in that lovely old story of George MacDonald's. Some night, Gilbert, I'll open my tower casement and just step into the arms of the wind...and Rebecca Dew will never know why my bed wasn't slept in that night.

"I hope when we find our 'house of dreams,' dearest, that there will be winds around it. I wonder where it is... that unknown house. Shall I love it best by moonlight or dawn? That home of the future where we will have love and friendship and work...and a few funny adventures to bring laughter in our old age. Old age! Can *we* ever be old, Gilbert? It seems impossible.

"From the left window in the tower I can see the roofs of the town...this place where I am to live for at least a year. People are living in those houses who will be my friends, though I don't know them yet. And perhaps my enemies. For the ilk of Pye are found everywhere, under all kinds of names, and I understand the Pringles are to be reckoned with. School begins tomorrow. I shall have to teach

The First Year

geometry! Surely that can't be any worse than learning it. I pray heaven there are no mathematical geniuses among the Pringles.

"I've been here only for half a day, but I feel as if I had known the widows and Rebecca Dew all my life. They've asked me to call them 'aunt' already and I've asked them to call me Anne. I called Rebecca Dew 'Miss Dew'...once.

"'Miss What?' quoth she.

"'Dew,' I said meekly. 'Isn't that your name?'

"'Well, yes, it is, but I ain't been called Miss Dew for so long it gave me quite a turn. You'd better not do it any more, Miss Shirley, me not being used to it.'

"'I'll remember, Rebecca...Dew,' I said, trying my hardest to leave off the Dew but not succeeding.

"Mrs. Braddock was quite right in saying Aunt Chatty was sensitive. I discovered that at supper-time. Aunt Kate had said something about 'Chatty's sixty-sixth birthday.' Happening to glance at Aunt Chatty I saw that she had... no, not *burst* into tears. That is entirely too explosive a term for her performance. She just overflowed. The tears welled up in her big brown eyes and brimmed over, effortlessly and silently.

"'What's the matter now, Chatty?' asked Aunt Kate rather dourly.

"'It...it was only my sixty-fifth birthday,' said Aunt Chatty.

"'I beg your pardon, Charlotte,' said Aunt Kate...and all was sunshine again.

"The cat is a lovely big Tommy-cat with golden eyes, an elegant coat of dusty Maltese and irreproachable linen. Aunts Kate and Chatty call him Dusty Miller, because that is his name, and Rebecca Dew calls him That Cat because she resents him and resents the fact that she has to give him a square inch of liver every morning and evening, clean his hairs off the parlor arm-chair seat with an old tooth-brush whenever he has sneaked in and hunt him up if he is out late at night.

"'Rebecca Dew has always hated cats,' Aunt Chatty tells me, 'and she hates Dusty especially. Old Mrs. Campbell's dog...she kept a dog then...brought him here two years ago in his mouth. I suppose he thought it was no use to take him to Mrs. Campbell. Such a poor miserable little kitten, all wet and cold, with its poor little bones almost sticking through its skin. A heart of stone couldn't have refused it shelter. So Kate and I adopted it, but Rebecca Dew has never really forgiven us. We were not diplomatic that time. We should have refused to take it in. I don't know if you've noticed...' Aunt Chatty looked cautiously around at the door between the dining room and kitchen...'how we manage Rebecca Dew.'

"I *had* noticed it...and it was beautiful to behold. Summerside and Rebecca Dew may think she rules the roost but the widows know differently.

"'We didn't want to take the banker...a young man would have been *so* unsettling and we would have had to worry so much if he didn't go to church regularly. But we pretended we did and Rebecca Dew simply wouldn't hear of it. I'm so glad we have you, dear. I feel sure you'll be a very nice person to cook for. I hope you'll like us all. Rebecca Dew has some very fine qualities. She was not so tidy when she came fifteen years ago as she is now. Once Kate had to write her name..."Rebecca Dew"...right across the parlor mirror to show the dust. But she never had to do it again. Rebecca Dew can take a hint. I hope you'll find your room comfortable, dear. You may have the window open at night. Kate does not approve of night air but she knows boarders

The First Year

must have privileges. She and I sleep together and we have arranged it so that one night the window is shut for her and the next it is open for me. One can always work out little problems like that, don't you think? Where there is a will there is always a way. Don't be alarmed if you hear Rebecca prowling a good deal in the night. She is always hearing noises and getting up to investigate them. I think that is why she didn't want the banker. She was afraid she might run into him in her nightgown. I hope you won't mind Kate not talking much. It's just her way. And she must have so many things to talk of...she was all over the world with Amasa MacComber in her young days. I wish I had the subjects for conversation she has, but I've never been off P. E. Island. I've often wondered why things should be arranged so...me loving to talk and with nothing to talk about and Kate with everything and hating to talk. But I suppose Providence knows best.'

"Although Aunt Chatty is a talker all right, she didn't say all this without a break. I interjected remarks at suitable intervals, but they were of no importance.

"They keep a cow which is pastured at Mr. James Hamilton's up the road and Rebecca Dew goes there to milk her. There is any amount of cream and every morning and evening I understand Rebecca Dew passes a glass of new milk through the opening in the wall gate to Mrs. Campbell's 'Woman.' It is for 'little Elizabeth,' who must have it under doctor's orders. Who the Woman is, or who little Elizabeth is, I have yet to discover. Mrs. Campbell is the inhabitant and owner of the fortress next door...which is called The Evergreens.

"I don't expect to sleep tonight...I never do sleep my first night in a strange bed and *this* is the very strangest bed I've ever seen. But I won't mind. I've always loved the night and I'll like lying awake and thinking over everything in life, past, present and to come. Especially *to come.*

"This is a merciless letter, Gilbert. I won't inflict such a long one on you again. But I wanted to tell you everything, so that you could picture my new surroundings for yourself. It has come to an end now, for far up the harbor the moon is 'sinking into shadow-land.' I must write a letter to Marilla yet. It will reach Green Gables the day after tomorrow and Davy will bring it home from the post-office, and he and Dora will crowd around Marilla while she opens it and Mrs. Lynde will have both ears open.... Ow...w...w! That has made me homesick. Good-night, dearest, from one who is now and ever will be,

"Fondestly yours,
"ANNE SHIRLEY."

2

(Extracts from various letters from the same to the same.)

"September 26th.

"Do you know where I go to read your letters? Across the road into the grove. There is a little dell there where the sun dapples the ferns. A brook meanders through it; there is a twisted mossy tree-trunk on which I sit, and the most delightful row of young sister birches. After this, when I have a dream of a certain kind...a golden-green, crimson-veined dream...a very

The First Year

dream of dreams...I shall please my fancy with the belief that it came from my secret dell of birches and was born of some mystic union between the slenderest, airiest of the sisters and the crooning brook. I love to sit there and listen to the silence of the grove. Have you ever noticed how many different silences there are, Gilbert? The silence of the woods...of the shore...of the meadows...of the night...of the summer afternoon. All different because all the undertones that thread them are different. I'm sure if I were totally blind and insensitive to heat and cold I could easily tell just where I was by the quality of the silence about me.

"School has been 'keeping' for two weeks now and I've got things pretty well organized. But Mrs. Braddock was right...the Pringles are my problem. And as yet I don't see exactly how I'm going to solve it in spite of my lucky clovers. As Mrs. Braddock says, they are as smooth as cream...and as slippery.

"The Pringles are a kind of clan who keeps tabs on each other and fight a good bit among themselves but stand shoulder to shoulder in regard to any outsider. I have come to the conclusion that there are just two kinds of people in Summerside...those who are Pringles and those who aren't.

"My room is full of Pringles and a good many students who bear another name have Pringle blood in them. The ring-leader of them seems to be Jen Pringle, a green-eyed bantling who looks as *Becky Sharp* must have looked at fourteen. I believe she is deliberately organizing a subtle campaign of insubordination and disrespect, with which I am going to find it hard to cope. She has a knack of making irresistibly comic faces and when I hear a smothered ripple of laughter running over the room behind my back I know perfectly well what has caused it, but so far I haven't been able to catch her out in it. She has brains, too...the little wretch!...can write compositions that are fourth cousins to literature and is quite brilliant in mathematics...woe is me! There is a certain *sparkle* in everything she says or does and she has a sense of humorous situations which would be a bond of kinship between us if she hadn't started out by hating me. As it is, I fear it will be a long time before Jen and I can laugh *together* over anything.

"Myra Pringle, Jen's cousin, is the beauty of the school... and apparently stupid. She does perpetrate some amusing howlers...as, for instance, when she said today in history class that the Indians thought Champlain and his men were gods or 'something inhuman.'

"Socially the Pringles are what Rebecca Dew calls 'the e-light' of Summerside. Already I have been invited to two Pringle homes for supper...because it is the proper thing to invite a new teacher to supper and the Pringles are not going to omit the required gestures. Last night I was at James Pringle's... the father of the aforesaid Jen. He looks like a college professor but is in reality stupid and ignorant. He talked a great deal about 'dis*cip*line,' tapping the tablecloth with a finger the nail of which was not impeccable and occasionally doing dreadful things to grammar. The Summerside High had always required a firm hand...an experienced teacher, male preferred. He was afraid I was a *leetle* too young...'a fault which time will cure all too soon,' he said sorrowfully. I didn't say anything because if I had said anything I might have said too much. So I was as smooth and creamy as any Pringle of them all could have been and contented myself with looking limpidly at him and saying inside of myself, 'You cantankerous, prejudiced old creature!'

"Jen must have got her brains from her mother...whom I found myself liking. Jen, in her parents' presence, was a model of decorum. But though her words were polite her tone was insolent. Every time she said 'Miss Shirley' she contrived to make it sound like an insult. And every time she looked at my hair I felt that it was just plain carroty red. No Pringle, I am certain, would ever admit it was auburn.

The First Year

"I liked the Morton Pringles much better...though Morton Pringle never really listens to anything you say. He says something to you and then, while you're replying, he is busy thinking out his next remark.

"Mrs. Stephen Pringle...the Widow Pringle...Summerside abounds in widows...wrote me a letter yesterday...a nice, polite, poisonous letter. Millie has too much home work...Millie is a delicate child and must not be overworked. Mr. Bell *never* gave her home work. She is a sensitive child that must be *understood*. Mr. Bell understood her so well! Mrs. Stephen is sure I will, too, if I try!

"I do not doubt Mrs. Stephen thinks I made Adam Pringle's nose bleed in class today by reason of which he had to go home. And I woke up last night and couldn't go to sleep again because I remembered an *i* I hadn't dotted in a question I wrote on the board. I'm certain Jen Pringle would notice it and a whisper will go around the clan about it.

"Rebecca Dew says that all the Pringles will invite me to supper, except the old ladies at Maplehurst, and then ignore me forever afterwards. As they are the 'e-light,' this may mean that socially I may be banned in Summerside. Well, we'll see. The battle is on but is not yet either won or lost. Still, I feel rather unhappy over it all. You can't reason with prejudice. I'm still just as I used to be in my childhood...I can't bear to have people not liking me. It isn't pleasant to think that the families of half my pupils hate me. And for no fault of my own. It is the *injustice* that stings me. There go more italics! But a few italics really do relieve your feelings.

"Apart from the Pringles I like my pupils very much. There are some clever, ambitious, hard-working ones who are really interested in getting an education. Lewis Allen is paying for his board by doing *housework* at his boarding-house and isn't a bit ashamed of it. And Sophy Sinclair rides bareback on her father's old gray mare six miles in and six miles out every day. There's pluck for you! If I can help a girl like that, am I to mind the Pringles?

"The trouble is...if I can't win the Pringles I won't have much chance of helping anybody.

"But I love Windy Poplars. It isn't a boarding-house...it's a home! And they like me...even Dusty Miller likes me, though he sometimes disapproves of me and shows it by deliberately sitting with his back turned towards me, occasionally cocking a golden eye over his shoulder at me to see how I'm taking it. I don't pet him much when Rebecca Dew is around because it really does irritate her. By day he is a homely, comfortable, meditative animal...but he is decidedly a weird creature at night. Rebecca says it is because he is never allowed to stay out after dark. She hates to stand in the back yard and call him. She says the neighbors will all be laughing at her. She calls in such fierce, stentorian tones that she really can be heard all over the town on a still night shouting for 'Puss...*puss*...PUSS!' The widows would have a conniption if Dusty Miller wasn't in when they went to bed. 'Nobody knows what I've gone through on account of That Cat...*nobody*,' Rebecca has assured me.

"The widows are going to wear well. Every day I like them better. Aunt Kate doesn't believe in reading novels, but informs me that she does not propose to censor my reading-matter. Aunt Chatty loves novels. She has a 'hidy-hole' where she keeps them...she smuggles them in from the town library...together with a pack of cards for solitaire and anything else she doesn't want Aunt Kate to see. It is in a chair seat which nobody but Aunt Chatty knows is more than a chair seat. She has shared the secret with me, because, I strongly suspect, she wants me to aid and abet her in the aforesaid smuggling. There shouldn't really be any need for hidy-holes at Windy Poplars, for I never saw a house with so many mysterious cupboards. Though to be sure, Rebecca Dew won't let them *be* mysterious. She is always cleaning them out ferociously. 'A house can't keep itself clean,' she says sorrowfully when either of the widows protests. I am

The First Year

sure she would make short work of a novel or a pack of cards if she found them. They are both a horror to her orthodox soul. Rebecca Dew says cards are the devil's books and novels even worse. The only things Rebecca ever reads, apart from her Bible, are the society columns of the Montreal *Guardian*. She loves to pore over the houses and furniture and doings of millionaires.

"'Just fancy soaking in a golden bathtub, Miss Shirley,' she said wistfully.

"But she's really an old duck. She has produced from somewhere a comfortable old wing chair of faded brocade that just fits my kinks and says, 'This is *your* chair. We'll keep it for *you*.' And she won't let Dusty Miller sleep on it lest I get hairs on my school skirt and give the Pringles something to talk about.

"The whole three are very much interested in my circlet of pearls...and what it signifies. Aunt Kate showed me her engagement ring (she can't wear it because it has grown too small) set with turquoises. But poor Aunt Chatty owned to me with tears in her eyes that she had never had an engagement ring...her husband thought it 'an unnecessary expenditure.' She was in my room at the time, giving her face a bath in buttermilk. She does it every night to preserve her complexion, and has sworn me to secrecy because she doesn't want Aunt Kate to know it.

"'She would think it ridiculous vanity in a woman of my age. And I am sure Rebecca Dew thinks that no Christian woman should try to be beautiful. I used to slip down to the kitchen to do it after Kate had gone to sleep but I was always afraid of Rebecca Dew coming down. She has ears like a cat's even when she is asleep. If I could just slip in here every night and do it... oh, thank you, my dear.'

"I have found out a little about our neighbors at The Evergreens. Mrs. Campbell (who was a Pringle!) is eighty. I haven't seen her but from what I can gather she is a very grim old lady. She has a maid, Martha Monkman, almost as ancient and grim as herself, who is generally referred to as 'Mrs. Campbell's Woman.' And she has her great-granddaughter, little Elizabeth Grayson, living with her. Elizabeth...on whom I have never laid eyes in spite of my two weeks' sojourn...is eight years old and goes to the public school by 'the back way'...a short cut through the back yards...so I never encounter her, going or coming. Her mother, who is dead, was a granddaughter of Mrs. Campbell, who brought her up also...*her* parents being dead. She married a certain Pierce Grayson, a 'Yankee,' as Mrs. Rachel Lynde would say. She died when Elizabeth was born and as Pierce Grayson had to leave America at once to take charge of a branch of his firm's business in Paris, the baby was sent home to old Mrs. Campbell. The story goes that he 'couldn't bear the sight of her' because she had cost her mother's life, and has never taken any notice of her. This of course may be sheer gossip because neither Mrs. Campbell nor the Woman ever opens her lips about him.

"Rebecca Dew says they are far too strict with little Elizabeth and she hasn't much of a time of it with them.

"'She isn't like other children...far too old for eight years. The things that she says sometimes! "Rebecca," she sez to me one day, "suppose just as you were ready to get into bed you felt your ankle *nipped*?" No wonder she's afraid to go to bed in the dark. And they make her do it. Mrs. Campbell says there are to be no cowards in *her* house. They watch her like two cats watching a mouse, and boss her within an inch of her life. If she makes a speck of noise they nearly pass out. It's "hush, hush" all the time. I tell you that child is being hush-hushed to death. And what is to be done about it?'

"What, indeed?

"I feel that I'd like to see her. She seems to me a bit pathetic. Aunt Kate says she is well looked after from a physical point of view...what Aunt Kate really said was, 'They feed and dress her well'...but a child can't live by bread alone. I can never forget

The First Year

what my own life was before I came to Green Gables.

"'I'm going home next Friday evening to spend two beautiful days in Avonlea. The only drawback will be that everybody I see will ask me how I like teaching in Summerside.

"But think of Green Gables now, Gilbert...the Lake of Shining Waters with a blue mist on it...the maples across the brook beginning to turn scarlet...the ferns golden brown in the Haunted Wood...and the sunset shadows in Lover's Lane, darling spot. I find it in my heart to wish I were there now with...with...guess whom?

"Do you know, Gilbert, there are times when I strongly suspect that I love you!"

"Windy Poplars,
"Spook's Lane,
"S'side,
"October 10th.

"HONORED AND RESPECTED SIR:—
"That is how a love letter of Aunt Chatty's grandmother began. Isn't it delicious? What a thrill of superiority it must have given the grandfather! Wouldn't you really prefer it to 'Gilbert darling, etc.'? But, on the whole, I think I'm glad you're not the grandfather...or *a* grandfather. It's wonderful to think we're young and have our whole lives before us... *together*...isn't it?"

(Several pages omitted, Anne's pen being evidently neither sharp, stub nor rusty.)

"I'm sitting on the window seat in the tower looking out into the trees waving against an amber sky and beyond them to the harbor. Last night I had such a lovely walk with myself. I really had to go somewhere for it was just a trifle dismal at Windy Poplars. Aunt Chatty was crying in the sitting-room because her feelings had been hurt and Aunt Kate was crying in her bedroom because it was the anniversary of Captain Amasa's death and Rebecca Dew was crying in the kitchen for no reason that I could discover. I've never seen Rebecca Dew cry before. But when I tried tactfully to find out what was wrong she pettishly wanted to know if a body couldn't enjoy a cry when she felt like it. So I folded my tent and stole away, leaving her to her enjoyment.

"I went out and down the harbor road. There was such a nice frosty, Octobery smell in the air, blent with the delightful odor of newly plowed fields. I walked on and on until twilight had deepened into a moonlit autumn night. I was alone but not lonely. I held a series of imaginary conversations with imaginary comrades and thought out so many epigrams that I was agreeably surprised at myself. I couldn't help enjoying myself in spite of my Pringle worries.

"The spirit moves me to utter a few yowls regarding the Pringles. I hate to admit it but things are not going any too well in Summerside High. There is no doubt that a cabal has been organized against me.

"For one thing, home work is never done by any of the Pringles or half Pringles. And there is no use in appealing to the parents. They are suave, polite, evasive. I know all the pupils who are not Pringles like me but the Pringle virus of disobedience is undermining the morale of the whole room. One morning I found my desk turned inside out and upside down. Nobody knew who did it, of course. And no one could or would tell who left on it another day the box out of which popped an artificial snake when I opened it. But every Pringle in the school screamed with laughter over my face. I suppose I did look wildly startled.

The First Year

"Jen Pringle comes late for school half the time, always with some perfectly water-tight excuse, delivered politely, with an insolent tilt to her mouth. She passes notes in class under my very nose. I found a peeled onion in the pocket of my coat when I put it on today. I should love to lock that girl up on bread and water until she learned how to behave herself.

"The worst thing to date was the caricature of myself I found on the blackboard one morning...done in white chalk with *scarlet* hair. Everybody denied doing it, Jen among the rest, but I knew Jen was the only pupil in the room who could draw like that. It *was* done well. My nose...which, as you know, has always been my one pride and joy...was humpbacked and my mouth was the mouth of a vinegary spinster who had been teaching a school full of Pringles for thirty years. But it was *me*. I woke up at three o'clock that night and writhed over the recollection. Isn't it queer that the things we writhe over at night are seldom wicked things? Just humiliating ones.

"All sorts of things are being said. I am accused of 'marking down' Hattie Pringle's examination papers just because she is a Pringle. I am said to 'laugh when the children make mistakes.' (Well, I *did* laugh when Fred Pringle defined a centurion as 'a man who had lived a hundred years.' I couldn't help it.)

"James Pringle is saying, 'There is no dis*cip*line in the school...no dis*cip*line whatever.' And a report is being circulated that I am a 'foundling.'

"I am beginning to encounter the Pringle antagonism in other quarters. Socially as well as educationally, Summerside seems to be under the Pringle thumb. No wonder they are called the Royal Family. I wasn't invited to Alice Pringle's walking party last Friday. And when Mrs. Frank Pringle got up a tea in aid of a church project (Rebecca Dew informs me that the ladies are going to 'build' the new spire!), I was the only girl in the Presbyterian church who was not asked to take a table. I have heard that the minister's wife, who is a newcomer in Summerside, suggested asking me to sing in the choir and was informed that all the Pringles would drop out of it if she did. That would leave such a skeleton that the choir simply couldn't carry on.

"Of course I'm not the only one of the teachers who has trouble with pupils. When the other teachers send theirs up to me to be 'disciplined'...how I hate that word!... half of them are Pringles. But there is never any complaint made about *them*.

"Two evenings ago I kept Jen in after school to do some work she had deliberately left undone. Ten minutes later the carriage from Maplehurst drew up before the school house and Miss Ellen was at the door...a beautifully dressed, sweetly smiling old lady, with elegant black lace mitts and a fine hawk-like nose, looking as if she had just stepped out of an 1840 band-box. She was so sorry but could she have Jen? She was going to visit friends in Lowvale and had promised to take Jen. Jen went off triumphantly and I realized afresh the forces arrayed against me.

"In my pessimistic moods I think the Pringles are a compound of Sloanes and Pyes. But I know they're not. I feel that I could like them if they were not my enemies. They are, for the most part, a frank, jolly, loyal set. I could even like Miss Ellen. I've never seen Miss Sarah. Miss Sarah has not left Maplehurst for ten years.

"'Too delicate...or thinks she is,' says Rebecca Dew with a sniff. 'But there ain't anything the matter with her pride. All the Pringles are proud but those two old girls pass everything. You should hear them talk about their

The First Year

ancestors. Well, their old father, Captain Abraham Pringle, *was* a fine old fellow. His brother Myrom wasn't quite so fine, but you don't hear the Pringles talking much about *him*. But I'm desprit afraid you're going to have a hard time with them all. When they make up their mind about anything or anybody they've never been known to change it. But keep your chin up, Miss Shirley...keep your chin up.'

"I wish I could get Miss Ellen's recipe for pound cake,' sighed Aunt Chatty. 'She's promised it to me time and again but it never comes. It's an old English family recipe. They're *so* exclusive about their recipes.'

"In wild fantastic dreams I see myself compelling Miss Ellen to hand that recipe over to Aunt Chatty on bended knee and make Jen mind her p's and q's. The maddening thing is that I could easily make Jen do it myself if her whole clan weren't backing her up in her deviltry."

(Two pages omitted.)

"Your obedient servant,
"ANNE SHIRLEY.

"P.S. That was how Aunt Chatty's grandmother signed her love letters."

"October 15th.

"We heard today that there had been a burglary at the other end of the town last night. A house was entered and some money and a dozen silver spoons stolen. So Rebecca Dew has gone up to Mr. Hamilton's to see if she can borrow a dog. She will tie him on the back veranda and she advises me to lock up my engagement ring!

"By the way, I found out why Rebecca Dew cried. It seems there had been a domestic convulsion. Dusty Miller had 'misbehaved again' and Rebecca Dew told Aunt Kate she would really have to do something about That Cat. He was wearing her to a fiddle-string. It was the third time in a year and she knew he did it on purpose. And Aunt Kate said that if Rebecca Dew would always let the cat out when he meowed there would be no danger of his misbehaving.

"'Well, this *is* the last straw,' said Rebecca Dew.

"Consequently, tears!

"The Pringle situation grows a little more acute every week. Something very impertinent was written across one of my books yesterday and Homer Pringle turned handsprings all the way down the aisle when leaving school. Also, I got an anonymous letter recently full of nasty innuendoes. Somehow, I don't blame Jen for either the book or the letter. Imp as she is, there are things she wouldn't stoop to. Rebecca Dew is furious and I shudder to think what she would do to the Pringles if she had them in her power. Nero's wish isn't to be compared to it. I really don't blame her, for there are times when I feel myself that I could cheerfully hand any and all of the Pringles a poisoned philter of Borgia brewing.

"I don't think I've told you much about the other teachers. There are two, you know...the Vice-principal, Katherine Brooke of the Junior Room, and George MacKay of the Prep. Of George I have little to say. He is a shy, good-natured lad of twenty, with a slight, delicious Highland accent suggestive of low shielings and misty islands...his grandfather 'was Isle of Skye'...and does very well with the Preps. So far as I know him I like him. But I'm afraid I'm going to have a hard time liking Katherine Brooke.

"Katherine is a girl of, I think, about twenty-eight, though she looks thirty-five. I have been told she cherished hopes of promotion to the Principalship and I suppose she resents my getting it, especially when I am considerably her junior. She is a good teacher...a bit of a martinet...but she is not popular with any one. And doesn't worry over it! She doesn't seem to have any friends or relations and boards in a gloomy-looking house on grubby little Temple Street. She dresses very dowdily, never goes out socially and is said to be 'mean.' She is very sarcastic and her pupils dread her biting remarks. I am told that her way of raising her thick black eyebrows and drawling at them reduces them to a pulp. I wish I could work it on the Pringles. But I really shouldn't like to govern by fear as she does. I want my pupils to love me.

"In spite of the fact that she has apparently no trouble in making them toe the line she is constantly sending some of them up to me...especially Pringles. I know she does it purposely and I feel miserably certain that she exults in my difficulties and would be glad to see me worsted.

"Rebecca Dew says that no one can make friends with her. The widows have invited her several times to Sunday supper...the dear souls are always doing that for lonely people, and always have the most delicious chicken salad for them...but she never came. So they have given it up because, as Aunt Kate says, 'there are limits.'

"There are rumors that she is very clever and can sing and recite...'elocute,' *a la* Rebecca Dew...but will not do either. Aunt Chatty once asked her to recite at a church supper.

"'We thought she refused very ungraciously,' said Aunt Kate.

"'Just growled,' said Rebecca Dew.

"Katherine has a deep throaty voice...almost a man's voice...and it does sound like a growl when she isn't in good humor.

"She isn't pretty but she might make more of herself. She is dark and swarthy, with magnificent black hair always dragged back from her high forehead and coiled in a clumsy knot at the base of her neck. Her eyes don't match her hair, being a clear, light amber under her black brows. She has ears she needn't be ashamed to show and the most beautiful hands I've ever seen. Also, she has a well-cut mouth. But she dresses terribly. Seems to have a positive genius for getting the colors and lines she should not wear. Dull dark greens and drab grays, when she is too shallow for greens and grays, and stripes which make her tall, lean figure even taller and leaner. And her clothes always look as if she'd slept in them.

"Her manner is very repellent...as Rebecca Dew would say, she always has a chip on her shoulder. Every time I pass her on the stairs I feel that she is thinking horrid things about me. Every time I speak to her she makes me feel I've said the wrong thing. And yet I'm very sorry for her... though I know she would resent my pity furiously. And I can't do anything to help her because she doesn't want to be helped. She is really hateful to me. One day, when we three teachers were all in the staff room, I did something which, it seems, transgressed one of the unwritten laws of the school, and Katherine said cuttingly, 'Perhaps you think *you* are above rules, Miss Shirley.' At another time, when I was suggesting some changes which I thought would be for the good of the school, she said with a scornful smile, 'I'm not interested in fairy tales.' Once, when I said some nice things about her and methods, she said, 'And what is to be the pill in all this jam?'

"But the thing that annoyed me most...well, one day when I happened to pick up a book of hers in the staff room and glanced at the flyleaf I said,

"'I'm glad you spell your name with a K. Katherine is so much more alluring than Catherine, just as K is ever so much gypsier a letter than smug C.'

"She made no response, but the next note she sent up was signed 'Catherine Brooke'!

"I sneezed all the way home.

"I really would give up trying to be friends with her if I hadn't a queer, unaccountable feeling that under all her bruskness and aloofness she is actually starved for companionship.

"Altogether, what with Katherine's antagonism and the Pringle attitude, I don't know just what I'd do if it wasn't for dear Rebecca Dew and your letters...and little Elizabeth.

"Because I've got acquainted with little Elizabeth. And she is a darling.

"Three nights ago I took the glass of milk to the wall door and little Elizabeth herself was there to get it instead of the Woman, her head just coming above the solid part of the door, so that her face was framed in the ivy. She is small, pale, golden and wistful. Her eyes, looking at me through the autumn twilight, are large and golden-hazel. Her silver-gold hair was parted in the middle, sleeked plainly down over her head with a circular comb, and fell in waves on her shoulders. She wore a pale blue gingham dress and the expression of a princess of elf-land. She had what Rebecca Dew calls 'a delicate air,' and gave me the impression of a child who was more or less undernourished...not in body, but in soul. More of a moonbeam than a sunbeam.

"'And this is Elizabeth?' I said.

"'Not tonight,' she answered gravely. 'This is my night for being Betty because I love everything in the world tonight. I was Elizabeth last night and tomorrow night I'll prob'ly be Beth. It all depends on how I feel.'

"There was the touch of the kindred spirit for you. I thrilled to it at once.

"'How very nice to have a name you can change so easily and still feel it's your own.'

"Little Elizabeth nodded.

"'I can make so many names out of it. Elsie and Betty and Bess and Elisa and Lisbeth and Beth...but not Lizzie. I never can feel like Lizzie.'

"'Who could?' I said.

"'Do you think it silly of me, Miss Shirley? Grandmother and the Woman do.'

"'Not silly at all...very wise and very delightful,' I said.

"Little Elizabeth made saucer eyes at me over the rim of her glass. I felt that I was being weighed in some secret spiritual balance and presently I realized thankfully that I had not been found wanting. For little Elizabeth asked a favor of me...and little Elizabeth does not ask favors of people she does not like.

"'Would you mind lifting up the cat and letting me pat him?' she asked shyly.

"Dusty Miller was rubbing against my legs. I lifted him and little Elizabeth put out a tiny hand and stroked his head delightedly.

"'I like kittens better than babies,' she said, looking at me with an odd little air of defiance, as if she knew I would be shocked but tell the truth she must.

"'I suppose you've never had much to do with babies, so you don't know how sweet they are,' I said, smiling. 'Have you a kitten of your own?'

"Elizabeth shook her head.

"'Oh, no; Grandmother doesn't like cats. And the Woman hates them. The Woman is out tonight, so that is why I could come for the milk. I love coming for the milk because Rebecca Dew is such an agree'ble person.'

The First Year

"'Are you sorry she didn't come tonight?' I laughed.

"Little Elizabeth shook her head.

"'No. You are very agree'ble, too. I've been wanting to get 'quainted with you but I was afraid it mightn't happen before Tomorrow comes.'

"We stood there and talked while Elizabeth sipped her milk daintily and she told me all about Tomorrow. The Woman had told her that Tomorrow never comes, but Elizabeth knows better. It *will* come sometime. Some beautiful morning she will just wake up and find it is Tomorrow. Not Today but Tomorrow. And then things will happen... wonderful things. She may even have a day to do exactly as she likes in, with nobody watching her...though I think Elizabeth feels *that* is too good to happen even in Tomorrow. Or she may find out what is at the end of the harbor road... that wandering, twisting road like a nice red snake, that leads, so Elizabeth thinks, to the end of the world. Perhaps the Island of Happiness is there. Elizabeth feels sure there is an Island of Happiness somewhere where all the ships that never come back are anchored, and she will find it when Tomorrow comes.

"'And when Tomorrow comes,' said Elizabeth, 'I will have a million dogs and forty-five cats. I told Grandmother that when she wouldn't let me have a kitten, Miss Shirley, and she was angry and said, "I'm not 'customed to be spoken to like that, Miss Impert'nence." I was sent to bed without supper...but I didn't mean to be impert'nent. And I couldn't sleep, Miss Shirley, because the Woman told me that she knew a child once that died in her sleep after being impert'nent.'

"When Elizabeth had finished her milk there came a sharp tapping at some unseen window behind the spruces. I think we had been watched all the time. My elf-maiden ran, her golden head glimmering along the dark spruce aisle until she vanished.

"'She's a fanciful little creature,' said Rebecca Dew when I told her of my adventure...really, it somehow had the quality of an adventure, Gilbert. 'One day she said to me, "Are you scared of lions, Rebecca Dew?"

"I never met any so I can't tell you," sez I. "There will be any amount of lions in Tomorrow," sez she, "but they will be nice friendly lions."

"Child, you'll turn into eyes if you look like that," sez I. She was looking clean through me at something she saw in that Tomorrow of hers. "I'm thinking deep thoughts, Rebecca Dew," she sez. The trouble with that child is she doesn't laugh enough.'

"I remembered Elizabeth had never laughed once during our talk. I feel that she hasn't learned how. The great house is so still and lonely and laughterless. It looks dull and gloomy even now when the world is a riot of autumn color. Little Elizabeth is doing too much listening to lost whispers.

"I think one of my missions in Summerside will be to teach her how to laugh.

"Your tenderest, most faithful friend,
"ANNE SHIRLEY.

"P.S. More of Aunt Chatty's grandmother!"

3

"Windy Poplars,
"Spook's Lane,
"S'side,
"October 25th.

"GILBERT DEAR:—
"What do you think? I've been to supper at Maplehurst!

"Miss Ellen herself wrote the invitation. Rebecca Dew was really excited...she had never believed they would take any notice of me. And she was quite sure it was not out of friendliness.

"'They have some sinister motive, that I'm certain of!' she exclaimed.

"I really had some such feeling in my own mind.

"'Be sure you put on your best,' ordered Rebecca Dew.

"So I put on my pretty cream challis dress with the purple violets in it and did my hair the new way with the dip in the forehead. It's very becoming.

"The ladies of Maplehurst are positively delightful in their own way, Gilbert. I could love them if they'd let me. Maplehurst is a proud, exclusive house which draws its trees around it and won't associate with common houses. It has a big, white, wooden woman off the bow of old Captain Abraham's famous ship, the *Go and Ask Her,* in the orchard and billows of southernwood about the front steps, which was brought out from the old country over a hundred years ago by the first emigrating Pringle. They have another ancestor who fought at the battle of Minden and his sword is hanging on the parlor wall beside Captain

Abraham's portrait. Captain Abraham was their father and they are evidently tremendously proud of him.

"They have stately mirrors over the old, black, fluted mantels, a glass case with wax flowers in it, pictures full of the beauty of the ships of long ago, a hair-wreath containing the hair of every known Pringle, big conch shells and a quilt on the spare-room bed quilted in infinitesimal fans.

"We sat in the parlor on mahogany Sheraton chairs. It was hung with silver-stripe wallpaper. Heavy brocade curtains at the windows. Marble-topped tables, one bearing a beautiful model of a ship with crimson hull and snow-white sails—the *Go and Ask Her.* An enormous chandelier, all glass and dingle-dangles, suspended from the ceiling. A round mirror with a clock in the center...something Captain Abraham had brought home from 'foreign parts.' It was wonderful. I'd like something like it in our house of dreams.

"The very shadows were eloquent and traditional. Miss Ellen showed me millions...more or less...of Pringle photographs, many of them daguerreotypes in leather cases. A big tortoise-shell cat came in, jumped on my knee and was at once whisked out to the kitchen by Miss Ellen. She apologized to me. But I expect she had previously apologized to the cat in the kitchen.

"Miss Ellen did most of the talking. Miss Sarah, a tiny thing in a black silk dress and starched petticoat, with snow-white hair and eyes as black as her dress, thin, veined hands folded on her lap amid fine lace ruffles, sad, lovely, gentle, looked almost too fragile to talk. And yet I got the impression, Gilbert, that Pringle of the clan, including Miss Ellen herself, danced to her piping.

"We had a delicious supper. The water was cold, the linen beautiful, the dishes and glassware thin. We were waited on

The First Year

by a maid, quite as aloof and aristocratic as themselves. But Miss Sarah pretended to be a little deaf whenever I spoke to her and I thought every mouthful would choke me. All my courage oozed out of me. I felt just like a poor fly caught on fly-paper. Gilbert, I can never, never conquer or win the Royal Family. I can see myself resigning at New Year's. I haven't a chance against a clan like that.

"And yet I couldn't help feeling a little sorry for the old ladies as I looked around their house. It had once *lived*... people had been born there...died there...exulted there... known sleep, despair, fear, joy, love, hope, hate. And now it has nothing but the memories by which they live...and their pride in them.

"Aunt Chatty is much upset because when she unfolded clean sheets for my bed today she found a diamond-shaped crease in the center. She is sure it foretells a death in the household. Aunt Kate is very much disgusted with such superstition. But I believe I rather like superstitious people. They lend color to life. Wouldn't it be a rather drab world if everybody was wise and sensible...and *good*? What would we find to talk about?

"We had a *cat*astrophe here two nights ago. Dusty Miller stayed out all night, in spite of Rebecca Dew's stentorian shouts of 'Puss' in the back yard. And when he turned up in the morning...oh, such a looking cat! One eye was closed completely and there was a lump as big as an egg on his jaw. His fur was stiff with mud and one paw was bitten through. But what a triumphant, unrepentant look he had in his one good eye! The widows were horrified but Rebecca Dew said exultantly, 'That Cat has never had a good fight in his life before. And I'll bet the other cat looks far worse than he does!'

"A fog is creeping up the harbor tonight, blotting out the red road that little Elizabeth wants to explore.

Weeds and leaves are burning in all the town gardens and the combination of smoke and fog is making Spook's Lane an eerie, fascinating, enchanted place. It is growing late and my bed says, 'I have sleep for you.' I've grown used to climbing a flight of steps into bed...and climbing down them. Oh, Gilbert, I've never told any one this, but it's too funny to keep any longer. The first morning I woke up in Windy Poplars I forgot all about the steps and made a blithe morning-spring out of bed. I came down like a thousand of brick, as Rebecca Dew would say. Luckily I didn't break any bones, but I was black and blue for a week.

"Little Elizabeth and I are very good friends by now. She comes every evening for her milk because the Woman is laid up with what Rebecca Dew calls 'brownkites.' I always find her at the wall gate, waiting for me, her big eyes full of twilight. We talk with the gate, which has never been opened for years, between us. Elizabeth sips the glass of milk as slowly as possible in order to spin our conversation out. Always, when the last drop is drained, comes the tap-tap on the window.

"I have found that one of the things that is going to happen in Tomorrow is that she will get a letter from her father. She had never got one. I wonder what the man can be thinking of.

"'You know, he couldn't bear the sight of me, Miss Shirley,' she told me, 'but he mightn't mind writing to me.'

"'Who told you he couldn't bear the sight of you?' I asked indignantly.

"'The Woman.' (Always when Elizabeth says 'the Woman,' I can see her like a great big forbidding 'W,' all angles and corners.) 'And it must be true or he would come to see me sometimes.'

"She was Beth that night...it is only when she is Beth that she will talk of her father. When she is Betty she makes faces at her grandmother and the Woman behind their backs; but when she turns into Elsie she is sorry for it and thinks she ought to confess, but is scared to. Very rarely she is Elizabeth and then she has the face of one who listens to fairy music and knows what roses and clovers talk about. She's the quaintest thing, Gilbert...as sensitive as one of the leaves of the windy poplars, and I love her. It infuriates me to know that those two terrible old women make her go to bed in the dark.

"'The Woman said I was big enough to sleep without a light. But I feel so small, Miss Shirley, because the night is so big and awful. And there is a stuffed crow in my room and I am afraid of it. The Woman told me it would pick my eyes out if I cried. Of course, Miss Shirley, I don't believe that, but still I'm scared. Things *whisper* so to each other at night. But in Tomorrow I'll never be scared of anything...not even of being kidnaped!'

"'But there is no danger of your being kidnaped, Elizabeth.'

"'The Woman said there was if I went anywhere alone or talked to strange persons. But you're not a strange person, are you, Miss Shirley?'

"'No, darling. We've always known each other in Tomorrow,' I said."

4

"Windy Poplars,
"Spook's Lane,
"S'side,
"November 10th.

"DEAREST:

"It used to be that the person I hated most in the world was the person who spoiled my pen-nib. But I can't hate Rebecca Dew in spite of her habit of using my pen to copy recipes when I'm in school. She's been doing it again and as a result you won't get a long or a loving letter this time. (Belovedest.)

"The last cricket song has been sung. The evenings are so chilly now that I have a small chubby, oblong wood-stove in my room. Rebecca Dew put it up...I forgive her the pen for it. There's nothing that woman can't do; and she always has a fire lighted for me in it when I come home from school. It is the tiniest of stoves...I could pick it up in my hands. It looks just like a pert little black dog on its four bandy iron legs. But when you fill it with hardwood sticks it blooms rosy red and throws a wonderful heat and you can't think how cozy it is. I'm sitting before it now, with my feet on its tiny hearth, scribbling to you on my knee.

"Every one else in S'side...more or less...is at the Hardy Pringles' dance. *I* was not invited. And Rebecca Dew is so cross about it that I'd hate to be Dusty Miller. But when I think of Hardy's daughter Myra, beautiful and brainless, trying to prove in an examination paper that the *angels* at the base of an isosceles triangle are equal, I forgive the entire Pringle clan. And last week she included 'gallows tree' quite seriously in a list of trees! But, to be just, all the howlers don't originate with the Pringles. Blake Fenton defined an alligator recently as 'a large kind of insect.' Such are the high lights of a teacher's life!

"It feels like snow tonight. I like an evening when it feels like snow. The wind is blowing 'in turret and tree' and making my cozy room seem even cozier. The last golden leaf will be blown from the aspens tonight.

"I think I've been invited to supper everywhere by now....I mean to the homes of all my pupils, both in town and country. And oh, Gilbert darling, I am *so* sick of pumpkin preserves! Never, never let us have pumpkin preserves in our house of dreams.

"Almost everywhere I've gone for the last month I've had P. P. for supper. The first time I had it I loved it...it was so golden that I felt I was eating preserved sunshine...and I incautiously raved about it. It got bruited about that I was very fond of P. P. and people had it on purpose for me. Last night I was going to Mr. Hamilton's and Rebecca Dew assured me that I wouldn't have to eat P. P. there because none of the Hamiltons liked it. But when we sat down to supper, there on the sideboard was the inevitable cut-glass bowl full of P. P.

"'I hadn't any punkin preserves of my own,' said Mrs. Hamilton, ladling me out a generous dishful, 'but I heard you was terrible partial to it, so when I was to my cousin's in Lowvale last Sunday I sez to her, "I'm having Miss Shirley to supper this week and she's terrible partial to punkin preserves. I wish you'd lend me a jar for her." So she did and here it is and you can take home what's left.'

"You should have seen Rebecca Dew's face when I arrived home from the Hamiltons' bearing a glass jar two-thirds full of P. P.! Nobody likes it here so we buried it darkly at dead of night in the garden.

"'You won't put this in a story, will you?' she asked anxiously. Ever since Rebecca Dew discovered that I do an occasional bit of fiction for the magazines she has lived in the fear...or hope, I don't know which...that I'll put everything that happens at Windy Poplars into a story. She wants me to 'write up the Pringles and blister them.' But alas, it's the Pringles that are doing the blistering and between them and my work in school I have scant time for writing fiction.

"There are only withered leaves and frosted stems in the garden now. Rebecca Dew has done the standard roses up in straw and potato bags, and in the twilight they look exactly like a group of humped-back old men leaning on staffs.

"I got a post-card from Davy today with ten kisses crossed on it and a letter from Priscilla written on some paper that 'a friend of hers in Japan' sent her...silky thin paper with dim cherry blossoms on it like ghosts. I'm beginning to have my suspicions about that friend of hers. But your big fat letter was the purple gift the day gave me. I read it four times over to get every bit of its savor...like a dog polishing off a plate! *That* certainly isn't a romantic simile, but it's the one that just popped into my head. Still, letters, even the nicest, aren't *satisfactory*. I want to see *you*. I'm glad it's only five weeks to Christmas holidays."

5

Anne, sitting at her tower window one late November evening, with her pen at her lip and dreams in her eyes, looked out on a twilight world and suddenly thought she would like a walk to the old graveyard. She had never visited it yet, preferring the birch and maple grove or the harbor road for her evening rambles. But there is always a November space after the leaves have fallen when she felt it was almost indecent to intrude on the woods...for their glory terrestrial had departed and their glory celestial of spirit and purity and whiteness had not yet come upon them. So Anne betook herself to the graveyard instead. She was feeling for the time so dispirited and hopeless that she thought a graveyard would be a comparatively cheerful place. Besides, it was full of Pringles, so Rebecca Dew said. They had buried there for generations, keeping it up in preference to the new graveyard until "no more of them could be squeezed in." Anne felt that it would be positively encouraging to see how many Pringles were where they couldn't annoy anybody any more.

In regard to the Pringles Anne felt that she was at the end of her tether. More and more the whole situation was coming to seem like a nightmare. The subtle campaign of insubordination and disrespect which Jen Pringle had organized had at last come to a head. One day, a week previously, she had asked the Seniors to write a composition on "The Most Important Happenings of the Week." Jen Pringle had written a brilliant one...the little imp *was* clever...and had inserted in it a sly insult to her teacher...one so pointed that it was impossible to ignore it. Anne had sent her home, telling her that she would have to apologize before she would be allowed to come back. The fat was fairly in the fire.

It was open warfare now between her and the Pringles. And poor Anne had no doubt on whose banner victory would perch. The school board would back the Pringles up and she would be given her choice between letting Jen come back or being asked to resign.

She felt very bitter. She had done her best and she knew she could have succeeded if she had had even a fighting chance.

"It's not my fault," she thought miserably. "Who *could* succeed against such a phalanx and such tactics?"

But to go home to Green Gables defeated! To endure Mrs. Lynde's indignation and the Pyes' exultation! Even the sympathy of friends would be an anguish. And with her Summerside failure bruited abroad she would never be able to get another school.

But at least they had not got the better of her in the matter of the play. Anne laughed a little wickedly and her eyes filled with mischievous delight over the memory.

She had organized a High School Dramatic Club and directed it in a little play hurriedly gotten up to provide some funds for one of her pet schemes...buying some good engravings for the rooms. She had made herself ask Katherine Brooke to help her because Katherine always seemed so left out of everything. She could not help regretting it many times, for Katherine was even more brusk and sarcastic than usual. She seldom let a practice pass without some corrosive remark and she overworked her eyebrows. Worse still, it was Katherine who had insisted on having Jen Pringle take the part of Mary Queen of Scots.

"There's no one else in the school who can play it," she said impatiently. "No one who has the necessary personality."

Anne was not so sure of this. She rather thought that Sophy Sinclair, who was tall and had hazel eyes and rich chestnut hair, would make a far better Queen Mary than Jen. But Sophy was not even a member of the club and had never taken part in a play.

The First Year

"We don't want absolute greenhorns in this. I'm not going to be associated with anything that is not successful," Katherine had said disagreeably, and had yielded. She could not deny that Jen was very good in the part. She had a natural flair for acting and she apparently threw herself into it wholeheartedly. They practiced four evenings a week and on the surface things went along very smoothly. Jen seemed to be so interested in her part that she behaved herself as far as the play was concerned. Anne did not meddle with her but left her to Katherine's coaching. Once or twice, though, she surprised a certain look of sly triumph on Jen's face that puzzled her. She could not guess just what it meant.

One afternoon, soon after the practices had begun, Anne found Sophy Sinclair in tears in a corner of the girls' coatroom. At first she had blinked her hazel eyes vigorously and denied it... then broke down.

"I did so want to be in the play...to be Queen Mary," she sobbed. "I've never had a chance...father wouldn't let me join the club because there are dues to pay and every cent counts so much. And of course I haven't had any experience. I've always loved Queen Mary...her very name just thrills me to my finger tips. I don't believe...I never will believe she had anything to do with murdering Damley. It would have been wonderful to fancy I was she for a little while!"

Afterwards Anne concluded that it was her guardian angel who prompted her reply.

"I'll write the part out for you, Sophy, and coach you in it. It will be good training for you. And, as we plan to give the play in other places if it goes well here, it will be just as well to have an understudy in case Jen shouldn't always be able to go. But we'll say nothing about it to any one."

Sophy had the part memorized by the next day. She went home to Windy Poplars with Anne every afternoon when school came out and rehearsed it in the tower. They had a lot of fun together, for Sophy was full of quiet vivacity. The play was to be put on the last Friday in November in the town hall; it was widely advertised and the reserved seats were sold to the last one. Anne and Katherine spent two evenings decorating the hall, the band was hired, and a noted soprano was coming up from Charlottetown to sing between the acts. The dress rehearsal was a success. Jen was really excellent and the whole cast played up to her. Friday morning Jen was not in school; and in the afternoon her mother sent word that Jen was ill with a very sore throat...they were afraid it was tonsillitis. Everybody concerned was very sorry, but it was out of the question that she should take part in the play that night.

Katherine and Anne stared at each other, drawn together for once in their common dismay.

"We'll have to put it off," said Katherine slowly. "And that means failure. Once we're into December there's so much going on. Well, I always thought it was foolish to try to get up a play this time of the year."

"We are not going to postpone it," said Anne, her eyes as green as Jen's own. She was not going to say it to Katherine Brooke, but she knew as well as she had ever known anything in her life that Jen Pringle was in no more danger of tonsillitis than she was. It was a deliberate device, whether any of the other Pringles were a party to it or not, to ruin the play because she, Anne Shirley, had sponsored it.

"Oh, if you feel that way about it!" said Katherine with a nasty shrug. "But what do you intend to do? Get some one to read the part? That would ruin it...Mary is the whole play."

"Sophy Sinclair can play the part as well as Jen. The costume will fit her and, thanks be, you made it and have it, not Jen."

The play was put on that night before a packed audience. A delighted Sophy played Mary...*was* Mary, as Jen Pringle could never have been...*looked* Mary in her velvet robes and ruff and jewels. Students of Summerside High, who had never seen Sophy in anything but her plain, dowdy, dark serge dresses, shapeless coat and shabby hats, stared at her in amazement. It was insisted on the spot that she become a permanent member of the Dramatic Club—Anne herself paid the membership fee—and from then on she was one of the pupils who "counted" in Summerside High. But nobody knew or dreamed, Sophy herself least of all, that she had taken the first step that night on a pathway that was to lead to the stars. Twenty years later Sophy Sinclair was to be one of the leading actresses in America. But probably no plaudits ever sounded so sweet in her ears as the wild applause amid which the curtain fell that night in Summerside town hall.

Mrs. James Pringle took a tale home to her daughter Jen which would have turned that damsel's eyes green if they had not been already so. For once, as Rebecca Dew said feelingly, Jen had got her come-uppance. And the eventual result was the insult in the composition on Important Happenings.

Anne went down to the old graveyard along a deep-rutted lane between high, mossy stone dykes, tasseled with frosted ferns. Slim, pointed lombardies, from which November winds had not yet stripped all the leaves, grew along it at intervals, coming out darkly against the amethyst of the far hills; but the old graveyard, with half its tombstones leaning at a drunken slant, was surrounded by a four-square row of tall, somber fir trees. Anne had not expected to find any one there and was a little taken aback when she met Miss Valentine Courtaloe, with her long delicate nose, her thin delicate mouth, her sloping delicate shoulders and her general air of invincible lady-likeness, just inside the gate. She knew Miss Valentine, of course, as did everyone in Summerside. She was "the" local dressmaker and what she didn't know about people, living or dead, was not worth taking into account. Anne had wanted to wander about by herself, read the odd old epitaphs and puzzle out the names of forgotten lovers under the lichens that were growing over them. But she could not escape when Miss Valentine slipped an arm through hers and proceeded to do the honors of the graveyard, where there were evidently as many Courtaloes buried as Pringles. Miss Valentine had not a drop of Pringle blood in her and one of Anne's favorite pupils was her nephew. So it was no great mental strain to be nice to her, except that one must be very careful never to hint that she "sewed for a living." Miss Valentine was said to be very sensitive on that point.

"I'm glad I happened to be here this evening," said Miss Valentine. "I can tell you all about everybody buried here. I always say you have to know the ins and outs of the corpses to find a graveyard real enjoyable. I like a walk here better than in the new. It's only the *old* families that are buried here but every Tom, Dick and Harry is being buried in the new. The Courtaloes are buried in this corner. My, we've had a terrible lot of funerals in our family."

"I suppose every old family has," said Anne, because Miss Valentine evidently expected her to say something.

"Don't tell me *any* family has ever had as many as ours," said Miss Valentine jealously. "We're *very* consumptive. Most of us died of a cough. This is my Aunt Bessie's grave. She was a saint if ever there was one. But there's no doubt her sister, Aunt Cecilia, was the more interesting to talk to. The last time I ever saw her she said to me, 'Sit down, my dear, sit down. I'm going to die tonight at ten minutes past eleven but that's no reason why we shouldn't have a real good gossip for the last.' The strange thing, Miss Shirley, is that she did die that night at ten minutes past eleven. Can you tell me how she knew it?"

Anne couldn't.

"My Great-great-grandfather Courtaloe is buried *here*. He came out in 1760 and he made spinning-wheels for a living. I've heard he made fourteen hundred in the course of his life. When he died the minister preached from the text, 'Their works do follow them,' and old Myrom Pringle said in that case the road to heaven behind my great-great-grandfather would be choked with spinning-wheels. Do you think such a remark was in good taste, Miss Shirley?"

Had any one but a Pringle said it, Anne might not have remarked so decidedly, "I certainly do not," looking at a gravestone adorned with a skull and cross-bones as if she questioned the good taste of that also.

"My cousin Dora is buried *here*. She had three husbands but they all died very rapidly. Poor Dora didn't seem to have any luck picking a healthy man. Her last one was Benjamin Banning...*not* buried here...buried in Lowvale beside *his* first wife...and he wasn't reconciled to dying. Dora told him he was going to a better world. 'Mebbe, mebbe,' says poor Ben, 'but I'm sorter used to the imperfections of this one.' He took sixty-one different kinds of medicine but in spite of that he lingered for a good while. All Uncle David Courtaloe's family are *here*. There's a cabbage rose planted at the foot of every grave and, my, don't they bloom! I come here every summer and gather them for my rose-jar. It would be a pity to let them go to waste, don't you think?"

"I...I suppose so."

"My poor young sister Harriet lies *here,*" sighed Miss Valentine. "She had magnificent hair...about the color of yours...not so red perhaps. It reached to her knees. She was engaged when she died. They tell me you're engaged. I never much wanted to be married but I think it would have been nice to be engaged. Oh, I've had some chances of course...perhaps I was too fastidious...but a Courtaloe couldn't marry *everybody*, could she?"

It did not seem likely she could.

"Frank Digby...over in that corner under the sumacs...wanted me. I *did* feel a little regretful over refusing him...but a Digby, my dear! He married Georgina Troop. She always went to church a little late to show off her clothes. My, she was fond of clothes. She was buried in such a pretty blue dress...I made it for her to wear to a wedding but in the end she wore it to her own funeral. She had three darling little children. They used to sit in front of me at church and I always gave them candy. Do you think it wrong to give children candy in church, Miss Shirley? Not peppermints...that would be all right...there's something *religious* about peppermints, don't you think? But the poor things don't like them."

When the Courtaloe's plots were exhausted Miss Valentine's reminiscences became a bit spicier. It did not make so much difference if you weren't a Courtaloe.

"Old Mrs. Russell Pringle is here. I often wonder if she's in heaven or not."

"But why?" gasped a rather shocked Anne.

"Well, she always hated her sister, Mary Ann, who had died a few months before. 'If Mary Ann is in heaven I won't stay there,' says she. And she was a woman who always kept her word, my dear...Pringle-like. She was born a Pringle and married her cousin Russell. This is Mrs. Dan Pringle...Janetta Bird. Seventy to a day when she died. Folks say she would have thought it wrong to die a day older than three-score and ten because that is the Bible limit. People do say such funny things, don't they? I've heard that dying was the only thing she ever dared do without asking her husband. Do you know, my dear, what he did once when she bought a hat he didn't like?"

"I can't imagine."

"He *et* it," said Miss Valentine solemnly. "Of course it was only a small hat...lace and flowers...no feathers. Still, it must have been rather indigestible. I understand he had gnawing pains in his stomach for quite a time. Of course I didn't *see* him eat it, but I've always been assured the story was true. Do you suppose it was?"

"I'd believe anything of a Pringle," said Anne bitterly.

Miss Valentine pressed her arm sympathetically.

"I feel for you...indeed I do. It's terrible the way they're treating you. But Summerside isn't *all* Pringle, Miss Shirley."

"Sometimes I think it is," said Anne with a rueful smile.

"No, it isn't. And there are plenty of people would like to see you get the better of them. Don't you give in to them no matter what they do. It's just the old Satan that's got into them. But they hang together so and Miss Sarah did want that cousin of theirs to get the school.

"The Nathan Pringles are *here*. Nathan always believed his wife was trying to poison him but he didn't seem to mind. He said it made life kind of exciting. Once he kind of suspected she'd put arsenic in his porridge. He went out and fed it to a pig. The pig died three weeks afterwards. But he said maybe it was only a coincidence and anyway he couldn't be sure it was the same pig. In the end she died before him and he said she'd always been a real good wife to him except for that one thing. I think it would be charitable to believe that he was mistaken about *it*. "

"'Sacred to the memory of *Miss Kinsey*,'" read Anne in amazement. "What an extraordinary inscription! Had she no other name?"

"If she had, nobody ever knew it," said Miss Valentine. "She came from Nova Scotia and worked for the George Pringles for forty years. She gave her name as Miss Kinsey and everybody called her that. She died suddenly and then it was discovered that nobody knew her first name and she had no relations that anybody could find. So they put that on her stone...the George Pringles buried her very nicely and paid for the monument. She was a faithful, hard-working creature but if you'd ever seen her you'd have thought she was *born* Miss Kinsey. The James Morleys are *here*. I was at their golden wedding. Such a to-do... gifts and speeches and flowers...and their children all home... and them smiling and bowing and just hating each other as hard as they could."

"Hating each other?"

"Bitterly, my dear. Every one knew it. They had for years and years...almost all their married life in fact. They quarreled on the way home from church after the wedding. I often wonder how they manage to lie here so peaceably side by side."

Again Anne shivered. How terrible...sitting opposite each other at table...lying down beside each other at night...going to church with their babies to be christened...and hating each other through it all! Yet they must have loved to begin with. Was it possible she and Gilbert could ever...nonsense! The Pringles were getting on her nerves.

"Handsome John MacTabb is buried here. He was always suspected of being the reason why Annetta Kennedy drowned herself. The MacTabbs were all handsome but you could never believe a word they said. There used to be a stone here for his Uncle Samuel, who was reported drowned at sea fifty years ago. When he turned up alive the family took the stone down. The man they bought it from wouldn't take it back so Mrs. Samuel used it for a baking-board. Talk about a marble slab for mixing on! That old tombstone was just fine, she said. The MacTabb children were always bringing cookies to school with raised letters and figures on them...scraps of the epitaph. They gave them away real generous, but I never could bring myself to eat one. I'm peculiar that way. Mr. Harley Pringle is *here*. He had to wheel Peter MacTabb down Main Street once, in a wheelbarrow, wearing a bonnet, for an election bet. All Summerside turned out to see it...except the Pringles, of course. *They* nearly died of shame. Milly Pringle is *here*. I was very fond of Milly, even if she was a Pringle. She was so pretty and as light-footed as a fairy. Sometimes I think, my dear, on nights like this she must slip out of her grave and dance like she used to do. But I suppose a Christian shouldn't be harboring such thoughts. This is Herb Pringle's grave. He was one of the jolly Pringles. He always made you laugh. He laughed right out in church once...when the mouse dropped out of the flowers on Meta Pringle's hat when she bowed in prayer. *I* didn't feel much like laughing. I didn't know where the mouse had gone. I pulled my skirts tight about my ankles and held them there till church was out, but it spoiled the sermon for me. Herb sat behind me and such a shout as he gave. People who couldn't see the mouse thought he'd gone crazy. It seemed to me that laugh of his *couldn't* die. If *he* was alive he'd stand up for you, Sarah or no Sarah. *This,* of course, is Captain Abraham Pringle's monument."

It dominated the whole graveyard. Four receding platforms of stone formed a square pedestal on which rose a huge pillar of marble topped with a ridiculous draped urn beneath which a fat cherub was blowing a horn.

"How ugly!" said Anne candidly.

"Oh, do you think so?" Miss Valentine seemed rather shocked. "It was thought very handsome when it was erected. That is supposed to be Gabriel blowing his trumpet. I think it gives quite a touch of elegance to the graveyard. It cost nine hundred dollars. Captain Abraham was a very fine old man. It is a great pity he is dead. If he was living they wouldn't be persecuting you the way they are. I don't wonder Sarah and Ellen are proud of him, though I think they carry it a bit too far."

At the graveyard gate Anne turned and looked back. A strange, peaceful hush lay over the windless land. Long fingers of moonlight were beginning to pierce the darkling firs, touching a gravestone here and there, and making strange shadows among them. But the graveyard wasn't a sad place after all. Really, the people in it seemed alive after Miss Valentine's tales.

"I've heard you write," said Miss Valentine anxiously, as they went down the lane. "You won't put the things I've told you in your stories, will you?"

"You may be sure I won't," promised Anne.

"Do you think it is really wrong...or dangerous...to speak ill of the dead?" whispered Miss Valentine a bit anxiously.

"I don't suppose it's exactly either," said Anne. "Only...rather unfair...like hitting those who can't defend themselves. But you didn't say anything very dreadful of anybody, Miss Courtaloe."

"I told you Nathan Pringle thought his wife was trying to poison him..."

"But you give her the benefit of the doubt..." and Miss Valentine went her way reassured.

6

"I wended my way to the graveyard this evening," wrote Anne to Gilbert after she got home. "I think 'wend your way' is a lovely phrase and I work it in whenever I can. It sounds funny to say I enjoyed my stroll in the graveyard but I really did. Miss Courtaloe's stories were so funny. Comedy and tragedy are so mixed up in life, Gilbert. The only thing that haunts me is that tale of the two who lived together fifty years and hated each other all that time. I can't believe they really did. Somebody has said that 'hate is only love that has missed its way.' I feel sure that under the hatred they really loved each other...just as I really loved you all those years I thought I hated you...and I think death would show it to them. I'm glad *I* found out in life. And I have found out there *are* some decent Pringles...dead ones.

"Last night when I went down late for a drink of water I found Aunt Kate buttermilking her face in the pantry. She asked me not to tell Chatty...she would think it so silly. I promised I wouldn't.

"Elizabeth still comes for the milk, though the Woman is pretty well over her bronchitis. I wonder they let her, especially since old Mrs. Campbell is a Pringle. Last Saturday night Elizabeth...she was Betty that night I think...ran in singing when she left me and I distinctly heard the Woman say to her at the porch door, 'It's too near the Sabbath for you to be singing *that* song.' I am sure that Woman would prevent Elizabeth from singing on any day if she could!

"Elizabeth had on a new dress that night, a dark wine color... they *do* dress her nicely...and she said wistfully, 'I thought I looked a little bit pretty when I put it on tonight, Miss Shirley, and I wished father could see me. Of course he will see me in Tomorrow...but it sometimes seems so slow in coming. I wish we could hurry time a bit, Miss Shirley.'

"Now, dearest, I must work out some geometrical exercises. Geometry exercises have taken the place of what Rebecca calls my 'literary efforts.' The specter that haunts my daily path now is the dread of an exercise popping up in class that I can't do. And what would the Pringles say then, oh, then...oh, what would the Pringles say then!

"Meanwhile, as you love me and the cat tribe, pray for a poor broken-hearted, ill-used Thomas cat. A mouse ran over Rebecca Dew's foot in the pantry the other day and she has fumed ever since. 'That Cat does nothing but eat and sleep and let mice overrun everything. This *is* the last straw.' So she chivies him from pillar to post, routs him off his favorite cushion and...I know, for I caught her at it...assists him none too gently with her foot when she lets him out."

7

One Friday evening, at the end of a mild, sunny December day Anne went out to Lowvale to attend a turkey supper. Wilfred Bryce's home was in Lowvale, where he lived with an uncle, and he had asked her shyly if she would go out with him after school, go to the turkey supper in the church and spend Saturday at his home. Anne agreed, hoping that she might be able to influence the uncle to let Wilfred keep on going to High School. Wilfred was afraid that he would not be able to go back after New Year. He was a clever, ambitious boy and Anne felt a special interest in him.

It could not be said that she enjoyed her visit overmuch, except in the pleasure it gave Wilfred. His uncle and aunt were a rather odd and uncouth pair. Saturday morning was windy and dark, with showers of snow, and at first Anne wondered how she was going to put in the day. She felt tired and sleepy after the late hours of the turkey supper; Wilfred had to help thrash; and there was not even a book in sight. Then she thought of the battered old seaman's chest she had seen in the back of the hall upstairs and recalled Mrs. Stanton's request. Mrs. Stanton was writing a history of Prince County and had asked Anne if she knew of, or could find, any old diaries or documents that might be helpful.

"The Pringles, of course, have lots that I could use," she told Anne. "But I can't ask *them*. You know the Pringles and Stantons have never been friends."

"*I* can't ask them either, unfortunately," said Anne.

"Oh, I'm not expecting you to. All I want is for you to keep your eyes open when you are visiting round in other people's homes and if you find or hear of any old diaries or maps or anything like that, try to get the loan of them for me. You've no idea what interesting things I've found in old diaries...little bits of real life that make the old pioneers live again. I want to get things like that for my book as well as statistics and genealogical tables."

Anne asked Mrs. Bryce if they had any such old records. Mrs. Bryce shook her head.

"Not as I knows on. In course..." brightening up..."there's old Uncle Andy's chist up there. There might be something in it. He used to sail with old Captain Abraham Pringle. I'll go out and ask Duncan if ye kin root in it."

Duncan sent word back that she could "root" in it all she liked and if she found any "dockyments" she could have them. He'd been meaning to bum the hull contents anyway and take the chest for a tool-box. Anne accordingly rooted, but all she found was an old yellowed diary or "log" which Andy Bryce seemed to have kept all through his years at sea. Anne beguiled the stormy forenoon away by reading it with interest and amusement. Andy was learned in sea lore and had gone on many voyages with Captain Abraham Pringle, whom he evidently admired immensely. The diary was full of ill-spelled, ungrammatical tributes to the Captain's courage and resourcefulness, especially in one wild enterprise of beating round the Horn. But his admiration had not, it seemed, extended to Abraham's brother Myrom, who was also a captain but of a different ship.

"Up to Myrom Pringle's tonight. His wife made him mad and he up and threw a glass of water in her face."

"Myrom is home. His ship was burned and they took to the boats. Nearly starved. In the end they et up Jonas Selkirk, who had shot himself. They lived on him till the *Mary G.* picked them up. Myrom told me this himself. Seemed to think it a good joke."

Anne shivered over this last entry, which seemed all the more horrifying for Andy's unimpassioned statement of the grim facts. Then she fell into a reverie. There was nothing in the book that could be of any use to Mrs. Stanton, but wouldn't Miss Sarah and Miss Ellen be interested in it since it contained so much about their adored old father? Suppose she sent it to them? Duncan Bryce had said she could do as she liked with it.

No, she wouldn't. Why should she try to please them or cater to their absurd pride, which was great enough now without any more food? They had set themselves to drive her out of the school and they were succeeding. They and their clan had beaten her.

Wilfred took her back to Windy Poplars that evening, both of them feeling happy. Anne had talked Duncan Bryce into letting Wilfred finish out his year in High School.

"Then I'll manage Queen's for a year and after that teach and educate myself," said Wilfred. "How can I ever repay you, Miss Shirley? Uncle wouldn't have listened to any one else, but he likes you. He said to me out in the barn, 'Red-haired women could always do what they liked with me.' But I don't think it was your hair, Miss Shirley, although it is so beautiful. It was just...*you.*"

At two o'clock that night Anne woke up and decided that she would send Andy Bryce's diary to Maplehurst. After all, she had a bit of liking for the old ladies. And they had so little to make life warm...only their pride in their father. At three she woke again and decided she wouldn't. Miss Sarah pretending to be deaf, indeed! At four she was in the swithers again. Finally she determined she would send it to them. She wouldn't be petty. Anne had a horror of being petty...like the Pyes.

Having settled this, Anne went to sleep for keeps, thinking how lovely it was to wake up in the night and hear the first snowstorm of the winter around your tower and then snuggle down in your blankets and drift into dreamland again.

Monday morning she wrapped up the old diary carefully and sent it to Miss Sarah with a little note.

"DEAR MISS PRINGLE:

"I wonder if you would be interested in this old diary. Mr. Bryce gaved it to me for Mrs. Stanton, who is writing a history of the county, but I don't think it would be of any use to her and I thought you might like to have it.

"Yours sincerely,

"ANNE SHIRLEY."

"That's a horribly stiff note," thought Anne, "but I can't write naturally to them. And I wouldn't be a bit surprised if they sent it haughtily back to me."

In the fine blue of the early winter evening Rebecca Dew got the shock of her life. The Maplehurst carriage drove along Spook's Lane, over the powdery snow, and stopped at the front gate. Miss Ellen got out of it and then...to every one's amazement... Miss Sarah, who had not left Maplehurst for ten years.

"They're coming to the front door," gasped Rebecca Dew, panic-stricken.

"Where else would a Pringle come to?" asked Aunt Kate.

"Of course...of course...but it sticks," said Rebecca tragically. "It *does* stick...you know it does. And it hasn't been opened since we house-cleaned last spring. This *is* the last straw."

The front door did stick...but Rebecca Dew wrenched it open with desperate violence and showed the Maplehurst ladies into the parlor.

"Thank heaven, we've had a fire in it today," she thought, "and all I hope is That Cat hasn't haired up the sofa. If Sarah Pringle got cat hairs on her dress in our parlor..."

Rebecca Dew dared not imagine the consequences. She called Anne from the tower room, Miss Sarah having asked if Miss Shirley were in, and then betook herself to the kitchen, half mad with curiosity as to what on earth was bringing the old Pringle girls to see Miss Shirley.

"If there's any more persecution in the wind..." said Rebecca Dew darkly.

Anne herself descended with considerable trepidation. Had they come to return the diary with icy scorn?

It was little, wrinkled, inflexible Miss Sarah who rose and spoke without preamble when Anne entered the room.

"We have come to capitulate," she said bitterly. "We can do nothing else...of course you knew that when you found that scandalous entry about poor Uncle Myrom. It wasn't true...it *couldn't* be true. Uncle Myrom was just taking a rise out of Andy Bryce...Andy was *so* credulous. But everybody outside of our family will be glad to believe it. You knew it would make us all a laughing stock...and worse. Oh, you are very clever. We admit *that*. Jen will apologize and behave herself in future...I, Sarah Pringle, assure you of that. If you will only promise not to tell Mrs. Stanton...not to tell any one...we will do anything ...*anything*."

Miss Sarah wrung her fine lace handkerchief in her little blue-veined hands. She was literally trembling.

Anne stared in amazement...and horror. The poor old darlings! They thought she had been threatening them!

"Oh, you've misunderstood me dreadfully," she exclaimed, taking Miss Sarah's poor, piteous hands. "I...I never dreamed you would think I was trying to...oh, it was just because I thought you would like to have all those interesting details about your splendid father. I never dreamed of showing or telling that other little item to any one. I didn't think it was of the least importance. And I never will."

There was a moment's silence. Then Miss Sarah freed her hands gently, put her handkerchief to her eyes and sat down, with a faint blush on her fine wrinkled face.

"We...we *have* misunderstood you, my dear. And we've... we've been abominable to you. Will you forgive us?"

The First Year

Half an hour later…a half hour which nearly was the death of Rebecca Dew…the Misses Pringle went away. It had been a half hour of friendly chat and discussion about the non-combustible items of Andy's diary. At the front door Miss Sarah…who had not had the least trouble with her hearing during the interview…turned back for a moment and took a bit of paper, covered with very fine, sharp writing, from her reticule.

"I had almost forgotten…we promised Mrs. MacLean our recipe for pound cake some time ago. Perhaps you won't mind handing it to her? And tell her the sweating process is very important…quite indispensable, indeed. Ellen, your bonnet is slightly over one ear. You had better adjust it before we leave. We…we were somewhat agitated while dressing."

Anne told the widows and Rebecca Dew that she had given Andy Bryce's old diary to the ladies of Maplehurst and that they had come to thank her for it. With this explanation they had to be contented, although Rebecca Dew always felt that there was more behind it than that…much more. Gratitude for an old faded, tobacco-stained diary would never have brought Sarah Pringle to the front door of Windy Poplars. Miss Shirley was deep…very deep!

"I'm going to open that front door once a day after this," vowed Rebecca. "Just to keep it in practice. I all but went over flat when it *did* give way. Well, we've got the recipe for the pound cake anyway. Thirty-six eggs! If you'd dispose of That Cat and let me keep hens we might be able to afford it once a year."

Whereupon Rebecca Dew marched to the kitchen and got square with fate by giving That Cat milk when she knew he wanted liver.

The Shirley-Pringle feud was over. Nobody outside of the Pringles ever knew why, but Summerside people understood that Miss Shirley, single-handed, had, in some mysterious way, routed the whole clan, who ate out of her hand from then on.

Jen came back to school the next day and apologized meekly to Anne before the whole room. She was a model pupil thereafter and every Pringle student followed her lead. As for the adult Pringles, their antagonism vanished like mist before the sun. There were no more complaints regarding "discipline" or home work. No more of the fine, subtle snubs characteristic of the ilk. They fairly fell over one another trying to be nice to Anne. No dance or skating party was complete without her. For, although the fatal diary had been committed to the flames by Miss Sarah herself, memory was memory and Miss Shirley had a tale to tell if she chose to tell it. It would never do to have that nosey Mrs. Stanton know that Captain Myrom Pringle had been a cannibal!

8

(Extract from letter to Gilbert)

"I am in my tower and Rebecca Dew is caroling *Could I but climb?* in the kitchen. Which reminds me that the minister's wife has asked me to sing in the choir! Of course the Pringles have told her to do it. I may do it on the Sundays I don't spend at Green Gables. The Pringles have held out the right hand of fellowship with a vengeance... accepted me lock, stock and barrel. What a clan!

"I've been to three Pringle parties. I set nothing down in malice but I think all the Pringle girls are imitating my style of hair-dressing. Well, 'imitation is the sincerest flattery.' And, Gilbert, I'm really liking them...as I always knew I would if they would give me a chance. I'm even beginning to suspect that sooner or later I'll find myself liking Jen. She can be charming when she wants to be and it is very evident she wants to be.

"Last night I bearded the lion in his den...in other words, I went boldly up the front steps of The Evergreens to the square porch with the four whitewashed iron urns in its corners, and rang the bell. When Miss Monkman came to the door I asked her if she would lend little Elizabeth to me for a walk. I expected a refusal, but after the Woman had gone in and conferred with Mrs. Campbell, she came back and said dourly that Elizabeth could go but, please, I wasn't to keep her out late. I wonder if even Mrs. Campbell has got her orders from Miss Sarah.

"Elizabeth came dancing down the dark stairway, looking like a pixy in a red coat and little green cap, and almost speechless for joy.

"'I feel all squirmy and excited, Miss Shirley,' she whispered as soon as we got away. 'I'm Betty...I'm always Betty when I feel like that.'

"We went as far down the Road that Leads to the End of the World as we dared and then back. Tonight the harbor, lying dark under a crimson sunset, seemed full of implications of 'fairylands forlorn' and mysterious isles in uncharted seas. I thrilled to it and so did the mite I held by the hand.

"'If we ran hard, Miss Shirley, could we get into the sunset?' she wanted to know. I remembered Paul and his fancies about the 'sunset land.'

"'We must wait for Tomorrow before we can do that,' I said. 'Look, Elizabeth, at that golden island of cloud just over the harbor mouth. Let's pretend that's your island of Happiness.'

"'There is an island down there somewhere,' said Elizabeth dreamily. 'Its name is Flying Cloud. Isn't that a lovely name...a name just out of Tomorrow? I can see it from the garret windows. It belongs to a gentleman from Boston and he has a summer home there. But I pretend it's mine.'

"At the door I stooped and kissed Elizabeth's cheek before she went in. I shall never forget her eyes. Gilbert, that child is just starved for love.

"Tonight, when she came over for her milk, I saw that she had been crying.

"'They...they made me wash your kiss off, Miss Shirley,' she sobbed. 'I didn't want ever to wash my face again. I *vowed* I wouldn't. Because, you see, I didn't want to wash your kiss off. I got away to school this morning without doing it, but tonight the Woman just took me and *scrubbed* it off.'

"I kept a straight face.

"'You couldn't go through life without washing your face occasionally, darling. But never mind about the kiss. I'll kiss you every night when you come for the milk and then it won't matter if it is washed off the next morning.'

"'You are the only person who loves me in the world,' said Elizabeth. 'When you talk to me I smell violets.'

"Was anybody ever paid a prettier compliment? But I couldn't quite let the first sentence pass.

"'Your grandmother loves you, Elizabeth.'

"'She doesn't...she hates me.'

"'You're just a wee bit foolish, darling. Your grandmother and Miss Monkman are both old people and old people are easily disturbed and worried. Of course you annoy them sometimes. And...of course...when *they* were young, children were brought up much more strictly than they are now. They cling to the old way.'

"But I felt I was not convincing Elizabeth. After all, they *don't* love her and she knows it. She looked carefully back at the house to see if the door was shut. Then she said deliberately:

"'Grandmother and the Woman are just two old tyrants and when Tomorrow comes I'm going to escape them forever.'

"I think she expected I'd die of horror....I really suspect Elizabeth said it just to make a sensation. I merely laughed and kissed her. I hope Martha Monkman saw it from the kitchen window.

"I can see over Summerside from the left window in the tower. Just now it is a huddle of friendly white roofs... friendly at last since the Pringles are my friends. Here and there a light is gleaming in gable and dormer. Here and there is a suggestion of gray-ghost smoke. Thick stars are low over it all. It is 'a dreaming town.' Isn't that a lovely phrase? You remember...'Galahad through dreaming towns did go'?

"I feel so happy, Gilbert. I won't have to go home to Green Gables at Christmas, defeated and discredited. Life is good...good!

"So is Miss Sarah's pound cake. Rebecca Dew made one and 'sweated' it according to directions...which simply means that she wrapped it in several thicknesses of brown paper and several more towels and left it for three days. I can recommend it.

"(Are there, or are there not, two 'c's' in 'recommend'? In spite of the fact that I am a B.A. I can never be certain. Fancy if the Pringles had discovered that before I found Andy's diary!)"

9

Trix Taylor was curled up in the tower one night in February, while little flurries of snow hissed against the windows and that absurdly tiny stove purred like a red-hot black cat. Trix was pouring out her woes to Anne. Anne was beginning to find herself the recipient of confidences on all sides. She was known to be engaged, so that none of the Summerside girls feared her as a possible rival, and there was something about her that made you feel it was safe to tell her secrets.

Trix had come up to ask Anne to dinner the next evening. She was a jolly, plump little creature, with twinkling brown eyes and rosy cheeks, and did not look as if life weighed too heavily on her twenty years. But it appeared that she had troubles of her own.

"Dr. Lennox Carter is coming to dinner tomorrow night. That is why we want you especially. He is the new Head of the Modern Languages Department at Redmond and dreadfully clever, so we want somebody with brains to talk to him. You know I haven't any to boast of, nor Pringle either. As for Esme...well, you know, Anne, Esme is the sweetest thing and she's really clever, but she's so shy and timid she can't even make use of what brains she has when Dr. Carter is around. She's so terribly in love with him. It's pitiful. *I'm* very fond of Johnny...but before I'd dissolve into such a liquid state for him!"

"Are Esme and Dr. Carter engaged?"

"Not yet"...significantly. "But, oh, Anne, she's hoping he means to ask her this time. Would he come over to the Island to visit his cousin right in the middle of the term if he didn't intend to? I hope he will for Esme's sake, because she'll just die if he doesn't. But between you and me and the bed-post I'm

The First Year

not terribly struck on him for a brother-in-law. He's awfully fastidious, Esme says, and she's desperately afraid he won't approve of *us*. If he doesn't, she thinks he'll never ask her to marry him. So you can't imagine how she's hoping everything will go well at the dinner tomorrow night. I don't see why it shouldn't...Mamma is the most wonderful cook...and we have a good maid and I've bribed Pringle with half my week's allowance to behave himself. Of course he doesn't like Dr. Carter either... says he's got swelled head...but he's fond of Esme. If only Papa won't have a sulky fit on!"

"Have you any reason to fear it?" asked Anne. Every one in Summerside knew about Cyrus Taylor's sulky fits.

"You never can tell when he'll take one," said Trix dolefully. "He was frightfully upset tonight because he couldn't find his new flannel nightshirt. Esme had put it in the wrong drawer. He may be over it by tomorrow night or he may not. If he's not, he'll disgrace us all and Dr. Carter will conclude he can't marry into such a family. At least, that is what Esme says and I'm afraid she may be right. I think, Anne, that Lennox Carter is very fond of Esme...thinks she would make a 'very suitable wife' for him... but doesn't want to do anything rash or throw his wonderful self away. I've heard that he told his cousin a man couldn't be too careful what kind of family he married into. He's just at the point where he might be turned either way by a trifle. And, if it comes to that, one of Papa's sulky fits isn't any trifle."

"Doesn't he like Dr. Carter?"

"Oh, he does. He thinks it would be a wonderful match for Esme. But when Father has one of his spells on, *nothing* has any influence over him while it lasts. That's the Pringle for you, Anne. Grandmother Taylor was a Pringle, you know. You just can't imagine what we've gone through as a family. He never goes into rages, you know...like Uncle George. Uncle George's family don't mind his rages. When he goes into a temper he blows off...you can hear him roaring three blocks away...and then he's like a lamb and brings every one a new dress for a peace offering. But Father just sulks and glowers, and won't say a word to *anybody* at meal times. Esme says that, after all, that's better than cousin Richard Taylor, who is always saying sarcastic things at the table and insulting his wife; but it seems to me *nothing* could be worse than those awful silences of Papa's. They rattle us and we're terrified to open our mouths. It wouldn't be so bad, of course, if it was only when we are alone. But it's just as apt to be where we have company. Esme and I are simply tired of trying to explain away Papa's insulting silences. She's just sick with fear that he won't have got over the nightshirt before tomorrow night...and what will Lennox think? And she wants you to wear your blue dress. Her new dress is blue, because Lennox likes blue. But Papa hates it. Yours may reconcile him to hers."

"Wouldn't it be better for her to wear something else?"

"She hasn't anything else fit to wear at a company dinner except the green poplin Father gave her at Christmas. It's a lovely dress in itself...Father likes us to have pretty dresses...but you can't think of anything as awful as Esme in green. Pringle says it makes her look as if she was in the last stages of consumption. And Lennox Carter's cousin told Esme he would never marry a delicate person. I'm more than glad Johnny isn't so 'fastidious.'"

"Have you told your father about your engagement to Johnny yet?" asked Anne, who knew all about Trix's love affair.

"No," poor Trix groaned. "I can't summon up the courage, Anne. I know he'll make a frightful scene. Papa has always been so down on Johnny because he's poor. Papa forgets that he was poorer than Johnny when he started out in the hardware business. Of course he'll have to be told soon...but I want to wait until Esme's affair is settled. I know Papa won't speak to *any* of us for weeks after I tell him, and Mamma will worry so...she can't *bear* Father's sulky fits. We're all such cowards before Papa. Of course, Mamma and Esme are naturally timid with every one, but Pringle and I have lots of ginger. It's only Papa who can cow us. Sometimes I think if we had any one to back us up...but we haven't, and we just feel paralyzed. You can't imagine, Anne darling, what a company dinner is like at our place when Papa is sulking. But if he only behaves tomorrow night I'll forgive him for everything. He *can* be very agreeable when he wants to be... Papa is really just like Longfellow's little girl...'when he's good he's very, very good and when he's bad he's horrid.' I've seen him the life of the party."

"He was very nice the night I had dinner with you last month."

"Oh, he likes you, as I've said. That's one of the reasons why we want you so much. It may have a good influence on him. We're not neglecting *anything* that may please him. But when he has a really bad fit of sulks on he seems to hate everything and everybody. Anyhow, we've got a bang-up dinner planned, with an elegant orange-custard dessert. Mamma wanted pie because she says every man in the world but Papa likes pie for dessert better than anything else...even Professors of Modern Languages. But Papa doesn't, so it would never do to take a chance on it tomorrow night, when so much depends on it. Orange custard is Papa's favorite dessert. As for poor Johnny and me, I suppose I'll just have to elope with him some day and Papa will never forgive me."

"I believe if you'd just get up enough spunk to tell him and endure his resulting sulks you'd find he'd come round to it beautifully and you'd be saved months of anguish."

"You don't know Papa," said Trix darkly.

"Perhaps I know him better than you do. You've lost your perspective."

"Lost my...what? Anne darling, remember I'm not a B.A. I only went through the High. I'd have loved to go to college, but Papa doesn't believe in the Higher Education of women."

"I only meant that you're too close to him to understand him. A stranger could very well see him more clearly...understand him better."

"I understand that nothing can induce Papa to speak if he has made up his mind not to...*nothing*. He prides himself on that."

"Then why don't the rest of you just go on and talk as if nothing was the matter?"

"We *can't*...I've told you he paralyzes us. You'll find it out for yourself tomorrow night if he hasn't got over the nightshirt. I don't know how he does it but he does. I don't believe we'd mind so much how cranky he was if he would only talk. It's the silence that shatters us. I'll never forgive Papa if he acts up tomorrow night when so much is at stake."

"Let's hope for the best, dear."

"I'm trying to. And I know it will help to have you there. Mamma thought we ought to have Katherine Brooke too, but I knew it wouldn't have a good effect on Papa. He hates her. I don't blame him for *that*, I must say. I haven't any use for her myself. I don't see how you can be as nice to her as you are."

"I'm sorry for her, Trix."

"Sorry for her! But it's all her own fault she isn't liked. Oh, well, it takes all kinds of people to make a world...but Summerside could spare Katherine Brooke...glum old cat!"

"She's an excellent teacher, Trix...."

"Oh, do I know it? I was in her class. She *did* hammer things into my head...and flayed the flesh off my bones with sarcasm as well. And the way she dresses! Papa can't bear to see a woman badly dressed. He says he has no use for dowds and he's sure God hasn't either. Mamma would be horrified if she knew I told you that, Anne. She excused it in Papa because he is a man. If that was all we had to excuse in him! And poor Johnny hardly daring to come to the house now because Papa is so rude to him. I slip out on fine nights and we walk round and round the square and get half frozen."

Anne drew what was something like a breath of relief when Trix had gone, and slipped down to coax a snack out of Rebecca Dew.

"Going to the Taylors for dinner, are you? Well, I hope old Cyrus will be decent. If his family weren't all so afraid of him in his sulky fits he wouldn't indulge in them so often, of that I feel certain. I tell you, Miss Shirley, he *enjoys* his sulks. And now I suppose I must warm That Cat's milk. Pampered animal!"

10

When Anne arrived at the Cyrus Taylor house the next evening she felt the chill in the atmosphere as soon as she entered the door. A trim maid showed her up to the guest room but as Anne went up the stairs she caught sight of Mrs. Cyrus Taylor scuttling from the dining-room to the kitchen and Mrs. Cyrus was wiping tears away from her pale, careworn, but still rather sweet face. It was all too clear that Cyrus had not yet "got over" the nightshirt.

This was confirmed by a distressed Trix creeping into the room and whispering nervously,

"Oh, Anne, he's in a dreadful humor. He seemed pretty amiable this morning and our hopes rose. But Hugh Pringle beat him at a game of checkers this afternoon and Papa can't *bear* to lose a checker game. And it had to happen today, of course. He found Esme 'admiring herself in the mirror,' as he put it, and just walked her out of her room and locked the door. The poor darling was only wondering if she looked nice enough to please Lennox Carter, Ph.D. She hadn't even a chance to put her pearl string on. And look at me. I didn't dare curl my hair...Papa doesn't like curls that are not natural...and I look like a fright. Not that it matters about me...only it just shows you. Papa threw out the flowers Mamma put on the dining-room table and she feels it so...she took such trouble with them...and he wouldn't let her put on her garnet earrings. He hasn't had such a bad spell since he came home from the west last spring and found Mamma had put red curtains in the sitting-room, when he preferred mulberry. Oh, Anne, do talk as hard as you can at dinner, if he won't. If you don't, it will be *too* dreadful."

"I'll do my best," promised Anne, who certainly had never found herself at a loss for something to say. But then never had she found herself in such a situation as presently confronted her.

They were all gathered around the table...a very pretty and well appointed table in spite of the missing flowers. Timid Mrs. Cyrus, in a gray silk dress, had a face that was grayer than her dress. Esme, the beauty of the family...a very pale beauty, pale gold hair, pale pink lips, pale forget-me-not eyes...was so much paler than usual that she looked as if she were going to faint. Pringle, ordinarily a fat, cheerful urchin of fourteen, with round eyes and glasses and hair so fair it looked almost white, looked like a tied dog, and Trix had the air of a terrified school-girl.

Dr. Carter, who was undeniably handsome and distinguished-looking, with crisp dark hair, brilliant dark eyes and silver-rimmed glasses, but whom Anne, in the days of his Assistant Professorship at Redmond, had thought a rather pompous young bore, looked ill at ease. Evidently he felt that

The First Year

something was wrong somewhere...a reasonable conclusion when your host simply stalks to the head of the table and drops into his chair without a word to you or anybody.

Cyrus would not say grace. Mrs. Cyrus, blushing beet-red, murmured almost inaudibly, "For what we are about to receive the Lord make us truly thankful." The meal started badly by nervous Esme dropping her fork on the floor. Everybody except Cyrus jumped, because their nerves were likewise keyed up to the highest pitch. Cyrus glared at Esme out of his bulging blue eyes in a kind of enraged stillness. Then he glared at everybody and froze them into dumbness. He glared at poor Mrs. Cyrus, when she took a helping of horseradish sauce, with a glare that reminded her of her weak stomach. She couldn't eat any of it after that...and she was so fond of it. She didn't believe it would hurt her. But for that matter she couldn't eat anything, nor could Esme. They only pretended. The meal proceeded in a ghastly silence, broken by spasmodic speeches about the weather from Trix and Anne. Trix implored Anne with her eyes to talk, but Anne found herself for once in her life with absolutely nothing to say. She felt desperately that she *must* talk, but only the most idiotic things came into her head...things it would be impossible to utter aloud. Was everyone bewitched? It was curious, the effect one sulky, stubborn man had on you. Anne couldn't have believed it possible. And there was no doubt that he was really quite happy in the knowledge that he had made everybody at his table horribly uncomfortable. What on earth was going on in his mind? Would he jump if any one stuck a pin in him? Anne wanted to slap him...rap his knuckles...stand him in a corner...treat him like the spoiled child he really was, in spite of his spiky gray hair and truculent mustache.

Above all she wanted to make him *speak*. She felt instinctively that nothing in the world would punish him so much as to be tricked into speaking when he was determined not to.

Suppose she got up and deliberately smashed that huge, hideous, old-fashioned vase on the table in the corner...an ornate thing covered with wreaths of roses and leaves which it was most difficult to dust but which must be kept immaculately clean. Anne knew that the whole family hated it, but Cyrus Taylor would not hear of having it banished to the attic, because it had been his mother's. Anne thought she would do it fearlessly if she really believed that it would make Cyrus explode into vocal anger.

Why didn't Lennox Carter talk? If he would, she, Anne, could talk, too, and perhaps Trix and Pringle would escape from the spell that bound them and some kind of conversation would be possible. But he simply sat there and ate. Perhaps he thought it was really the best thing to do...perhaps he was afraid of saying something that would still further enrage the evidently already enraged parent of his lady.

"Will you please start the pickles, Miss Shirley?" said Mrs. Taylor faintly.

Something wicked stirred in Anne. She started the pickles... and something else. Without letting herself stop to think she bent forward, her great, gray-green eyes glimmering limpidly, and said gently,

"Perhaps you would be surprised to hear, Dr. Carter, that Mr. Taylor went deaf very suddenly last week?"

Anne sat back, having thrown her bomb. She could not tell precisely what she expected or hoped. If Dr. Carter got the impression that his host was deaf instead of in a towering rage of silence, it might loosen his tongue. She had *not* told a falsehood...she had *not* said Cyrus Taylor *was* deaf. As for Cyrus Taylor, if she had hoped to make him speak she had failed. He merely glared at her, still in silence.

But Anne's remark had an effect on Trix and Pringle that she had never dreamed of. Trix was in a silent rage herself. She had,

The First Year

the moment before Anne had hurled her rhetorical question, seen Esme furtively wipe away a tear that had escaped from one of her despairing blue eyes. Everything was hopeless...Lennox Carter would never ask Esme to marry him now...it didn't matter any more what any one said or did. Trix was suddenly possessed with a burning desire to get square with her brutal father. Anne's speech gave her a weird inspiration, and Pringle, a volcano of suppressed impishness, blinked his white eyelashes for a dazed moment and then promptly followed her lead. Never, as long as they might live, would Anne, Esme or Mrs. Cyrus forget the dreadful quarter of an hour that followed.

"Such an affliction for poor papa," said Trix, addressing Dr. Carter across the table. "And him only sixty-eight."

Two little white dents appeared at the corners of Cyrus Taylor's nostrils when he heard his age advanced six years. But he remained silent.

"It's such a treat to have a decent meal," said Pringle, clearly and distinctly. "What would you think, Dr. Carter, of a man who makes his family live on fruit and eggs...nothing but fruit and eggs...just for a fad?"

"Does your father...?" began Dr. Carter bewilderedly.

"What would you think of a husband who bit his wife when she put up curtains he didn't like...deliberately bit her?" demanded Trix.

"Till the blood came," added Pringle solemnly.

"Do you mean to say your father...?"

"What would you think of a man who would cut up a silk dress of his wife's just because the way it was made didn't suit him?" said Trix.

"What would you think," said Pringle, "of a man who refuses to let his wife have a dog?"

"When she would so love to have one," sighed Trix.

"What would you think of a man," continued Pringle, who was beginning to enjoy himself hugely, "who would give his wife a pair of goloshes for a Christmas present...nothing but a pair of goloshes?"

"Goloshes don't exactly warm the heart," admitted Dr. Carter. His eyes met Anne's and he smiled. Anne reflected that she had never seen him smile before. It changed his face wonderfully for the better. What *was* Trix saying? Who would have thought she could be such a demon?

"Have you ever wondered, Dr. Carter, how awful it must be to live with a man who thinks nothing...*nothing*—of picking up the roast, if it isn't perfectly done, and hurling it at the maid?"

Dr. Carter glanced apprehensively at Cyrus Taylor, as if he feared Cyrus might throw the skeletons of the chickens at somebody. Then he seemed to remember comfortingly that his host was deaf.

"What would you think of a man who believed the earth was flat?" asked Pringle.

Anne thought Cyrus *would* speak then. A tremor seemed to pass over his rubicund face, but no words came. Still, she was sure his mustaches were a little less defiant.

"What would you think of a man who let his aunt...his only aunt...go to the poorhouse?" asked Trix.

"And pastured his cow in the graveyard?" said Pringle. "Summerside hasn't got over that sight yet."

"What would you think of a man who would write down in his diary every day what he had for dinner?" asked Trix.

"The great Pepys did that," said Dr. Carter with another smile. His voice sounded as if he would like to laugh. Perhaps after all he was not pompous, thought Anne...only young and shy and overserious. But she was feeling positively aghast. She had never meant things to go as far as this. She was finding out that it is much easier to start things than finish them. Trix and Pringle were being diabolically clever. They had not said that their father did a single one of these things. Anne could fancy Pringle saying, his round eyes rounder still with pretended innocence, "I just asked those questions of Dr. Carter for *information.*"

"What would you think," kept on Trix, "of a man who opens and reads his wife's letters?"

"What would you think of a man who would go to a funeral…his father's funeral…in overalls?" asked Pringle.

What *would* they think of next? Mrs. Cyrus was crying openly and Esme was quite calm with despair. Nothing mattered any more. She turned and looked squarely at Dr. Carter, whom she had lost forever. For once in her life she was stung into saying a really clever thing.

"What," she asked quietly, "would you think of a man who spent a whole day hunting for the kittens of a poor cat who had been shot, because he couldn't bear to think of them starving to death?"

A strange silence descended on the room. Trix and Pringle looked suddenly ashamed of themselves. And then Mrs. Cyrus piped up, feeling it her wifely duty to back up Esme's unexpected defense of her father.

"And he can crochet so beautifully…he made the loveliest centerpiece for the parlor table last winter when he was laid up with lumbago."

Every one has some limit of endurance and Cyrus Taylor had reached his. He gave his chair such a furious backward push that it shot instantly across the polished floor and struck the table on which the vase stood. The table went over and the vase broke in the traditional thousand pieces. Cyrus, his bushy white eyebrows fairly bristling with wrath, stood up and exploded at last.

"I don't crochet, woman! Is one contemptible doily going to blast a man's reputation forever? I was so bad with that blamed lumbago I didn't know what I was doing. And I'm deaf, am I, Miss Shirley? I'm deaf?"

"She didn't *say* you were, Papa," cried Trix, who was never afraid of her father when his temper was vocal.

"Oh, no, she didn't say it. None of you said anything! *You* didn't say I was sixty-eight when I'm only sixty-two, did you? *You* didn't say I wouldn't let your mother have a dog! Good Lord, woman, you can have forty thousand dogs if you want to and you know it! When did I ever deny you anything you wanted...when?"

"Never, Poppa, never," sobbed Mrs. Cyrus brokenly. "And I never wanted a dog. I never even *thought* of wanting a dog, Poppa."

"When did I open your letters? When have I ever kept a diary? A diary! When did I ever wear overalls to anybody's funeral? When did I pasture a cow in the graveyard? What aunt of mine is in the poorhouse? Did I ever throw a roast at anybody? Did I ever make you live on fruit and eggs?"

"Never, Poppa, never," wept Mrs. Cyrus. "You've always been a good provider...the best."

"Didn't you tell me you *wanted* goloshes last Christmas?"

"Yes, oh, yes; of course I did, Poppa. And my feet have been so nice and warm all winter."

"Well, then!" Cyrus threw a triumphant glance around the room. His eyes encountered Anne's. Suddenly the unexpected happened. Cyrus chuckled. His cheeks actually dimpled. Those dimples worked a miracle with his whole expression. He brought his chair back to the table and sat down.

"I've got a very bad habit of sulking, Dr. Carter. Every one has some bad habit...that's mine. The only one. Come, come, Momma, stop crying. I admit I deserved all I got except that crack of yours about crocheting. Esme, my girl, I won't forget that you were the only one who stood up for me. Tell Maggie to come and clear up that mess...I know you're all glad the darn thing is smashed...and bring on the pudding."

Anne could never have believed that an evening which began so terribly could end up so pleasantly. Nobody could have been more genial or better company than Cyrus: and there was evidently no aftermath of reckoning, for when Trix came down a few evenings later it was to tell Anne that she had at last scraped up enough courage to tell her father about Johnny.

"Was he very dreadful, Trix?"

"He...he wasn't dreadful at all," admitted Trix sheepishly. "He just snorted and said it was about time Johnny came to the point after hanging around for two years and keeping every one else away. I think he felt he couldn't go into another spell of sulks so soon after the last one. And you know, Anne, between sulks Papa really is an old duck."

"I think he is a great deal better father to you than you deserve," said Anne, quite in Rebecca Dew's manner. "You were simply outrageous at that dinner, Trix."

"Well, you know you started it," said Trix. "And good old Pringle helped a bit. All's well that ends well...and thank goodness I'll never have to dust that vase again."

11

(Extract from letter to Gilbert two weeks later.)

"Esme Taylor's engagement to Dr. Lennox Carter is announced. By all I can gather from various bits of local gossip I think he decided that fatal Friday night that he wanted to protect her, and save her from her father and her family...and perhaps from her friends! Her plight evidently appealed to his sense of chivalry. Trix persists in thinking I was the means of bringing it about and perhaps I did take a hand, but I don't think I'll ever try an experiment like that again. It's too much like picking up a lightning flash by the tail.

"I really don't know what got into me, Gilbert. It must have been a hangover from my old detestation of anything savoring of Pringleism. It *does* seem old now. I've almost forgotten it. But other folks are still wondering. I hear Miss Valentine Courtaloe says she isn't at all surprised I have won the Pringles over, because I have 'such a way with me'; and the minister's wife thinks it is an answer to the prayer she put up. Well, who knows but that it was?

"Jen Pringle and I walked part of the way home from school yesterday and talked of 'ships and shoes and sealing wax'...of almost everything but geometry. We avoid that subject. Jen knows I don't know too much about geometry, but my own wee bit of knowledge about Captain Myrom balances that. I lent Jen my Foxe's *Book of Martyrs*. I hate to lend a book I *love*...it never seems quite the same when it comes back to me...but I love Foxe's *Martyrs* only because dear Mrs. Allan gave it to me for a Sunday-school prize years ago. I don't like reading about martyrs because they always make me feel petty and ashamed...ashamed to admit I hate to get out of bed on frosty mornings and shrink from a visit to the dentist!

"Well, I'm glad Esme and Trix are both happy. Since my own little romance is in flower I am all the more interested in other people's. A *nice* interest, you know. Not curious or malicious but just glad there's such a lot of happiness spread about.

"It's still February and 'on the convent roof the snows are sparkling to the moon'...only it isn't a convent...just the roof of Mr. Hamilton's barn. But I'm beginning to think,

The First Year

'Only a few more weeks till spring...and a few more weeks then till summer...and holidays...and Green Gables...and golden sunlight on Avonlea meadows...and a gulf that will be silver at dawn and sapphire at noon and crimson at sunset...and *you*.'

"Little Elizabeth and I have no end of plans for spring. We are such good friends. I take her milk every evening and once in so long she is allowed to go for a walk with me. We have discovered that our birthdays are on the same day and Elizabeth flushed 'divinest rosy red' with the excitement of it. She is so sweet when she blushes. Ordinarily she is far too pale and doesn't get any pinker because of the new milk. Only when we come back from our twilight trysts with evening winds does she have a lovely rose color in her little cheeks. Once she asked me gravely, 'Will I have a lovely creamy skin like yours when I grow up, Miss Shirley, if I put buttermilk on my face every night?' Buttermilk seems to be the preferred cosmetic in Spook's Lane. I have discovered that Rebecca Dew uses it. She has bound me over to keep it secret from the widows because they would think it too frivolous for her age. The number of secrets I have to keep at Windy Poplars is aging me before my time. I wonder if I buttermilked my nose if it would banish those seven freckles. By the way, did it ever occur to you, sir, that I had a 'lovely creamy skin'? If it did, you never told me so. And have you realized to the full that I am 'comparatively beautiful'? Because I have discovered that I am.

"'What is it like to be beautiful, Miss Shirley?' asked Rebecca Dew gravely the other day...when I was wearing my new biscuit-colored voile.

"'I've often wondered,' said I.

"'But you *are* beautiful,' said Rebecca Dew.

"'I never thought you could be sarcastic, Rebecca,' I said reproachfully.

"'I did not mean to be sarcastic, Miss Shirley. You are beautiful...comparatively.'

"'Oh! Comparatively!' said I.

"'Look in the sideboard glass,' said Rebecca Dew, pointing. 'Compared to *me*, you are.'

"Well, I was!

"But I hadn't finished with Elizabeth. One stormy evening when the wind was howling along Spook's Lane, we couldn't go for a walk, so we came up to my room and drew a map of fairyland. Elizabeth sat on my blue doughnut cushion to make her higher, and looked like a serious little gnome as she bent over the map. (By the way, no phonetic spelling for me! 'Gnome' is far eerier and fairy-er than 'nome.')

"Our map isn't completed yet...every day we think of something more to go in it. Last night we located the house of the Witch of the Snow and drew a triple hill, covered completely with wild cherry trees in bloom, behind it. (By the way, I want some wild cherry trees near our house of dreams, Gilbert.) Of course we have a Tomorrow on the map...located east of Today and west of Yesterday...and we have no end of 'times' in fairyland. Spring-time, long time, short time, new-moon time, good-night time, next time...but no last time, because that is too sad a time for fairyland; old time, young time...because if there is an old time there ought to be a young time, too; mountain time... because that has such a fascinating sound; night-time and day-time...but no bedtime or school-time; Christmas-time; no only time, because that also is too sad...but lost time, because it is so nice to find it; some time, good time, fast time, slow time, half-past kissing-time, going-home time, and time immemorial...which is one of the most beautiful phrases in the world. And we have cunning little red arrows everywhere, pointing to the different 'times.' I know Rebecca Dew thinks I'm quite childish. But, oh, Gilbert, don't let's ever grow too old and wise...no, not too old and *silly* for fairyland.

"Rebecca Dew, I feel sure, is not quite certain that I am an influence for good in Elizabeth's life. She thinks I encourage her in being 'fanciful.' One evening when I was away Rebecca Dew took the milk to her and found her already at the gate, looking at the sky so intently that she never heard Rebecca's (anything but) fairy footfalls.

"'I was *listening,* Rebecca,' she explained.

"'You do too much listening,' said Rebecca disapprovingly.

"Elizabeth smiled, remotely, austerely. (Rebecca Dew didn't use those words but I know exactly how Elizabeth smiled.)

"'You would be surprised, Rebecca, if you knew what I hear sometimes,' she said, in a way that made Rebecca Dew's flesh creep on her bones...or so she avers.

"But Elizabeth is always touched with faery and what can be done about it?

"Your Very Anne-est ANNE.

"P.S.1. Never, never, never shall I forget Cyrus Taylor's face when his wife accused him of crocheting. But I shall always like him because he hunted for those kittens. And I like Esme for standing up for her father under the supposed wreck of all her hopes.

"P.S.2. I have put in a new pen. And I love you because you aren't pompous like Dr. Carter...and I love you because you haven't got sticky-out ears like Johnny. And...the very best reason of all...I love you for just being Gilbert!"

12

"Windy Poplars,
"Spook's Lane,
"May 30th.

"DEAREST-AND-THEN-MORE-DEAR:
"It's spring!

"Perhaps you, up to your eyes in a welter of exams in Kingsport, don't know it. But I am aware of it from the crown of my head to the tips of my toes. Summerside is aware of it. Even the most unlovely streets are transfigured by arms of bloom reaching over old board fences and a ribbon of dandelions in the grass that borders the sidewalks. Even the china lady on my shelf is aware of it and I know if I could only wake up suddenly enough some night I'd catch her dancing a *pas seul* in her pink, gilt-heeled shoes.

"Everything is calling 'spring' to me...the little laughing brooks, the blue hazes on the Storm King, the maples in the grove when I go to read your letters, the white cherry trees along Spook's Lane, the sleek and saucy robins hopping defiance to Dusty Miller in the back yard, the creeper hanging greenly down over the half-door to which little Elizabeth comes for milk, the fir trees preening in new tassel tips around the old graveyard...even the old graveyard itself, where all sorts of flowers planted at the heads of the graves are budding into leaf and bloom, as if to say, 'Even here life is triumphant over death.' I had a really lovely prowl about the graveyard the other night. (I'm sure Rebecca Dew thinks my taste in walks frightfully

The First Year

morbid. 'I can't think why you have such a hankering after that unchancy place,' she says.) I roamed over it in the scented green cat's light and wondered if Nathan Pringle's wife really had tried to poison him. Her grave looked so innocent with its new grass and its June lilies that I concluded she had been entirely maligned.

"Just another month and I'll be home for vacation! I keep thinking of the old orchard at Green Gables with its trees now in full snow...the old bridge over the Lake of Shining Waters...the murmur of the sea in your ears...a summer afternoon in Lover's Lane...and *you!*

"I have just the right kind of pen tonight, Gilbert, and so...

(Two pages omitted.)

"I was around at the Gibsons' this evening for a call. Marilla asked me some time ago to look them up because she once knew them when they lived in White Sands. Accordingly I looked them up and have been looking them up weekly ever since because Pauline seems to enjoy my visits and I'm so sorry for her. She is simply a slave to her mother...who is a terrible old woman.

"Mrs. Adoniram Gibson is eighty and spends her days in a wheel-chair. They moved to Summerside fifteen years ago. Pauline, who is forty-five, is the youngest of the family, all her brothers and sisters being married and all of them determined not to have Mrs. Adoniram in their homes. She keeps the house and waits on her mother hand and foot. She is a little pale, fawn-eyed thing with golden-brown hair that is still glossy and pretty. They are quite comfortably off and if it were not for her mother Pauline could have a very pleasant easy life. She just loves church work and would be perfectly happy attending Ladies' Aids and Missionary Societies, planning for church suppers and

Welcome socials, not to speak of exulting proudly in being the possessor of the finest wandering-jew in town. But she can hardly ever get away from the house, even to go to church on Sundays. I can't see any way of escape for her, for old Mrs. Gibson will probably live to be a hundred. And, while she may not have the use of her legs, there is certainly nothing the matter with her tongue. It always fills me with helpless rage to sit there and hear her making poor Pauline the target for her sarcasm. And yet Pauline has told me that her mother 'thinks quite highly' of me and is much nicer to her when I am around. If this be so I shiver to think what she must be when I am not around.

"Pauline dares not do *anything* without asking her mother. She can't even buy her own clothes...not so much as a pair of stockings. Everything has to be sent up for Mrs. Gibson's approval; everything has to be worn until it has been turned twice. Pauline has worn the same hat for four years.

"Mrs. Gibson can't bear any noise in the house or a breath of fresh air. It is said she never smiled in her life...I've never caught her at it, anyway, and when I look at her I find myself wondering what would happen to her face if she did smile. Pauline can't even have a room to herself. She has to sleep in the same room with her mother and be up almost every hour of the night rubbing Mrs. Gibson's back or giving her a pill or getting a hot-water bottle for her...*hot,* not lukewarm!...or changing her pillows or seeing what that mysterious noise is in the back yard. Mrs. Gibson does her sleeping in the afternoons and spends her nights devising tasks for Pauline.

"Yet nothing has ever made Pauline bitter. She is sweet and unselfish and patient and I am glad she has a dog to love. The only thing she has ever had her own way about

The First Year

is keeping that dog...and then only because there was a burglary somewhere in town and Mrs. Gibson thought it would be a protection. Pauline never dares to let her mother see how much she loves the dog. Mrs. Gibson hates him and complains of his bringing bones in but she never actually says he must go, for her own selfish reason.

"But at last I have a chance to give Pauline something and I'm going to do it. I'm going to give her a *day*, though it will mean giving up my next week-end at Green Gables.

"Tonight when I went in I could see that Pauline had been crying. Mrs. Gibson did not long leave me in doubt why.

"'Pauline wants to go and leave me, Miss Shirley,' she said. 'Nice, grateful daughter I've got, haven't I?'

"'Only for a day, Ma,' said Pauline, swallowing a sob and trying to smile.

"'Only for a day,' says she! 'Well, *you* know what my days are like, Miss Shirley...every one knows what my days are like. But you don't know...*yet*...Miss Shirley, and I hope you never will, how long a day can be when you are suffering.'

"I knew Mrs. Gibson didn't suffer at all now, so I didn't try to be sympathetic.

"'I'd get some one to stay with you, of course, Ma,' said Pauline. 'You see,' she explained to me, 'my cousin Louisa is going to celebrate her silver wedding at White Sands next Saturday week and she wants me to go. I was her bridesmaid when she was married to Maurice Hilton. I *would* like to go so much if Ma would give her consent.'

"'If I must die alone I must,' said Mrs. Gibson. 'I leave it to your conscience, Pauline.'

"I knew Pauline's battle was lost the moment Mrs. Gibson left it to her conscience. Mrs. Gibson has got her way all her life by leaving things to people's consciences. I've heard that years ago somebody wanted to marry Pauline and Mrs. Gibson prevented it by leaving it to her conscience.

"Pauline wiped her eyes, summoned up a piteous smile and picked up a dress she was making over...a hideous green and black plaid.

"'Now don't sulk, Pauline,' said Mrs. Gibson. 'I can't abide people who sulk. And mind you put a collar on that dress. Would you believe it, Miss Shirley, she actually wanted to make the dress without a collar? She'd wear a low-necked dress, that one, if I'd let her.'

"I looked at poor Pauline with her slender little throat...which is rather plump and pretty yet...enclosed in a high, stiff-boned net collar.

"'Collarless dresses are coming in,' I said.

"'Collarless dresses,' said Mrs. Gibson, 'are indecent.'

"(Item:—I was wearing a collarless dress.)

"'Moreover,' went on Mrs. Gibson, as if it were all of a piece. 'I never liked Maurice Hilton. His mother was a Crockett. He never had any sense of decorum...always kissing his wife in the most unsuitable places!'

"(Are you sure you kiss me in suitable places, Gilbert? I'm afraid Mrs. Gibson would think the nape of the neck, for instance, most unsuitable.)

"'But, Ma, you know that was the day she nearly escaped being trampled by Harvey Wither's horse running amuck on the church green. It was only natural Maurice should feel a little excited.'

"'Pauline, please don't contradict me. I *still* think the church steps were an unsuitable place for any one to be kissed. But of course *my* opinions don't matter to *any one* any longer. Of course every one wishes I was dead. Well, there'll be room for me in the grave. I know what a burden I am to you. I might as well die. Nobody wants me.'

"'Don't say that, Ma,' begged Pauline.

"'I *will* say it. Here you are, determined to go to that silver wedding although you know I'm not willing.'

"'Ma dear. I'm not going...I'd never think of going if you weren't willing. Don't excite yourself so....'

"'Oh, I can't even have a little excitement, can't I, to brighten my dull life? Surely you're not going so soon, Miss Shirley?'

"I felt that if I stayed any longer I'd either go crazy or slap Mrs. Gibson's nut-cracker face. So I said I had exam papers to correct.

"'Ah well, I suppose two old women like us are very poor company for a young girl,' sighed Mrs. Gibson. 'Pauline isn't very cheerful...are you, Pauline? Not very cheerful. I don't wonder Miss Shirley doesn't want to stay long.'

"Pauline came out to the porch with me. The moon was shining down on her little garden and sparkling on the harbor. A soft, delightful wind was talking to a white apple tree. It was spring...spring...spring! Even Mrs. Gibson can't stop plum trees from blooming. And Pauline's soft gray-blue eyes were full of tears.

"'I *would* like to go to Louie's wedding so much,' she said, with a long sigh of despairing resignation.

"'You are going,' I said.

"'Oh, no, dear, I can't go. Poor Ma will never consent. I'll just put it out of my mind. Isn't the moon beautiful tonight?' she added, in a loud, cheerful tone.

"'I've never heard of any good that came from moon gazing,' called out Mrs. Gibson from the sitting-room. 'Stop chirruping there, Pauline, and come in and get my red bedroom slippers with the fur round the tops for me. These shoes pinch my feet something terrible. But nobody cares how I suffer.'

"I felt that *I* didn't care how much she suffered. Poor darling Pauline! But a day off is certainly coming to Pauline and she is going to have her silver wedding. I, Anne Shirley, have spoken it.

"I told Rebecca Dew and the widows all about it when I came home and we had such fun, thinking up all the lovely, insulting things I might have said to Mrs. Gibson. Aunt Kate does not think I will succeed in getting Mrs. Gibson to let Pauline go but Rebecca Dew has faith in me. 'Anyhow, if *you* can't, nobody can,' she said.

"I was at supper recently with Mrs. Tom Pringle who wouldn't take me to board. (Rebecca says I am the best paying boarder she ever heard of because I am invited out to supper so often.) I'm very glad she didn't. She's nice and purry and her pies praise her in the gates, but her home isn't Windy Poplars and she doesn't live in Spook's Lane and she isn't Aunt Kate and Aunt Chatty and Rebecca Dew. I love them all three and I'm going to board here next year and the year after. My chair is always called 'Miss Shirley's chair' and Aunt Chatty tells me that when I'm not here Rebecca Dew sets my place at the table just the same, 'so it won't seem so lonesome.' Sometimes Aunt Chatty's feelings have complicated matters a bit but she says she understands me now and knows I would never hurt her intentionally.

"Little Elizabeth and I go out for a walk twice a week now. Mrs. Campbell has agreed to that, but it must not be oftener and *never* on Sundays. Things are better for little Elizabeth in spring. Some sunshine gets into even that grim old house and outwardly it is even beautiful because of the dancing shadows of tree tops. Still, Elizabeth likes to escape from it whenever she can. Once in a while we go up-town so that Elizabeth can see the lighted shop windows. But mostly we go as far as we dare down the Road that Leads to the End of the World, rounding every corner adventurously and expectantly, as if we were going to find Tomorrow behind it, while all the little green evening hills neatly nestle together in the distance. One of the things Elizabeth is going to do in Tomorrow is 'go to Philadelphia and see the angel in the church.' I haven't told her...I never will tell her...that the Philadelphia St. John was writing about was *not* Phila., Pa. We lose our illusions soon enough. And anyhow, if we *could* get into Tomorrow, who knows what we might find there? Angels everywhere, perhaps.

"Sometimes we watch the ships coming up the harbor before a fair wind, over a glistening pathway, through the transparent spring air, and Elizabeth wonders if her father may be on board one of them. She clings to the hope that he may come some day. I can't imagine why he doesn't. I'm sure he would if he knew what a darling little daughter he has here longing for him. I suppose he never realizes she is quite a girl now....I suppose he still thinks of her as the little baby who cost his wife her life.

"I'll soon have finished my first year in Summerside High. The first term was a nightmare, but the last two have been very pleasant. The Pringles are *delightful people*. How could I ever have compared them to the Pyes? Sid Pringle brought me a bunch of trilliums today. Jen is going to lead her class and Miss Ellen is reported to have said that I am the only teacher who ever *really understood* the child! The only fly in my ointment is Katherine Brooke, who continues unfriendly and distant. I'm going to give up trying to be friends with her. After all, as Rebecca Dew says, there *are* limits.

"Oh, I nearly forgot to tell you....Sally Nelson has asked me to be one of her bridesmaids. She is going to be married the last of June at Bonnyview, Dr. Nelson's summer home down at the jumping-off place. She is marrying Gordon Hill. Then Nora Nelson will be the only one of Dr. Nelson's six girls left unmarried. Jim Wilcox has been going with her for years...'off and on' as Rebecca Dew says...but it never seems to come to anything and nobody thinks it will now. I'm very fond of Sally, but I've never made much headway getting acquainted with Nora. She's a good deal older than I am, of course, and rather reserved and proud. Yet I'd like to be friends with her. She isn't pretty or clever or charming but somehow she's got a *tang*. I've a feeling she'd be worth while.

"Speaking of weddings, Esme Taylor was married to her Ph.D. last month. As it was on Wednesday afternoon I couldn't go to the church to see her, but every one says she looked very beautiful and happy and Lennox looked as if he knew he had done the right thing and had the approval of his conscience. Cyrus Taylor and I are great friends. He often refers to the dinner which he has come to consider a great joke on everybody. 'I've never dared sulk since,' he told me. 'Momma might accuse me of sewing patchwork next time.' And then he tells me to be sure and give his love to 'the widows.' Gilbert, people are delicious and life is delicious and I am

"Forevermore
'Yours!

"P.S. Our old red cow down at Mr. Hamilton's has a spotted calf. We've been buying our milk for three months from Lew Hunt. Rebecca says we'll have cream again now...and that she has always heard the Hunt well was inexhaustible and now she believes it. Rebecca didn't want that calf to be born at all. Aunt Kate had to get Mr. Hamilton to tell her that the cow was really too old to have a calf before she would consent."

13

"Ah, when you've been old and bed-rid as long as me you'll have more sympathy," whined Mrs. Gibson.

"Please don't think I'm lacking in sympathy, Mrs. Gibson," said Anne, who, after half an hour's vain effort, felt like wringing Mrs. Gibson's neck. Nothing but poor Pauline's pleading eyes in the background kept her from giving up in despair and going home. "I assure you, you won't be lonely and neglected. I will be here all day and see that you lack nothing in any way."

"Oh, I know I'm of no use to any one," said Mrs. Gibson, apropos of nothing that had been said. "You don't need to rub that in, Miss Shirley. I'm ready to go any time...any time. Pauline can gad round all she wants to then. I won't be here to feel neglected. None of the young people of today have any sense. Giddy...very giddy."

Anne didn't know whether it was Pauline or herself who was the giddy young person without sense, but she tried the last shot in her locker.

"Well, you know, Mrs. Gibson, people will talk so terribly if Pauline doesn't go to her cousin's silver wedding."

"Talk!" said Mrs. Gibson sharply. "What will they talk about?"

"Dear Mrs. Gibson..." ('May I be forgiven the adjective!' thought Anne) "in your long life you have learned, I know, just what idle tongues can say."

"You needn't be casting my age up to me," snapped Mrs. Gibson. "And I don't need to be told it's a censorious world. Too well...too well I know it. And I don't need to be told that this town is full of tattling toads neither. But I dunno's I fancy them jabbering about me...saying, I s'pose, that I'm an old tyrant. *I* ain't stopping Pauline from going. Didn't I leave it to her conscience?"

"So few people will believe that," said Anne, carefully sorrowful.

Mrs. Gibson sucked a peppermint lozenge fiercely for a minute or two. Then she said,

"I hear there's mumps at White Sands."

"Ma, dear, you know I've had the mumps."

"There's folks as takes them twice. You'd be just the one to take them twice, Pauline. You always took everything that come round. The nights I've set up with you, not expecting you'd see the morning! Ah me, a mother's sacrifices ain't long remembered. Besides, how would you get to White Sands? You ain't been on a train for years. And there ain't any train back Saturday night."

"She could go on the Saturday morning train," said Anne. "And I'm sure Mr. James Gregor will bring her back."

"I never liked Jim Gregor. His mother was a Tarbush."

"He is taking his double-seated buggy and going down Friday, or else he would take her down, too. But she'll be quite safe on the train, Mrs. Gibson. Just step on at Summerside... step off at White Sands...no changing."

"There's something behind all this," said Mrs. Gibson suspiciously. "Why are you so set on her going, Miss Shirley? Just tell me that."

The First Year

Anne smiled into the beady-eyed face.

"Because I think Pauline is a good, kind daughter to you, Mrs. Gibson, and needs a day off now and then, just as everybody does."

Most people found it hard to resist Anne's smile. Either that, or the fear of gossip vanquished Mrs. Gibson.

"I s'pose it never occurs to any one *I'd* like a day off from this wheel-chair if I could get it. But I can't...I just have to bear my affliction patiently. Well, if she must go she must. She's always been one to get her own way. If she catches mumps or gets poisoned by strange mosquitoes, don't blame me for it. I'll have to get along as best I can. Oh, I s'pose you'll be here, but you ain't used to my ways as Pauline is. I s'pose I can stand it for one day. If I can't...well, I've been living on borrowed time many's the year now so what's the difference?" Not a gracious assent by any means but still an assent. Anne in her relief and gratitude found herself doing something she could never have imagined herself doing...she bent over and kissed Mrs. Gibson's leathery cheek. "Thank you," she said.

"Never mind your wheedling ways," said Mrs. Gibson. "Have a peppermint."

"How can I ever thank you, Miss Shirley?" said Pauline, as she went a little way down the street with Anne.

"By going to White Sands with a light heart and enjoying every minute of the time."

"Oh, I'll do that. You don't know what this means to me, Miss Shirley. It's not only Louisa I want to see. The old Luckley place next to her home is going to be sold and I did so want to see it once more before it passed into the hands of strangers. Mary Luckley...she's Mrs. Howard Flemming now and lives out west...was my dearest friend when I was a girl. We were like sisters. I used to be at the Luckley place so much and I loved it so. I've often dreamed of going back. Ma says I'm getting too old to dream. Do you think I am, Miss Shirley?"

"Nobody is ever too old to dream. And dreams never grow old."

"I'm so glad to hear you say that. Oh, Miss Shirley, to think of seeing the gulf again. I haven't seen it for fifteen years. The harbor is beautiful, but it isn't the gulf. I feel as if I was walking on air. And I owe it all to you. It was just because Ma likes you she let me go. You've made me happy...you are always making people happy. Why, whenever you come into a room, Miss Shirley, the people in it feel happier."

"That's the very nicest compliment I've ever had paid me, Pauline."

"There's just one thing, Miss Shirley...I've nothing to wear but my old black taffeta. It's too gloomy for a wedding, isn't it? And it's too big for me since I got thin. You see it's six years since I got it."

"We must try to induce your mother to let you have a new dress," said Anne hopefully.

But that proved to be beyond her powers. Mrs. Gibson was adamant. Pauline's black taffeta was plenty good for Louisa Hilton's wedding.

"I paid two dollars a yard for it six years ago and three to Jane Sharp for making it. Jane was a good dressmaker. Her mother was a Smiley. The idea of you wanting something 'light,' Pauline Gibson! She'd go dressed in scarlet from head to foot, that one, if she was let, Miss Shirley. She's just waiting till I'm dead to do it. Ah, well, you'll soon be shet of all the trouble I am to you, Pauline. Then you can dress as gay and giddy as you like, but as long as I'm alive you'll be decent. And what's the matter with your hat? It's time you wore a bonnet, anyhow."

Poor Pauline had a lively horror of having to wear a bonnet. She would wear her old hat for the rest of her life before she would do that.

"I'm just going to be glad inside and forget all about my clothes," she told Anne, when they went out to the garden to

The First Year

pick a bouquet of June lilies and bleeding-heart for the widows.

"I've a plan," said Anne, with a cautious glance to make sure Mrs. Gibson couldn't hear her, though she was watching from the sitting-room window. "You know that silver-gray poplin of mine? I'm going to lend you that for the wedding."

Pauline dropped the basket of flowers in her agitation, making a pool of pink and white sweetness at Anne's feet.

"Oh, my dear, I couldn't....Ma wouldn't let me."

"She won't know a thing about it. Listen. Saturday morning you'll put it on under your black taffeta. I know it will fit you. It's a little long, but I'll run some tucks in it tomorrow...tucks are fashionable now. It's collarless, with elbow sleeves so no one will suspect. As soon as you get to Gull Cove, take off the taffeta. When the day is over you can leave the poplin at Gull Cove and I can get it the next week-end I'm home."

"But wouldn't it be too young for me?"

"Not a bit of it. Any age can wear gray."

"Do you think it would be...right...to deceive Ma?" faltered Pauline.

"In this case entirely right," said Anne shamelessly. "You know, Pauline, it would never do to wear a black dress to a wedding. It might bring the bride bad luck."

"Oh, I wouldn't do that for anything. And of course it won't hurt Ma. I do hope she'll get through Saturday all right. I'm afraid she won't eat a bite when I'm away...she didn't the time I went to Cousin Matilda's funeral. Miss Prouty told me she didn't....Miss Prouty stayed with her. She was so provoked at Cousin Matilda for dying...Ma was, I mean."

"She'll eat....I'll see to that."

"I know you've a great knack of managing her," conceded Pauline. "And you won't forget to give her her medicine at the regular times, will you, dear? Oh, perhaps I oughtn't to go after all."

"You've been out there long enough to pick forty bokays," called Mrs. Gibson irately. "I dunno what the widows want of your flowers. They've plenty of their own. I'd go a long time without flowers if I waited for Rebecca Dew to send me any. I'm dying for a drink of water. But then I'm of no consequence."

Friday night Pauline telephoned Anne in terrible agitation. She had a sore throat and did Miss Shirley think it could possibly be the mumps? Anne ran down to reassure her, taking the gray poplin in a brown paper parcel. She hid it in the lilac bush and late that night Pauline, in a cold perspiration, managed to smuggle it upstairs to the little room where she kept her clothes and dressed, though she was never permitted to sleep there. Pauline was not quite easy about the dress. Perhaps her sore throat was a judgment on her for deception. But she couldn't go to Louisa's silver wedding in that dreadful old black taffeta... she simply couldn't.

Saturday morning Anne was at the Gibson house bright and early. Anne always looked her best on a sparkling summer morning such as this. She seemed to sparkle with it and she moved through the golden air like a slender figure on a Grecian urn. The dullest room sparkled, too...*lived*...when she came into it.

"Walking as if you owned the earth," commented Mrs. Gibson sarcastically.

"So I do," said Anne gayly.

"Ah, you're very young," said Mrs. Gibson maddeningly.

"'I withhold not my heart from any joy,'" quoted Anne. "That is Bible authority for you, Mrs. Gibson."

"'Man is born to trouble as the sparks fly upward.' That's in the Bible, too," retorted Mrs. Gibson. The fact that she had so neatly countered Miss Shirley, B.A., put her in comparatively good humor. "I never was one to flatter, Miss Shirley, but that chip hat of yours with the blue flower kind of sets you. Your

The First Year

hair don't look so red under it, seems to me. Don't you admire a fresh young girl like this, Pauline? Wouldn't you like to be a fresh young girl yourself, Pauline?"

Pauline was too happy and excited to want to be anyone but herself just then. Anne went to the upstairs room with her to help her dress.

"It's so lovely to think of all the pleasant things that must happen today, Miss Shirley. My throat is quite well and Ma is in such a good humor. You mightn't think so, but I know she is because she is talking, even if she is sarcastic. If she was mad or riled she'd be sulking. I've peeled the potatoes and the steak is in the ice-box and Ma's blanc mange is down cellar. There's canned chicken for supper and a sponge cake in the pantry. I'm just on tenterhooks Ma'll change her mind yet. I couldn't bear it if she did. Oh, Miss Shirley, do you think I'd better wear that gray dress...really?"

"Put it on," said Anne in her best school-teacherish manner.

Pauline obeyed and emerged a transformed Pauline. The gray dress fitted her beautifully. It was collarless and had dainty lace ruffles in the elbow sleeves. When Anne had done her hair Pauline hardly knew herself.

"I hate to cover it up with that horrid old black taffeta, Miss Shirley."

But it had to be. The taffeta covered it very securely. The old hat went on...but it would be taken off, too, when she got to Louisa's...and Pauline had a new pair of shoes. Mrs. Gibson had actually allowed her to get a new pair of shoes, though she thought the heels "scandalous high."

"I'll make quite a sensation going away on the train *alone*. I hope people won't think it's a death. I wouldn't want Louisa's silver wedding to be connected in any way with the thought of death. Oh, perfume, Miss Shirley! Apple-blossom! Isn't that lovely? Just a whiff...so lady-like, I always think. Ma won't let me buy any. Oh, Miss Shirley, you won't forget to feed my dog, will you? I've left his bones in the pantry in the covered dish. I do hope"...dropping her voice to a shamed whisper..."that he won't...misbehave...in the house while you're here."

Pauline had to pass her mother's inspection before leaving. Excitement over her outing and guilt in regard to the hidden poplin combined to give her a very unusual flush. Mrs. Gibson gazed at her discontentedly.

"Oh me, oh my! Going to London to look at the Queen, are we? You've got too much color. People will think you're painted. Are you sure you ain't?"

"Oh, no, Ma...*no,* " in shocked tones.

"Mind your manners now and when you set down, cross your ankles decently. Mind you don't set in a draught or talk too much."

"I won't, Ma," promised Pauline earnestly, with a nervous glance at the clock.

"I'm sending Louisa a bottle of my sarsaparilla wine to drink the toasts in. I never cared for Louisa, but her mother was a Tackaberry. Mind you bring back the bottle and don't let her give you a kitten. Louisa's always giving people kittens."

"I won't, Ma."

"You're sure you didn't leave the soap in the water?"

"Quite sure, Ma," with another anguished glance at the clock.

"Are your shoe-laces tied?"

"Yes, Ma."

"You don't smell respectable...drenched with scent."

"Oh, no, Ma dear...just a little...the tiniest bit..."

"I said drenched and I mean drenched. There isn't a rip under your arm, is there?"

"Oh, no, Ma."

"Let me see..." inexorably.

The First Year

Pauline quaked. Suppose the skirt of the gray dress showed when she lifted her arms!

"Well, go, then." With a long sigh. "If I ain't here when you come back, remember that I want to be laid out in my lace shawl and my black satin slippers. And see that my hair is crimped."

"Do you feel any worse, Ma?" The poplin dress had made Pauline's conscience very sensitive. "If you do...I'll not go..."

"And waste the money for them shoes! 'Course you're going. And mind you don't slide down the banister."

But at this the worm turned.

"Ma! Do you think I would?"

"You did at Nancy Parker's wedding."

"Thirty-five years ago! Do you think I would do it now?"

"It's time you were off. What are you jabbering here for? Do you want to miss your train?"

Pauline hurried away and Anne sighed with relief. She had been afraid that old Mrs. Gibson had, at the last moment, been taken with a fiendish impulse to detain Pauline until the train was gone.

"Now for a little peace," said Mrs. Gibson. "This house is in an awful condition of untidiness, Miss Shirley. I hope you realize it ain't always so. Pauline hasn't known which end of her was up these last few days. Will you please set that vase an inch to the left? No, move it back again. That lamp shade is crooked. Well, that's a *little* straighter. But that blind is an inch lower than the other. I wish you'd fix it."

Anne unluckily gave the blind too energetic a twist; it escaped her fingers and went whizzing to the top. "Ah, now you see," said Mrs. Gibson.

Anne didn't see but she adjusted the blind meticulously.

"And now wouldn't you like me to make you a nice cup of tea, Mrs. Gibson?"

"I *do* need something....I'm clean wore out with all this worry and fuss. My stomach seems to be dropping out of me," said Mrs. Gibson pathetically. "Kin you make a decent cup of tea? I'd as soon drink mud as the tea some folks make."

"Marilla Cuthbert taught me how to make tea. You'll see. But first I'm going to wheel you out to the porch so that you can enjoy the sunshine."

"I ain't been out on the porch for years," objected Mrs. Gibson.

"Oh, it's so lovely today, it can't hurt you. I want you to see the crab tree in bloom. You can't see it unless you go out. And the wind is south today, so you'll get the clover scent from Norman Johnson's field. I'll bring you your tea and we'll drink it together and then I'll get my embroidery and we'll sit there and criticize everybody who passes."

"I don't hold with criticizing people," said Mrs. Gibson virtuously. "It ain't Christian. Would you mind telling me if that is all your own hair?"

"Every bit," laughed Anne.

"Pity it's red. Though red hair seems to be gitting popular now. I sort of like your laugh. That nervous giggle of poor Pauline's always gits on my nerves. Well, if I've got to git out, I s'pose I've got to. I'll likely ketch my death of cold, but the responsibility is yours, Miss Shirley. Remember I'm eighty... every day of it, though I hear old Davy Ackham has been telling all around Summerside I'm only seventy-nine. His mother was a Watt. The Watts were always jealous."

Anne moved the wheel-chair deftly out, and proved that she had a knack of arranging pillows. Soon after she brought out the tea and Mrs. Gibson deigned approval.

"Yes, this is drinkable, Miss Shirley. Ah me, for one year I had to live entirely on liquids. They never thought I'd pull through. I often think it might have been better if I hadn't. Is that the crab tree you was raving about?"

"Yes...isn't it lovely...so white against that deep blue sky?"

"It ain't poetical," was Mrs. Gibson's sole comment. But she became rather mellow after two cups of tea and the forenoon wore away until it was time to think of dinner.

"I'll go and get it ready and then I'll bring it out here on a little table."

"No, you won't, miss. No crazy monkey-shines like that for me! People would think it awful queer, us eating out here in public. I ain't denying it's kind of nice out here...though the smell of clover always makes me kind of squalmish...and the forenoon's passed awful quick to what it mostly does, but I ain't eating my dinner out-of-doors for any one. I ain't a gypsy. Mind you wash your hands clean before you cook the dinner. My, Mrs. Storey must be expecting more company. She's got all the spare-room bed-clothes airing on the line. It ain't real hospitality...just a desire for sensation. Her mother was a Carey."

The dinner Anne produced pleased even Mrs. Gibson.

"I didn't think any one who wrote for the papers could cook. But of course Marilla Cuthbert brought you up. Her mother was a Johnson. I s'pose Pauline will eat herself sick at that wedding. She don't know when she's had enough...just like her father. I've seen him gorge on strawberries when he knew he'd be doubled up with pain an hour afterwards. Did I ever show you his picture, Miss Shirley? Well, go to the spare-room and bring it down. You'll find it under the bed. Mind you don't go prying into the drawers while you're up there. But take a peep and see if there's any dust curls under the bureau. I don't trust Pauline...Ah, yes, that's him. His mother was a Walker. There's no men like that nowadays. This is a degenerate age, Miss Shirley."

"Homer said the same thing eight hundred years, B.C.," smiled Anne.

"Some of them Old Testament writers was always croaking," said Mrs. Gibson. "I daresay you're shocked to hear me say so,

Miss Shirley, but my husband was very broad in his views. I hear you're engaged...to a medical student. Medical students mostly drink, I believe...have to, to stand the dissecting-room. Never marry a man who drinks, Miss Shirley. Nor one who ain't a good provider. Thistledown and moonshine ain't much to live on, I kin tell you. Mind you clean the sink and rinse the dish-towels. I can't abide greasy dish-towels. I s'pose you'll have to feed the dog. He's too fat now, but Pauline just stuffs him. Sometimes I think I'll have to get rid of him."

"Oh, I wouldn't do that, Mrs. Gibson. There are always burglaries, you know...and your house is lonely, off here by itself. You really do need protection."

"Oh, well, have it your own way. I'd rather do anything than argue with people, 'specially when I've such a queer throbbing in the back of my neck. I s'pose it means I'm going to have a stroke."

"You need your nap. When you've had it you'll feel better. I'll tuck you up and lower your chair. Would you like to go out on the porch for your nap?"

"Sleeping in public! That'd be worse than eating. You do have the queerest ideas. You just fix me up right here in the sitting-room and draw the blinds down and shut the door to keep the flies out. I daresay you'd like a quiet spell yourself... your tongue's been going pretty steady."

Mrs. Gibson had a good long nap, but woke up in a bad humor. She would not let Anne wheel her out to the porch again.

"Want me to ketch my death in the night air, I s'pose," she grumbled, although it was only five o'clock. Nothing suited her. The drink Anne brought her was too cold...the next one wasn't cold enough...of course *anything* would do for *her*. Where was the dog? Misbehaving, no doubt. Her back ached...her knees ached...her head ached...her breast-bone ached. Nobody sympathized with her...nobody knew what she went through. Her chair was too high...her chair was too low....She wanted a shawl for her shoulders and an afghan for her knees and a cushion for her feet. And *would* Miss Shirley see where that awful draught was coming from? She could do with a cup of tea, but she didn't want to be a trouble to any one and she would soon be at rest in her grave. Maybe they might appreciate her when she was gone.

"Be the day short or be the day long, at last it weareth to evening song." There were moments when Anne thought it never would, but it did. Sunset came and Mrs. Gibson began to wonder why Pauline wasn't coming. Twilight came...still no Pauline. Night and moonshine and no Pauline.

"I knew it," said Mrs. Gibson cryptically.

"You know she can't come till Mr. Gregor comes and he's generally the last dog hung," soothed Anne. "Won't you let me put you to bed, Mrs. Gibson? You're tired...I know it's a bit of a strain having a stranger round instead of some one you're accustomed to."

The little puckery lines about Mrs. Gibson's mouth deepened obstinately.

"I'm not going to bed till that girl comes home. But if you're so anxious to be gone, *go. I* can stay alone...or die alone."

At half past nine Mrs. Gibson decided that Jim Gregor was not coming home till Monday.

"Nobody could ever depend on Jim Gregor to stay in the same mind twenty-four hours. And he thinks it's wrong to travel on Sunday even to come home. He's on your school board, ain't he? What do you really think of him and his opinions on eddication?"

Anne went wicked. After all, she had endured a good deal at Mrs. Gibson's hands that day.

"I think he's a psychological anachronism," she answered gravely.

Mrs. Gibson did not bat an eyelash.

"I agree with you," she said. But she pretended to go to sleep after that.

14

It was ten o'clock when Pauline came at last...a flushed, starry-eyed Pauline, looking ten years younger, in spite of the resumed taffeta and the old hat, and carrying a beautiful bouquet which she hurriedly presented to the grim lady in the wheel-chair.

"The bride sent you her bouquet, Ma. Isn't it lovely? Twenty-five white roses."

"Cat's hindfoot! I don't s'pose any one thought of sending me a crumb of wedding-cake. People nowadays don't seem to have any family feeling. Ah, well, I've seen the day..."

"But they did. I've a great big piece here in my bag. And everybody asked about you and sent you their love, Ma."

"Did you have a nice time?" asked Anne.

Pauline sat down on a hard chair because she knew her mother would resent it if she sat on a soft one.

"Very nice," she said cautiously. "We had a lovely wedding-dinner and Mr. Freeman, the Gull Cove minister, married Louisa and Maurice over again...."

"I call that sacrilegious...."

"And then the photographer took all our pictures. The flowers were simply wonderful. The parlor was a bower..."

"Like a funeral I s'pose..."

"And, oh, Ma. Mary Luckley was there from the west...Mrs. Flemming, you know. You remember what friends she and I always were. We used to call each other Polly and Molly...."

"Very silly names..."

"And it was so nice to see her again and have a long talk over old times. Her sister Em was there, too, with such a delicious baby."

The First Year

"You talk as if it was something to eat," grunted Mrs. Gibson. "Babies are common enough."

"Oh, no, babies are never common," said Anne, bringing a bowl of water for Mrs. Gibson's roses. "Every one is a miracle."

"Well, I had ten and I never saw much that was miraculous about any of them. Pauline, do sit still if you kin. You fidget me. I notice you ain't asking how *I* got along. But I s'pose I couldn't expect it."

"I can tell how you got along without asking, Ma...you look so bright and cheerful." Pauline was still so uplifted by the day that she could be a little arch even with her mother. "I'm sure you and Miss Shirley had a nice time together."

"We got on well enough. I just let her have her own way. I admit it's the first time in years I've heard some interesting conversation. I ain't so near the grave as some people would like to make out. Thank heaven I've never got deaf or childish. Well, I s'pose the next thing you'll be off to the moon. And I s'pose they didn't care for my sarsaparilla wine by any chance?"

"Oh, they did. They thought it delicious."

"You've taken your own time telling me that. Did you bring back the bottle...or would it be too much to expect you'd remember that?"

"The...the bottle got broke," faltered Pauline. "Some one knocked it over in the pantry. But Louisa gave me another just exactly the same, Ma, so you needn't worry."

"I've had that bottle ever since I started housekeeping. Louisa's can't be exactly the same. They don't make such bottles nowadays. I wish you'd bring me another shawl. I'm sneezing...I expect I've got a terrible cold. You can't either of you seem to remember not to let the night air git at me. Likely it'll bring my neuritis back."

An old neighbor up the street dropped in at this juncture and Pauline snatched at the chance to go a little way with Anne.

"Good night, Miss Shirley," said Mrs. Gibson quite graciously. "I'm much obliged to you. If there was more people like you in this town, it would be the better for it." She grinned toothlessly and pulled Anne down to her. "I don't care what people say...I think you're real nice-looking," she whispered.

Pauline and Anne walked along the street, through the cool, green night, and Pauline let herself go, as she had not dared do before her mother.

"Oh, Miss Shirley, it was heavenly. How can I ever repay you? I've never spent such a wonderful day...I'll live on it for years. It was such fun being a bridesmaid again. And Captain Isaac Kent was groomsman. He...he used to be an old beau of mine....well, no, hardly a beau....I don't think he ever had any real intentions but we drove round together...and he paid me two compliments. He said, 'I remember how pretty you looked at Louisa's wedding in that wine-colored dress.' Wasn't it wonderful his remembering the dress? And he said, 'Your hair looks just as much like molasses taffy as it ever did.' There wasn't anything improper in his saying that, was there, Miss Shirley?"

"Nothing whatever."

"Lou and Molly and I had such a nice supper together after everybody had gone. I was so hungry...I don't think I've been so hungry for years. It was so nice to eat just what I wanted and nobody to warn me about things that wouldn't agree with my stomach. After supper Mary and I went over to her old home and wandered around the garden, talking over old times. We saw the lilac bushes we planted years ago. We had some beautiful summers together when we were girls. Then when it came sunset we went down to the dear old shore and sat there on a rock in silence. There was a bell ringing down at the harbor and it was lovely to feel the wind from the sea again and see the stars trembling in the water. I had forgotten night on the gulf could be so beautiful. When it got quite dark we went back and

Mr. Gregor was ready to start...and so," concluded Pauline with a laugh, "The Old Woman Got Home That Night."

"I wish...I wish you didn't have such a hard time at home, Pauline...."

"Oh, dear Miss Shirley, I won't mind it now," said Pauline quickly. "After all, poor Ma needs me. And it's nice to be needed, my dear."

Yes, it was nice to be needed. Anne thought of this in her tower room, where Dusty Miller, having evaded both Rebecca Dew and the widows, was curled up on her bed. She thought of Pauline trotting back to her bondage but companied by "the immortal spirit of one happy day."

"I hope some one will always need me," said Anne to Dusty Miller. "And it's wonderful, Dusty Miller, to be able to give happiness to somebody. It has made me feel so rich, giving Pauline this day. But, oh, Dusty Miller, you don't think I'll ever be like Mrs. Adoniram Gibson, even if I live to be eighty? Do you, Dusty Miller?"

Dusty Miller, with rich, throaty purrs, assured her he didn't.

15

Anne went down to Bonnyview on the Friday night before the wedding. The Nelsons were giving a dinner for some family friends and wedding-guests arriving by the boat train. The big, rambling house which was Dr. Nelson's "summer home" was built among spruces on a long point with the bay on both sides and a stretch of golden-breasted dunes beyond that knew all there was to be known about winds.

Anne liked it the moment she saw it. An old stone house always looks reposeful and dignified. It fears not what rain or wind or changing fashion can do. And on this June evening it was bubbling over with young life and excitement, the laughter of girls, the greetings of old friends, buggies coming and going, children running everywhere, gifts arriving, every one in the delightful turmoil of a wedding, while Dr. Nelson's two black cats, who rejoiced in the names of Barnabas and Saul, sat on the railing of the veranda and watched everything like two imperturbable sable sphinxes.

Sally detached herself from a mob and whisked Anne upstairs.

"We've saved the north gable room for you. Of course you'll have to share it with at least three others. There's a perfect riot here. Father's having a tent put up for the boys down among the spruces and later on we can have cots in the glassed-in porch at the back. And we can pack most of the children in the hay-loft of course. Oh, Anne, I'm so excited. It's really no end of fun getting married. My wedding-dress just came from Montreal today. It's a *dream*...cream corded silk with a lace bertha and pearl embroidery. The loveliest gifts have come. This is your bed. Mamie Gray and Dot Fraser and Sis Palmer have the others. Mother wanted to put Amy Stewart here but I wouldn't let her. Amy hates you because she wanted to be my bridesmaid. But I couldn't have any one so fat and dumpy, could I now? Besides, she looks like somebody seasick in Nile green. Oh, Anne, Aunt Mouser is here. She came just a few minutes ago and we're simply horror-stricken. Of course we had to invite her, but we never thought of her coming before tomorrow."

"Who in the world is Aunt Mouser?"

"Dad's aunt, Mrs. James Kennedy. Oh, of course she's really Aunt Grace, but Tommy nicknamed her Aunt Mouser because she's always mousing round pouncing on things we don't want her to find out. There's no escaping her. She even gets up early in the morning for fear of missing something and she's the last to go to bed at night. But that isn't the worst. If there's a wrong thing to say she's certain to say it and she's never learned that there are questions that mustn't be asked. Dad calls her speeches 'Aunt Mouser's felicities.' I know she'll spoil the dinner. Here she comes now."

The door opened and Aunt Mouser came in...a fat, brown, pop-eyed little woman, moving in an atmosphere of moth-balls and wearing a chronically worried expression. Except for the expression she really did look a good deal like a hunting pussy-cat.

"So you're the Miss Shirley I've always heard so much of. You ain't a bit like a Miss Shirley I once knew. *She* had such beautiful eyes. Well, Sally, so you're to be married at last. Poor Nora is the only one left. Well, your mother is lucky to be rid of five of you. Eight years ago I said to her, 'Jane,' sez I, 'do you think you'll *ever* get all those girls married off?' Well, a man is nothing but trouble as I sees it and of all the uncertain things marriage is the uncertainest, but what else is there for a woman in this world? That's what I've just been saying to poor Nora. 'Mark my words, Nora,' I said to her, 'there isn't much fun in being an old maid. What's Jim Wilcox thinking of?' I said to her."

"Oh, Aunt Grace, I wish you hadn't! Jim and Nora had some sort of a quarrel last January and he's never been round since."

"I believe in saying what I think. Things is better said. I'd heard of that quarrel. That's why I asked her about him. 'It's only right,' I told her, 'that you should know they say he's driving Eleanor Pringle.' She got red and mad and flounced off. What's Vera Johnson doing here? She ain't any relation."

"Vera's always been a great friend of mine, Aunt Grace. She's going to play the wedding-march."

"Oh, she is, is she? Well, all I hope is she won't make a mistake and play the Dead March like Mrs. Tom Scott did at

Dora Best's wedding. Such a bad omen. I don't know where you're going to put the mob you've got here for the night. Some of us will have to sleep on the clothes-line I reckon."

"Oh, we'll find a place for every one, Aunt Grace."

"Well, Sally, all I hope is you won't change your mind at the last moment like Helen Summers did. It clutters things up so. Your father is in terrible high spirits. I never was one to go looking for trouble but all I hope is it ain't the forerunner of a stroke. I've seen it happen that way."

"Oh, Dad's fine, Aunt Mouser. He's just a bit excited."

"Ah, you're too young, Sally, to know all that can happen. Your mother tells me the ceremony is at high noon tomorrow. The fashions in weddings are changing like everything else and not for the better. When *I* was married it was in the evening and my father laid in twenty gallons of liquor for the wedding. Ah, dear me, times ain't what they used to be. What's the matter with Mercy Daniels? I met her on the stairs and her complexion has got terrible muddy."

"'The quality of mercy is not strained,'" giggled Sally, wriggling into her dinner-dress.

"Don't quote the Bible flippantly," rebuked Aunt Mouser. "You must excuse her, Miss Shirley. She just ain't used to getting married. Well, all I hope is the groom won't have a hunted look like so many of them do. I s'pose they do feel that way, but they needn't show it so plain. And I hope he won't forget the ring. Upton Hardy did. Him and Flora had to be married with a ring off one of the curtain poles. Well, I'll be taking another look at the wedding-presents. You've got a lot of nice things, Sally. All I hope is it won't be as hard to keep the handles of them spoons polished as I think likely."

Dinner that night in the big, glassed-in porch was a gay affair. Chinese lanterns had been hung all about it, shedding mellow-tinted lights on the pretty dresses and glossy hair and

The First Year

white, unlined brows of girls. Barnabas and Saul sat like ebony statues on the broad arms of the Doctor's chair, where he fed them tidbits alternately.

"Just about as bad as Parker Pringle," said Aunt Mouser. "*He* has his dog sit at the table with a chair and napkin of his own. Well, sooner or later there'll be a judgment."

It was a large party, for all the married Nelson girls and their husbands were there, besides ushers and bridesmaids; and it was a merry one, in spite of Aunt Mouser's "felicities"...or perhaps because of them. Nobody took Aunt Mouser very seriously; she was evidently a joke among the young fry. When she said, on being introduced to Gordon Hill, "Well, well, you ain't a bit like I expected. I always thought Sally would pick out a tall handsome man," ripples of laughter ran through the porch. Gordon Hill, who was on the short side and called no more than "pleasant-faced" by his best friends, knew he would never hear the last of it. When she said to Dot Fraser, "Well, well, a new dress every time I see you! All I hope is your father's purse will be able to stand it for a few years yet," Dot could, of course, have boiled her in oil, but some of the other girls found it amusing. And when Aunt Mouser mournfully remarked, apropos of the preparations of the wedding-dinner, "All I hope is everybody will get her teaspoons afterwards. Five were missing after Gertie Paul's wedding. They never turned up," Mrs. Nelson, who had borrowed three dozen and the sisters-in-law she had borrowed them from all looked harried. But Dr. Nelson haw-hawed cheerfully.

"We'll make everyone turn out their pockets before they go, Aunt Grace."

"Ah, you may laugh, Samuel. It is no joking-matter to have anything like that happen in the family. *Some one* must have those teaspoons. I never go anywhere but I keep my eyes open for them. I'd know them wherever I saw them, though it was twenty-eight years ago. Poor Nora was just a baby then. You remember you had her there, Jane, in a little white embroidered dress? Twenty-eight years! Ah, Nora, you're getting on, though in this light you don't show your age so much."

Nora did not join in the laugh that followed. She looked as if she might flash lightning at any moment. In spite of her daffodil-hued dress and the pearls in her dark hair, she made Anne think of a black moth. In direct contrast with Sally, who was a cool, snowy blonde, Nora Nelson had magnificent black hair, dusky eyes, heavy black brows and velvety red cheeks. Her nose was beginning to look a trifle hawk-like and she had never been accounted pretty, but Anne felt an odd attraction to her in spite of her sulky, smoldering expression. She felt that she would prefer Nora as a friend to the popular Sally.

They had a dance after dinner and music and laughter came tumbling out of the broad low windows of the old stone house in a flood. At ten Nora had disappeared. Anne was a little tired of the noise and merriment. She slipped through the hall to a back door that opened almost on the bay, and flitted down a flight of rocky steps to the shore, past a little grove of pointed firs. How divine the cool salt air was after the sultry evening! How exquisite the silver patterns of moonlight on the bay! How dream-like that ship which had sailed at the rising of the moon and was now approaching the harbor bar! It was a night when you might expect to stray into a dance of mermaids.

Nora was hunched up in the grim black shadow of a rock by the water's edge, looking more like a thunderstorm than ever.

"May I sit with you for a while?" asked Anne. "I'm a little tired of dancing and it's a shame to miss this wonderful night. I envy you with the whole harbor for a back yard like this."

"What would you feel like at a time like this if you had no beau?" asked Nora abruptly and sullenly. "Or any likelihood of one," she added still more sullenly.

The First Year

"I think it must be your own fault if you haven't," said Anne, sitting down beside her. Nora found herself telling Anne her troubles. There was always something about Anne that made people tell her their troubles.

"You're saying that to be polite of course. You needn't. You know as well as I do that I'm not a girl men are likely to fall in love with...I'm 'the plain Miss Nelson.' It *isn't* my fault that I haven't anybody. I couldn't stand it in there any longer. I had to come down here and just let myself be unhappy. I'm tired of smiling and being agreeable to every one and pretending not to care when they give me digs about not being married. I'm not going to pretend any longer. I *do* care...I care horribly. I'm the only one of the Nelson girls left. Five of us are married or will be tomorrow. You heard Aunt Mouser casting my age up to me at the dinnertable. And I heard her telling Mother before dinner that I had 'aged quite a bit' since last summer. Of course I have. I'm twenty-eight. In twelve more years I'll be forty. How will I endure life at forty, Anne, if I haven't got any roots of my own by that time?"

"I wouldn't mind what a foolish old woman said."

"Oh, wouldn't you? You haven't a nose like mine. I'll be as beaky as Father in ten more years. And I suppose you wouldn't care, either, if you'd waited years for a man to propose...and he just wouldn't?"

"Oh, yes, I think I would care about *that.*"

"Well, that's my predicament exactly. Oh, I know you've heard of Jim Wilcox and me. It's such an old story. He's been hanging around me for years...but he's never said anything about getting married."

"Do you care for him?"

"Of course I care. I've always pretended I didn't but, as I've told you, I'm through with pretending. And he's never been near me since last January. We had a fight...but we've had hundreds of fights. He always came back before...but he hasn't come this time...and he never will. He doesn't want to. Look at his house across the bay, shining in the moonlight. I suppose he's there... and I'm here...and all the harbor between us. That's the way it always will be. It...it's terrible! And I can't do a thing."

"If you sent for him, wouldn't he come back?"

"Send for him! Do you think I'd do *that*? I'd die first. If he wants to come, there's nothing to prevent him coming. If he doesn't, *I* don't want him to. Yes, I do...I do! I love Jim...and I want to get married. I want to have a home of my own and be 'Mrs.' and shut Aunt Mouser's mouth. Oh, I wish I could be Barnabas or Saul for a few moments just to swear at her! If she calls me 'poor Nora' again I'll throw a scuttle at her. But after all, she only says what everybody thinks. Mother has despaired long ago of my ever marrying, so she leaves me alone, but the rest rag me. I hate Sally...of course I'm dreadful...but I hate her. She's getting a nice husband and a lovely home. It isn't fair she should have everything and I nothing. She isn't better or cleverer or much prettier than me...only luckier. I suppose you think I'm awful...not that I care what you think."

"I think you're very, very tired, after all these weeks of preparation and strain, and that things which were always hard have become *too* hard all at once."

"You understand...oh, yes, I always knew you would. I've wanted to be friends with you, Anne Shirley. I like the way you laugh. I've always wished I could laugh like that. I'm not as sulky as I look...it's these eyebrows. I really think they're what scare the men away. I never had a real girl friend in my life. But of course I always had Jim. We've been...friends...ever since we were kids. Why, I used to put a light up in that little window in the attic whenever I wanted him over particularly and he'd sail across at once. We went everywhere together. No other boy ever had a chance...not that any one wanted it, I suppose. And now it's all over. He was just tired of me and was glad of the excuse of a quarrel to get free. Oh, won't I hate you tomorrow because I've told you this!"

"Why?"

"We always hate people who surprise our secrets, I suppose," said Nora drearily. "But there's something gets into you at a wedding...and I just don't care...I don't care for anything. Oh, Anne Shirley, I'm so miserable! Just let me have a good cry on your shoulder. I've *got* to smile and look happy all day tomorrow. Sally thinks it's because I'm superstitious that I wouldn't be her bridesmaid....Three times a bridesmaid, never a bride,' you know. 'Tisn't! I just couldn't endure to stand there and hear her saying, 'I will,' and know I'd never have a chance to say it for Jim. I'd have flung back my head and howled. I want to be a bride...and have a trousseau...and monogrammed linen...and lovely presents. Even Aunt Mouser's silver butter-dish. She always gives a butter-dish to every bride...awful things with tops like the dome of St. Peter's. We could have had it on the breakfast table just for Jim to make fun of. Anne, I think I'm going crazy."

The dance was over when the girls went back to the house, hand in hand. People were being stowed away for the night. Tommy Nelson was taking Barnabas and Saul to the barn. Aunt Mouser was still sitting on a sofa, thinking of all the dreadful things she hoped wouldn't happen on the morrow.

"I hope nobody will get up and give a reason why they shouldn't be joined together. *That* happened at Tillie Hatfield's wedding."

"No such good luck for Gordon as that," said the groomsman. Aunt Mouser fixed him with a stony brown eye.

"Young man, marriage isn't exactly a joke."

"You bet it isn't," said the unrepentant. "Hello, Nora, when are we going to have a chance to dance at your wedding?"

Nora did not answer in words. She went closer up to him and deliberately slapped him, first on one side of his face and then on the other. The slaps were not make-believe ones. Then she went upstairs without looking behind her.

"That girl," said Aunt Mouser, "is overwrought."

16

The forenoon of Saturday passed in a whirl of last-minute things. Anne, shrouded in one of Mrs. Nelson's aprons, spent it in the kitchen helping Nora with the salads. Nora was all prickles, evidently repenting, as she had foretold, her confidences of the night before.

"We'll be all tired out for a month," she snapped, "and Father can't really afford all this splurge. But Sally was set on having what she calls a 'pretty wedding' and Father gave in. He's always spoiled her."

"Spite and jealousy," said Aunt Mouser, suddenly popping her head out of the pantry, where she was driving Mrs. Nelson frantic with her hopings against hope.

"She's right," said Nora bitterly to Anne. "Quite right. I *am* spiteful and jealous...I hate the very look of happy people. But all the same I'm not sorry I slapped Jud Taylor's face last night. I'm only sorry I didn't tweak his nose into the bargain. Well, that finishes the salads. They do look pretty. I love fussing things up when I'm normal. Oh, after all, I hope everything will go off nicely for Sally's sake. I suppose I do love her underneath everything, though just now I feel as if I hated every one and Jim Wilcox worst of all."

"Well, all I hope is the groom won't be missing just before the ceremony," floated out from the pantry in Aunt Mouser's lugubrious tones. "Austin Creed was. He just forgot he was to be married that day. The Creeds were always forgetful, but I call that carrying things too far."

The two girls looked at each other and laughed. Nora's whole face changed when she laughed...lightened...glowed...rippled. And then some one came out to tell her that Barnabas had been sick on the stairs...too many chicken livers probably. Nora rushed off to repair the damage and Aunt Mouser came out of the pantry to hope that the wedding-cake wouldn't disappear as had happened at Alma Clark's wedding ten years before.

By noon everything was in immaculate readiness...the table laid, the beds beautifully dressed, baskets of flowers everywhere; and in the big north room upstairs Sally and her three bridesmaids were in quivering splendor. Anne, in her Nile green dress and hat, looked at herself in the mirror, and wished that Gilbert could see her.

"You're wonderful," said Nora half enviously.

"You're looking wonderful yourself, Nora. That smoke-blue chiffon and that picture hat bring out the gloss of your hair and the blue of your eyes."

"There's nobody to care how I look," said Nora bitterly. "Well, watch me grin, Anne. I mustn't be the death's head at the feast, I suppose. I have to play the wedding-march after all... Vera's got a terrible headache. I feel more like playing the Dead March, as Aunt Mouser foreboded."

Aunt Mouser, who had wandered round all the morning, getting in everybody's way, in a none too clean old kimono and a wilted "boudoir cap," now appeared resplendent in maroon grosgrain and told Sally one of her sleeves didn't fit and she hoped nobody's petticoat would show below her dress as had happened at Annie Crewson's wedding. Mrs. Nelson came in and cried because Sally looked so lovely in her wedding-dress.

"Now, now, don't be sentimental, Jane," soothed Aunt Mouser. "You've still got one daughter left...and likely to have her by all accounts. Tears ain't lucky at weddings. Well, all I hope is nobody'll drop dead like old Uncle Cromwell at Roberta Pringle's wedding, right in the middle of the ceremony. The bride spent two weeks in bed from shock."

With this inspiring send-off the bridal party went downstairs, to the strains of Nora's wedding-march somewhat stormily played, and Sally and Gordon were married without anybody dropping dead or forgetting the ring. It *was* a pretty wedding group and even Aunt Mouser gave up worrying about the universe for a few moments. "After all," she told Sally hopefully later on, "even if you ain't very happy married, it's likely you'd be more unhappy not." Nora alone continued to glower from the piano stool, but she went up to Sally and gave her a fierce hug, wedding-veil and all.

"So that's finished," said Nora drearily, when the dinner was over and the bridal party and most of the guests had gone. She glanced around at the room which looked as forlorn and disheveled as rooms always do in the aftermath...a faded, trampled corsage lying on the floor...chairs awry...a torn piece of lace...two dropped handkerchiefs...crumbs the children had scattered...a dark stain on the ceiling where the water from a jug Aunt Mouser had overturned in a guest-room had seeped through.

"I must clear up this mess," went on Nora savagely. "There's a lot of young fry waiting for the boat train and some staying over Sunday. They're going to wind up with a bonfire on the shore and a moonlit rock dance. You can imagine how much I feel like moonlight dancing. *I* want to go to bed and cry."

"A house after a wedding is over does seem a rather forsaken place," said Anne. "But I'll help you clear up and then we'll have a cup of tea."

The First Year

"Anne Shirley, do you think a cup of tea is a panacea for everything? It's you who ought to be the old maid, not me. Never mind. I don't want to be horrid, but I suppose it's my native disposition. I hate the thought of this shore dance more than the wedding. Jim always used to be at our shore dances. Anne, I've made up my mind to go and train for a nurse. I know I'll hate it...and heaven help my future patients...but I'm not going to hang around Summerside and be teased about being on the shelf any longer. Well, let's tackle this pile of greasy plates and look as if we liked it."

"I do like it...I've always liked washing dishes. It's fun to make dirty things clean and shining again."

"Oh, you ought to be in a museum," snapped Nora.

By moonrise everything was ready for the shore dance. The boys had a huge bonfire of driftwood ablaze on the point, and the waters of the harbor were creaming and shimmering in the moonlight. Anne was expecting to enjoy herself hugely, but a glimpse of Nora's face, as the latter went down the steps carrying a basket of sandwiches, gave her pause.

"She's so unhappy. If there was anything I could do!"

An idea popped into Anne's head. She had always been a prey to impulse. Darting into the kitchen, she snatched up a little hand-lamp alight there, sped up the back stairs and up another flight to the attic. She set the light in the dormer-window that looked out across the harbor. The trees hid it from the dancers.

"He may see it and come. I suppose Nora will be furious with me, but that won't matter if he only comes. And now to wrap up a bit of wedding-cake for Rebecca Dew."

Jim Wilcox did not come. Anne gave up looking for him after a while and forgot him in the merriment of the evening. Nora had disappeared and Aunt Mouser had for a wonder gone to bed. It was eleven o'clock when the revelry ceased and the tired moonlighters yawned their way upstairs. Anne was so sleepy, she never thought of the light in the attic. But at two o'clock Aunt Mouser crept into the room and flashed a candle in the girls' faces.

"Goodness, what's the matter?" gasped Dot Fraser, sitting up in bed.

"S-s-s-sh," warned Aunt Mouser, her eyes nearly popping out of her head, "I think there's some one in the house...I *know* there is. What is that noise?"

"Sounds like a cat mewing or a dog barking," giggled Dot.

"Nothing of the sort," said Aunt Mouser severely. "I know there's a dog barking in the barn, but that is not what wakened me. It was a bump...a loud, distinct bump."

"'From ghosties and ghoulies and long-legged beasties and things that go bump in the night, good Lord, deliver us,'" murmured Anne.

"Miss Shirley, this ain't any laughing-matter. There's burglars in this house. I'm going to call Samuel."

Aunt Mouser disappeared and the girls looked at each other.

"Do you suppose...all the wedding-presents are down in the library..." said Anne.

"I'm going to get up, anyhow," said Mamie. "Anne, did you ever see anything like Aunt Mouser's face when she held the candle low and the shadows fell upward...and all those wisps of hair hanging about it? Talk of the Witch of Endor!"

Four girls in kimonos slipped out into the hall. Aunt Mouser was coming along it, followed by Dr. Nelson in dressing-gown and slippers. Mrs. Nelson, who couldn't find her kimono, was sticking a terrified face out of her door.

"Oh, Samuel...don't take any risks...if it's burglars they may shoot...."

"Nonsense! I don't believe there's anything," said the Doctor.

"I tell you I heard a bump," quavered Aunt Mouser.

A couple of boys joined the party. They crept cautiously down the stairs with the Doctor at the head and Aunt Mouser, candle in one hand and poker in the other, bringing up the rear.

There were undoubtedly noises in the library. The Doctor opened the door and walked in.

Barnabas, who had contrived to be overlooked in the library when Saul had been taken to the barn, was sitting on the back of the chesterfield, blinking amused eyes. Nora and a young man were standing in the middle of the room, which was dimly lighted by another flickering candle. The young man had his arms around Nora and was holding a large white handkerchief to her face.

"He's chloroforming her!" shrieked Aunt Mouser, letting the poker fall with a tremendous crash.

The young man turned, dropped the handkerchief and looked foolish. Yet he was a rather nice-looking young man, with crinkly russet eyes and crinkly red-brown hair, not to mention a chin that gave the world assurance of a chin.

Nora snatched the handkerchief up and applied it to her face.

"Jim Wilcox, what does this mean?" said the Doctor, with exceeding sternness.

"*I* don't know what it means," said Jim Wilcox rather sulkily. "All I know is Nora signaled for me. I didn't see the light till I got home at one from a Masonic banquet in Summerside. And I sailed right over."

"I didn't signal for you," stormed Nora. "For pity's sake don't look like that, Father. I wasn't asleep...I was sitting at my window...I hadn't undressed...and I saw a man coming up from the shore. When he got near the house I knew it was Jim, so I ran down. And I...I ran into the library door and made my nose bleed. He's just been trying to stop it."

"I jumped in at the window and knocked over that bench...."

"I told you I heard a bump," said Aunt Mouser.

"... and now Nora says she didn't signal for me, so I'll just relieve you of my unwelcome presence, with apologies to all concerned."

"It's really too bad to have disturbed your night's rest and brought you all the way over the bay on a wild-goose chase," said Nora as icily as possible, consistent with hunting for a bloodless spot on Jim's handkerchief.

"Wild-*goose* chase is right," said the Doctor.

"You'd better try a door-key down your back," said Aunt Mouser.

"It was I who put the light in the window," said Anne shamefacedly, "and then I forgot..."

"You dared!" cried Nora, "I'll never forgive you..."

"Have you all gone crazy?" said the Doctor irritably. "What's all this fuss about, anyhow? For heaven's sake put that window down, Jim...there's a wind blowing in fit to chill you to the bone. Nora, hang your head back and your nose will be all right."

Nora was shedding tears of rage and shame. Mingled with the blood on her face they made her a fearsome sight. Jim Wilcox looked as if he wished the floor would open and gently drop him in the cellar.

"Well," said Aunt Mouser belligerently, "all you can do now is marry her, Jim Wilcox. She'll never get a husband if it gets round that she was found here with you at two o'clock at night."

"Marry her!" cried Jim in exasperation. "What have I wanted all my life but to marry her...never wanted anything else!"

"Then why didn't you say so long ago?" demanded Nora, whirling about to face him.

"Say so? You've snubbed and frozen and jeered at me for years. You've gone out of your way times without number to show me how you despised me. I didn't think it was the least use to ask you. And last January you said..."

"You goaded me into saying it..."

The First Year

"*I* goaded you! I like that! You picked a quarrel with me just to get rid of me...."

"I didn't...I..."

"And yet I was fool enough to tear over here in the dead of night because I thought you'd put our old signal in the window and wanted me! Ask you to marry me! Well, I'll ask you now and have done with it and you can have the fun of turning me down before all this gang. Nora Edith Nelson, will you marry me?"

"Oh, won't I...won't I!" cried Nora so shamelessly that even Barnabas blushed for her.

Jim gave her one incredulous look...then sprang at her. Perhaps her nose had stopped bleeding...perhaps it hadn't. It didn't matter.

"I think you've all forgotten that this is the Sabbath morn," said Aunt Mouser, who had just remembered it herself. "I could do with a cup of tea if any one would make it. I ain't used to demonstrations like this. All I hope is poor Nora has really landed him at last. At least, she has witnesses."

They went to the kitchen and Mrs. Nelson came down and made tea for them...all except Jim and Nora, who remained closeted in the library with Barnabas for chaperon. Anne did not see Nora until the morning...such a different Nora, ten years younger, flushed with happiness.

"I owe this to you, Anne. If you hadn't set the light...though just for two and a half minutes last night I could have chewed your ears off!"

"And to think I slept through it all," moaned Tommy Nelson heart-brokenly.

But the last word was with Aunt Mouser.

"Well, all I hope is it won't be a case of marrying in haste and repenting at leisure."

17

(Extract from letter to Gilbert.)

"School closed today. Two months of Green Gables and dew-wet, spicy ferns ankle-deep along the brook and lazy, dappling shadows in Lover's Lane and wild strawberries in Mr. Bell's pasture and the dark loveliness of firs in the Haunted Wood! My very soul has wings.

"Jen Pringle brought me a bouquet of lilies of the valley and wished me a happy vacation. She's coming down to spend a week-end with me some time. Talk of miracles!

"But little Elizabeth is heart-broken. I wanted her for a visit, too, but Mrs. Campbell did not 'deem it advisable.' Luckily, I hadn't said anything to Elizabeth about it, so she was spared that disappointment.

"I believe I'll be Lizzie all the time you're away, Miss Shirley,' she told me. 'I'll *feel* like Lizzie anyway.'

"'But think of the fun we'll have when I come back,' I said. 'Of course you won't be Lizzie. There's no such person as Lizzie in you. And I'll write you every week, little Elizabeth.'

"'Oh, Miss Shirley, will you! I've never had a letter in my life. Won't it be fun! And I'll write you if they'll let me have a stamp. If they don't, you'll know I'm thinking of you just the same. I've called the chipmunk in the back yard after you...Shirley. You don't mind, do you? I thought at first of calling it Anne Shirley...but then I thought that mightn't be respectful...and, anyway, Anne doesn't sound chipmunky. Besides, it might be a gentleman chipmunk. Chipmunks are such darling things, aren't they? But the Woman says they eat the rosebush roots.'

"'She would!' I said.

"I asked Katherine Brooke where she was going to spend the summer and she briefly answered, 'Here. Where did you suppose?'

"I felt as if I ought to ask her to Green Gables, but I just couldn't. Of course I don't suppose she'd have come, anyway. And she's such a kill-joy. She'd spoil everything. But when I think of her alone in that cheap boarding-house all summer, my conscience gives me unpleasant jabs.

"Dusty Miller brought in a live snake the other day and dropped it on the floor of the kitchen. If Rebecca Dew could have turned pale she would have. 'This *is* really the last straw!' she said. But Rebecca Dew is just a little peevish these days because she has to spend all her spare time picking big gray-green beetles off the rose trees and dropping them in a can of kerosene. She thinks there are entirely too many insects in the world.

"'It's just going to be eaten up by them some day,' she predicts mournfully.

"Nora Nelson is to be married to Jim Wilcox in September. Very quietly...no fuss, no guests, no bridesmaids. Nora told me that was the only way to escape Aunt Mouser, and she will *not* have Aunt Mouser to see her married. I'm to be present, however, sort of unofficially. Nora says Jim would never have come back if I hadn't set that light in the window. He was going to sell his store and go west. Well, when I think of all the matches I'm supposed to have made...

"Sally says they'll fight most of their time but that they'll be happier fighting with each other than agreeing with anybody else. But I don't think they'll fight...much. I think it is just misunderstanding that makes most of the trouble in the world. You and I for so long, now...

"Good night, belovedest. Your sleep will be sweet if there is any influence in the wishes of

"YOUR OWN.

"P.S. The above sentence is quoted verbatim from a letter of Aunt Chatty's grandmother."

The Second Year

1

"Windy Poplars,
"Spook's Lane,
"September 14th.

"I can hardly reconcile myself to the fact that our beautiful two months are over. They *were* beautiful, weren't they, dearest? And now it will be only two years before...

(Several paragraphs omitted.)

"But there has been a good deal of pleasure in coming back to Windy Poplars...to my own private tower and my own special chair and my own lofty bed...and even Dusty Miller basking on the kitchen window-sill.

"The widows were glad to see me and Rebecca Dew said frankly, 'It's good to have you back.' Little Elizabeth felt the same way. We had a rapturous meeting at the green gate.

"'I was a little afraid you might have got into Tomorrow before me,' said little Elizabeth.

"'Isn't this a lovely evening?' I said.

"'Where you are it's always a lovely evening, Miss Shirley,' said little Elizabeth.

"Talk of compliments!

"'How have you put in the summer, darling?' I asked.

"'Thinking,' said little Elizabeth softly, 'of all the lovely things that will happen in Tomorrow.'

"Then we went up to the tower room and read a story about elephants. Little Elizabeth is very much interested in elephants at present.

The Second Year

"'There is something bewitching about the very name of elephant, isn't there?' she said gravely, holding her chin in her small hands after a fashion she has. 'I expect to meet lots of elephants in Tomorrow.'

"We put an elephant park in our map of fairyland. It is no use looking superior and disdainful, my Gilbert, as I know you will be looking when you read this. Not a bit of use. The world always *will* have fairies. It can't get along without them. And somebody has to supply them.

"It's rather nice to be back in school, too. Katherine Brooke isn't any more companionable but my pupils seemed glad to see me and Jen Pringle wants me to help her make the tin halos for the angels' heads in a Sunday-school concert.

"I think the course of study this year will be much more interesting than last year. Canadian History has been added to the curriculum. I have to give a little 'lecturette' tomorrow on the War of 1812. It seems so strange to read over the stories of those old wars...things that can never happen again. I don't suppose any of us will ever have more than an academic interest in 'battles long ago.' It's impossible to think of Canada ever being at war again. I am so thankful that phase of history is over.

"We are going to reorganize the Dramatic Club at once and canvass every family connected with the school for a subscription. Lewis Allen and I are going to take the Dawlish Road as our territory and canvass it next Saturday afternoon. Lewis will try to kill two birds with one stone, as he is competing for a prize offered by *Country Homes* for the best photograph of an attractive farmhouse. The prize is twenty-five dollars and that will mean a badly needed new suit and overcoat for Lewis. He worked on a farm all summer and is doing housework and waiting on the table at his boarding-house again this year. He must hate it, but he never says a word about it. I do like Lewis...he is so plucky and ambitious, with a charming grin in place of a smile. And he really isn't over-strong. I was afraid last year he would break down. But his summer on the farm seems to have built him up a bit. This is his last year in High and then he hopes to achieve a year at Queen's. The widows are going to ask him to Sunday-night supper as often as possible this winter. Aunt Kate and I have had a conference on ways and means and I persuaded her to let me put up the extras. Of course we didn't try to persuade Rebecca Dew. I merely asked Aunt Kate in Rebecca's hearing if I could have Lewis Allen in on Sunday nights at least twice a month. Aunt Kate said coldly she was afraid they couldn't afford it, in addition to their usual lonely girl.

"Rebecca Dew uttered a cry of anguish.

"This *is* the last straw. Getting so poor we can't afford a bite now and again to a poor, hard-working, sober boy who is trying to get an education! You pay more for liver for That Cat and him ready to burst. Well, take a dollar off my wages and have him.'

"The gospel according to Rebecca was accepted. Lewis Allen is coming and neither Dusty Miller's liver nor Rebecca Dew's wages will be less. Dear Rebecca Dew!

"Aunt Chatty crept into my room last night to tell me she wanted to get a beaded cape but that Aunt Kate thought she was too old for it and her feelings had been hurt.

"'Do you think I am, Miss Shirley? I don't want to be undignified...but I've always wanted a beaded cape so much. I always thought they were what you might call jaunty...and now they're in again."

"Too old! Of course you're not too old, dearest,' I assured her. 'Nobody is ever too old to wear just what she wants to wear. You wouldn't *want* to wear it if you were too old.' 'I shall get it and defy Kate,' said Aunt Chatty, anything but defiantly. But I think she will...and I think I know how to reconcile Aunt Kate.

"I'm alone in my tower. Outside there is a still, still night and the silence is velvety. Not even the poplars are stirring. I have just leaned out of my window and blown a kiss in the direction of somebody not a hundred miles away from Kingsport."

2

The Dawlish Road was a meandering sort of road, and the afternoon was made for wanderers...or so Anne and Lewis thought as they prowled along it, now and then pausing to enjoy a sudden sapphire glimpse of the strait through the trees or to snap a particularly lovely bit of scenery or picturesque little house in a leafy hollow. It was not, perhaps, quite so pleasant to call at the houses themselves and ask for subscriptions for the benefit of the Dramatic Club, but Anne and Lewis took turns doing the talking...he taking on the women while Anne manipulated the men.

"Take the men if you're going in that dress and hat," Rebecca Dew had advised. "I've had a good bit of experience in canvassing in my day and it all went to show that the better-dressed and better-looking you are the more money...or promise of it...you'll get, if it's the men you have to tackle. But if it's the women, put on the oldest and ugliest things you have."

"Isn't a road an interesting thing, Lewis?" said Anne dreamily. "Not a straight road, but one with ends and kinks around which anything of beauty and surprise may be lurking. I've always loved bends in roads."

"Where does this Dawlish Road go to?" asked Lewis practically...though at the same moment he was reflecting that Miss Shirley's voice always made him think of spring.

"I might be horrid and school-teacherish, Lewis, and say that it doesn't go anywhere...it stays right here. But I won't. As to where it goes or where it leads to...who cares? To the end of the world and back, perhaps. Remember what Emerson says...'Oh, what have I to do with time?' That's our motto for today. I expect the universe will muddle on if we let it alone for a while. Look at those cloud shadows...and that tranquillity of green valleys...and that house with an apple tree at each of its corners. Imagine it in spring. This is one of the days people *feel* alive and every wind of the world is a sister. I'm glad there are so many clumps of spice ferns along this road...spice ferns with gossamer webs on them. It brings back the days when I pretended...or believed...I think I really did believe...that gossamer webs were fairies' table-cloths."

They found a wayside spring in a golden hollow and sat down on a moss that seemed made of tiny ferns, to drink from a cup that Lewis twisted out of birch bark.

"You never know the real joy of drinking till you're dry with thirst and find water," he said. "That summer I worked out west on the railroad they were building, I got lost on the prairie one hot day and wandered for hours. I thought I'd die of thirst and then I came to a settler's shack, and he had a little spring like this in a clump of willows. How I drank! I've understood the Bible and its love of good water better ever since."

The Second Year

"We're going to get some water from another quarter," said Anne rather anxiously. "There's a shower coming up and...Lewis, I love showers, but I've got on my best hat and my second-best dress. And there isn't a house within half a mile."

"There's an old deserted blacksmith's forge over there," said Lewis, "but we'll have to run for it."

Run they did and from its shelter enjoyed the shower as they had enjoyed everything else on that carefree, gypsying afternoon. A veiled hush had fallen over the world. All the young breezes that had been whispering and rustling so importantly along the Dawlish Road had folded their wings and become motionless and soundless. Not a leaf stirred, not a shadow flickered. The maple leaves at the bend of the road turned wrong side out until the trees looked as if they were turning pale from fear. A huge cool shadow seemed to engulf them like a green wave... the cloud had reached them. Then the rain, with a rush and sweep of wind. The shower pattered sharply down on the leaves, danced along the smoking red road and pelted the roof of the old forge right merrily.

"If this lasts..." said Lewis.

But it didn't. As suddenly as it had come up, it was over and the sun was shining on the wet, glistening trees. Dazzling glimpses of blue sky appeared between the torn white clouds. Far away they could see a hill still dim with rain, but below them the cup of the valley seemed to brim over with peach-tinted mists. The woods around were pranked out with a sparkle and glitter as of springtime, and a bird began to sing in the big maple over the forge as if he were cheated into believing it really was springtime, so amazingly fresh and sweet did the world seem all at once.

"Let's explore this," said Anne, when they resumed their tramp, looking along a little side road running between old rail fences smothered in goldenrod.

"I don't think there's anybody living along that road," said Lewis doubtfully. "I think it's only a road running down to the harbor."

"Never mind...let's go along it. I've always had a weakness for side roads...something off the beaten track, lost and green and lonely. Smell the wet grass, Lewis. Besides, I feel in my bones that there *is* a house on it...a certain kind of house...a very snappable house."

Anne's bones did not deceive her. Soon there was a house... and a snappable house to boot. It was a quaint, old-fashioned one, low in the eaves, with square, small-paned windows. Big willows stretched patriarchal arms over it and an apparent wilderness of perennials and shrubs crowded all about it. It was weather-gray and shabby, but the big barns beyond it were snug and prosperous-looking, up-to-date in every respect. "I've always heard, Miss Shirley, that when a man's barns are better than his house, it's a sign that his income exceeds his expenditure," said Lewis, as they sauntered up the deep-rutted grassy lane.

"I should think it was a sign that he thought more of his horses than of his family," laughed Anne. "I'm not expecting a subscription to our club here, but that's the most likely house for a prize contest we've encountered yet. It's grayness won't matter in a photograph."

"This lane doesn't look as if it were much traveled," said Lewis with a shrug. "Evidently the folks who live here aren't strongly sociable. I'm afraid we'll find they don't even know what a dramatic club is. Anyhow, I'm going to secure my picture before we rouse any of them from their lair."

The house seemed deserted, but after the picture was taken they opened a little white gate, crossed the yard and knocked on a faded blue kitchen door, the front door evidently being like that of Windy Poplars, more for show than for use...if a door literally hidden in Virginia creeper could be said to be for show.

The Second Year 381

They expected at least the civility which they had hitherto met in their calls, whether backed up with generosity or not. Consequently they were decidedly taken aback when the door was jerked open and on the threshold appeared, not the smiling farmer's wife or daughter they had expected to see, but a tall, broad-shouldered man of fifty, with grizzled hair and bushy eyebrows, who demanded unceremoniously,

"What do you want?"

"We have called, hoping to interest you in our High School Dramatic Club," began Anne, rather lamely. But she was spared further effort.

"Never heard of it. Don't want to hear about it. Nothing to do with it," was the uncompromising interruption, and the door was promptly shut in their faces.

"I believe we've been snubbed," said Anne as they walked away.

"Nice amiable gentleman, that," grinned Lewis. "I'm sorry for his wife, if he has one."

"I don't think he can have, or she would civilize him a trifle," said Anne, trying to recover her shattered poise. "I wish Rebecca Dew had the handling of him. But we've got his house, at least, and I've a premonition that it's going to win the prize. Bother! I've just got a pebble in my shoe and I'm going to sit down on my gentleman's stone dyke, with or without his permission, and remove it."

"Luckily it's out of sight of the house," said Lewis. Anne had just retied her shoe-lace when they heard something pushing softly through the jungle of shrubbery on their right. Then a small boy about eight years of age came into view and stood surveying them bashfully, with a big apple turnover clasped tightly in his chubby hands. He was a pretty child, with glossy brown curls, big trustful brown eyes and delicately modeled features. There was an air of refinement about him, in spite of the fact that he was bare-headed and barelegged, with only a faded blue cotton shirt and a pair of threadbare velvet knickerbockers between head and legs. But he looked like a small prince in disguise.

Just behind him was a big black Newfoundland dog whose head was almost on a level with the lad's shoulder.

Anne looked at him with a smile that always won children's hearts.

"Hello, sonny," said Lewis. "Who belongs to you?"

The boy came forward with an answering smile, holding out his turnover.

"This is for you to eat," he said shyly. "Dad made it for me, but I'd rather give it to you. I've lots to eat."

Lewis, rather tactlessly, was on the point of refusing to take the little chap's snack, but Anne gave him a quick nudge. Taking the hint, he accepted it gravely and handed it to Anne, who, quite as gravely, broke it in two and gave half of it back to him. They knew they must eat it and they had painful doubts as to "Dad's" ability in the cooking line, but the first mouthful reassured them. "Dad" might not be strong on courtesy but he could certainly make turnovers.

"This is delicious," said Anne. "What is your name, dear?"

"Teddy Armstrong," said the small benefactor. "But Dad always calls me Little Fellow. I'm all he has, you know. Dad is awful fond of me and I'm awful fond of Dad. I'm afraid you think my dad is impolite 'cause he shut that door so quick, but he doesn't mean to be. I heard you asking for something to eat." ("We didn't but it doesn't matter," thought Anne.)

"I was in the garden behind the hollyhocks, so I just thought I'd bring you my turnover 'cause I'm always so sorry for poor people who haven't plenty to eat. I have, always. My dad is a splendid cook. You ought to see the rice puddings he can make."

"Does he put raisins in them?" asked Lewis with a twinkle.

The Second Year

"Lots and lots. There's nothing mean about my dad."

"Haven't you any mother, darling?" asked Anne.

"No. My mother is dead. Mrs. Merrill told me once she'd gone to heaven, but my dad says there's no such place and I guess he ought to know. My dad is an awful wise man. He's read thousands of books. I mean to be just 'zackly like him when I grow up...only I'll always give people things to eat when they want them. My dad isn't very fond of people, you know, but he's awful good to me."

"Do you go to school?" asked Lewis.

"No. My dad teaches me at home. The trustees told him I'd have to go next year, though. I think I'd like to go to school and have some other boys to play with. 'Course I've got Carlo and Dad himself is splendid to play with when he has time. My dad is pretty busy, you know. He has to run the farm and keep the house clean, too. That's why he can't be bothered having people around, you see. When I get bigger I'll be able to help him lots and then he'll have more time to be polite to folks."

"That turnover was just about right, Little Fellow," said Lewis, swallowing the last crumb.

The Little Fellow's eyes beamed.

"I'm so glad you liked it," he said.

"Would you like to have your picture taken?" said Anne, feeling that it would never do to offer this generous small soul money. "If you would, Lewis will take it."

"Oh, wouldn't I!" said the Little Fellow eagerly. "Carlo, too?"

"Certainly Carlo, too."

Anne posed the two prettily before a background of shrubs, the little lad standing with his arm about his big, curly playmate's neck, both dog and boy seeming equally well pleased, and Lewis took the picture with his last remaining plate.

"If it comes out well I'll send you one by mail," he promised. "How shall I address it?"

"Teddy Armstrong, care of Mr. James Armstrong, Glencove Road," said the Little Fellow. "Oh, won't it be fun to have something coming to me mineself through the post-office! I tell you I'll feel awful proud. I won't say a word to Dad about it so that it'll be a splendid surprise for him."

"Well, look out for your parcel in two or three weeks," said Lewis, as they bade him good-by. But Anne suddenly stooped and kissed the little sunburned face. There was something about it that tugged at her heart. He was so sweet...so gallant...so motherless!

They looked back at him before a curve in the lane and saw him standing on the dyke, with his dog, waving his hand to them.

Of course Rebecca Dew knew all about the Armstrongs.

"James Armstrong has never got over his wife's death five years ago," she said. "He wasn't so bad before that...agreeable enough, though a bit of a hermit. Kind of built that way. He was just wrapped up in his bit of a wife...she was twenty years younger than he was. Her death was an awful shock to him I've heard...just seemed to change his nature completely. He got sour and cranky. Wouldn't even get a housekeeper...looked after his house and child himself. He kept bachelor's hall for years before he was married, so he ain't a bad hand at it."

"But it's no life for the child," said Aunt Chatty. "His father never takes him to church or anywhere he'd see people."

"He worships the boy, I've heard," said Aunt Kate.

"'Thou shalt have no other gods before me,'" quoted Rebecca Dew suddenly.

3

It was almost three weeks before Lewis found time to develop his pictures. He brought them up to Windy Poplars the first Sunday night he came to supper. Both the house and the Little Fellow came out splendidly. The Little Fellow smiled up from the picture "as real as life," said Rebecca Dew.

"Why, he looks like you, Lewis!" exclaimed Anne.

"He does that," agreed Rebecca Dew, squinting at it judicially. "The minute I saw it, his face reminded me of somebody but I couldn't think who."

"Why, the eyes...the forehead...the whole expression...are yours, Lewis," said Anne.

"It's hard to believe I was ever such a good-looking little chap," shrugged Lewis. "I've got a picture of myself somewhere, taken when I was eight. I must hunt it out and compare it. You'd laugh to see it, Miss Shirley. I'm the most sober-eyed kid, with long curls and a lace collar, looking stiff as a ramrod. I suppose I had my head clamped in one of those three-clawed contraptions they used to use. If this picture really resembles me, it must be only a coincidence. The Little Fellow can't be any relation of mine. I haven't any relative on the Island...now."

"Where were you born?" asked Aunt Kate.

"N. B. Father and Mother died when I was ten and I came over here to live with a cousin of mother's...I called her Aunt Ida. She died too, you know...three years ago."

"Jim Armstrong came from New Brunswick," said Rebecca Dew. "*He* ain't a real islander...wouldn't be such a crank if he was. We have our peculiarities but we're *civilized.*"

"I'm not sure that I want to discover a relation in the amiable Mr. Armstrong," grinned Lewis, attacking Aunt

Chatty's cinnamon toast. "However, I think when I get the photograph finished and mounted I'll take it out to Glencove Road myself and investigate a little. He may be a distant cousin or something. I really know nothing about my mother's people, if she had any living. I've always been under the impression that she hadn't. Father hadn't, I know."

"If you take the picture out in person, won't the Little Fellow be a bit disappointed over losing his thrill of getting something through the post-office?" said Anne.

"I'll make it up to him...I'll send him something else by mail."

The next Saturday afternoon Lewis came driving along Spook's Lane in an antiquated buggy behind a still more antiquated mare.

"I'm going out to Glencove to take little Teddy Armstrong his picture, Miss Shirley. If my dashing turn-out doesn't give you heart-failure I'd like to have you come, too. I don't *think* any of the wheels will fall off."

"Where on earth did you pick up that relic, Lewis?" demanded Rebecca Dew.

"Don't poke fun at my gallant steed, Miss Dew. Have some respect for age. Mr. Bender lent me both mare and buggy on condition I'd do an errand for him along the Dawlish Road. I hadn't time to walk out to Glencove today and back."

"Time!" said Rebecca Dew. "I could walk there and back myself faster than that animal."

"And carry a bag of potatoes back for Mr. Bender? You wonderful woman!"

Rebecca Dew's red cheeks grew even redder.

"It ain't nice to make fun of your elders," she said rebukingly. Then, by way of coals of fire..."Could you do with a few doughnuts afore you start out?"

The Second Year

The white mare, however, developed surprising powers of locomotion when they were once more out in the open. Anne giggled to herself as they jogged along the road. What would Mrs. Gardiner or even Aunt Jamesina say if they could see her now? Well, she didn't care. It was a wonderful day for a drive through a land that was keeping its old lovely ritual of autumn, and Lewis was a good companion. Lewis would attain his ambitions. Nobody else of her acquaintance, she reflected, would dream of asking her to go driving in the Bender buggy behind the Bender mare. But it never occurred to Lewis that there was anything odd about it. What difference *how* you traveled as long as you got there? The calm rims of the upland hills were as blue, the roads as red, the maples as gorgeous, no matter what vehicle you rode in. Lewis was a philosopher and cared as little what people might say as he did when some of the High School pupils called him "Sissy" because he did housework for his board. Let them call! Some day the laugh would be on the other side. His pockets might be empty but his head wasn't. Meanwhile the afternoon was an idyl and they were going to see the Little Fellow again. They told Mr. Bender's brother-in-law about their errand when he put the bag of potatoes in the back of the buggy.

"Do you mean to say you've got a photo of little Teddy Armstrong?" exclaimed Mr. Merrill.

"That I have and a good one." Lewis unwrapped it and held it proudly out. "I don't believe a professional photographer could have taken a better."

Mr. Merrill slapped his leg resoundingly.

"Well, if that don't beat all! Why, little Teddy Armstrong is dead..."

"Dead!" exclaimed Anne in horror. "Oh, Mr. Merrill...no...don't tell me...that dear little boy..."

"Sorry, miss, but it's a fact. And his father is just about wild and all the worse that he hasn't got any kind of a picture of him at all. And now you've got a good one. Well, well!"

"It...it seems impossible," said Anne, her eyes full of tears. She was seeing the slender little figure waving his farewell from the dyke.

"Sorry to say it's only too true. He died nearly three weeks ago. Pneumonia. Suffered awful but he was just as brave and patient as any one could be, they say. I dunno what'll become of Jim Armstrong now. They say he's like a crazy man—just moping and muttering to himself all the time. 'If I only had a picture of my Little Fellow,' he keeps saying."

"I'm sorry for that man," said Mrs. Merrill suddenly. She had not hitherto spoken, standing by her husband, a gaunt, square-built gray woman in wind-whipped calico and check apron. "He's well-to-do and I've always felt he looked down on us because we were poor. But we have our boy...and it don't never matter how poor you are as long as you've got something to love."

Anne looked at Mrs. Merrill with a new respect. Mrs. Merrill was not beautiful, but as her sunken gray eyes met Anne's, something of spirit kinship was acknowledged between them. Anne had never seen Mrs. Merrill before and never saw her again, but she always remembered her as a woman who had attained to the ultimate secret of life. You were never poor as long as you had something to love.

The golden day was spoiled for Anne. Somehow, the Little Fellow had won her heart in their brief meeting. She and Lewis drove in silence down the Glencove Road and up the grassy lane. Carlo was lying on the stone before the blue door. He got up and came down over to them, as they descended from the buggy, licking Anne's hand and looking up at her with big wistful eyes as if asking for news of his little playmate. The door

The Second Year

was open and in the dim room beyond they saw a man with his head bowed on the table.

At Anne's knock he started up and came to the door. She was shocked at the change in him. He was hollow-cheeked, haggard and unshaven, and his deep- set eyes flashed with a fitful fire.

She expected a repulse at first, but he seemed to recognize her, for he said listlessly,

"So you're back? The Little Fellow said you talked to him and kissed him. He liked you. I was sorry I'd been so churlish to you. What is it you want?"

"We want to show you something," said Anne gently.

"Will you come in and sit down?" he said drearily. Without a word Lewis took the Little Fellow's picture from its wrappings and held it out to him. He snatched it up, gave it one amazed, hungry look, then dropped on his chair and burst into tears and sobs. Anne had never seen a man weep so before. She and Lewis stood in mute sympathy until he had regained his self-control.

"Oh, you don't know what this means to me," he said brokenly at last. "I hadn't any picture of him. And I'm not like other folks...I can't recall a face...I can't see faces as most folks can in their mind. It's been awful since the Little Fellow died....I couldn't even remember what he looked like. And now you've brought me this...after I was so rude to you. Sit down... sit down. I wish I could express my thanks in some way. I guess you've saved my reason...maybe my life. Oh, miss, isn't it like him? You'd think he was going to speak. My dear Little Fellow! How am I going to live without him? I've nothing to live for now. First his mother...now him."

"He was a dear little lad," said Anne tenderly.

"That he was. Little Teddy...Theodore, his mother named him...her 'gift of Gods' she said he was. And he was so patient and never complained. Once he smiled up in my face and said, 'Dad, I think you've been mistaken in one thing...just one. I guess there is a heaven, isn't there? Isn't there, Dad?' I said to him, yes, there was....God forgive me for ever trying to teach him anything else. He smiled again, contented like, and said, 'Well, Dad, I'm going there and Mother and God are there, so I'll be pretty well off. But I'm worried about you, Dad. You'll be so awful lonesome without me. But just do the best you can and be polite to folks and come to us by and by.' He made me promise I'd try, but when he was gone I couldn't stand the blankness of it. I'd have gone mad if you hadn't brought me this. It won't be so hard now."

He talked about his Little Fellow for some time, as if he found relief and pleasure in it. His reserve and gruffness seemed to have fallen from him like a garment. Finally Lewis produced the small faded photograph of himself and showed it to him.

"Have you ever seen anybody who looked like that, Mr. Armstrong?" asked Anne.

Mr. Armstrong peered at it in perplexity.

"It's awful like the Little Fellow," he said at last. "Whose might it be?"

"Mine," said Lewis, "when I was seven years old. It was because of the strange resemblance to Teddy that Miss Shirley made me bring it to show you. I thought it possible that you and I or the Little Fellow might be some distant relation. My name is Lewis Allen and my father was George Allen. I was born in New Brunswick."

James Armstrong shook his head. Then he said,

"What was your mother's name?"

"Mary Gardiner."

James Armstrong looked at him for a moment in silence.

"She was my half-sister," he said at last. "I hardly knew her... never saw her but once. I was brought up in an uncle's family after my father's death. My mother married again and moved away. She came to see me once and brought her little daughter.

The Second Year

She died soon after and I never saw my half-sister again. When I came over to the Island to live, I lost all trace of her. You are my nephew and the Little Fellow's cousin."

This was surprising news to a lad who had fancied himself alone in the world. Lewis and Anne spent the whole evening with Mr. Armstrong and found him to be a well-read and intelligent man. Somehow, they both took a liking to him. His former inhospitable reception was quite forgotten and they saw only the real worth of the character and temperament below the unpromising shell that had hitherto concealed them.

"Of course the Little Fellow couldn't have loved his father so much if it hadn't been so," said Anne, as she and Lewis drove back to Windy Poplars through the sunset.

When Lewis Allen went the next week-end to see his uncle, the latter said to him,

"Lad, come and live with me. You are my nephew and I can do well for you...what I'd have done for my Little Fellow if he'd lived. You're alone in the world and so am I. I need you. I'll grow hard and bitter again if I live here alone. I want you to help me keep my promise to the Little Fellow. His place is empty. Come you and fill it."

"Thank you, Uncle; I'll try," said Lewis, holding out his hand.

"And bring that teacher of yours here once in a while. I like that girl. The Little Fellow liked her. 'Dad,' he said to me, 'I didn't think I'd ever like anybody but you to kiss me, but I liked it when she did. There was something in her eyes, Dad.'"

4

"The old porch thermometer says it's zero and the new side-door one says it's ten above," remarked Anne, one frosty December night. "So I don't know whether to take my muff or not."

"Better go by the old thermometer," said Rebecca Dew cautiously. "It's probably more used to our climate. Where are you going this cold night, anyway?"

"I'm going round to Temple Street to ask Katherine Brooke to spend the Christmas holidays with me at Green Gables."

"You'll spoil your holidays, then," said Rebecca Dew solemnly. "She'd go about snubbing the angels, that one...that is, if she ever condescended to enter heaven. And the worst of it is, she's proud of her bad manners...thinks it shows her strength of mind no doubt!"

"My brain agrees with every word you say but my heart simply won't," said Anne. "I feel, in spite of everything, that Katherine Brooke is only a shy, unhappy girl under her disagreeable rind. I can never make any headway with her in Summerside, but if I can get her to Green Gables I believe it will thaw her out."

"You won't get her. She won't go," predicted Rebecca Dew. "Probably she'll take it as an insult to be asked...think you're offering her charity. *We* asked her here once to Christmas dinner...the year afore you came...you remember, Mrs. MacComber, the year we had two turkeys give us and didn't know how we was to get 'em et...and all she said was, 'No, thank you. If there's anything I hate, it's the word Christmas!'"

"But that is so dreadful...hating Christmas! Something *has* to be done, Rebecca Dew. I'm going to ask her and I've a queer feeling in my thumbs that tells me she will come."

The Second Year

"Somehow," said Rebecca Dew reluctantly, "when you say a thing is going to happen, a body believes it will. You haven't got a second sight, have you? Captain MacComber's mother had it. Useter give me the creeps."

"I don't think I have anything that need give you creeps. It's only just...I've had a feeling for some time that Katherine Brooke is almost crazy with loneliness under her bitter outside and that my invitation will come pat to the psychological moment, Rebecca Dew."

"I am not a B.A.," said Rebecca with awful humility, "and I do not deny your right to use words I cannot always understand. Neither do I deny that you can wind people round your little finger. Look how you managed the Pringles. But I do say I pity you if you take that iceberg and nutmeg grater combined home with you for Christmas."

Anne was by no means as confident as she pretended to be during her walk to Temple Street. Katherine Brooke had really been unbearable of late. Again and again Anne, rebuffed, had said, as grimly as Poe's raven, "Nevermore." Only yesterday Katherine had been positively insulting at a staff meeting. But in an unguarded moment Anne had seen something looking out of the older girl's eyes...a passionate, half-frantic something like a caged creature mad with discontent. Anne spent the first half of the night trying to decide whether to invite Katherine Brooke to Green Gables or not. Finally she fell asleep with her mind irrevocably made up.

Katherine's landlady showed Anne into the parlor and shrugged a fat shoulder when she asked for Miss Brooke.

"I'll tell her you're here but I dunno if she'll come down. She's sulking. I told her at dinner tonight that Mrs. Rawlins says its scandalous the way she dresses, for a teacher in Summerside High, and she took it high and mighty as usual."

"I don't think you should have told Miss Brooke that," said Anne reproachfully.

"But I thought she ought to know," said Mrs. Dennis somewhat waspishly.

"Did you also think she ought to know that the Inspector said she was one of the best teachers in the Maritimes?" asked Anne. "Or didn't you know it?"

"Oh, I heard it. But she's stuck-up enough now without making her any worse. Proud's no name for it...though what she's got to be proud of, *I* dunno. Of course she was mad anyhow tonight because I'd said she couldn't have a dog. She's took a notion into her head she'd like to have a dog. Said she'd pay for his rations and see he was no bother. But what'd I do with him when she was in school? I put my foot down. 'I'm boarding no dogs,' sez I."

"Oh, Mrs. Dennis, won't you let her have a dog? He wouldn't bother you...much. You could keep him in the basement while she was in school. And a dog really is such a protection at night. I wish you would...*please.*"

There was always something about Anne Shirley's eyes when she said "please" that people found hard to resist. Mrs. Dennis, in spite of fat shoulders and a meddlesome tongue, was not unkind at heart. Katherine Brooke simply got under her skin at times with her ungracious ways.

"I dunno why you should worry as to her having a dog or not. I didn't know you were such friends. She hasn't *any* friends. I never had such an unsociable boarder."

"I think that is why she wants a dog, Mrs. Dennis. None of us can live without some kind of companionship."

"Well, it's the first human thing I've noticed about her," said Mrs. Dennis. "I dunno's I have any awful objection to a dog, but she sort of vexed me with her sarcastic way of asking...'I s'pose you wouldn't consent if I asked you if I might have a dog, Mrs. Dennis,' she sez, haughty like. Set her up with it! 'You're s'posing right,' sez I, as haughty as herself. I don't like eating my words any more than most people, but you can tell her she can have a dog if she'll guarantee he won't misbehave in the parlor."

Anne did not think the parlor could be much worse if the dog did misbehave. She eyed the dingy lace curtains and the hideous purple roses on the carpet with a shiver.

"I'm sorry for any one who has to spend Christmas in a boarding-house like this," she thought. "I don't wonder Katherine hates the word. I'd like to give this place a good airing...it smells of a thousand meals. *Why* does Katherine go on boarding here when she has a good salary?"

"She says you can come up," was the message Mrs. Dennis brought back, rather dubiously, for Miss Brooke had run true to form.

The narrow, steep stair was repellent. It didn't want you. Nobody would go up who didn't have to. The linoleum in the hall was worn to shreds. The little back hall-bedroom where Anne presently found herself was even more cheerless than the parlor. It was lighted by one glaring unshaded gas jet. There was an iron bed with a valley in the middle of it and a narrow, sparsely draped window looking out on a backyard garden where a large crop of tin cans flourished. But beyond it was a marvelous sky and a row of lombardies standing out against long, purple, distant hills.

"Oh, Miss Brooke, look at that sunset," said Anne rapturously from the squeaky, cushionless rocker to which Katherine had ungraciously pointed her.

"I've seen a good many sunsets," said the latter coldly, without moving. ("Condescending to me with your sunsets!" she thought bitterly.)

"You haven't seen this one. No two sunsets are alike. Just sit down here and let us let it sink into our souls," *said* Anne. *Thought* Anne, "Do you *ever* say anything pleasant?"

"Don't be ridiculous, please."

The most insulting words in the world! With an added edge of insult in Katherine's contemptuous tones. Anne turned from her sunset and looked at Katherine, much more than half inclined to get up and walk out. But Katherine's eyes looked a trifle strange. *Had* she been crying? Surely not...you couldn't imagine Katherine Brooke crying.

"You don't make me feel very welcome," Anne said slowly.

"I can't pretend things. I haven't *your* notable gift for doing the queen act...saying exactly the right thing to every one. You're *not* welcome. What sort of room is this to welcome any one to?"

Katherine made a scornful gesture at the faded walls, the shabby bare chairs and the wobbly dressing-table with its petticoat of limp muslin.

"It isn't a nice room, but why do you stay here if you don't like it?"

"Oh...why...Why? *You* wouldn't understand. It doesn't matter. I don't care what anybody thinks. What brought you here tonight? I don't suppose you came just to soak in the sunset."

"I came to ask if you would spend the Christmas holidays with me at Green Gables."

("Now," thought Anne, "for another broadside of sarcasm! I do wish she'd sit down at least. She just stands there as if waiting for me to go.")

But there was silence for a moment. Then Katherine said slowly,

"Why do you ask me? It isn't because you like me...even you couldn't pretend *that.* "

"It's because I can't bear to think of any human being spending Christmas in a place like *this,*" said Anne candidly.

The sarcasm came then.

"Oh, I see. A seasonable outburst of charity. I'm hardly a candidate for that *yet,* Miss Shirley."

The Second Year

Anne got up. She was out of patience with this strange, aloof creature. She walked across the room and looked Katherine squarely in the eye. "Katherine Brooke, whether you know it or not, what *you* want is a good spanking."

They gazed at each other for a moment.

"It must have relieved you to say that," said Katherine. But somehow the insulting tone had gone out of her voice. There was even a faint twitch at the corner of her mouth.

"It has," said Anne. "I've been wanting to tell you just that for some time. I didn't ask you to Green Gables out of charity... you know that perfectly well. I told you my true reason. *Nobody* ought to spend Christmas here...the very idea is indecent."

"You asked me to Green Gables just because you are sorry for me."

"I *am* sorry for you. Because you've shut out life...and now life is shutting you out. Stop, it, Katherine. Open your doors to life...and life will come in."

"The Anne Shirley version of the old bromide, 'If you bring a smiling visage to the glass you meet a smile,'" said Katherine with a shrug.

"Like all bromides, that's absolutely true. Now, are you coming to Green Gables or are you not?"

"What would you say if I accepted...to yourself, not to me?"

"I'd say you were showing the first faint glimmer of common sense I'd ever detected in you," retorted Anne.

Katherine laughed...surprisingly. She walked across to the window, scowled at the fiery streak which was all that was left of the scorned sunset and then turned.

"Very well...I'll go. Now you can go through the motions of telling me you're delighted and that we'll have a jolly time."

"I *am* delighted. But I don't know if you'll have a jolly time or not. That will depend a good deal on yourself, Miss Brooke."

"Oh, I'll behave myself decently. You'll be surprised. You won't find me a very exhilarating guest, I suppose, but I promise you I won't eat with my knife or insult people when they tell me it's a fine day. I tell you frankly that the only reason I'm going is because even I can't stick the thought of spending the holidays here alone. Mrs. Dennis is going to spend Christmas week with her daughter in Charlottetown. It's a bore to think of getting my own meals. I'm a rotten cook. So much for the triumph of matter over mind. But will you give me your word of honor that you won't wish me a merry Christmas? I just don't want to be merry at Christmas."

"I won't. But I can't answer for the twins."

"I'm not going to ask you to sit down here...you'd freeze... but I see that there's a very fine moon in place of your sunset and I'll walk home with you and help you to admire it if you like."

"I do like," said Anne, "but I want to impress on your mind that we have *much* finer moons in Avonlea."

"So she's going?" said Rebecca Dew as she filled Anne's hot-water bottle. "Well, Miss Shirley, I hope you'll never try to induce me to turn Mohammedan...because you'd likely succeed. Where *is* That Cat? Out frisking round Summerside and the weather at zero."

"Not by the new thermometer. And Dusty Miller is curled up on the rocking-chair by my stove in the tower, snoring with happiness."

"Ah well," said Rebecca Dew with a little shiver as she shut the kitchen door, "I wish every one in the world was as warm and sheltered as we are tonight."

5

Anne did not know that a wistful little Elizabeth was watching out of one of the mansard windows of The Evergreens as she drove away from Windy Poplars...an Elizabeth with tears in her eyes who felt as if everything that made life worth living had gone out of her life for the time being and that she was the very Lizziest of Lizzies. But when the livery sleigh vanished from her sight around the corner of Spook's Lane Elizabeth went and knelt down by her bed.

"Dear God," she whispered, "I know it isn't any use to ask You for a merry Christmas for me because Grandmother and The Woman couldn't be merry, but please let my dear Miss Shirley have a merry, merry Christmas and bring her back safe to me when it's over.

"Now," said Elizabeth, getting up from her knees, "I've done all that I can."

Anne was already tasting Christmas happiness. She fairly sparkled as the train left the station. The ugly streets slipped past her...she was going home...home to Green Gables. Out in the open country the world was all golden-white and pale violet, woven here and there with the dark magic of spruces and the leafless delicacy of birches. The low sun behind the bare woods seemed rushing through the trees like a splendid god, as the train sped on. Katherine was silent but did not seem ungracious.

"Don't expect me to talk," she had warned Anne curtly.

"I won't. I hope you don't think I'm one of those terrible people who make you feel that you *have* to talk to them all the time. We'll just talk when we feel like it. I admit I'm likely to feel like it a good part of the time, but you're under no obligation to take any notice of what I'm saying."

Davy met them at Bright River with a big two-seated sleigh full of furry robes...and a bear hug for Anne. The two girls snuggled down in the back seat. The drive from the station to Green Gables had always been a very pleasant part of Anne's week-ends home. She always recalled her first drive home from Bright River with Matthew. That had been in spring and this was December, but everything along the road kept saying to her, "Do you remember?" The snow crisped under the runners; the music of the bells tinkled through the ranks of tall pointed firs, snow-laden. The White Way of Delight had little festoons of stars tangled in the trees. And on the last hill but one they saw the great gulf, white and mystical under the moon but not yet ice-bound.

"There's just one spot on this road where I always feel suddenly...'I'm *home*,'" said Anne. "It's the top of the next hill, where we'll see the lights of Green Gables. I'm just thinking of the supper Marilla will have ready for us. I believe I can smell it here. Oh, it's good...good...good to be home again!"

At Green Gables every tree in the yard seemed to welcome her back...every lighted window was beckoning. And how good Marilla's kitchen smelled as they opened the door. There were hugs and exclamations and laughter. Even Katherine seemed somehow no outsider, but one of them. Mrs. Rachel Lynde had set her cherished parlor lamp on the supper-table and lighted it. It was really a hideous thing with a hideous red globe, but what a warm rosy becoming light it cast over everything! How warm and friendly were the shadows! How pretty Dora was growing! And Davy really seemed almost a man.

There was news to tell. Diana had a small daughter...Josie Pye actually had a young man...and Charlie Sloane was said to be engaged. It was all just as exciting as news of empire could have been. Mrs. Lynde's new patchwork quilt, just completed, containing five thousand pieces, was on display and received its meed of praise.

The Second Year

"When you come home, Anne," said Davy, "everything seems to come alive."

"Ah, this is how life should be," purred Dora's kitten.

"I've always found it hard to resist the lure of a moonlight night," said Anne after supper. "How about a snow-shoe tramp, Miss Brooke? I think that I've heard that you snow-shoe."

"Yes...it's the only thing I *can* do...but I haven't done it for six years," said Katherine with a shrug.

Anne rooted out her snow-shoes from the garret and Davy shot over to Orchard Slope to borrow an old pair of Diana's for Katherine. They went through Lover's Lane, full of lovely tree shadows, and across fields where little fir trees fringed the fences and through woods which were full of secrets they seemed always on the point of whispering to you but never did...and through open glades that were like pools of silver.

They did not talk or want to talk. It was as if they were afraid to talk for fear of spoiling something beautiful. But Anne had never felt so *near* Katherine Brooke before. By some magic of its own the winter night had brought them together...*almost* together but not quite.

When they came out to the main road and a sleigh flashed by, bells ringing, laughter tinkling, both girls gave an involuntary sigh. It seemed to both that they were leaving behind a world that had nothing in common with the one to which they were returning...a world where time was not...which was young with immortal youth...where souls communed with each other in some medium that needed nothing so crude as words.

"It's been wonderful," said Katherine so obviously to herself that Anne made no response.

They went down the road and up the long Green Gables lane but just before they reached the yard gate, they both paused as by a common impulse and stood in silence, leaning against the old mossy fence and looked at the brooding, motherly old house seen dimly through its veil of trees. How beautiful Green Gables was on a winter night!

Below it the Lake of Shining Waters was locked in ice, patterned around its edges with tree shadows. Silence was everywhere, save for the staccato clip of a horse trotting over the bridge. Anne smiled to recall how often she had heard that sound as she lay in her gable room and pretended to herself that it was the gallop of fairy horses passing in the night.

Suddenly another sound broke the stillness.

"Katherine...you're...why, you're not crying!"

Somehow, it seemed impossible to think of Katherine crying. But she was. And her tears suddenly humanized her. Anne no longer felt afraid of her.

"Katherine...dear Katherine...what is the matter? Can I help?"

"Oh...you can't understand!" gasped Katherine. "Things have always been made easy for *you*. You...you seem to live in a little enchanted circle of beauty and romance. 'I wonder what delightful discovery I'll make today'...that seems to be your attitude to life, Anne. As for me, I've forgotten how to live...no, I never knew how. I'm...I'm like a creature caught in a trap. I can never get out...and it seems to me that somebody is always poking sticks at me through the bars. And you...you have more happiness than you know what to do with...friends everywhere, a lover! Not that I want a lover...I hate men...but if I died tonight, not one living soul would miss me. How would you like to be absolutely friendless in the world?"

Katherine's voice broke in another sob.

"Katherine, you say you like frankness. I'm going to be frank. If you are as friendless as you say, it is your own fault. I've wanted to be friends with you. But you've been all prickles and stings."

"Oh, I know...I know. How I hated you when you came first! Flaunting your circlet of pearls..."

The Second Year

"Katherine, I didn't 'flaunt' it!"

"Oh, I suppose not. That's just my natural hatefulness. But it seemed to flaunt itself...not that I envied you your beau...I've never wanted to be married...I saw enough of that with father and mother...but I hated your being over me when you were younger than I...I was glad when the Pringles made trouble for you. You seemed to have everything I hadn't...charm... friendship.... youth. Youth! I never had anything but starved youth. You know nothing about it. You don't know...you haven't the least idea what it is like not to be wanted by any one...any one!"

"Oh, haven't I?" cried Anne.

In a few poignant sentences she sketched her childhood before coming to Green Gables.

"I wish I'd known that," said Katherine. "It would have made a difference. To me you seemed one of the favorites of fortune. I've been eating my heart out with envy of you. You got the position I wanted...oh, I know you're better qualified than I am, but there it was. You're pretty...at least you make people believe you're pretty. *My* earliest recollection is of some one saying, 'What an ugly child!' You come into a room delightfully...oh, I remember how you came into school that first morning. But I think the real reason I've hated you so is that you always seemed to have some secret delight...as if every day of life was an adventure. In spite of my hatred there were times when I acknowledged to myself that you might just have come from some far-off star."

"Really, Katherine, you take my breath with all these compliments. But you don't hate me any longer, do you? We can be friends now."

"I don't know...I've never had a friend of any kind, much less one of anything like my own age. I don't belong anywhere... never have belonged. I don't think I know how to *be* a friend.

No, I don't hate you any longer...I don't know how I feel about you...oh, I suppose it's your noted charm beginning to work on me. I only know that I feel I'd like to tell you what my life has been like. I could never have told you if you hadn't told me about your life before you came to Green Gables. I want you to understand what has made me as I am. I don't know why I should want you to understand...but I do."

"Tell me, Katherine dear. I do want to understand you."

"You *do* know what it is like not to be wanted, I admit... but not what it is like to know that your father and mother don't want you. Mine didn't. They hated me from the moment I was born...and before...and they hated each other. Yes, they did. They quarreled continually...just mean, nagging, petty quarrels. My childhood was a nightmare. They died when I was seven and I went to live with Uncle Henry's family. *They* didn't want me either. They all looked down on me because I was 'living on their charity.' I remember all the snubs I got...every one. I can't remember a single kind word. I had to wear my cousins' castoff clothes. I remember one hat in particular...it made me look like a mushroom. And they made fun of me whenever I put it on. One day I tore it off and threw it on the fire. I had to wear the most awful old tam to church all the rest of the winter. I never even had a dog...and I wanted one so. I had some brains...I longed so for a B.A. course...but naturally I might just as well have yearned for the moon. However, Uncle Henry agreed to put me through Queen's if I would pay him back when I got a school. He paid my board in a miserable third-rate boarding-house where I had a room over the kitchen that was ice cold in winter and boiling hot in summer, and full of stale cooking smells in all seasons. And the clothes I had to wear to Queen's! But I got my license and I got the second room in Summerside High...the only bit of luck I've ever had. Ever since then I've been pinching and scrimping to pay Uncle Henry...not only

The Second Year

what he spent putting me through Queen's, but what my board through all the years I lived there cost him. I was determined I would not owe him one cent. That is why I've boarded with Mrs. Dennis and dressed shabbily. And I've just finished paying him. For the first time in my life I feel *free*. But meanwhile I've developed the wrong way. I know I'm unsocial...I know I can never think of the right thing to say. I know it's my own fault that I'm always neglected and overlooked at social functions. I know I've made being disagreeable into a fine art. I know I'm sarcastic. I know I'm regarded as a tyrant by my pupils. I know they hate me. Do you think it doesn't hurt me to know it? They always look afraid of me...I hate people who look as if they were afraid of me. Oh, Anne...hate's got to be a disease with me. I do want to be like other people...and I never can now. *That* is what makes me so bitter."

"Oh, but you can!" Anne put her arm about Katherine. "You can put hate out of your mind...cure yourself of it. Life is only beginning for you now...since at last you're quite free and independent. And you never know what may be around the next bend in the road."

"I've heard you say that before...I've laughed at your 'bend in the road.' But the trouble is there aren't any bends in my road. I can see it stretching straight out before me to the sky-line... endless monotony. Oh, does life ever *frighten* you, Anne, with its *blankness*...its swarms of cold, uninteresting people? No, of course it doesn't. *You* don't have to go on teaching all the rest of your life. And you seem to find *everybody* interesting, even that little round red being you call Rebecca Dew. The truth is, I hate teaching...and there's nothing else I can do. A schoolteacher is simply a slave of time. Oh, I know you like it...I don't see how you can. Anne, I want to travel. It's the one thing I've always longed for. I remember the one and only picture that hung on the wall of my attic room at Uncle Henry's...a faded old print that had been discarded from the other rooms with scorn. It was a picture of palms around a spring in the desert, with a string of camels marching away in the distance. It literally fascinated me. I've always wanted to go and find it...I want to see the Southern Cross and the Taj Mahal and the pillars of Karnak. I want to *know*...not just *believe*...that the world is round. And I can never do it on a teacher's salary. I'll just have to go on forever, prating of King Henry the Eighth's wives and the inexhaustible resources of the Dominion."

Anne laughed. It was safe to laugh now, for the bitterness had gone out of Katherine's voice. It sounded merely rueful and impatient.

"Anyhow, we're going to be friends...and we're going to have a jolly ten days here to begin our friendship. I've always wanted to be friends with you, Katherine...spelled with a K! I've always felt that underneath all your prickles was something that would make you worth while as a friend."

"So that is what you've really thought of me? I've often wondered. Well, the leopard will have a go at changing its spots if it's at all possible. Perhaps it is. I can believe almost anything at this Green Gables of yours. It's the first place I've ever been in that felt like a *home.* I should like to be more like other people...if it isn't too late. I'll even practice a sunny smile for that Gilbert of yours when he arrives tomorrow night. Of course I've forgotten how to talk to young men...if I ever knew. He'll just think me an old-maid gooseberry. I wonder if, when I go to bed tonight, I'll feel furious with myself for pulling off my mask and letting you see into my shivering soul like this."

"No, you won't. You'll think, 'I'm glad she's found out I'm human.' We're going to snuggle down among the warm fluffy blankets, probably with two hot-water bottles, for likely Marilla and Mrs. Lynde will each put one in for us for fear the other has forgotten it. And you'll feel deliciously sleepy after this walk in the frosty moonshine...and first thing you'll know, it will be morning and you'll feel as if you were the first person to discover that the sky is blue. And you'll grow learned in lore of plum puddings because you're going to help me make one for Tuesday...a great big plummy one."

Anne was amazed at Katherine's good looks when they went in. Her complexion was radiant after her long walk in the keen air and color made all the difference in the world to her.

"Why, Katherine would be handsome if she wore the right kind of hats and dresses," reflected Anne, trying to imagine Katherine with a certain dark, richly red velvet hat she had seen in a Summerside shop, on her black hair and pulled over her amber eyes. "I've simply got to see what can be done about it."

6

Saturday and Monday were full of gay doings at Green Gables. The plum pudding was concocted and the Christmas tree brought home. Katherine and Anne and Davy and Dora went to the woods for it...a beautiful little fir to whose cutting down Anne was only reconciled by the fact that it was in a little clearing of Mr. Harrison's which was going to be stumped and plowed in the spring anyhow.

They wandered about, gathering creeping spruce and ground pine for wreaths...even some ferns that kept green in a certain deep hollow of the woods all winter...until day smiled back at night over white-bosomed hills and they came back to Green Gables in triumph...to meet a tall young man with hazel eyes and the beginnings of a mustache which made him look so much older and maturer that Anne had one awful moment of wondering if it were really Gilbert or a stranger.

Katherine, with a little smile that tried to be sarcastic but couldn't quite succeed, left them in the parlor and played games with the twins in the kitchen all the evening. To her amazement she found she was enjoying it. And what fun it was to go down to the cellar with Davy and find that there were really such things as sweet apples still left in the world.

Katherine had never been in a country cellar before and had no idea what a delightful, spooky, shadowy place it could be by candle-light. Life already seemed *warmer*. For the first time it came home to Katherine that life might be beautiful, even for her.

Davy made enough noise to wake the Seven Sleepers, at an unearthly hour Christmas morning, ringing an old cowbell up and down the stairs. Marilla was horrified at his doing such a thing when there was a guest in the house, but Katherine came down laughing. Somehow, an odd camaraderie had sprung up between her and Davy. She told Anne candidly that she had no use for the impeccable Dora but that Davy was somehow tarred with her own brush.

They opened the parlor and distributed the gifts before breakfast because the twins, even Dora, couldn't have eaten anything if they hadn't. Katherine, who had not expected anything except, perhaps, a duty gift from Anne, found herself getting presents from every one. A gay, crocheted afghan from Mrs. Lynde...a sachet of orris root from Dora...a paper-knife from Davy...a basketful of tiny jars of jam and jelly from Marilla...even a little bronze chessy cat for a paper-weight from Gilbert.

And, tied under the tree, curled up on a bit of warm and woolly blanket, a dear little brown-eyed puppy, with alert, silken ears and an ingratiating tail. A card tied to his neck bore the legend, "From Anne, who dares, after all, to wish you a Merry Christmas." Katherine gathered his wriggling little body up in her arms and spoke shakily.

"Anne...he's a darling! But Mrs. Dennis won't let me keep him. I asked her if I might get a dog and she refused."

"I've arranged it all with Mrs. Dennis. You'll find she won't object. And, anyway, Katherine, you're not going to be there long. You *must* find a decent place to live, now that you've paid off what you thought were your obligations. Look at the lovely box of stationery Diana sent me. Isn't it fascinating to look at the blank pages and wonder what will be written on them?"

Mrs. Lynde was thankful it was a white Christmas...there would be no fat graveyards when Christmas was white... but to Katherine it seemed a purple and crimson and golden Christmas. And the week that followed was just as beautiful. Katherine had often wondered bitterly just what it would be like to be happy and now she found out. She bloomed out in the most astonishing way. Anne found herself enjoying their companionship.

"To think I was afraid she would spoil my Christmas holiday!" she reflected in amazement.

"To think," said Katherine to herself, "that I was on the verge of refusing to come here when Anne invited me!"

They went for long walks...through Lover's Lane and the Haunted Wood, where the very silence seemed friendly...over hills where the light snow whirled in a winter dance of goblins... through old orchards full of violet shadows...through the glory of sunset woods. There were no birds to chirp or sing, no brooks to gurgle, no squirrels to gossip. But the wind made occasional music that had in quality what it lacked in quantity.

"One can always find something lovely to look at or listen to," said Anne.

They talked of "cabbages and kings," and hitched their wagons to stars, and came home with appetites that taxed even the Green Gables pantry. One day it stormed and they couldn't go out. The east wind was beating around the eaves and the gray gulf was roaring. But even a storm at Green Gables had charms of its own. It was cozy to sit by the stove and dreamily watch the firelight flickering over the ceiling while you munched apples and candy. How jolly supper was with the storm wailing outside!

One night Gilbert took them to see Diana and her new baby daughter.

"I never held a baby in my life before," said Katherine as they drove home. "For one thing, I didn't want to, and for another I'd have been afraid of it going to pieces in my grasp. You can't imagine how I felt...so big and clumsy with that tiny, exquisite thing in my arms. I know Mrs. Wright thought I was going to drop it every minute. I could see her striving heroically to conceal her terror. But it did something to me...the baby I mean...I haven't decided just what."

"Babies are such fascinating creatures," said Anne dreamily. "They are what I heard somebody at Redmond call 'terrific bundles of potentialities.' Think of it, Katherine...Homer must have been a baby once...a baby with dimples and great eyes full of light...he couldn't have been blind then, of course."

"What a pity his mother didn't know he was to be Homer," said Katherine.

"But I think I'm glad Judas' mother didn't know he was to be Judas," said Anne softly. "I hope she never did know."

There was a concert in the hall one night, with a party at Abner Sloane's after it, and Anne persuaded Katherine to go to both.

"I want you to give us a reading for our program, Katherine. I've heard you read beautifully."

The Second Year

"I used to recite...I think I rather liked doing it. But the summer before last I recited at a shore concert which a party of summer resorters got up...and I heard them laughing at me afterwards."

"How do you know they were laughing at you?"

"They must have been. There wasn't anything else to laugh at."

Anne hid a smile and persisted in asking for the reading.

"Give *Genevra* for an encore. I'm told you do that splendidly. Mrs. Stephen Pringle told me she never slept a wink the night after she heard you give it."

"No; I've never liked *Genevra*. It's in the reading, so I try occasionally to show the class how to read it. I really have no patience with Genevra. Why didn't she scream when she found herself locked in? When they were hunting everywhere for her, surely somebody would have heard her."

Katherine finally promised the reading but was dubious about the party. "I'll go, of course. But nobody will ask me to dance and I'll feel sarcastic and prejudiced and ashamed. I'm always miserable at parties...the few I've ever gone to. Nobody seems to think I can dance...and you know I can fairly well, Anne. I picked it up at Uncle Henry's, because a poor bit of a maid they had wanted to learn, too, and she and I used to dance together in the kitchen at night to the music that went on in the parlor. I think I'd like it...with the right kind of partner."

"You won't be miserable at this party, Katherine. You won't be outside looking in. There's all the difference in the world, you know, between being inside looking out and outside looking in. You have such lovely hair, Katherine. Do you mind if I try a new way of doing it?"

Katherine shrugged.

"Oh, go ahead. I suppose my hair does look dreadful...but I've no time to be always primping. I haven't a party dress. Will my green taffeta do?"

"It will have to do...though green is the one color above all others that you should never wear, my Katherine. But you're going to wear a red, pin-tucked chiffon collar I've made for you. Yes, you *are*. You ought to have a red dress, Katherine."

"I've always hated red. When I went to live with Uncle Henry, Aunt Gertrude always made me wear aprons of bright turkey-red. The other children in school used to call out 'Fire,' when I came in with one of those aprons on. Anyway, I can't be bothered with clothes."

"Heaven grant me patience! Clothes are *very* important," said Anne severely, as she braided and coiled. Then she looked at her work and saw that it was good. She put her arm about Katherine's shoulders and turned her to the mirror.

"Don't you truly think we are a pair of quite good-looking girls?" she laughed. "And isn't it really nice to think people will find some pleasure in looking at us? There are so many homely people who would actually look quite attractive if they took a little pains with themselves. Three Sundays ago in church...you remember the day poor old Mr. Milvain preached and had such a terrible cold in his head that nobody could make out what he was saying?... well, I passed the time making the people around me beautiful. I gave Mrs. Brent a new nose, I waved Mary Addison's hair and gave Jane Marden's a lemon rinse...I dressed Emma Dill in blue instead of brown...I dressed Charlotte Blair in stripes instead of checks...I removed several moles...and I shaved off Thomas Anderson's long, sandy Piccadilly weepers. You couldn't have known them when I got through with them. And, except perhaps for Mrs. Brent's nose, they could have done everything I did, themselves. Why, Katherine, your eyes are just the color of tea...amber tea. Now, live up to your name this evening...a brook should be sparkling...limpid...merry."

"Everything I'm not."

"Everything you've been this past week. So you *can* be it."

"That's only the magic of Green Gables. When I go back to Summerside, twelve o'clock will have struck for Cinderella."

"You'll take the magic back with you. Look at yourself... looking for once as you ought to look all the time."

Katherine gazed at her reflection in the mirror as if rather doubting her identity.

"I do look years younger," she admitted. "You were right... clothes *do* do things to you. Oh, I know I've been looking older than my age. I didn't care. Why should I? Nobody else cared. And I'm not like you, Anne. Apparently you were born knowing how to live. And I don't know anything about it...not even the A B C. I wonder if it's too late to learn. I've been sarcastic so long, I don't know if I can be anything else. Sarcasm seemed to me to be the only way I could make any impression on people. And it seems to me, too, that I've always been afraid when I was in the company of other people...afraid of saying something stupid...afraid of being laughed at."

"Katherine Brooke, look at yourself in that mirror; carry that picture of yourself with you...magnificent hair framing your face instead of trying to pull it backward...eyes sparkling like dark stars...a little flush of excitement on your cheeks...and you won't feel afraid. Come, now. We're going to be late, but fortunately all the performers have what I heard Dora referring to as 'preserved' seats."

Gilbert drove them to the hall. How like old times it was... only Katherine was with her in place of Diana. Anne sighed. Diana had so many other interests now. No more running round to concerts and parties for her.

But what an evening it was! What silvery satin roads with a pale green sky in the west after a light snowfall! Orion was treading his stately march across the heavens, and hills and fields and woods lay around them in a pearly silence.

Katherine's reading captured her audience from the first line, and at the party she could not find dances for all her would-be partners. She suddenly found herself laughing without bitterness.

Then home to Green Gables, warming their toes at the sitting-room fire by the light of two friendly candles on the mantel; and Mrs. Lynde tiptoeing into their room, late as it was, to ask them if they'd like another blanket and assure Katherine that her little dog was snug and warm in a basket behind the kitchen stove.

"I've got a new outlook on life," thought Katherine as she drifted off to slumber. "I didn't know there were people like this."

"Come again," said Marilla when she left.

Marilla never said that to any one unless she meant it.

"Of course she's coming again," said Anne. "For weekends... and for *weeks* in the summer. We'll build bonfires and hoe in the garden...and pick apples and go for the cows...and row on the pond and get lost in the woods. I want to show you Little Hester Gray's garden, Katherine, and Echo Lodge and Violet Vale when it's full of violets."

7

"Windy Poplars,
"January 5th,
"The street where ghosts (should) walk.

"MY ESTEEMED FRIEND:

"That isn't anything Aunt Chatty's grandmother wrote. It's only something she would have written if she'd thought of it.

"I've made a New Year resolution to write sensible love-letters. Do you suppose such a thing is possible?

The Second Year

"I have left dear Green Gables but I have returned to dear Windy Poplars. Rebecca Dew had a fire lighted in the tower room for me and a hot-water bottle in the bed.

"I'm so glad I like Windy Poplars. It would be dreadful to live in a place I didn't like...that didn't seem friendly to me...that didn't say, 'I'm glad you're back.' Windy Poplars does. It's a bit old-fashioned and a bit prim, but it likes me.

"And I was glad to see Aunt Kate and Aunt Chatty and Rebecca Dew again. I can't help seeing their funny sides but I love them well for all that.

"Rebecca Dew said such a nice thing to me yesterday.

"'Spook's Lane has been a different place since you came here, Miss Shirley.'

"I'm glad you liked Katherine, Gilbert. She was surprisingly nice to you. It's amazing to find how nice she can be when she tries. And I think she is just as much amazed at it herself as any one else. She had no idea it would be so easy.

"It's going to make so much difference in school, having a Vice you can really work with. She is going to change her boarding-house, and I have already persuaded her to get that velvet hat and have not yet given up hope of persuading her to sing in the choir.

"Mr. Hamilton's dog came down yesterday and chivied Dusty Miller. 'This *is* the last straw,' said Rebecca Dew. And with her red cheeks redder still, her chubby back shaking with anger, and in such a hurry that she put her hat on hindside before and never knew it, she toddled up the road and gave Mr. Hamilton quite a large piece of her mind. I can just see his foolish, amiable face while he was listening to her.

"'I do not like That Cat,' she told me, 'but he is OURS and no Hamilton dog is going to come here and give him impudence in his own back yard. "He only chased your cat in fun," said Jabez Hamilton. "The Hamilton ideas of fun are different from the MacComber ideas of fun or the MacLean ideas of fun or, if it comes to that, the Dew ideas of fun," I told him. "Tut, tut, you must have had cabbage for dinner, Miss Dew," said he. "No," I said, "but I *could* have had. Mrs. Captain MacComber didn't sell all her cabbages last fall and leave her family without any because the price was so good. There are some people," sez I, "that can't hear anything because of the jingle in their pocket." And I left that to sink in. But what could you expect from a Hamilton? Low scum!'

"There is a crimson star hanging low over the white Storm King. I wish you were here to watch it with me. If you were, I really think it would be more than a moment of esteem and friendship."

"January 12th.

"Little Elizabeth came over two nights ago to find out if I could tell her what peculiar kind of terrible animals Papal bulls were, and to tell me tearfully that her teacher had asked her to sing at a concert the public school is getting up but that Mrs. Campbell put her foot down and said 'no' most decidedly. When Elizabeth attempted to plead, Mrs. Campbell said,

"'Have the goodness not to talk back to me, Elizabeth, if you please.'

"Little Elizabeth wept a few bitter tears in the tower room that night and said she felt it would make her Lizzie forever. She could never be any of her other names again.

"'Last week I loved God, this week I don't,' she said defiantly.

The Second Year 417

"All her class were taking part in the program and she felt 'like a leopard.' I think the sweet thing meant she felt like a leper and that was sufficiently dreadful. Darling Elizabeth must not feel like a leper.

"So I manufactured an errand to The Evergreens next evening. The Woman...who might really have lived before the flood, she looks so ancient...gazed at me coldly out of great gray, expressionless eyes, showed me grimly into the drawing-room and went to tell Mrs. Campbell that I had asked for her.

"I don't think there has been any sunshine in that drawing-room since the house was built. There was a piano, but I'm sure it could never have been played on. Stiff chairs, covered with silk brocade, stood against the wall...*all* the furniture stood against the wall except a central marble-topped table, and none of it seemed to be acquainted with the rest.

"Mrs. Campbell came in. I had never seen her before. She has a fine, sculptured old face that might have been a man's, with black eyes and black bushy brows under frosty hair. She has not quite eschewed *all* vain adornment of the body, for she wore large black onyx earrings that reached to her shoulders. She was painfully polite to me and I was painlessly polite to her. We sat and exchanged civilities about the weather for a few moments...both, as Tacitus remarked a few thousand years ago, 'with countenances adjusted to the occasion.' I told her, truthfully, that I had come to see if she would lend me the Rev. James Wallace Campbell's *Memoirs* for a short time, because I understood there was a good deal about the early history of Prince County in them which I wished to make use of in school.

"Mrs. Campbell thawed quite markedly and summoning Elizabeth, told her to go up to her room and bring down the *Memoirs*. Elizabeth's face showed signs of tears and Mrs. Campbell condescended to explain that it was because little Elizabeth's teacher had sent another note begging that she be allowed to sing at the concert, and that she, Mrs. Campbell, had written a very stinging reply which little Elizabeth would have to carry to her teacher the next morning.

"'I do not approve of children of Elizabeth's age singing in public,' said Mrs. Campbell. 'It tends to make them bold and forward.'

"As if anything could make little Elizabeth bold and forward!

"'I think perhaps you are wise, Mrs. Campbell,' I remarked in my most patronizing tone. 'In any event Mabel Phillips is going to sing, and I am told that her voice is really so wonderful that she will make all the others seem as nothing. No doubt it is *much* better that Elizabeth should not appear in competition with her.'

"Mrs. Campbell's face was a study. She may be Campbell outside but she is Pringle at the core. She said nothing, however, and I knew the psychological moment for stopping. I thanked her for the *Memoirs* and came away.

"The next evening when little Elizabeth came to the garden gate for her milk, her pale, flower-like face was literally a-star. She told me that Mrs. Campbell had told her she might sing after all, if she were careful not to let herself get puffed up about it.

"You see, Rebecca Dew had told me that the Phillips and the Campbell clans have always been rivals in the matter of good voices!

"I gave Elizabeth a bit of a picture for Christmas to hang above her bed...just a light-dappled woodland path leading up a hill to a quaint little house among some trees.

The Second Year

Little Elizabeth says she is not so frightened now to go to sleep in the dark, because as soon as she gets into bed she pretends that she is walking up the path to the house and that she goes inside and it is all lighted and her father is there.

"Poor darling! I can't help detesting that father of hers!"

"January 19th.

"There was a dance at Carry Pringle's last night. Katherine was there in a dark red silk with the new side flounces and her hair had been done by a hairdresser. Would you believe it, people who had known her ever since she came to teach in Summerside actually asked one another who she was when she came into the room. But I think it was less the dress and hair that made the difference than some indefinable change in herself.

"Always before, when she was out with people, her attitude seemed to be, 'These people bore me. I expect I bore them and I hope I do.' But last night it was as if she had set lighted candles in all the windows of her house of life.

"I've had a hard time winning Katherine's friendship. But nothing worth while is ever easy come by and I have always felt that her friendship would be worth while.

"Aunt Chatty has been in bed for two days with a feverish cold and thinks she may have the doctor tomorrow, in case she is taking pneumonia. So Rebecca Dew, her head tied up in a towel, has been cleaning the house madly all day to get it in perfect order before the doctor's possible visit. Now she is in the kitchen ironing Aunt Chatty's white cotton nighty with the crochet yoke, so that it will be ready for her to slip over her flannel one. It was spotlessly clean before, but Rebecca Dew thought it was not quite a good color from lying in the bureau drawer."

"January 28th.

"January so far has been a month of cold gray days, with an occasional storm whirling across the harbor and filling Spook's Lane with drifts. But last night we had a silver thaw and today the sun shone. My maple grove was a place of unimaginable splendors. Even the commonplaces had been made lovely. Every bit of wire fencing was a wonder of crystal lace.

"Rebecca Dew has been poring this evening over one of my magazines containing an article on 'Types of Fair Women,' illustrated by photographs.

"'Wouldn't it be lovely, Miss Shirley, if some one could just wave a wand and make everybody beautiful?' she said wistfully. 'Just fancy my feelings, Miss Shirley, if I suddenly found myself beautiful! But then'...with a sigh...'if we were all beauties who would do the work?'"

8

"I'm so tired," sighed Cousin Ernestine Bugle, dropping into her chair at the Windy Poplars supper-table. "I'm afraid sometimes to sit down for fear I'll never be able to git up again."

Cousin Ernestine, a cousin three times removed of the late Captain MacComber, but still, as Aunt Kate used to reflect, much too close, had walked in from Lowvale that afternoon

The Second Year

for a visit to Windy Poplars. It cannot be said that either of the widows had welcomed her very heartily, in spite of the sacred ties of family. Cousin Ernestine was not an exhilarating person, being one of those unfortunates who are constantly worrying not only about their own affairs but everybody else's as well and will not give themselves or others any rest at all. The very look of her, Rebecca Dew declared, made you feel that life was a vale of tears.

Certainly Cousin Ernestine was not beautiful and it was extremely doubtful if she ever had been. She had a dry, pinched little face, faded, pale blue eyes, several badly placed moles and a whining voice. She wore a rusty black dress and a decrepit neck-piece of Hudson seal which she would not remove even at the table, because she was afraid of draughts.

Rebecca Dew might have sat at the table with them had she wished, for the widows did not regard Cousin Ernestine as any particular "company." But Rebecca always declared she couldn't "savor her victuals" in that old kill-joy's society. She preferred to "eat her morsel" in the kitchen, but that did not prevent her from saying her say as she waited on the table.

"Likely it's the spring getting into your bones," she remarked unsympathetically.

"Ah, I hope it's only that, Miss Dew. But I'm afraid I'm like poor Mrs. Oliver Gage. She et mushrooms last summer but there must-a been a toadstool among them, for she's never felt the same since."

"But you can't have been eating mushrooms as early as this," said Aunt Chatty.

"No, but I'm afraid I've et something else. Don't try to cheer me up, Charlotte. You mean well, but it ain't no use. I've been through too much. Are you sure there ain't a spider in that cream jug, Kate? I'm afraid I saw one when you poured my cup."

"We never have spiders in *our* cream jugs," said Rebecca Dew ominously, and slammed the kitchen door.

"Mebbe it was only a shadder," said Cousin Ernestine meekly. "My eyes ain't what they were. I'm afraid I'll soon be blind. That reminds me...I dropped in to see Martha MacKay this afternoon and she was feeling feverish and all out in some kind of a rash. 'Looks to me as though you had the measles,' I told her. 'Likely they'll leave you almost blind. Your family all have weak eyes.' I thought she ought to be prepared. Her mother isn't well either. The doctor says it's indigestion, but I'm afraid it's a *growth*. 'And if you have to have an operation and take chloroform,' I told her, 'I'm afraid you'll never come out of it. Remember you're a Hillis and the Hillises all had weak hearts. Your father died of heart-failure, you know.'"

"At eighty-seven!" said Rebecca Dew, whisking away a plate.

"And you know three score and ten is the Bible limit," said Aunt Chatty cheerfully.

Cousin Ernestine helped herself to a third teaspoonful of sugar and stirred her tea sadly.

"So King David said, Charlotte, but I'm afraid David wasn't a very nice man in some respects." Anne caught Aunt Chatty's eye and laughed before she could help herself.

Cousin Ernestine looked at her disapprovingly.

"I've heerd you was a great girl to laugh. Well, I hope it'll last, but I'm afraid it won't. I'm afraid you'll find out all too soon that life's a melancholy business. Ah well, I was young myself once."

"Was you really?" inquired Rebecca Dew sarcastically, bringing in the muffins. "Seems to me you must always have been afraid to be young. It takes courage, I can tell you that, Miss Bugle."

"Rebecca Dew has such an odd way of putting things," complained Cousin Ernestine. "Not that I mind her of course. And it's well to laugh when you can, Miss Shirley, but I'm afraid you're tempting Providence by being so happy. You're awful like

The Second Year

our last minister's wife's aunt...she was always laughing and she died of a parralattic stroke. The third one kills you. I'm afraid our new minister out at Lowvale is inclined to be frivolous. The minute I saw him I sez to Louisy, 'I'm afraid a man with legs like that must be addicted to dancing.' I s'pose he's give it up since he turned minister, but I'm afraid the strain will come out in his family. He's got a young wife and they say she's scandalously in love with him. I can't seem to git over the thought of any one marrying a minister for love. I'm afraid it's awful irreverent. He preaches pretty fair sermons, but I'm afraid from what he said of Elijah the Tidbit last Sunday that he's far too liberal in his views of the Bible."

"I see by the papers that Peter Ellis and Fanny Bugle were married last week," said Aunt Chatty.

"Ah, yes. I'm afraid that'll be a case of marrying in haste and repenting at leisure. They've only known each other three years. I'm afraid Peter'll find out that fine feathers don't always make fine birds. I'm afraid Fanny's very shiftless. She irons her table napkins on the right side first and only. Not much like her sainted mother. Ah, *she* was a thorough woman if ever there was one. When she was in mourning she always wore black nightgowns. Said she felt as bad in the night as in the day. I was down at Andy Bugle's, helping them with the cooking, and when I come downstairs on the wedding morning if there wasn't Fanny eating an egg for her breakfast...and her gitting married that day. I don't s'pose you'll believe that...I wouldn't if I hadn't a-seen it with my own eyes. My poor dead sister never et a thing for three days afore she was married. And after her husband died we was all afraid she was never going to eat again. There are times when I feel I can't understand the Bugles any longer. There was a time when you knew where you was with your own connection, but it ain't that way now."

"Is it true that Jean Young is going to be married again?" asked Aunt Kate.

"I'm afraid it is. Of course Fred Young is supposed to be dead, but I'm dreadful afraid he'll turn up yet. You could never trust that man. She's going to marry Ira Roberts. I'm afraid he's only marrying her to make her happy. His Uncle Philip once wanted to marry me, but I sez to him, sez I, 'Bugle I was born and Bugle I will die. Marriage is a leap in the dark,' sez I, 'and I ain't going to be drug into it.' There's been an awful lot of weddings in Lowvale this winter. I'm afraid there'll be funerals all summer to make up for it. Annie Edwards and Chris Hunter were married last month. I'm afraid they won't be as fond of each other in a few years' time as they are now. I'm afraid she was just swept off her feet by his dashing ways. His Uncle Hiram was crazy...he belieft he was a dog for years."

"If he did his own barking nobody need have grudged him the fun of it," said Rebecca Dew, bringing in the pear preserves and the layer cake.

"I never heerd that he barked," said Cousin Ernestine. "He just gnawed bones and buried them when nobody was looking. His wife felt it."

"Where is Mrs. Lily Hunter this winter?" asked Aunt Chatty.

"She's been spending it with her son in San Francisco and I'm awful afraid there'll be another earthquake afore she gits out of it. If she does, she'll likely try to smuggle and have trouble at the border. If it ain't one thing, it's another when you're traveling. But folks seem to be crazy for it. My cousin Jim Bugle spent the winter in Florida. I'm afraid he's gitting rich and worldly. I said to him afore he went, sez I...I remember it was the night afore the Colemans' dog died...or was it?...yes, it was...'Pride goeth afore destruction and a haughty spirit afore a fall,' sez I. His daughter is teaching over in the Bugle Road school and she can't make up her mind which of her beaus to take. 'There's one thing

I can assure you of, Mary Annetta,' sez I, 'and that is you'll never git the one you love best. So you'd better take the one as loves you...if you kin be sure he does.' I hope she'll make a better choice than Jessie Chipman did. I'm afraid *she's* just going to marry Oscar Green because he was always round. 'Is *that* what you've picked out?' I sez to her. His brother died of galloping consumption. 'And don't be married in May,' sez I, 'for May's awful unlucky for a wedding.'"

"How encouraging you always are!" said Rebecca Dew, bringing in a plate of macaroons.

"Can you tell me," said Cousin Ernestine, ignoring Rebecca Dew and taking a second helping of pears, "if a calceolaria is a flower or a disease?"

"A flower," said Aunt Chatty.

Cousin Ernestine looked a little disappointed. "Well, whatever it is, Sandy Bugle's widow's got it. I heerd her telling her sister in church last Sunday that she had a calceolaria at last. Your geraniums are dreadful scraggy, Charlotte. I'm afraid you don't fertilize them properly. Mrs. Sandy's gone out of mourning and poor Sandy only dead four years. Ah well, the dead are soon forgot nowadays. My sister wore crape for her husband twenty-five years."

"Did you know your placket was open?" said Rebecca, setting a coconut pie before Aunt Kate.

"I haven't time to be always staring at my face in the glass," said Cousin Ernestine acidly. "What if my placket is open? I've got three petticoats on, haven't I? They tell me the girls nowadays only wear one. I'm afraid the world is gitting dreadful gay and giddy. I wonder if they ever think of the judgment day."

"Do you s'pose they'll ask us at the judgment day how many petticoats we've got on?" asked Rebecca Dew, escaping to the kitchen before any one could register horror. Even Aunt Chatty thought Rebecca Dew really had gone a little too far.

"I s'pose you saw old Alec Crowdy's death last week in the paper," sighed Cousin Ernestine. "His wife died two years ago, lit'rally harried into her grave, poor creetur. They say he's been awful lonely since she died, but I'm afraid that's too good to be true. And I'm afraid they're not through with their troubles with him yet, even if he is buried. I hear he wouldn't make a will and I'm afraid there'll be awful ructions over the estate. They say Annabel Crowdy is going to marry a jack-of-all-trades. Her mother's first husband was one, so mebbe it's heredit'ry. Annabel's had a hard life of it, but I'm afraid she'll find it's out of the frying-pan into the fire, even if it don't turn out he's got a wife already."

"What is Jane Goldwin doing with herself this winter?" asked Aunt Kate. "She hasn't been in to town for a long time."

"Ah, poor Jane! She's just pining away mysteriously. They don't know what's the matter with her, but I'm afraid it'll turn out to be an alibi. What is Rebecca Dew laughing like a hyenus out in the kitchen for? I'm afraid you'll have her on your hands yet. There's an awful lot of weak minds among the Dews."

"I see Thyra Cooper has a baby," said Aunt Chatty.

"Ah, yes, poor little soul. Only one, thank mercy. I was afraid it would be twins. Twins run so in the Coopers."

"Thyra and Ned are such a nice young couple," said Aunt Kate, as if determined to salvage something from the wreck of the universe.

But Cousin Ernestine would not admit that there was any balm in Gilead much less in Lowvale.

"Ah, she was real thankful to git him at last. There was a time she was afraid he wouldn't come back from the west. I warned her. 'You may be sure he'll disappoint you,' I told her. 'He's always disappointed people. Every one expected him to die afore he was a year old, but you see he's alive yet.' When he bought the Holly place I warned her again. 'I'm afraid that well is full of typhoid,' I told her. The Holly hired man died of

The Second Year

typhoid there five years ago.' They can't blame *me* if anything happens. Joseph Holly has some misery in his back. He calls it lumbago, but I'm afraid it's the beginning of spinal meningitis."

"Old Uncle Joseph Holly is one of the best men in the world," said Rebecca Dew, bringing in a replenished teapot.

"Ah, he's good," said Cousin Ernestine lugubriously. "Too good! I'm afraid his sons will all go to the bad. You see it like that so often. Seems as if an average has to be struck. No, thank you, Kate, I won't have any more tea...well, mebbe a macaroon. They don't lie heavy on the stomach, but I'm afraid I've et far too much. I must be taking French leave, for I'm afraid it'll be dark afore I git home. I don't want to git my feet wet; I'm so afraid of ammonia. I've had something traveling from my arm to my lower limbs all winter. Night after night I've laid awake with it. Ah, nobody knows what I've gone through, but I ain't one of the complaining sort. I was determined I'd git up to see you once more, for I may not be here another spring. But you've both failed terrible, so you may go afore me yet. Ah well, it's best to go while there's some one of your own left to lay you out. Dear me, how the wind is gitting up! I'm afraid our barn roof will blow off if it comes to a gale. We've had so much wind this spring I'm afraid the climate is changing. Thank you, Miss Shirley..." as Anne helped her into her coat..."Be careful of yourself. You look awful washed out. I'm afraid people with red hair never have real strong constitutions."

"I think my constitution is all right," smiled Anne, handing Cousin Ernestine an indescribable bit of millinery with a stringy ostrich feather dripping from its back. "I have a touch of sore throat tonight, Miss Bugle, that's all."

"Ah!" Another of Cousin Ernestine's dark forebodings came to her. "You want to watch a sore throat. The symptoms of diptheria and tonsillitis are exactly the same till the third day. But there's one consolation...you'll be spared an awful lot of trouble if you die young."

9

> "Tower Room,
> "Windy Poplars,
> "April 20th.

"POOR DEAR GILBERT:

"'I said of laughter, it is mad, and of mirth, what doeth it?' I'm afraid I'll turn gray young...I'm afraid I'll end up in the poorhouse...I'm afraid none of my pupils will pass their finals...Mr. Hamilton's dog barked at me Saturday night and I'm afraid I'll have hydrophobia...I'm afraid my umbrella will turn inside out when I keep a tryst with Katherine tonight...I'm afraid Katherine likes me so much now that she can't always like me as much...I'm afraid my hair isn't auburn after all...I'm afraid I'll have a mole on the end of my nose when I'm fifty...I'm afraid my school is a fire-trap...I'm afraid I'll find a mouse in my bed tonight...I'm afraid you got engaged to me just because I was always around...I'm afraid I'll soon be picking at the counterpane.

"No, dearest, I'm not crazy...not yet. It's only that Cousin Ernestine Bugle is catching.

"I know now why Rebecca Dew has always called her 'Miss Much-afraid.' The poor soul has borrowed so much trouble, she must be hopelessly in debt to fate.

"There are so many Bugles in the world...not many quite so far gone in Buglism as Cousin Ernestine, perhaps, but so many kill-joys, afraid to enjoy today because of what tomorrow will bring.

"Gilbert darling, don't let's ever be afraid of things. It's such dreadful slavery. Let's be daring and adventurous and expectant. Let's dance to meet life and all it can bring to us, even if it brings scads of trouble and typhoid and twins!

"Today has been a day dropped out of June into April. The snow is all gone and the fawn meadows and golden

The Second Year

hills just sing of spring. I know I heard Pan piping in the little green hollow in my maple bush and my Storm King was bannered with the airiest of purple hazes. We've had a great deal of rain lately and I've loved sitting in my tower in the still, wet hours of the spring twilights. But tonight is a gusty, hurrying night...even the clouds racing over the sky are in a hurry and the moonlight that gushes out between them is in a hurry to flood the world.

"Suppose, Gilbert, we were walking hand in hand down one of the long roads in Avonlea tonight!

"Gilbert, I'm afraid I'm scandalously in love with you. You don't think it's irreverent, do you? But then, you're not a minister."

10

"I'm *so* different," sighed Hazel.

It was really dreadful to be so different from other people... and yet rather wonderful, too, as if you were a being strayed from another star. Hazel would not have been one of the common herd for *anything*...no matter what she suffered by reason of her differentness.

"Everybody is different," said Anne amusedly.

"You are smiling." Hazel clasped a pair of very white, very dimpled hands and gazed adoringly at Anne. She emphasized at least one syllable in every word she uttered. "You have such a fascinating smile...such a *haunting* smile. I knew the moment I first saw you that you would understand *everything*. We are on the *same plane*. Sometimes I think I must be *psychic*, Miss Shirley. I always know so *instinctively* the moment I meet any one whether I'm going to like them or not. I felt at once that you were sympathetic...that you would *understand*. It's so sweet to be understood. Nobody understands me, Miss Shirley... *nobody*. But when I saw you, some inner voice whispered to me, '*She* will understand...with her you can be your *real self*.' Oh, Miss Shirley, let's be *real*...let's *always* be real. Oh, Miss Shirley, do you love me the leastest, tiniest bit?"

"I think you're a dear," said Anne, laughing a little and ruffling Hazel's golden curls with her slender fingers. It was quite easy to be fond of Hazel.

Hazel had been pouring out her soul to Anne in the tower room, from which they could see a young moon hanging over the harbor and the twilight of a late May evening filling the crimson cups of the tulips below the windows.

"Don't let's have any light yet," Hazel had begged, and Anne had responded,

"No...it's lovely here when the dark is your friend, isn't it? When you turn on the light, it makes the dark your enemy...and it glowers in at you resentfully."

"I can *think* things like that but I can never express them so beautifully," moaned Hazel in an anguish of rapture. "You talk in the language of the violets, Miss Shirley."

Hazel couldn't have explained in the least what she meant by that, but it didn't matter. It sounded *so* poetic.

The tower room was the only peaceful room in the house. Rebecca Dew had said that morning, with a hunted look, "We *must* get the parlor and spare-room papered before the Ladies' Aid meets here," and had forthwith removed all the furniture from both to make way for a paper-hanger who then refused to come until the next day. Windy Poplars was a wilderness of confusion, with one sole oasis in the tower room.

The Second Year

Hazel Marr had a notorious "crush" on Anne. The Marrs were new-comers in Summerside, having moved there from Charlottetown during the winter. Hazel was an "October blonde," as she liked to describe herself, with hair of golden bronze and brown eyes, and, so Rebecca Dew declared, had never been much good in the world since she found out she was pretty. But Hazel was popular, especially among the boys, who found her eyes and curls a quite irresistible combination.

Anne liked her. Earlier in the evening she had been tired and a trifle pessimistic, with the fag that comes with late afternoon in a schoolroom, but she felt rested now; whether as a result of the May breeze, sweet with apple blossom, blowing in at the window, or of Hazel's chatter, she could not have told. Perhaps both. Somehow, to Anne, Hazel recalled her own early youth, with all its raptures and ideals and romantic visions.

Hazel caught Anne's hand and pressed her lips to it reverently.

"I *hate* all the people you have loved before me, Miss Shirley. I hate all the other people you love *now*. I want to possess you *exclusively.*"

"Aren't you a bit unreasonable, honey? *You* love other people besides me. How about Terry, for example?"

"Oh, Miss Shirley! It's that I want to talk to you about. I can't endure it in silence any longer...I *cannot*. I *must* talk to some one about it...some one who *understands*. I went out the night before last and walked round and round the pond all night...well, nearly...till twelve, anyhow. I've suffered everything...*everything.*"

Hazel looked as tragic as a round, pink-and-white face, long-lashed eyes and a halo of curls would let her.

"Why, Hazel dear, I thought you and Terry were so happy... that everything was settled."

Anne could not be blamed for thinking so. During the preceding three weeks, Hazel had raved to her about Terry Garland, for Hazel's attitude was, what was the use of having a beau if you couldn't talk to some one about him?

"*Everybody* thinks that," retorted Hazel with great bitterness. "Oh, Miss Shirley, life seems so full of perplexing problems. I feel sometimes as if I wanted to lie down somewhere...*anywhere*...and fold my hands and never *think* again."

"My dear girl, what has gone wrong?"

"Nothing...and *everything*. Oh, Miss Shirley, *can* I tell you all about it...*can* I pour out my whole soul to you?"

"Of course, dear."

"I have really no place to pour out my soul," said Hazel pathetically. "Except in my journal, of course. Will you let me show you my journal some day, Miss Shirley? It is a self-revelation. And yet I cannot write out what burns in my soul. It...it *stifles* me!"

Hazel clutched dramatically at her throat.

"Of course I'd like to see it if you want me to. But what is this trouble between you and Terry?"

"Oh, Terry! Miss Shirley, will you believe me when I tell you that Terry seems like a *stranger* to me? A stranger! Some one I'd never seen before," added Hazel, so that there might be no mistake.

"But, Hazel...I thought you loved him...you said..."

"Oh, I know. I *thought* I loved him, too. But now I know it was all a terrible mistake. Oh, Miss Shirley, you can't dream how *difficult* my life is...how *impossible.*"

"I know something about it," said Anne sympathetically, remembering Roy Gardner.

"Oh, Miss Shirley, I'm sure I don't love him enough to marry him. I realize that now...now that it is too late. I was just moonlighted into thinking I loved him. If it hadn't been for the moon I'm sure I would have asked for time to think it over. But I was swept off my feet...I can see that now. Oh, I'll run away...I'll do something desperate!"

"But, Hazel dear, if you feel you've made a mistake, why not just tell him..."

The Second Year

"Oh, Miss Shirley, I couldn't! It would kill him. He simply adores me. There isn't any way out of it really. And Terry's beginning to talk of getting married. Think of it...a child like me...I'm only eighteen. All the friends I've told about my engagement as a secret are congratulating me...and it's such a farce. They think Terry is a great catch because he comes into ten thousand dollars when he is twenty-five. His grandmother left it to him. As if I cared about such a sordid thing as *money*! Oh, Miss Shirley, *why* is it such a mercenary world...*why?*"

"I suppose it is mercenary in some respects, but not in all, Hazel. And if you feel like this about Terry...we all make mistakes...it's very hard to know our own minds sometimes...."

"Oh, isn't it? I *knew* you'd understand. I *did* think I cared for him, Miss Shirley. The first time I saw him I just sat and gazed at him the whole evening. *Waves* went over me when I met his eyes. He was *so* handsome...though I thought even then that his hair was *too* curly and his eyelashes too white. *That* should have warned me. But I always put my soul into everything, you know...I'm so intense. I felt little shivers of ecstasy whenever he came near me. And now I feel nothing...*nothing*! Oh, I've grown old these past few weeks, Miss Shirley...*old*! I've hardly eaten anything since I got engaged. Mother could tell you. I'm *sure* I don't love him enough to marry him. Whatever else I may be in doubt about, I know *that*."

"Then you shouldn't..."

"Even that moonlight night he proposed to me, I was thinking of what dress I'd wear to Joan Pringle's fancy dress party. I thought it would be lovely to go as Queen of the May in pale green, with a sash of darker green and a cluster of pale pink roses in my hair. And a May-pole decked with tiny roses and hung with pink and green ribbons. Wouldn't it have been fetching? And then Joan's uncle had to go and die and Joan couldn't have the party after all, so it all went for nothing. But the point is...I really couldn't have loved him when my thoughts were wandering like that, could I?"

"I don't know...our thoughts play us curious tricks sometimes."

"I really don't think I ever want to get married at all, Miss Shirley. Do you happen to have an orangewood stick handy? Thanks. My half-moons are getting ragged. I might as well do them while I'm talking. Isn't it just lovely to be exchanging confidences like this? It's so seldom one gets the opportunity... the world intrudes itself so. Well, what was I talking of...oh, yes, Terry. What am I to do, Miss Shirley? I want your advice. Oh, I feel like a trapped creature!"

"But, Hazel, it's so very simple..."

"Oh, it isn't simple at all, Miss Shirley! It's dreadfully complicated. Mamma is so outrageously pleased, but Aunt Jean isn't. *She* doesn't like Terry, and everybody says she has such good judgment. I don't want to marry anybody. I'm ambitious...I want a career. Sometimes I think I'd like to be a nun. Wouldn't it be wonderful to be the bride of heaven? I think the Catholic church is *so* picturesque, don't you? But of course I'm not a Catholic...and anyway, I suppose you could hardly call it a career. I've always felt I'd love to be a nurse. It's such a romantic profession, don't you think? Smoothing fevered brows and all that...and some handsome millionaire patient falling in love with you and carrying you off to spend a honeymoon in a villa on the Riviera, facing the morning sun and the blue Mediterranean. I've *seen* myself in it. Foolish dreams, perhaps, but, oh, so sweet. I *can't* give them up for the prosaic reality of marrying Terry Garland and settling down in *Summerside!*"

Hazel shivered at the very idea and scrutinized a half-moon critically.

"I suppose..." began Anne.

The Second Year

"We haven't *anything* in common, you know, Miss Shirley. He doesn't care for poetry and romance, and they're my very *life*. Sometimes I think I must be a reincarnation of Cleopatra... or would it be Helen of Troy?...one of those languorous, seductive creatures, anyhow. I have such *wonderful* thoughts and feelings...I don't know where I get them if that isn't the explanation. And Terry is so terribly matter-of-fact...he can't be a reincarnation of anybody. What he said when I told him about Vera Fry's quill pen proves that, doesn't it?"

"But I never heard of Vera Fry's quill pen," said Anne patiently.

"Oh, haven't you? I thought I'd told you. I've told you so much. Vera's fiancé gave her a quill pen he'd made out of a feather he'd picked up that had fallen from a crow's wing. He said to her, 'Let your spirit soar to heaven with it whenever you use it, like the bird who once bore it.' Wasn't that just *wonderful*? But Terry said the pen would wear out very soon, especially if Vera wrote as much as she talked, and anyway he didn't think crows ever soared to heaven. He just missed the meaning of the whole thing completely...it's very essence."

"What *was* its meaning?"

"Oh...why...why...*soaring*, you know...getting away from the clods of earth. Did you notice Vera's ring? A sapphire. I think sapphires are too dark for engagement rings. I'd rather have your dear, romantic little hoop of pearls. Terry wanted to give me my ring right away...but I said not yet a while...it would seem like a fetter...so *irrevocable*, you know. I wouldn't have felt like that if I'd really loved him, would I?"

"No, I'm afraid not..."

"It's been so *wonderful* to tell somebody what I really feel like. Oh, Miss Shirley, if I could only find myself free again...free to seek the deeper meaning of life! Terry wouldn't understand what I meant if I said *that* to him. And I know he has a temper...

all the Garlands have. Oh, Miss Shirley...if you would just talk to him...tell him what I feel like...he thinks you're wonderful... he'd be guided by what you say."

"Hazel, my dear little girl, how could I do that?"

"I don't see why not." Hazel finished the last new moon and laid the orangewood stick down tragically. "If you can't, there isn't any help *anywhere*. But I can never, *never*, NEVER marry Terry Garland."

"If you don't love Terry, you ought to go to him and tell him so...no matter how badly it will make him feel. Some day you'll meet some one you can really love, Hazel dear...you won't have any doubts then...you'll *know.*"

"I shall never love *anybody* again," said Hazel, stonily calm. "Love brings only sorrow. Young as I am I have learned *that*. This would make a wonderful plot for one of your stories, wouldn't it, Miss Shirley? I must be going...I'd no idea it was so late. I feel *so* much better since I've confided in you...'touched your soul in shadowland,' as Shakespeare says."

"I think it was Pauline Johnson," said Anne gently.

"Well, I knew it was somebody...somebody who had *lived*. I think I shall sleep tonight, Miss Shirley. I've hardly slept since I found myself engaged to Terry, without the *least* notion how it had all come about."

Hazel fluffed out her hair and put on her hat, a hat with a rosy lining to its brim and rosy blossoms around it. She looked so distractingly pretty in it that Anne kissed her impulsively. "You're the prettiest thing, darling," she said admiringly.

Hazel stood very still.

Then she lifted her eyes and stared clear through the ceiling of the tower room, clear through the attic above it, and sought the stars.

"I shall never, *never* forget this *wonderful* moment, Miss Shirley," she murmured rapturously. "I feel that my beauty...

The Second Year

if I have any...has been *consecrated*. Oh, Miss Shirley, you don't know how really terrible it is to have a reputation for beauty and to be always afraid that when people meet you they will not think you as pretty as you were reported to be. It's *torture.* Sometimes I just *die* of mortification because I fancy I can see they're disappointed. Perhaps it's only my imagination...I'm *so* imaginative...too much so for my own good, I fear. I *imagined* I was in love with Terry, you see. Oh, Miss Shirley, *can* you smell the apple-blossom fragrance?"

Having a nose, Anne could.

"Isn't it just *divine?* I hope heaven will be *all* flowers. One could be good if one lived in a lily, couldn't one?"

"I'm afraid it might be a little confining," said Anne perversely.

"Oh, Miss Shirley, don't...*don't* be sarcastic with your little adorer. Sarcasm just *shrivels* me up like a leaf."

"I see she hasn't talked you quite to death," said Rebecca Dew, when Anne had come back after seeing Hazel to the end of Spook's Lane. "I don't see how you put up with her."

"I like her, Rebecca, I really do. *I* was a dreadful little chatterbox when I was a child. I wonder if I sounded as silly to the people who had to listen to me as Hazel does sometimes."

"I didn't know you when you was a child but I'm sure you didn't," said Rebecca. "Because you would *mean* what you said no matter how you expressed it and Hazel Marr doesn't. She's nothing but skim milk pretending to be cream."

"Oh, of course she dramatizes herself a bit as most girls do, but I think she means some of the things she says," said Anne, thinking of Terry. Perhaps it was because she had a rather poor opinion of the said Terry that she believed Hazel was quite in earnest in all she said about him. Anne thought Hazel was throwing herself away on Terry in spite of the ten thousand he was "coming into." Anne considered Terry a good-looking, rather weak youth who would fall in love with the first pretty girl who made eyes at him and would, with equal facility, fall in love with the next one if Number One turned him down or left him alone too long.

Anne had seen a good deal of Terry that spring, for Hazel had insisted on her playing gooseberry frequently; and she was destined to see more of him, for Hazel went to visit friends in Kingsport and during her absence Terry rather attached himself to Anne, taking her out for rides and "seeing her home" from places. They called each other "Anne" and "Terry," for they were about the same age, although Anne felt quite motherly towards him. Terry felt immensely flattered that "the clever Miss Shirley" seemed to like his companionship and he became so sentimental the night of May Connelly's party, in a moonlit garden, where the shadows of the acacias blew crazily about, that Anne amusedly reminded him of the absent Hazel.

"Oh, Hazel!" said Terry. "That child!"

"You're engaged to 'that child,' aren't you?" said Anne severely.

"Not really engaged...nothing but some boy-and-girl nonsense. I...I guess I was just swept off my feet by the moonlight."

Anne did a bit of rapid thinking. If Terry really cared so little for Hazel as this, the child was far better freed from him. Perhaps this was a heaven-sent opportunity to extricate them both from the silly tangle they had got themselves into and from which neither of them, taking things with all the deadly seriousness of youth, knew how to escape.

"Of course," went on Teriy, misinterpreting her silence. "I'm in a bit of a predicament, I'll own. I'm afraid Hazel has taken me a little bit too seriously, and I don't just know the best way to open her eyes to her mistake."

Impulsive Anne assumed her most maternal look.

"Terry, you are a couple of children playing at being grown up. Hazel doesn't really care anything more for you than you do for her. Apparently the moonlight affected both of you. *She* wants to be free but is afraid to tell you so for fear of hurting your feelings. She's just a bewildered, romantic girl and you're a boy in love with love, and some day you'll both have a good laugh at yourselves."

("I think I've put that very nicely," thought Anne complacently.)

Terry drew a long breath.

"You've taken a weight off my mind, Anne. Hazel's a sweet little thing, of course, I hated to think of hurting her, but I've realized my...our...mistake for some weeks. When one meets a *woman...the* woman...you're not going in yet, Anne? Is all this good moonlight to be wasted? You look like a white rose in the moonlight...Anne...

But Anne had flown.

11

Anne, correcting examination papers in the tower room one mid-June evening, paused to wipe her nose. She had wiped it so often that evening that it was rosy-red and rather painful. The truth was that Anne was the victim of a very severe and very unromantic cold in the head. It would not allow her to enjoy the soft green sky behind the hemlocks of The Evergreens, the silver-white moon hanging over the Storm King, the haunting perfume of the lilacs below her window or the frosty, blue-penciled irises in the vase on her table. It darkened all her past and overshadowed all her future.

"A cold in the head in June is an immoral thing," she told Dusty Miller, who was meditating on the window-sill. "But in two weeks from today I'll be in dear Green Gables instead of stewing here over examination papers full of howlers and wiping a worn-out nose. Think of it, Dusty Miller."

Apparently Dusty Miller thought of it. He may also have thought that the young lady who was hurrying along Spook's Lane and down the road and along the perennial path looked angry and disturbed and un-June-like. It was Hazel Marr, only a day back from Kingsport, and evidently a much disturbed Hazel Marr, who, a few minutes later, burst stormily into the tower room without waiting for a reply to her sharp knock.

"Why, Hazel dear..." *(Kershoo!)* "...are you back from Kingsport already? I didn't expect you till next week."

"No, I suppose you didn't," said Hazel sarcastically. "Yes, Miss Shirley, I *am* back. And what do I find? That you have been doing your best to lure Terry away from me...and all but succeeding."

"Hazel!" *(Kershoo!)*

"Oh, I know it all! You told Terry I didn't love him...that I wanted to break our engagement...our *sacred* engagement!"

"Hazel...child!" *(Kershoo!)*

"Oh, yes, sneer at me...sneer at everything. But don't try to deny it. You did it...and you did it *deliberately.* "

"Of course, I did. You asked me to."

"I...asked...you...to!"

"Here, in this very room. You told me you didn't love him and could never marry him."

"Oh, just a mood, I suppose. I never dreamed you'd take me seriously. I thought *you* would understand the artistic temperament. You're ages older than I am, of course, but even

The Second Year

you can't have forgotten the crazy ways girls talk...feel. *You* who pretended to be my friend!"

"This must be a nightmare," thought poor Anne, wiping her nose. "Sit down, Hazel...do."

"Sit down!" Hazel flew wildly up and down the room. "How can I sit down...how can *anybody* sit down when her life is in ruins all about her? Oh, if that is what being old does to you... jealous of younger people's happiness and determined to wreck it...I shall pray never to grow old."

Anne's hand suddenly tingled to box Hazel's ears with a strange horrible primitive tingle of desire. She slew it so instantly that she would never believe afterwards that she had really felt it. But she did think a little gentle chastisement was indicated.

"If you can't sit down and talk sensibly, Hazel, I wish you would go away." (A very violent *kershoo.*) "I have work to do." (Sniff...sniff...snuffle!)

"I am not going away till I have told you just what I think of you. Oh, I know I've only myself to blame...I should have known...I *did* know. I felt instinctively the first time I saw you that you were *dangerous.* That red hair and those green eyes! But I never *dreamed* you'd go so far as to make trouble between me and Terry. I thought you were a *Christian* at least. I never *heard* of any one doing such a thing. Well, you've broken my heart, if that is any satisfaction to you."

"You little goose..."

"I won't talk to you! Oh, Terry and I were so happy before you spoiled everything. *I* was so happy...the first girl of my set to be engaged. I even had my wedding all planned out...four bridesmaids in lovely pale blue silk dresses with black velvet ribbon on the flounces. So chic! Oh, I don't know if I hate you the most or pity you the most! Oh, how *could* you treat me like this...after I've *loved* you so...*trusted* you so...*believed* in you so!"

Hazel's voice broke...her eyes filled with tears...she collapsed on a rocking-chair.

"You can't have many exclamation points left," thought Anne, "but no doubt the supply of italics is inexhaustible."

"This will just about kill poor Momma," sobbed Hazel. "She was so pleased...*everybody* was so pleased...they all thought it an *ideal* match. Oh, can *anything* ever again be like it used to be?"

"Wait till the next moonlight night and try," said Anne gently.

"Oh, yes, laugh, Miss Shirley...laugh at my suffering. I have not the least doubt that you find it all very amusing...very amusing indeed! *You* don't know what suffering is! It is terrible... *terrible!*"

Anne looked at the clock and sneezed.

"Then don't suffer," she said unpityingly.

"I *will* suffer. My feelings are *very* deep. Of course a *shallow* soul wouldn't suffer. But I am thankful I am *not* shallow whatever else I am. Have you *any* idea what it means to be in love, Miss Shirley? Really, terribly deeply, *wonderfully* in love? And then to trust and be deceived? I went to Kingsport *so* happy...loving all the world! I told Terry to be good to you while I was away... not to let you be lonesome. I came home last night *so* happy. And he told me he didn't love me any longer...that it was all a mistake...a *mistake!*...and that *you* had told him I didn't care for him any longer, and wanted to be free!"

"My intentions were honorable," said Anne, laughing. Her impish sense of humor had come to her rescue and she was laughing as much at herself as at Hazel.

"Oh, *how* did I live through the night?" said Hazel wildly. "I just walked the floor. And you don't know...you can't even *imagine* what I've gone through today. I've had to sit and listen... actually *listen*...to people talking about Terry's infatuation for *you*. Oh, people have been watching you! *They* know what you've been doing. And why...*why*! That is what I *cannot* understand.

The Second Year

You had your own lover...why couldn't you have left me mine? What had you against me? What had I ever *done* to you?"

"I think," said Anne, thoroughly exasperated, "that you and Terry both need a good spanking. If you weren't too angry to listen to reason..."

"Oh, I'm not *angry*, Miss Shirley...only *hurt*...terribly hurt," said Hazel in a voice positively foggy with tears. "I feel that I have been betrayed in *everything*...in friendship as well as in love. Well, they say after your heart is broken you never suffer any more. I hope it's true, but I fear it isn't."

"What has become of your ambition, Hazel? And what about the millionaire patient and the honeymoon villa on the blue Mediterranean?"

"I'm sure I don't know what you're talking about, Miss Shirley. I'm not a bit ambitious...I'm not one of those dreadful new women. *My* highest ambition was to be a happy wife and make a happy home for my husband. *Was...was!* To think it should be in the past tense! Well, it doesn't do to trust *any one*. I've learned t*hat*. A bitter, bitter lesson!"

Hazel wiped her eyes and Anne wiped her nose, and Dusty Miller glared at the evening star with the expression of a misanthrope.

"You'd better go, I think, Hazel. I'm really very busy and I can't see that there is anything to be gained by prolonging this interview."

Hazel walked to the door with the air of Mary Queen of Scots advancing to the scaffold, and turned there dramatically.

"Farewell, Miss Shirley. I leave you to your conscience."

Anne, left alone with her conscience, laid down her pen, sneezed three times and gave herself a plain talking-to.

"You may be a B.A., Anne Shirley, but you have a few things to learn yet...things that even Rebecca Dew could have told you...*did* tell you. Be honest with yourself, my dear girl, and take your medicine like a gallant lady. Admit that you were carried off your feet by flattery. Admit that you really liked Hazel's professed adoration for you. Admit you found it pleasant to be worshiped. Admit that you liked the idea of being a sort of *dea ex machina*...saving people from their own folly when they didn't in the least want to be saved from it. And having admitted all this and feeling wiser and sadder and a few thousand years older, pick up your pen and proceed with your examination papers, pausing to note in passing that Myra Pringle thinks a seraph is 'an animal that abounds in Africa.'"

12

A week later a letter came for Anne, written on pale blue paper edged with silver.

"DEAR MISS SHIRLEY:

"I am writing this to tell you that *all misunderstanding* is cleared away between Terry and me and we are so deeply, intensely, *wonderfully* happy that we have decided we can forgive you. Terry says he was just moonlighted into making love to you but that his heart never *really* swerved in its allegiance to me. He says he really likes *sweet, simple* girls...that *all men* do...and has no use for *intriguing, designing ones*. We don't understand why you behaved to us as you did...we never will understand. Perhaps you just wanted material for a story and thought you could find it in tampering with the first sweet, tremulous love of a girl. But we thank you for *revealing us to ourselves*. Terry says he never realized the deeper meaning of life before. So really it

The Second Year   **445**

was all for the best. We are *so* sympathetic...we can *feel* each other's thoughts. Nobody understands him but me and I want to be a *source of inspiration* to him forever. *I* am not clever like y*ou* but I feel I can be *that,* for we are *soul-mates* and have vowed eternal *truth and constancy* to each other, no matter how many *jealous people* and *false friends* may try to make trouble between us.

"We are going to be married as soon as I have my trousseau ready. I am going up to Boston to get it. There really isn't *anything* in Summerside. My dress is to be *white moire* and my traveling-suit will be dove gray with hat, gloves and blouse of *delphinium blue.* Of course I'm very young, but I want to be married when I *am* young, before the *bloom* goes off life.

"Terry is all that my *wildest dreams* could picture and every *thought* of my heart is for him alone. I *know* we are going to be *rapturously happy. Once* I believed all my friends would *rejoice* with me in my happiness, but I have learned a *bitter lesson* in *worldly wisdom* since then.

"Yours *Truly,*
HAZEL MARR.

"P.S. 1. You told me Terry had *such a temper.* Why, he's a perfect lamb, his sister says.

"H.M.

"P.S. 2. I've heard that *lemon juice* will bleach freckles. You might try it on your nose.

"H.M."

"To quote Rebecca Dew," remarked Anne to Dusty Miller, "postscript Number Two *is* the last straw."

13

Anne went home for her second Summerside vacation with mixed feelings. Gilbert was not to be in Avonlea that summer. He had gone west to work on a new railroad that was being built. But Green Gables was still Green Gables and Avonlea was still Avonlea. The Lake of Shining Waters shone and sparkled as of old. The ferns still grew as thickly over the Dryad's Bubble, and the log-bridge, though it was a little crumblier and mossier every year, still led up to the shadows and silences and wind-songs of the Haunted Wood.

And Anne had prevailed on Mrs. Campbell to let little Elizabeth go home with her for a fortnight...no more. But Elizabeth, looking forward to two whole weeks with Miss Shirley, asked no more of life.

"I feel like *Miss* Elizabeth today," she told Anne with a sigh of delightful excitement, as they drove away from Windy Poplars. "Will you please call me 'Miss Elizabeth' when you introduce me to your friends at Green Gables? It would make me feel so grown up."

"I will," promised Anne gravely, remembering a small, red-headed damsel who had once begged to be called Cordelia.

Elizabeth's drive from Blight River to Green Gables, over a road which only Prince Edward Island in June can show, was almost as ecstatic a thing for her as it had been for Anne that memorable spring evening so many years ago. The world was beautiful, with wind-rippled meadows on every hand and surprises lurking around every corner. She was with her beloved Miss Shirley; she would be free from the Woman for two whole weeks; she had a new pink gingham dress and a pair of lovely new brown boots. It was almost as if Tomorrow were already

The Second Year

there...with fourteen Tomorrows to follow. Elizabeth's eyes were shining with dreams when they turned into the Green Gables lane where the pink wild roses grew.

Things seemed to change magically for Elizabeth the moment she got to Green Gables. For two weeks she lived in a world of romance. You couldn't step outside the door without stepping into something romantic. Things were just bound to happen in Avonlea...if not today, then tomorrow. Elizabeth knew she hadn't *quite* got into Tomorrow yet, but she knew she was on the very fringes of it.

Everything in and about Green Gables seemed to be acquainted with her. Even Manila's pink rosebud teaset was like an old friend. The rooms looked at her as if she had always known and loved them; the very grass was greener than grass anywhere else; and the people who lived at Green Gables were the kind of people who lived in Tomorrow. She loved them and was beloved by them. Davy and Dora adored her and spoiled her; Marilla and Mrs. Lynde approved of her. She was neat, she was lady-like, she was polite to her elders. They knew Anne did not like Mrs. Campbell's methods, but it was plain to be seen that she had trained her great-granddaughter properly.

"Oh, I don't want to sleep, Miss Shirley," Elizabeth whispered when they were in bed in the little porch gable, after a rapturous evening. "I don't want to sleep away a single minute of these wonderful two weeks. I wish I could get along without any sleep while I'm here."

For a while she didn't sleep. It was heavenly to lie there and listen to the splendid low thunder Miss Shirley had told her was the sound of the sea. Elizabeth loved it and the sigh of the wind around the eaves as well. Elizabeth had always been "afraid of the night." Who knew what queer thing might jump at you out of it? But now she was afraid no longer. For the first time in her life the night seemed like a friend to her.

They would go to the shore tomorrow, Miss Shirley had promised, and have a dip in those silver-tipped waves they had seen breaking beyond the green dunes of Avonlea when they drove over the last hill. Elizabeth could see them coming in, one after the other. One of them was a great dark wave of sleep...it rolled right over her...Elizabeth drowned in it with a delicious sigh of surrender.

"It's...so...easy...to...love...God...here," was her last conscious thought.

But she lay awake for a while every night of her stay at Green Gables, long after Miss Shirley had gone to sleep, thinking over things. Why couldn't life at The Evergreens be like life at Green Gables?

Elizabeth had never lived where she could make a noise if she wanted to. Everybody at The Evergreens had to move softly... speak softly...even, so Elizabeth felt, *think* softly. There were times when Elizabeth desired perversely to yell loud and long.

"You may make all the noise you want to here," Anne had told her. But it was strange...she no longer wanted to yell, now that there was nothing to prevent her. She liked to go quietly, stepping gently among all the lovely things around her. But Elizabeth learned to laugh during that sojourn at Green Gables. And when she went back to Summerside she carried delightful memories with her and left equally delightful ones behind her. To the Green Gables folks Green Gables seemed for months full of memories of little Elizabeth. For "little Elizabeth" she was to them in spite of the fact that Anne had solemnly introduced her as "Miss Elizabeth." She was so tiny, so golden, so elf-like, that they couldn't think of her as anything but little Elizabeth... little Elizabeth dancing in a twilight garden among the white June lilies...coiled up on a bough of the big Duchess apple tree reading fairy tales, unlet and unhindered...little Elizabeth half drowned in a field of buttercups where her golden head seemed

The Second Year

just a larger buttercup...chasing silver-green moths or trying to count the fireflies in Lover's Lane...listening to the bumblebees zooming in the canterburybells...being fed strawberries and cream by Dora in the pantry or eating red currants with her in the yard..."Red currants are such beautiful things, aren't they, Dora? It's just like eating jewels, isn't it?"...little Elizabeth singing to herself in the haunted dusk of the firs...with fingers sweet from gathering the big, fat, pink "cabbage roses"...gazing at the great moon hanging over the brook valley..."I think the moon has *worried eyes,* don't you, Mrs. Lynde?"...crying bitterly because a chapter in the serial story in Davy's magazine left the hero in a sad predicament..."Oh, Miss Shirley, I'm sure he can never live through it!"...little Elizabeth curled up, all flushed and sweet like a wild rose, for an afternoon nap on the kitchen sofa with Dora's kittens cuddled about her...shrieking with laughter to see the wind blowing the dignified old hens' tails over their backs...*could* it be little Elizabeth laughing like that?...helping Anne frost cupcakes, Mrs. Lynde cut the patches for a new "double Irish chain" quilt, and Dora rub the old brass candlesticks till they could see their faces in them...cutting out tiny biscuits with a thimble under Manila's tutelage. Why, the Green Gables folks could hardly look at a place or thing without being reminded of little Elizabeth.

"I wonder if I'll ever have such a happy fortnight again," thought little Elizabeth, as she drove away from Green Gables. The road to the station was just as beautiful as it had been two weeks before, but half the time little Elizabeth couldn't see it for tears.

"I couldn't have believed I'd miss a child so much," said Mrs. Lynde.

When little Elizabeth went, Katherine Brooke and her dog came for the rest of the summer. Katherine had resigned from the staff of the High School at the close of the year and meant to go to Redmond in the fall to take a secretarial course at Redmond University. Anne had advised this.

"I know you'd like it and you've never liked teaching," said the latter, as they sat one evening in a ferny corner of a clover field and watched the glories of a sunset sky.

"Life owes me something more than it has paid me and I'm going out to collect it," said Katherine decidedly. "I feel so much younger than I did this time last year," she added with a laugh.

"I'm sure it's the best thing for you to do, but I hate to think of Summerside and the High without you. What will the tower room be like next year without our evenings of confab and argument, and our hours of foolishness, when we turned everybody and everything into a joke?"

The Third Year

1

"Windy Poplars,
"Spook's Lane,
"September 8th.

"DEAREST:
"The summer is over...the summer in which I have seen you only that week-end in May. And I am back at Windy Poplars for my third and last year in Summerside High. Katherine and I had a delightful time together at Green Gables and I'm going to miss her dreadfully this year. The new Junior teacher is a jolly little personage, chubby and rosy and friendly as a puppy...but somehow, there's nothing more to her than that. She has sparkling shallow blue eyes with no thought behind them. I like her...I'll always like her...neither more nor less...there's nothing to *discover* in her. There was so much to discover in Katherine, when you once got past her guard.

"There is no change at Windy Poplars...yes there is. The old red cow has gone to her long home, so Rebecca Dew sadly informed me when I came down to supper Monday night. The widows have decided not to bother with another one but to get milk and cream from Mr. Cherry. This means that little Elizabeth will come no more to the garden gate for her new milk. But Mrs. Campbell seems to have grown reconciled to her coming over here when she wants to, so that does not make so much difference now.

"And another change is brewing. Aunt Kate told me, much to my sorrow, that they have decided to give Dusty Miller away as soon as they can find a suitable home for him.

When I protested, she said they were really driven to it for peace' sake. Rebecca Dew has been constantly complaining about him all summer and there seems to be no other way of satisfying her. Poor Dusty Miller...and he is such a nice, prowly, purry darling!

"Tomorrow, being Saturday, I'm going to look after Mrs. Raymond's twins while she goes to Charlottetown to the funeral of some relative. Mrs. Raymond is a widow who came to our town last winter. Rebecca Dew and the Windy Poplars widows...really, Summerside is a great place for widows...think her a 'little too grand' for Summerside, but she was really a wonderful help to Katherine and me in our Dramatic Club activities. One good turn deserves another.

"Gerald and Geraldine are eight and are a pair of angelic-looking youngsters, but Rebecca Dew 'pulled a mouth,' to use one of her own expressions, when I told her what I was going to do.

"'But I love children, Rebecca.'

"'Children, yes, but them's holy terrors, Miss Shirley. Mrs. Raymond doesn't believe in punishing children no matter what they do. She says she's determined they'll have a "natural" life. They take people in by that saintly look of theirs, but I've heard what her neighbors have to say of them. The minister's wife called one afternoon...well, Mrs. Raymond was sweet as sugar pie to her, but when she was leaving a shower of Spanish onions came flying down the stairs and one of them knocked her hat off. "Children always behave so abominably when you 'specially want them to be good," was all Mrs. Raymond said...kinder as if she was rather proud of them being so unmanageable. They're from the States, you know'...as if that explained everything. Rebecca has about as much use for 'Yankees' as Mrs. Lynde has."

The Third Year

2

Saturday forenoon Anne betook herself to the pretty, old-fashioned cottage on a street that straggled out into the country, where Mrs. Raymond and her famous twins lived. Mrs. Raymond was all ready to depart...rather gayly dressed for a funeral, perhaps...especially with regard to the beflowered hat perched on top of the smooth brown waves of hair that flowed around her head...but looking very beautiful. The eight-year-old twins, who had inherited her beauty, were sitting on the stairs, their, delicate faces wreathed with a quite cherubic expression. They had complexions of pink and white, large China-blue eyes and aureoles of fine, fluffy, pale yellow hair.

They smiled with engaging sweetness when their mother introduced them to Anne and told them that dear Miss Shirley had been so kind as to come and take care of them while Mother was away at dear Aunty Ella's funeral, and of course they would be good and not give her one teeny-weeny bit of trouble, wouldn't they, darlings?

The darlings nodded gravely and contrived, though it hadn't seemed possible, to look more angelic than ever.

Mrs. Raymond took Anne down the walk to the gate with her.

"They're all I've got...now," she said pathetically. "Perhaps I may have spoiled them a little...I know people say I have... people always know so much better how you ought to bring up your children than you know yourself, haven't you noticed, Miss Shirley? But *I* think loving is better than spanking any day, don't you, Miss Shirley? I'm sure *you* will have no trouble with them. Children always *know* whom they can play on and whom they can't, don't you think? That poor old Miss Prouty up the street...I had her to stay with them one day, but the poor darlings couldn't bear her. So of course they teased her a good bit...*you* know what children are. She has revenged herself by telling the most ridiculous tales about them all over town. But they'll just love you and I know they'll be angels. Of course, they have high spirits...but children should have, don't you think? It's so pitiful to see children with a cowed appearance, isn't it? I like them to be natural, don't you? Too good children don't seem natural, *do* they? Don't let them sail their boats in the bathtub or go wading in the pond, will you? I'm *so* afraid of them catching cold...their father died of pneumonia."

Mrs. Raymond's large blue eyes looked as if they were going to overflow, but she gallantly blinked the tears away.

"Don't worry if they quarrel a little—children always *do* quarrel, don't you think? But if any outsider attacks them...my dear!! They really just worship each other, you know. I could have taken *one* of them to the funeral, but they simply wouldn't hear of it. They've never been separated a day in their lives. And I *couldn't* look after twins at a funeral, could I now?"

"Don't worry, Mrs. Raymond," said Anne kindly. "I'm sure Gerald and Geraldine and I will have a beautiful day together. I love children."

"I know it. I felt sure the minute I saw you that you loved children. One can always tell, don't you think? There's *something* about a person who loves children. Poor old Miss Prouty detests them. She looks for the worst in children and so of course she finds it. You can't conceive what a comfort it is to me to reflect that my darlings are under the care of one who loves and understands children. I'm sure I'll quite enjoy the day."

"You might take *us* to the funeral," shrieked Gerald, suddenly sticking his head out of an upstairs window. "We never have any fun like that."

The Third Year

"Oh, they're in the bathroom!" exclaimed Mrs. Raymond tragically. "Dear Miss Shirley, please go and take them out. Gerald darling, you know mother couldn't take you *both* to the funeral. Oh, Miss Shirley, he's got that coyote skin from the parlor floor tied round his neck by the paws again. He'll ruin it. Please make him take it off at once. I *must* hurry or I'll miss the train."

Mrs. Raymond sailed elegantly away and Anne ran upstairs to find that the angelic Geraldine had grasped her brother by the legs and was apparently trying to hurl him bodily out of the window.

"Miss Shirley, make Gerald stop putting out his tongue at me," she demanded fiercely.

"Does it hurt you?" asked Anne smilingly.

"Well, he's not going to put out his tongue at *me,*" retorted Geraldine, darting a baleful look at Gerald, who returned it with interest.

"My tongue's my own and *you* can't stop me from putting it out when I like...can she, Miss Shirley?"

Anne ignored the question.

"Twins dear, it's just an hour till lunch-time. Shall we go and sit in the garden and play games and tell stories? And, Gerald, won't you put that coyote skin back on the floor?"

"But I want to play wolf," said Gerald.

"He wants to play wolf," cried Geraldine, suddenly aligning herself on her brother's side.

"We want to play wolf," they both cried together.

A peal from the door-bell cut the knot of Anne's dilemma.

"Come on and see who it is," cried Geraldine. They flew to the stairs and by reason of sliding down the banisters, got to the front door much quicker than Anne, the coyote skin coming unloosed and drifting away in the process.

"We never buy anything from peddlers," Gerald told the lady standing on the door-stone.

"Can I see your mother?" asked the caller.

"No, you can't. Mother's gone to Aunt Ella's funeral. Miss Shirley's looking after us. That's her coming down the stairs. *She'll* make you scat."

Anne *did* feel rather like making the caller "scat" when she saw who it was. Miss Pamela Drake was not a popular caller in Summerside. She was always "canvassing" for something and it was generally quite impossible to get rid of her unless you bought it, since she was utterly impervious to snubs and hints and had apparently all the time in the world at her command.

This time she was "taking orders" for an encyclopedia... something no school-teacher could afford to be without. Vainly Anne protested that she did not need an encyclopedia...the High School already possessed a very good one.

"Ten years out of date," said Miss Pamela firmly.

"We'll just sit down here on this rustic bench, Miss Shirley, and I'll show you my prospectus."

"I'm afraid I haven't time, Miss Drake. I have the children to look after."

"It won't take but a few minutes. I've been meaning to call on you, Miss Shirley, and I call it real fortunate to find you here. Run away and play, children, while Miss Shirley and I skim over this beautiful prospectus."

"Mother's hired Miss Shirley to look after us," said Geraldine, with a toss of her aerial curls. But Gerald had tugged her backward and they slammed the door shut.

"You see, Miss Shirley, what this encyclopedia *means*. Look at the beautiful paper...*feel* it...the splendid engravings...no other encyclopedia on the market has half the number of engravings... the wonderful print—a blind man could read it—and all for eighty dollars...eight dollars down and eight dollars a month till it's all paid. You'll never have such another chance...we're just doing this to introduce it...next year it will be a hundred and twenty."

"But I don't want an encyclopedia, Miss Drake," said Anne desperately.

"Of course you want an encyclopedia...*every one* wants an encyclopedia...a *National* encyclopedia. *I* don't know how I lived before I became acquainted with the *National* encyclopedia. *Live!* I didn't live...I merely existed. *Look* at that engraving of the cassowary, Miss Shirley. Did you ever really *see* a cassowary before?"

"But, Miss Drake, I..."

"If you think the terms a little too onerous I feel sure I can make a special arrangement for you, being a school-teacher...six a month instead of eight. You simply can't refuse an offer like that, Miss Shirley."

Anne almost felt she couldn't. Wouldn't it be worth six dollars a month to get rid of this terrible woman who had so evidently made up her mind not to go until she had got an order? Besides, *what* were the twins doing? They were alarmingly quiet. Suppose they were sailing their boats in the bathtub. Or had sneaked out of the back door and gone wading in the pond.

She made one more pitiful effort to escape.

"I'll think this over, Miss Drake, and let you know..."

"There's no time like the present," said Miss Drake, briskly getting out her fountain-pen. "You *know* you're going to take the *National,* so you might just as well sign for it now as any other time. Nothing is ever gained by putting things off. The price may go up any moment and then you'd have to pay a hundred and twenty. Sign here, Miss Shirley."

Anne felt the fountain-pen being forced into her hand... another moment...and then there was such a blood-curdling shriek from Miss Drake that Anne dropped the fountain-pen under the clump of golden glow that flanked the rustic seat, and gazed in amazed horror at her companion.

Was *that* Miss Drake...that indescribable object, hatless, spectacleless, almost hairless? Hat, spectacles, false front were floating in the air above her head halfway up to the bathroom window, out of which two golden heads were hanging. Gerald was grasping a fishing-rod to which were tied two cords ending in fishhooks. By what magic he had contrived to make a triple catch, only he could have told. Probably it was sheer luck.

Anne flew into the house and upstairs. By the time she reached the bathroom the twins had fled. Gerald had dropped the fishing-rod and a peep from the window revealed a furious Miss Drake retrieving her belongings, including the fountain-pen, and marching to the gate. For once in her life Miss Pamela Drake had failed to land her order.

Anne discovered the twins seraphically eating apples on the back porch. It was hard to know what to do. Certainly, such behavior could not be allowed to pass without a rebuke...but Gerald had undoubtedly rescued her from a difficult position and Miss Drake *was* an odious creature who needed a lesson. Still...

"You've et a great big worm!" shrieked Gerald. "I saw it disappear down your throat."

Geraldine laid down her apple and promptly turned sick...very sick. Anne had her hands full for some time. And when Geraldine was better, it was lunch-hour and Anne suddenly decided to let Gerald off with a very mild reproof. After all, no lasting harm had been done Miss Drake, who would probably hold her tongue religiously about the incident for her own sake.

"Do you think, Gerald," she said gently, "that what you did was a gentlemanly action?"

"Nope," said Gerald, "but it was good fun. Gee, I'm some fisherman, ain't I?"

The lunch was excellent. Mrs. Raymond had prepared it before she left and whatever her shortcomings as a disciplinarian might be, she was a good cook. Gerald and Geraldine, being occupied with gorging, did not quarrel or display worse table manners than the general run of children. After lunch Anne washed the dishes, getting Geraldine to help dry them and Gerald to put them carefully away in the cupboard. They were both quite knacky at it and Anne reflected complacently that all they needed was wise training and a little firmness.

3

At two o'clock Mr. James Grand called. Mr. Grand was the chairman of the High School board of trustees and had matters of importance to talk of, which he wished to discuss fully before he left on Monday to attend an educational conference in Kingsport. Could he come to Windy Poplars in the evening? asked Anne. Unfortunately he couldn't.

Mr. Grand was a good sort of man in his own fashion, but Anne had long ago found out that he must be handled with gloves. Moreover, Anne was very anxious to get him on her side in a battle royal over new equipment that was looming up. She went out to the twins.

"Darlings, will you play nicely out in the back yard while I have a little talk with Mr. Grand? I won't be very long...and then we'll have an afternoon-tea picnic on the banks of the pond... and I'll teach you to blow soap-bubbles with red dye in them... the loveliest things!"

"Will you give us a quarter apiece if we behave?" demanded Gerald.

"No, Gerald dear," said Anne firmly, "I'm not going to bribe you. I know you are going to be good, just because I ask you, as a gentleman should."

"We'll be good, Miss Shirley," promised Gerald solemnly.

"Awful good," echoed Geraldine, with equal solemnity.

It is possible they would have kept their promise if Ivy Trent had not arrived almost as soon as Anne was closeted with Mr. Grand in the parlor. But Ivy Trent did arrive and the Raymond twins hated Ivy Trent...the impeccable Ivy Trent who never did anything wrong and always looked as if she had just stepped out of a band-box.

On this particular afternoon there was no doubt that Ivy Trent had come over to show off her beautiful new brown boots and her sash and shoulder bows and hair bows of scarlet ribbon. Mrs. Raymond, whatever she lacked in some respects, had fairly sensible ideas about dressing children. Her charitable neighbors said she put so much money on herself that she had none to spend on the twins...and Geraldine never had a chance to parade the street in the style of Ivy Trent, who had a dress for every afternoon in the week. Mrs. Trent always arrayed her in "spotless white." At least. Ivy was always spotless when she left home. If she were not quite so spotless when she returned that, of course, was the fault of the "jealous" children with whom the neighborhood abounded.

Geraldine *was* jealous. She longed for scarlet sash and shoulder bows and white embroidered dresses. What would she not have given for buttoned brown boots like those?

"How do you like my new sash and shoulder bows?" asked Ivy proudly.

"How do you like my new sash and shoulder bows?" mimicked Geraldine tauntingly.

"But you haven't got shoulder bows," said Ivy grandly.

"But you haven't got shoulder bows," squeaked Geraldine.

The Third Year

Ivy looked puzzled.

"I have so. Can't you see them?"

"I have so. Can't you see them?" mocked Geraldine, very happy in this brilliant idea of repeating everything Ivy said scornfully.

"They ain't paid for," said Gerald.

Ivy Trent had a temper. It showed itself in her face, which grew as red as her shoulder bows.

"They are, too. *My* mother always pays her bills."

"*My* mother always pays her bills," chanted Geraldine.

Ivy was uncomfortable. She didn't know exactly how to cope with this. So she turned to Gerald, who was undoubtedly the handsomest boy on the street. Ivy had made up her mind about him.

"I came over to tell you I'm going to have you for my beau," she said, looking eloquently at him out of a pair of brown eyes that, even at seven, Ivy had learned had a devastating effect on most of the small boys of her acquaintance.

Gerald turned crimson.

"I won't be your beau," he said.

"But you've got to be," said Ivy serenely.

"But you've got to be," said Geraldine, wagging her head at him.

"I won't be," shouted Gerald furiously. "And don't you give me any more of your lip, Ivy Trent."

"You have to be," said Ivy stubbornly.

"You have to be," said Geraldine.

Ivy glared at her.

"You just shut up, Geraldine Raymond!"

"I guess I can talk in my own yard," said Geraldine.

"'Course she can," said Gerald. "And if *you* don't shut up, Ivy Trent, I'll just go over to your place and dig the eyes out of your doll."

"My mother would spank you if you did," cried Ivy.

"Oh, she would, would she? Well, do you know what *my* mother would do to her if she did? She'd just sock her on the nose."

"Well, anyway, you've got to be my beau," said Ivy, returning calmly to the vital subject.

"I'll...I'll duck your head in the rain-barrel," yelled the maddened Gerald..."I'll rub your face in an ant's nest...I'll...I'll tear them bows and sash off you..." triumphantly, for this at least was feasible.

"Let's do it," squealed Geraldine.

They pounced like furies on the unfortunate Ivy, who kicked and shrieked and tried to bite but was no match for the two of them. Together they hauled her across the yard and into the woodshed, where her howls could not be heard.

"Hurry," gasped Geraldine, "'fore Miss Shirley comes out."

No time was to be lost. Gerald held Ivy's legs while Geraldine held her wrists with one hand and tore off her hair bow and shoulder bows and sash with the other.

"Let's paint her legs," shouted Gerald, his eyes falling on a couple of cans of paint left there by some workmen the previous week. "I'll hold her and you paint her."

Ivy shrieked vainly in despair. Her stockings were pulled down and in a few moments her legs were adorned with wide stripes of red and green paint. In the process a good deal of the paint got spattered over her embroidered dress and new boots. As a finishing touch they filled her curls with burrs.

She was a pitiful sight when they finally released her. The twins howled mirthfully as they looked at her. Long weeks of airs and condescensions from Ivy had been avenged.

"Now you go home," said Gerald. "This'll teach you to go 'round telling people they have to be your beaus."

"I'll tell my mother," wept Ivy. "I'll go straight home and tell my mother on you, you horrid, horrid, hateful, *ugly* boy!"

"Don't you call my brother ugly, you stuck-up thing," cried Geraldine. "You and your shoulder bows! Here, take them with you. *We* don't want them cluttering up *our* woodshed."

Ivy, pursued by the bows, which Geraldine pelted after her, ran sobbing out of the yard and down the street.

"Quick...let's sneak up the back stairs to the bathroom and clean up 'fore Miss Shirley sees us," gasped Geraldine.

4

Mr. Grand had talked himself out and bowed himself away. Anne stood for a moment on the doorstone, wondering uneasily where her charges were. Up the street and in at the gate came a wrathful lady, leading a forlorn and still sobbing atom of humanity by the hand.

"Miss Shirley, where is Mrs. Raymond?" demanded Mrs. Trent.

"Mrs. Raymond is..."

"I insist on seeing Mrs. Raymond. She shall see with her own eyes what *her* children have done to poor, helpless, innocent Ivy. Look at her, Miss Shirley...just *look* at her!"

"Oh, Mrs. Trent...I'm so sorry! It is all my fault. Mrs. Raymond is away...and I promised to look after them...but Mr. Grand came..."

"No, it isn't your fault, Miss Shirley. I don't blame *you*. No one can cope with those diabolical children. The whole street knows them. If Mrs. Raymond isn't here, there is no point in my remaining. I shall take my poor child home. But Mrs. Raymond shall hear of this...indeed she shall. Listen to *that,* Miss Shirley. Are they tearing each other limb from limb?"

"That" was a chorus of shrieks, howls and yells that came echoing down the stairs. Anne ran upwards. On the hall floor was a twisting, writhing, biting, tearing, scratching mass. Anne separated the furious twins with difficulty and, holding each firmly by a squirming shoulder, demanded the meaning of such behavior.

"She says I've got to be Ivy Trent's beau," snarled Gerald.

"So he has got to be," screamed Geraldine.

"I won't be!"

"You've got to be!"

"Children!" said Anne. Something in her tone quelled them. They looked at her and saw a Miss Shirley they had not seen before. For the first time in their young lives they felt the force of authority.

"You, Geraldine," said Anne quietly, "will go to bed for two hours. You, Gerald, will spend the same length of time in the hall closet. Not a word. You have behaved abominably and you must take your punishment. Your mother left you in my charge and you will obey me."

"Then punish us *together*," said Geraldine, beginning to cry.

"Yes...you've no right to sep'rate us...we've never been sep'rated," muttered Gerald.

"You will be now." Anne was still very quiet. Meekly Geraldine took off her clothes and got into one of the cots in their room. Meekly Gerald entered the hall closet. It was a large airy closet with a window and a chair and nobody could have called the punishment an unduly severe one. Anne locked the door and sat down with a book by the hall window. At least, for two hours she would know a little peace of mind.

A peep at Geraldine a few minutes later showed her to be sound asleep, looking so lovely in her sleep that Anne almost

The Third Year

repented her sternness. Well, a nap would be good for her, anyway. When she wakened she should be permitted to get up, even if the two hours had not expired.

At the end of an hour Geraldine was still sleeping. Gerald had been so quiet that Anne decided that he had taken his punishment like a man and might be forgiven. After all, Ivy Trent was a vain little monkey and had probably been very irritating.

Anne unlocked the closet door and opened it.

There was no Gerald in the closet. The window was open and the roof of the side porch was just beneath it. Anne's lips tightened. She went downstairs and out into the yard. No sign of Gerald. She explored the woodshed and looked up and down the street. Still no sign.

She ran through the garden and through the gate into the lane that led through a patch of scrub woodland to the little pond in Mr. Robert Creedmore's field. Gerald was happily poling himself about on it in the small flat Mr. Creedmore kept there. Just as Anne broke through the trees Gerald's pole, which he had stuck rather deep in the mud, came away with unexpected ease at his third tug and Gerald promptly shot heels over head backward into the water.

Anne gave an involuntary shriek of dismay, but there was no real cause for alarm. The pond at its deepest would not come up to Gerald's shoulders and where he had gone over, it was little deeper than his waist. He had somehow got on his feet and was standing there rather foolishly, with his aureole plastered drippingly down on his head, when Anne's shriek was re-echoed behind her, and Geraldine, in her nightgown, tore through the trees and out to the edge of the little wooden platform to which the flat was commonly moored.

With a despairing shriek of "Gerald!" she took a flying leap that landed her with a tremendous splash by Gerald's side and almost gave him another ducking.

"Gerald, are you drowned?" cried Geraldine. "Are you drowned, darling?"

"No...no...darling," Gerald assured her through his chattering teeth.

They embraced and kissed passionately.

"Children, come in here this minute," said Anne. They waded to the shore. The September day, warm in the morning, had turned cold and windy in the late afternoon. They shivered terribly...their faces were blue. Anne, without a word of censure, hurried them home, got off their wet clothes and got them into Mrs. Raymond's bed, with hot-water bottles at their feet. They still continued to shiver. Had they got a chill? Were they headed for pneumonia?

"You should have taken better care of us, Miss Shirley," said Gerald, still chattering.

"'Course you should," said Geraldine.

A distracted Anne flew downstairs and telephoned for the doctor. By the time he came the twins had got warm, and he assured Anne that they were in no danger. If they stayed in bed till tomorrow they would be all right.

He met Mrs. Raymond coming up from the station on the way back, and it was a pale, almost hysterical lady who presently rushed in.

"Oh, Miss Shirley, how *could* you have let my little treasures get into such danger!"

"That's just what we told her, Mother," chorused the twins.

"I trusted you...I told you..."

"I hardly see how I was to blame, Mrs. Raymond," said Anne, with eyes as cold as gray mist. "You will realize this, I think, when you are calmer. The children are quite all right...I simply sent for the doctor as a precautionary measure. If Gerald and Geraldine had obeyed me, this would not have happened."

"I thought a *teacher* would have a little authority over children," said Mrs. Raymond bitterly.

The Third Year

"Over children perhaps...but not young demons," thought Anne. She said only, "Since you are here, Mrs. Raymond, I think I will go home. I don't think I can be of any further service and I have some school work to do this evening."

As one child the twins hurled themselves out of bed and flung their arms around her.

"I hope there'll be a funeral every week," cried Gerald. "'Cause I like you, Miss Shirley, and I hope you'll come and look after us every time Mother goes away."

"So do I," said Geraldine.

"I like you ever so much better than Miss Prouty."

"Oh, ever so much," said Geraldine.

"Will you put us in a story?" demanded Gerald.

"Oh, do," said Geraldine.

"I'm sure you *meant* well," said Mrs. Raymond tremulously.

"Thank you," said Anne icily, trying to detach the twins' clinging arms.

"Oh, don't let's quarrel about it," begged Mrs. Raymond, her enormous eyes filling with tears. "I *can't* endure quarreling with anybody."

"Certainly not." Anne was at her stateliest and Anne *could* be very stately. "I don't think there is the slightest necessity for quarreling. I think Gerald and Geraldine have quite enjoyed the day, though I don't suppose poor little Ivy Trent did."

Anne went home feeling years older.

"To think I ever thought Davy was mischievous," she reflected.

She found Rebecca in the twilight garden gathering late pansies.

"Rebecca Dew, I used to think the adage, 'Children should be seen and not heard,' entirely too harsh. But I see its points now."

"My poor darling. I'll get you a nice supper," said Rebecca Dew. And did *not* say, "I told you so."

5

(Extract from letter to Gilbert.)

"Mrs. Raymond came down last night and, with tears in her eyes, begged me to forgive her for her 'hasty behavior.' 'If you knew a mother's heart, Miss Shirley, you would not find it hard to forgive.'

"I didn't find it hard to forgive as it was...there is really something about Mrs. Raymond I can't help liking and she was a duck about the Dramatic Club. Just the same I did *not* say, 'Any Saturday you want to be away, I'll look after your offspring.' One learns by experience...even a person so incorrigibly optimistic and trustful as myself.

"I find that a certain section of Summerside society is at present very much exercised over the loves of Jarvis Morrow and Dovie Westcott...who, as Rebecca Dew says, have been engaged for over a year but can't get any 'forrader.' Aunt Kate, who is a distant aunt of Dovie's... to be exact, I think she's the aunt of a second cousin of Dovie's on the mother's side...is deeply interested in the affair because she thinks Jarvis is such an excellent match for Dovie...and also, I suspect, because she hates Franklin Westcott and would like to see him routed, horse, foot and artillery. Not that Aunt Kate would admit she 'hated' anybody, but Mrs. Franklin Westcott was a very dear girlhood friend of hers and Aunt Kate solemnly avers that he murdered her.

"I am interested in it, partly because I'm very fond of Jarvis and moderately fond of Dovie and partly, I begin to suspect, because I am an inveterate meddler in other people's business...always with excellent intentions, of course.

The Third Year

"The situation is briefly this:—Franklin Westcott is a tall, somber, hard-bitten merchant, close and unsociable. He lives in a big, old-fashioned house called Elmcroft just outside the town on the upper harbor road. I have met him once or twice but really know very little about him, except that he has an uncanny habit of saying something and then going off into a long chuckle of soundless laughter. He has never gone to church since hymns came in and he insists on having all his windows open even in winter storms. I confess to a sneaking sympathy with him in this, but I am probably the only person in Summerside who would. He has got into the habit of being a leading citizen and nothing municipal dares to be done without his approval.

"His wife is dead. It is common report that she was a slave, unable to call her soul her own. Franklin told her, it is said, when he brought her home that he would be master.

"Dovie, whose real name is Sibyl, is his only child...a very pretty, plump, lovable girl of nineteen, with a red mouth always falling a little open over her small white teeth, glints of chestnut in her brown hair, alluring blue eyes and sooty lashes so long you wonder if they can be real. Jen Pringle says it is her eyes Jarvis is really in love with. Jen and I have actually talked the affair over. Jarvis is her favorite cousin.

"(In passing, you wouldn't believe how fond Jen is of me...and I of Jen. She's really the cutest thing.)

"Franklin Westcott has never allowed Dovie to have any beaus and when Jarvis Morrow began to 'pay her attention,' he forbade him the house and told Dovie there was to be no more 'running round with that fellow.' But the mischief had been done. Dovie and Jarvis were already fathoms deep in love.

"Everybody in town is in sympathy with the lovers. Franklin Westcott is really unreasonable. Jarvis is a successful young lawyer, of good family, with good prospects, and a very nice, decent lad in himself.

"'Nothing could be more suitable,' declares Rebecca Dew. 'Jarvis Morrow could have *any* girl he wanted in Summerside. Franklin Westcott has just made up his mind that Dovie is to be an old maid. He wants to be sure of a housekeeper when Aunt Maggie dies.'

"'Isn't there any one who has any influence with him?' I asked.

"'Nobody can argue with Franklin Westcott. He's too sarcastical. And if you get the better of him he throws a tantrum. I've never seen him in one of his tantrums but I've heard Miss Prouty describe how he acted one time she was there sewing. He got mad over something...nobody knew what. He just grabbed everything in sight and flung it out of the window. Milton's poems went flying clean over the fence into George Clarke's lily pond. He's always kind of had a grudge at life. Miss Prouty says her mother told her that the yelps of him when he was born passed anything she ever heard. I suppose God has some reason for making men like that, but you'd wonder. No, I can't see any chance for Jarvis and Dovie unless they elope. It's a kind of low-down thing to do, though there's been a terrible lot of romantic nonsense talked about eloping. But this is a case where anybody would excuse it.'

"I don't know what to do but I must do something. I simply can't sit still and see people make a mess of their lives under my very nose, no matter how many tantrums Franklin Westcott takes. Jarvis Morrow is not going to wait forever...rumor has it that he is getting out of patience already and has been seen savagely cutting Dovie's name out of a tree on which he had cut it. There is an attractive Palmer girl who is reported to be throwing herself at his head, and his sister is said to have said that his mother has said that *her* son has no need to dangle for years at any girl's apron-string.

"Really, Gilbert, I'm quite unhappy about it.

"It's moonlight tonight, beloved...moonlight on the poplars of the yard...moonlit dimples all over the harbor where a phantom ship is drifting outwards...moonlight on the old graveyard...on my own private valley...on the Storm King. And it will be moonlight in Lover's Lane and on the Lake of Shining Waters and the old Haunted Wood and Violet Vale. There should be fairy dances on the hills tonight. But, Gilbert dear, moonlight with no one to share it is just...just *moonshine*.

"I wish I could take little Elizabeth for a walk. She loves a moonlight walk. We had some delightful ones when she was at Green Gables. But at home Elizabeth never sees moonlight except from the window.

"I am beginning to be a little worried about her, too. She is going on ten now and those two old ladies haven't the least idea what she needs, spiritually and emotionally. As long as she has good food and good clothes, they cannot imagine her needing anything more. And it will be worse with every succeeding year. What kind of girlhood will the poor child have?"

6

Jarvis Morrow walked home from the High School Commencement with Anne and told her his woes.

"You'll have to run away with her, Jarvis. Everybody says so. As a rule I don't approve of elopements" ("I said that like a teacher of forty years' experience," thought Anne with an unseen grin) "but there are exceptions to all rules."

"It takes two to make a bargain, Anne. I can't elope alone. Dovie is so frightened of her father, I can't get her to agree. And it wouldn't be an elopement...really. She'd just come to my sister Julia's...Mrs. Stevens, you know...some evening. I'd have the minister there and we could be married respectably enough to please anybody and go over to spend our honeymoon with Aunt Bertha in Kingsport. Simple as that. But I can't get Dovie to chance it. The poor darling has been giving in to her father's whims and crotchets so long, she hasn't any will-power left."

"You'll simply have to make her do it, Jarvis."

"Great Peter, you don't suppose I haven't tried, do you, Anne? I've begged till I was black in the face. When she's with me she'll almost promise it, but the minute she's home again she sends me word she can't. It seems odd, Anne, but the poor child is really fond of her father and she can't bear the thought of his never forgiving her."

"You must tell her she has to choose between her father and you."

"And suppose she chooses him?"

"I don't think there's any danger of that."

"You can never tell," said Jarvis gloomily. "But something has to be decided soon. I can't go on like this forever. I'm crazy about Dovie...everybody in Summerside knows that. She's like a little red rose just out of reach...I *must* reach her, Anne."

The Third Year

"Poetry is a very good thing in its place, but it won't get you anywhere in this instance, Jarvis," said Anne coolly. "That sounds like a remark Rebecca Dew would make, but it's quite true. What you need in this affair is plain, hard common sense. Tell Dovie you're tired of shilly-shallying and that she must take you or leave you. If she doesn't care enough for you to leave her father for you, it's just as well for you to realize it."

Jarvis groaned.

"You haven't been under the thumb of Franklin Westcott all your life, Anne. You haven't any realization of what he's like. Well, I'll make a last and final effort. As you say, if Dovie really cares for me she'll come to me...and if she doesn't, I might as well know the worst. I'm beginning to feel I've made myself rather ridiculous."

"If you're beginning to feel like that," thought Anne, "Dovie would better watch out."

Dovie herself slipped into Windy Poplars a few evenings later to consult Anne.

"What shall I do, Anne? What *can* I do? Jarvis wants me to elope...practically. Father is to be in Charlottetown one night next week attending a Masonic banquet...and it *would* be a good chance. Aunt Maggie would never suspect. Jarvis wants me to go to Mrs. Stevens' and be married there."

"And why don't you, Dovie?"

"Oh, Anne, do you really think I ought to?" Dovie lifted a sweet, coaxing face. "Please, *please* make up my mind for me. I'm just distracted." Dovie's voice broke on a tearful note. "Oh, Anne, you don't know Father. He just hates Jarvis...I can't imagine why...can you? How can *anybody* hate Jarvis? When he called on me the first time, Father forbade him the house and told him he'd set the dog on him if he ever came again...our big bull. You know they never let go once they take hold. And he'll never forgive me if I run away with Jarvis."

"You must choose between them, Dovie."

"That's just what Jarvis said," wept Dovie. "Oh, he was so stern...I never saw him like that before. And I can't...I *can't* li...i...i...ve without him, Anne."

"Then live with him, my dear girl. And don't call it eloping. Just coming into Summerside and being married among his friends isn't eloping."

"Father will call it so," said Dovie, swallowing a sob. "But I'm going to take your advice, Anne. I'm sure *you* wouldn't advise me to take any step that was wrong. I'll tell Jarvis to go ahead and get the license and I'll come to his sister's the night Father is in Charlottetown."

Jarvis told Anne triumphantly that Dovie had yielded at last.

"I'm to meet her at the end of the lane next Tuesday night... she won't have me go down to the house for fear Aunt Maggie might see me...and we'll just step up to Julia's and be married in a brace of shakes. All my folks will be there, so it will make the poor darling quite comfortable. Franklin Westcott said I should never get his daughter. I'll show him he was mistaken."

7

Tuesday was a gloomy day in late November. Occasional cold, gusty showers drifted over the hills. The world seemed a dreary outlived place, seen through a gray drizzle.

"Poor Dovie hasn't a very nice day for her wedding," thought Anne. "Suppose...suppose..." she quaked and shivered. "...suppose it doesn't turn out well, after all. It will be my fault.

The Third Year

Dovie would never have agreed to it if I hadn't advised her to. And suppose Franklin Westcott never forgives her. Anne Shirley, stop this! The weather is all that's the matter with you."

By night the rain had ceased but the air was cold and raw and the sky lowering. Anne was in her tower room, correcting school papers, with Dusty Miller coiled up under her stove. There came a thunderous knock at the front door.

Anne ran down. Rebecca Dew poked an alarmed head out of her bedroom door. Anne motioned her back.

"It's some one at *the front door*!" said Rebecca hollowly.

"It's all right, Rebecca dear. At least, I'm afraid it's all wrong... but, anyway, it's only Jarvis Morrow. I saw him from the side tower window and I know he wants to see me."

"Jarvis Morrow!" Rebecca went back and shut her door. "This *is* the last straw."

"Jarvis, whatever is the matter?"

"Dovie hasn't come," said Jarvis wildly. "We've waited *hours*...the minister's there...and my friends...and Julia has supper ready...and Dovie hasn't come. I waited for her at the end of the lane till I was half crazy. I didn't dare go down to the house because I didn't know what had happened. That old brute of a Franklin Westcott may have come back. Aunt Maggie may have locked her up. But I've got to *know*. Anne, you must go to Elmcroft and find out why she hasn't come."

"Me?" said Anne incredulously and ungrammatically.

"Yes, you. There's no one else I can trust...no one else who knows. Oh, Anne, don't fail me now. You've backed us up right along. Dovie says you are the only real friend she has. It isn't late...only nine. Do go."

"And be chewed up by the bulldog?" said Anne sarcastically.

"That old dog!" said Jarvis contemptuously. "He wouldn't say boo to a tramp. You don't suppose I was afraid of the dog, do you? Besides, he's always shut up at night. I simply don't want to make any trouble for Dovie at home if they've found out. Anne, please!"

"I suppose I'm in for it," said Anne with a shrug of despair.

Jarvis drove her to the long lane of Elmcroft, but she would not let him come further.

"As you say, it might complicate matters for Dovie in case her father has come home."

Anne hurried down the long, tree-bordered lane. The moon occasionally broke through the windy clouds, but for the most part it was gruesomely dark and she was not a little dubious about the dog.

There seemed to be only one light in Elmcroft...shining from the kitchen window. Aunt Maggie herself opened the side door to Anne. Aunt Maggie was a very old sister of Franklin Westcott's, a little bent, wrinkled woman who had never been considered very bright mentally, though she was an excellent housekeeper.

"Aunt Maggie, is Dovie home?"

"Dovie's in bed," said Aunt Maggie stolidly.

"In bed? Is she sick?"

"Not as I knows on. She seemed to be in a dither all day. After supper she says she was tired and ups and goes to bed."

"I must see her for a moment, Aunt Maggie. I...I just want a little important information."

"Better go up to her room then. It's the one on the right side as you go up."

Aunt Maggie gestured to the stairs and waddled out to the kitchen.

Dovie sat up as Anne walked in, rather unceremoniously, after a hurried rap. As could be seen by the light of a tiny candle, Dovie was in tears, but her tears only exasperated Anne.

"Dovie Westcott, did you forget that you promised to marry Jarvis Morrow tonight...*tonight?*"

The Third Year

"No...no..." whimpered Dovie. "Oh, Anne, I'm so unhappy...I've put in such a dreadful day. You can never, never know what I've gone through."

"I know what poor Jarvis has gone through, waiting for two hours at that lane in the cold and drizzle," said Anne mercilessly.

"Is he...is he very angry, Anne?"

"Just what you could notice"...bitingly.

"Oh, Anne, I just got frightened. I never slept one wink last night. I couldn't go through with it...I couldn't. I...there's really something disgraceful about eloping, Anne. And I wouldn't get any nice presents...well, not many, anyhow. I've always wanted to be m...m...arried in church...with lovely decorations...and a white veil and dress...and s...s...ilver slippers!"

"Dovie Westcott, get right out of that bed...*at once*...and get dressed...and come with me."

"Anne...it's too late now."

"It isn't too late. And it's now or never...you must know that, Dovie, if you've a grain of sense. You must know Jarvis Morrow will never speak to you again if you make a fool of him like this."

"Oh, Anne, he'll forgive me when he knows..."

"He won't. I know Jarvis Morrow. He isn't going to let you play indefinitely with his life. Dovie, do you want me to drag you bodily out of bed?"

Dovie shuddered and sighed.

"I haven't any suitable dress..."

"You've half-a-dozen pretty dresses. Put on your rose taffeta."

"And I haven't *any* trousseau. The Morrows will always cast that up to me...."

"You can get one afterwards. Dovie, didn't you weigh all these things in the balance before?"

"No...no...that's just the trouble. I only began to think of them last night. And Father...you don't know Father, Anne...."

"Dovie. I'll give you just ten minutes to get dressed!"

Dovie was dressed in the specified time.

"This dress is g...g...getting too tight for me," she sobbed as Anne hooked her up. "If I get much fatter I don't suppose Jarvis will l...l...love me. I wish I was tall and slim and pale, like you, Anne. Oh, Anne, what if Aunt Maggie hears us!"

"She won't. She's shut in the kitchen and you know she's a little deaf. Here's your hat and coat and I've tumbled a few things into this bag."

"Oh, my heart is fluttering so. Do I look terrible, Anne?"

"You look lovely," said Anne sincerely. Dovie's satin skin was rose and cream and all her tears hadn't spoiled her eyes. But Jarvis couldn't see her eyes in the dark and he was just a little annoyed with his adored fair one and rather cool during the drive to town.

"For Heaven's sake, Dovie, don't look so scared over having to marry me," he said impatiently as she came down the stairs of the Stevens house. "And don't cry...it will make your nose swell. It's nearly ten o'clock and we've got to catch the eleven o'clock train."

Dovie was quite all right as soon as she found herself irrevocably married to Jarvis. What Anne rather cattishly described in a letter to Gilbert as "the honeymoon look" was already on her face.

"Anne, darling, we owe it all to you. We'll never forget it, will we, Jarvis? And, oh, Anne darling, will you do just one more thing for me? Please break the news to Father. He'll be home early tomorrow evening...and *somebody* has got to tell him. You can smooth him over if anybody can. Please do your best to get him to forgive me."

Anne felt she rather needed some smoothing-over herself just then; but she also felt rather uneasily responsible for the outcome of the affair, so she gave the required promise.

"Of course he'll be terrible...simply terrible, Anne...but he can't kill you," said Dovie comfortingly. "Oh, Anne, you don't know...you can't realize...how *safe* I feel with Jarvis."

When Anne got home Rebecca Dew had reached the point where she had to satisfy her curiosity or go mad. She followed Anne to the tower room in her night-dress, with a square of flannel wrapped round her head, and heard the whole story.

"Well, I suppose this is what you might call 'life,'" she said sarcastically. "But I'm real glad Franklin Westcott has got his come-uppance at last, and so will Mrs. Captain MacComber be. But I don't envy you the job of breaking the news to him. He'll rage and utter vain things. If I was in your shoes, Miss Shirley, I wouldn't sleep one blessed wink tonight."

"I feel that it won't be a very pleasant experience," agreed Anne ruefully.

8

Anne betook herself to Elmcroft the next evening, walking through the dream-like landscape of a November fog with a rather sinking sensation pervading her being. It was not exactly a delightful errand. As Dovie had said, of course Franklin Westcott wouldn't kill her. Anne did not fear physical violence... though if all the tales told of him were true, he might throw something at her. Would he gibber with rage? Anne had never seen a man gibbering with rage and she imagined it must be a rather unpleasant sight. But he would probably exercise his noted gift for unpleasant sarcasm, and sarcasm, in man or woman, was the one weapon Anne dreaded. It always hurt her... raised blisters on her soul that smarted for months.

"Aunt Jamesina used to say, 'Never, if you can help it, be the bringer of ill news,'" reflected Anne. "She was as wise in that as in everything else. Well, here I am."

Elmcroft was an old-fashioned house with towers at every corner and a bulbous cupola on the roof. And at the top of the flight of front steps sat the dog.

"'If they take hold they never let go,'" remembered Anne. Should she try going round to the side door? Then the thought that Franklin Westcott might be watching her from the window braced her up. Never would she give him the satisfaction of seeing that she was afraid of his dog. Resolutely, her head held high, she marched up the steps, past the dog and rang the bell. The dog had not stirred. When Anne glanced at him over her shoulder he was apparently asleep.

Franklin Westcott, it transpired, was not at home but was expected every minute, as the Charlottetown train was due. Aunt Maggie convoyed Anne into what she called the "liberry" and left her there. The dog had got up and followed them in. He came and arranged himself at Anne's feet.

Anne found herself liking the "liberry." It was a cheerful, shabby room, with a fire glowing cozily in the grate, and bearskin rugs on the worn red carpet of the floor. Franklin Westcott evidently did himself well in regard to books and pipes.

Presently she heard him come in. He hung up his hat and coat in the hall: he stood in the library doorway with a very decided scowl on his brow. Anne recalled that her impression of him the first time she had seen him was that of a rather gentlemanly pirate, and she felt a repetition of it.

"Oh, it's you, is it?" he said rather gruffly. "Well, and what do you want?"

He had not even offered to shake hands with her. Of the two, Anne thought the dog had decidedly the better manners.

The Third Year

"Mr. Westcott, please hear me through patiently before..."

"I am patient...very patient. Proceed!"

Anne decided that there was no use beating about the bush with a man like Franklin Westcott.

"I have come to tell you," she said steadily, "that Dovie has married Jarvis Morrow."

Then she waited for the earthquake. None came. Not a muscle of Franklin Westcott's lean brown face changed. He came in and sat down in the bandylegged leather chair opposite Anne.

"When?" he said.

"Last night...at his sister's," said Anne.

Franklin Westcott looked at her for a moment out of yellowish brown eyes deeply set under penthouses of grizzled eyebrow. Anne had a moment of wondering what he had looked like when he was a baby. Then he threw back his head and went into one of his spasms of soundless laughter.

"You mustn't blame Dovie, Mr. Westcott," said Anne earnestly, recovering her powers of speech now that the awful revelation was over. "It wasn't her fault...."

"I'll bet it wasn't," said Franklin Westcott.

Was he trying to be sarcastic?

"No, it was all mine," said Anne, simply and bravely. "I advised her to elo...to be married....I *made* her do it. So please forgive her, Mr. Westcott."

Franklin Westcott coolly picked up a pipe and began to fill it.

"If you've managed to make Sibyl elope with Jarvis Morrow, Miss Shirley, you've accomplished more than I ever thought anybody could. I was beginning to be afraid she'd never have backbone enough to do it. And then I'd have had to back down... and Lord, how we Westcotts hate backing down! You've saved my face, Miss Shirley, and I'm profoundly grateful to you."

There was a very loud silence while Franklin Westcott tamped his tobacco down and looked with an amused twinkle at Anne's face. Anne was so much at sea she didn't know what to say.

"I suppose," he said, "that you came here in fear and trembling to break the terrible news to me?"

"Yes," said Anne, a trifle shortly.

Franklin Westcott chuckled soundlessly.

"You needn't have. You couldn't have brought me more welcome news. Why, I picked Jarvis Morrow out for Sibyl when they were kids. Soon as the other boys began taking notice of her, I shooed them off. That gave Jarvis his first notion of her. He'd show the old man! But he was so popular with the girls that I could hardly believe the incredible luck when he did really take a genuine fancy to her. Then I laid out my plan of campaign. I knew the Morrows root and branch. You don't. They're a good family, but the men don't want things they can get easily. And they're determined to get a thing when they're told they can't. They always go by contraries. Jarvis' father broke three girls' hearts because their families threw them at his head. In Jarvis' case I knew exactly what would happen. Sibyl would fall head over heels in love with him...and he'd be tired of her in no time. I knew he wouldn't keep on wanting her if she was too easy to get. So I forbade him to come near the place and forbade Sibyl to have a word to say to him and generally played the heavy parent to perfection. Talk about the charm of the uncaught! It's nothing to the charm of the uncatchable. It all worked out according to schedule, but I struck a snag in Sibyl's spinelessness. She's a nice child but she *is* spineless. I've been thinking she'd never have the pluck to marry him in my teeth. Now, if you've got your breath back, my dear young lady, unbosom yourself of the whole story."

The Third Year

Anne's sense of humor had again come to her rescue. She could never refuse an opportunity for a good laugh, even when it was on herself. And she suddenly felt very well acquainted with Franklin Westcott.

He listened to the tale, taking quiet, enjoyable whiffs of his pipe. When Anne had finished he nodded comfortably.

"I see I'm more in your debt even than I thought. She'd never have got up the courage to do it if it hadn't been for you. And Jarvis Morrow wouldn't have risked being made a fool of twice...not if I know the breed. Gosh, but I've had a narrow escape! I'm yours to command for life. You're a real brick to come here as you did, believing all the yarns gossip told you. You've been told a-plenty, haven't you now?"

Anne nodded. The bulldog had got his head on her lap and was snoring blissfully.

"Every one agreed that you were cranky, crabbed and crusty," she said candidly.

"And I suppose they told you I was a tyrant and made my poor wife's life miserable and ruled my family with a rod of iron?"

"Yes; but I really did take all that with a grain of salt, Mr. Westcott. I felt that Dovie couldn't be as fond of you as she was if you were as dreadful as gossip painted you."

"Sensible gal! My wife was a happy woman, Miss Shirley. And when Mrs. Captain MacComber tells you I bullied her to death, tick her off for me. Excuse my common way. Mollie was pretty...prettier than Sibyl. Such a pink-and-white skin...such golden-brown hair...such dewy blue eyes! She was the prettiest woman in Summerside. Had to be. I couldn't have stood it if a man had walked into church with a handsomer wife than me. I ruled my household as a man should but *not* tyrannically. Oh, of course, I had a spell of temper now and then, but Mollie didn't mind them after she got used to them. A man has a right to have a row with his wife now and then, hasn't he? Women get tired of monotonous husbands. Besides, I always gave her a ring or a necklace or some such gaud after I calmed down. There wasn't a woman in Summerside had more nice jewelry. I must get it out and give it to Sibyl."

Anne went wicked.

"What about Milton's poems?"

"Milton's poems? Oh, that! It wasn't Milton's poems...it was Tennyson's. I reverence Milton but I can't abide Alfred. He's too sickly sweet. Those last two lines of *Enoch Arden* made me so mad one night, I did fire the book through the window. But I picked it up the next day for the sake of the *Bugle Song*. I'd forgive anybody anything for that. It *didn't* go into George Clarke's lily pond—that was old Prouty's embroidery. You're not going? Stay and have a bite of supper with a lonely old fellow robbed of his only whelp."

"I'm really sorry I can't, Mr. Westcott, but I have to attend a meeting of the staff tonight."

"Well, I'll be seeing you when Sibyl comes back. I'll have to fling a party for them, no doubt. Good gosh, what a relief this has been to my mind. You've no idea how I'd have hated to have to back down and say, 'Take her.' *Now* all I have to do is to pretend to be heart-broken and resigned and forgive her sadly for the sake of her poor mother. I'll do it beautifully... Jarvis must never suspect. Don't *you* give the show away."

"I won't," promised Anne.

Franklin Westcott saw her courteously to the door. The bulldog sat up on his haunches and cried after her.

Franklin Westcott took his pipe out of his mouth at the door and tapped her on the shoulder with it.

"Always remember," he said solemnly, "there's more than one way to skin a cat. It can be done so that the animal'll never know he's lost his hide. Give my love to Rebecca Dew. A nice old puss, if you stroke her the right way. And thank you...thank you."

Anne betook herself home, through the soft, calm evening. The fog had cleared, the wind had shifted and there was a look of frost in the pale green sky.

"People told me I didn't know Franklin Westcott," reflected Anne. "They were right...I didn't. And neither did they."

"How did he take it?" Rebecca Dew was keen to know. She had been on tenterhooks during Anne's absence.

"Not so badly after all," said Anne confidentially. "I *think* he'll forgive Dovie in time."

"I never did see the beat of you, Miss Shirley, for talking people round," said Rebecca Dew admiringly. "You have certainly got a way with you."

"'Something attempted, something done has earned a night's repose,'" quoted Anne wearily as she climbed the three steps into her bed that night. "But just wait till the next person asks my advice about eloping!"

9

(Extract from, letter to Gilbert.)
"I am invited to have supper tomorrow night with a lady of Summerside. I know you won't believe me, Gilbert, when I tell you her name is Tomgallon...Miss Minerva Tomgallon. You'll say I've been reading Dickens too long and too late.

"Dearest, aren't you glad your name is Blythe? I am sure I could never marry you if it were Tomgallon. Fancy...Anne Tomgallon! No, you can't fancy it.

"This is the ultimate honor Summerside has to bestow... an invitation to Tomgallon House. It has no other name. No nonsense about Elms or Chestnuts or Crofts for the Tomgallons.

"I understand they were the 'Royal Family' in old days. The Pringles are mushrooms compared to them. And now there is left of them all only Miss Minerva, the sole survivor of six generations of Tomgallons. She lives alone in a huge house on Queen Street...a house with great chimneys, green shutters and the only stained-glass window in a private house in town. It is big enough for four families and is occupied only by Miss Minerva, a cook and a maid. It is very well kept up, but somehow whenever I walk past it I feel that it is a place which life has forgotten.

"Miss Minerva goes out very little, excepting to the Anglican church, and I had never met her until a few weeks ago, when she came to a meeting of staff and trustees to make a formal gift of her father's valuable library to the school. She looks exactly as you would expect a Minerva Tomgallon to look...tall and thin, with a long, narrow white face, a long thin nose and a long thin mouth. That doesn't sound very attractive, yet Miss Minerva is quite handsome in a stately, aristocratic style and is always dressed with great, though somewhat old-fashioned, elegance. She was quite a beauty when she was young, Rebecca Dew tells me, and her large black eyes are still full of fire and dark luster. She suffers from no lack of words, and I don't think I ever heard any one enjoy making a presentation speech more.

"Miss Minerva was especially nice to me, and yesterday I received a formal little note inviting me to have supper with her. When I told Rebecca Dew, she opened her eyes as widely as if I had been invited to Buckingham Palace.

The Third Year

"'It's a great honor to be asked to Tomgallon House,' she said in a rather awed tone. I never heard of Miss Minerva asking any of the principals there before. To be sure, they were all men, so I suppose it would hardly have been proper. Well, I hope she won't talk you to death, Miss Shirley. The Tomgallons could all talk the hind leg off a cat. And they liked to be in the front of things. Some folks think the reason Miss Minerva lives so retired is because now that she's old she can't take the lead as she used to do and she won't play second fiddle to any one. What are you going to wear, Miss Shirley? I'd like to see you wear your cream silk gauze with your black velvet bows. It's so dressy.'

"'I'm afraid it would be rather too "dressy" for a quiet evening out,' I said.

"'Miss Minerva would like it, I think. The Tomgallons all liked their company to be nicely arrayed. They say Miss Minerva's grandfather once shut the door in the face of a woman who had been asked there to a ball, because she came in her second-best dress. He told her her best was none too good for the Tomgallons.'

"Nevertheless, I think I'll wear my green voile, and the ghosts of the Tomgallons must make the best of it.

"I'm going to confess something I did last week, Gilbert. I suppose you'll think I'm meddling again in other folks' business. But I *had* to do something. I'll not be in Summerside next year and I can't bear the thought of leaving little Elizabeth to the mercy of those two unloving old women who are growing bitterer and narrower every year. What kind of a girlhood will she have with them in that gloomy old place?

"'I wonder,' she said to me wistfully, not long ago, 'what it would be like to have a grandmother you weren't afraid of.'

"This is what I did: *I wrote to her father.* He lives in Paris and I didn't know his address, but Rebecca Dew had heard and remembered the name of the firm whose branch he runs there, so I took a chance and addressed him in care of it. I wrote as diplomatic a letter as I could, but I told him plainly that he ought to take Elizabeth. I told him how she longs for and dreams about him and that Mrs. Campbell was really too severe and strict with her. Perhaps nothing will come of it, but if I hadn't written I would be forever haunted by the conviction that I ought to have done it.

"What made me think of it was Elizabeth telling me very seriously one day that she had 'written a letter to God,' asking Him to bring her father back to her and make him love her. She said she had stopped on the way home from school, in the middle of a vacant lot, and read it, looking up at the sky. I knew she had done something odd, because Miss Prouty had seen the performance and told me about it when she came to sew for the widows next day. She thought Elizabeth was getting 'queer'...'talking to the sky like that.' "I asked Elizabeth about it and she told me.

"'I thought God might pay more attention to a letter than a prayer,' she said. 'I've prayed so long. He must get so many prayers.'

"That night I wrote to her father.

"Before I close I must tell you about Dusty Miller. Some time ago Aunt Kate told me that she felt she must find another home for him because Rebecca Dew kept complaining about him so that she felt she really could not endure it any longer. One evening last week when I came home from school there was no Dusty Miller. Aunt Chatty said they had given him to Mrs. Edmonds, who lives on the other side of Summerside from Windy Poplars. I felt sorry, for Dusty Miller and I have been excellent friends. 'But, at least,' I thought, 'Rebecca Dew will be a happy woman.'

"Rebecca was away for the day, having gone to the country to help a relative hook rugs. When she returned at dusk nothing was said, but at bedtime when she was calling Dusty Miller from the back porch Aunt Kate said quietly:

"'You needn't call Dusty Miller, Rebecca. He is not here. We have found a home for him elsewhere. You will not be bothered with him any more.'

"If Rebecca Dew could have turned pale she would have done so.

"'Not here? Found a home for him? Good grief! Isn't this his home?'

"'We have given him to Mrs. Edmonds. She has been very lonely since her daughter married and thought a nice cat would be company.'

"Rebecca Dew came in and shut the door. She looked very wild.

"'This *is* the last straw,' she said. And indeed it seemed to be. I've never seen Rebecca Dew's eyes emit such sparkles of rage. 'I'll be leaving at the end of the month, Mrs. MacComber, and sooner if you can be suited.'

"'But, Rebecca,' said Aunt Kate in bewilderment, 'I don't understand. You've always disliked Dusty Miller. Only last week you said...'

"'That's right,' said Rebecca bitterly. 'Cast things up to me! Don't have any regard for my feelings! That poor dear Cat! I've waited on him and pampered him and got up nights to let him in. And now he's been spirited away behind my back without so much as a by-your-leave. And to Sarah Edmonds, who wouldn't buy a bit of liver for the poor creature if he was dying for it! The only company I had in the kitchen!'

"'But, Rebecca, you've always...'

"'Oh, keep on...keep on! Don't let *me* get a word in edgewise, Mrs. MacComber. I've raised that cat from a kitten...I've looked after his health and his morals...and what for? That Jane Edmonds should have a well-trained cat for company. Well, I hope she'll stand out in the frost at nights, as I've done, calling that cat for *hours* rather than leave him out to freeze, but I doubt it...I seriously doubt it. Well, Mrs. MacComber, all I hope is that your conscience won't trouble you the next time it's ten below zero. *I* won't sleep a wink when it happens, but of course *that* doesn't matter an old shoe to any one.'

"'Rebecca, if you would only...'

"'Mrs. MacComber, I am not a worm, neither am I a doormat. Well, this has been a lesson for me...a valuable lesson! Never again will I allow my affections to twine themselves around an animal of any kind or description. And if you'd done it open and aboveboard...but behind my back...taking advantage of me like that! I never heard of anything so dirt mean! But who am I that I should expect *my* feelings to be considered!'

"'Rebecca,' said Aunt Kate desperately, 'if you want Dusty Miller back we can get him back.'

"'Why didn't you say so before then?' demanded Rebecca Dew. 'And I doubt it. Jane Edmonds has got her claws in him. Is it likely she'll give him up?'

"'I think she will,' said Aunt Kate, who had apparently reverted to jelly. 'And if he comes back you won't leave us, will you, Rebecca?'

"'I may think it over,' said Rebecca, with the air of one making a tremendous concession.

"Next day, Aunt Chatty brought Dusty Miller home in a covered basket. I caught a glance exchanged between her and Aunt Kate after Rebecca had carried Dusty Miller out to the kitchen and shut the door. I wonder! Was it all a deep-laid plot on the part of the widows, aided and abetted by Jane Edmonds?

"Rebecca has never uttered a word of complaint about Dusty Miller since and there is a veritable clang of victory in her voice when she shouts for him at bedtime. It sounds as if she wanted all Summerside to know that Dusty Miller is back where he belongs and that she has once more got the better of the widows!"

10

It was on a dark, windy March evening, when even the clouds scudding over the sky seemed in a hurry, that Anne skimmed up the triple flight of broad, shallow steps flanked by stone urns and stonier lions, that led to the massive front door of Tomgallon House. Usually, when she had passed it after dark it was somber and grim, with a dim twinkle of light in one or two windows. But now it blazed forth brilliantly, even the wings on either side being lighted up, as if Miss Minerva were entertaining the whole town. Such an illumination in her honor rather overcame Anne. She almost wished she had put on her cream gauze.

Nevertheless she looked very charming in her green voile and perhaps Miss Minerva, meeting her in the hall, thought so, for her face and voice were very cordial. Miss Minerva herself was regal in black velvet, a diamond comb in the heavy coils of her iron-gray hair and a massive cameo brooch surrounded by a braid of some departed Tomgallon's hair. The whole costume was a little outmoded, but Miss Minerva wore it with such a grand air that it seemed as timeless as royalty's.

"Welcome to Tomgallon House, my dear," she said, giving Anne a bony hand, likewise well sprinkled with diamonds. "I am very glad to have you here as my guest."

"I am..."

"Tomgallon House was always the resort of beauty and youth in the old days. We used to have a great many parties and entertained all the visiting celebrities," said Miss Minerva, leading Anne to the big staircase over a carpet of faded red velvet. "But all is changed now. I entertain very little. I am the last of the Tomgallons. Perhaps it is as well. Our family, my dear, are *under a curse.*"

Miss Minerva infused such a gruesome tinge of mystery and horror into her tones that Anne almost shivered. The Curse of the Tomgallons! What a title for a story!

"This is the stair down which my Great-grandfather Tomgallon fell and broke his neck the night of his house-warming given to celebrate the completion of his new home. This house was consecrated by human blood. He fell *there...*" Miss Minerva pointed a long white finger so dramatically at a tiger-skin rug in the hall that Anne could almost see the departed Tomgallon dying on it. She really did not know what to say, so said inanely, "Oh!"

Miss Minerva ushered her along a hall, hung with portraits and photographs of faded loveliness, with the famous stained-glass window at its end, into a large, high-ceilinged, very stately guest-room. The high walnut bed, with its huge headboard, was covered with so gorgeous a silken quilt that Anne felt it was a desecration to lay her coat and hat on it.

The Third Year

"You have very beautiful hair, my dear," said Miss Minerva admiringly. "I always liked red hair. My Aunt Lydia had it...she was the only red-haired Tomgallon. One night when she was brushing it in the north room it caught fire from her candle and she ran shrieking down the hall wrapped in flames. All part of the Curse, my dear...all part of the Curse."

"Was she..."

"No, she wasn't burned to death, but she lost all her beauty. She was very handsome and vain. She never went out of the house from that night to the day of her death and she left directions that her coffin was to be shut so that no one might see her scarred face. Won't you sit down to remove your rubbers, my dear? This is a very comfortable chair. My sister died in it from a stroke. She was a widow and came back home to live after her husband's death. Her little girl was scalded in our kitchen with a pot of boiling water. Wasn't that a tragic way for a child to die?"

"Oh, how.. ."

"But at least we knew *how* it died. My half-aunt Eliza...at least, she would have been my half-aunt if she had lived...just *disappeared* when she was six years old. Nobody ever knew what became of her."

"But surely..."

"*Every* search was made but nothing was ever discovered. It was said that her mother...my step-grandmother...had been very cruel to an orphan niece of my grandfather's who was being brought up here. She locked it up in the closet at the head of the stairs, one hot summer day, for punishment and when she went to let it out she found it...*dead*. Some people thought it was a judgment on her when her own child vanished. But I think it was just Our Curse."

"Who put...?"

"What a high instep you have, my dear! My instep used to be admired too. It was said a stream of water could run under it...the test of an aristocrat."

Miss Minerva modestly poked a slipper from under her velvet skirt and revealed what was undoubtedly a very handsome foot.

"It certainly..."

"Would you like to see over the house, my dear, before we have supper? It used to be the Pride of Summerside. I suppose everything is very old-fashioned now, but perhaps there are a few things of interest. That sword hanging by the head of the stairs belonged to my great-great-grandfather who was an officer in the British Army and received a grant of land in Prince Edward Island for his services. He never lived in this house, but my great-great-grandmother did for a few weeks. She did not long survive her son's tragic death."

Miss Minerva marched Anne ruthlessly over the whole huge house, full of great square rooms...ballroom, conservatory, billiard-room, three drawingrooms, breakfast-room, no end of bedrooms and an enormous attic. They were all splendid and dismal.

"Those were my Uncle Ronald and my Uncle Reuben," said Miss Minerva, indicating two worthies who seemed to be scowling at each other from the opposite sides of a fireplace. "They were twins and they hated each other bitterly from birth. The house rang with their quarrels. It darkened their mother's whole life. And during their final quarrel in this very room, while a thunderstorm was going on, Reuben was killed by a flash of lightning. Ronald never got over it. He was a *haunted man* from that day. His wife," Miss Minerva added reminiscently, "swallowed her wedding-ring."

"What an ex..."

"Ronald thought it was very careless and wouldn't have anything done. A prompt emetic might have...but it was never heard of again. It spoiled her life. She always felt so *un*married without a wedding-ring."

"What a beautiful..."

The Third Year

"Oh, yes, that was my Aunt Emilia...not my aunt really, of course. Just the wife of Uncle Alexander. She was noted for her spiritual look, but she poisoned her husband with a stew of mushrooms...toadstools really. We always pretended it was an accident, because a murder is such a messy thing to have in a family, but we all knew the truth. Of course she married him against her will. She was a gay young thing and he was far too old for her. December and May, my dear. Still, that did not really justify toadstools. She went into a decline soon afterwards. They are buried together in Charlottetown...all the Tomgallons bury in Charlottetown. This was my Aunt Louise. She drank laudanum. The doctor pumped it out and saved her, but we all felt we could never trust her again. It was really rather a relief when she died respectably of pneumonia. Of course, some of us didn't blame her much. You see, my dear, her husband had spanked her."

"Spanked..."

"Exactly. There are really some things no gentleman should do, my dear, and one of them is spank his wife. Knock her down...possibly...but spank her, never! I would like," said Miss Minerva, very majestically, "to see the man who would dare to spank *me*."

Anne felt she would like to see him also. She realized that there are limits to the imagination after all. By no stretch of hers could she imagine a husband spanking Miss Minerva Tomgallon.

"This is the ballroom. Of course it is never used now. But there have been any number of balls here. The Tomgallon balls were famous. People came from all over the Island to them. That chandelier cost my father five hundred dollars. My Great-aunt Patience dropped dead while dancing here one night... right there in that corner. She had fretted a great deal over a man who had disappointed her. I cannot imagine any girl breaking her heart over a man. Men," said Miss Minerva, staring at a photograph of her father...a person with bristling side-whiskers and a hawklike nose..."have always seemed to me such *trivial* creatures."

11

The dining-room was in keeping with the rest of the house. There was another ornate chandelier, an equally ornate, gilt-framed mirror over the mantelpiece, and a table beautifully set with silver and crystal and old Crown Derby. The supper, served by a rather grim and ancient maid, was bountiful and exceedingly good, and Anne's healthy young appetite did full justice to it. Miss Minerva kept silence for a time and Anne dared say nothing for fear of starting another avalanche of tragedies. Once a large, sleek black cat came into the room and sat down by Miss Minerva with a hoarse meow. Miss Minerva poured a saucer of cream and set it down before him. She seemed so much more human after this that Anne lost a good deal of her awe of the last of the Tomgallons.

"Do have some more of the peaches, my dear. You've eaten nothing...positively nothing."

"Oh, Miss Tomgallon, I've enjoyed..."

"The Tomgallons always set a good table," said Miss Minerva complacently. "My Aunt Sophia made the best sponge-cake I ever tasted. I think the only person my father ever really hated to see come to our house was his sister Mary, because she had such a poor appetite. She just minced and tasted. He took it

The Third Year

as a personal insult. Father was a very unrelenting man. He never forgave my brother Richard for marrying against his will. He ordered him out of the house and he was never allowed to enter it again. Father always repeated the Lord's Prayer at family worship every morning, but after Richard flouted him he always left out the sentence, 'Forgive us our trespasses as we forgive those who trespass against us.' I can see him," said Miss Minerva dreamily, "kneeling there leaving it out."

After supper they went to the smallest of the three drawing-rooms...which was still rather big and grim...and spent the evening before the huge fire...a pleasant, friendly enough fire. Anne crocheted at a set of intricate doilies and Miss Minerva knitted away at an afghan and kept up what was practically a monologue composed in great part of colorful and gruesome Tomgallon history.

"This is a house of tragical memories, my dear."

"Miss Tomgallon, didn't *any* pleasant thing ever happen in this house?" asked Anne, achieving a complete sentence by a mere fluke. Miss Minerva had had to stop talking long enough to blow her nose.

"Oh, I suppose so," said Miss Minerva, as if she hated to admit it. "Yes, of course, we used to have gay times here when I was a girl. They tell me you're writing a book about every one in Summerside, my dear."

"I'm not...there isn't a word of truth..."

"Oh!" Miss Minerva was plainly a little disappointed. "Well, if ever you do you are at liberty to use any of our stories you like, perhaps with the names disguised. And now what do you say to a game of parchesi?"

"I'm afraid it is time I was going...."

"Oh, my dear, you can't go home tonight. It's pouring cats and dogs...and listen to the wind. I don't keep a carriage now...I have so little use for one...and you can't walk half a mile in that deluge. You must be my guest for the night."

Anne was not sure she wanted to spend a night in Tomgallon House. But neither did she want to walk to Windy Poplars in a March tempest. So they had their game of parchesi...in which Miss Minerva was so interested that she forgot to talk about horrors...and then a "bedtime snack." They ate cinnamon toast and drank cocoa out of old Tomgallon cups of marvelous thinness and beauty.

Finally Miss Minerva took her up to a guest-room which Anne at first was glad to see was not the one where Miss Minerva's sister had died of a stroke.

"This is Aunt Annabella's room," said Miss Minerva, lighting the candles in the silver candlesticks on a rather pretty green dressing-table and turning out the gas. Matthew Tomgallon had blown out the gas one night...whereupon exit Matthew Tomgallon. "She was the handsomest of all the Tomgallons. That's her picture above the mirror. Do you notice what a proud mouth she had? She made that crazy quilt on the bed. I hope you'll be comfortable, my dear. Mary has aired the bed and put two hot bricks in it. And she has aired this night-dress for you..." pointing to an ample flannel garment hanging over a chair and smelling strongly of moth balls. "I hope it will fit you. It hasn't been worn since poor Mother died in it. Oh, I nearly forgot to tell you..." Miss Minerva turned back at the door..."this is the room Oscar Tomgallon came back to life in—after being thought dead for two days. They *didn't want him to,* you know—*that* was the tragedy. I hope you'll sleep well, my dear."

Anne did not know if she could sleep at all or not. Suddenly there seemed something strange and alien in the room... something a little hostile. But is there not something strange about any room that has been occupied through generations? Death has lurked in it...love has been rosy red in it...births have been here...all the passions...all the hopes. It is full of wraiths.

The Third Year

But this was really rather a terrible old house, full of the ghosts of dead hatreds and heart-breaks, crowded with dark deeds that had never been dragged into light and were still festering in its corners and hidy-holes. Too many women must have wept here. The wind wailed very eerily in the spruces by the window. For a moment Anne felt like running out, storm or no storm.

Then she took herself resolutely in hand and commanded common sense. If tragic and dreadful things had happened here, many shadowy years agone, amusing and lovely things must have happened, too. Gay and pretty girls had danced here and talked over their charming secrets; dimpled babies had been born here; there had been weddings and balls and music and laughter. The sponge-cake lady must have been a comfortable creature and the unforgiven Richard a gallant lover.

"I'll think on these things and go to bed. What a quilt to sleep under! I wonder if I'll be as crazy as it by morning. And this is a spare room! I've never forgotten what a thrill it used to give me to sleep in any one's spare room."

Anne uncoiled and brushed her hair under the very nose of Annabella Tomgallon, who stared down at her with a face in which there were pride and vanity, and something of the insolence of great beauty. Anne felt a little creepy as she looked in the mirror. Who knew what faces might look out of it at her? All the tragic and haunted ladies who had ever looked into it, perhaps. She bravely opened the closet door, half expecting any number of skeletons to tumble out, and hung up her dress. She sat down calmly on a rigid chair, which looked as if it would be insulted if anybody sat on it, and took off her shoes. Then she put on the flannel nightgown, blew out the candles and got into the bed, pleasantly warm from Mary's bricks. For a little while the rain streaming on the panes and the shriek of the wind around the old eaves prevented her from sleeping. Then she forgot all the Tomgallon tragedies in dreamless slumber until she found herself looking at dark fir boughs against a red sunrise.

"I've enjoyed having you so much, my dear," said Miss Minerva when Anne left after breakfast. "We've had a real cheerful visit, haven't we? Though I've lived so long alone I've almost forgotten how to talk. And I need not say what a delight it is to meet a really charming and unspoiled young girl in this frivolous age. I didn't tell you yesterday but it was my birthday, and it was very pleasant to have a bit of youth in the house. There is nobody to remember my birthday now..." Miss Minerva gave a faint sigh..."and once there were so many."

"Well, I suppose you heard a pretty grim chronicle," said Aunt Chatty that night.

"Did all those things Miss Minerva told me really happen, Aunt Chatty?"

"Well, the queer thing is, they did," said Aunt Chatty. "It's a curious thing, Miss Shirley, but a lot of awful things did happen to the Tomgallons."

"I don't know that there were many more than happen in any large family in the course of six generations," said Aunt Kate.

"Oh, I think there were. They really did seem under a curse. So many of them died sudden or violent deaths. Of course there is a streak of insanity in them...every one knows that. That was curse enough...but I've heard an old story...I can't recall the details...of the carpenter who built the house cursing it. Something about the contract...old Paul Tomgallon held him to it and it ruined him, it cost so much more than he had figured."

"Miss Minerva seems rather proud of the curse," said Anne.

"Poor old thing, it's all she has," said Rebecca Dew.

Anne smiled to think of the stately Miss Minerva being referred to as a poor old thing. But she went to the tower room and wrote to Gilbert:

"I thought Tomgallon House was a sleepy old place where nothing ever happened. Well, perhaps things don't happen now but evidently they *did*. Little Elizabeth is always talking of Tomorrow. But the old Tomgallon house is Yesterday. I'm glad I don't live in Yesterday...that Tomorrow is still a friend.

"Of course I think Miss Minerva has all the Tomgallon liking for the spotlight and gets no end of satisfaction out of her tragedies. They are to her what husband and children are to other women. But, oh, Gilbert, no matter how old we get in years to come, don't let's ever see life as *all* tragedy and revel in it. I think I'd hate a house one hundred and twenty years old. I hope when we get our house of dreams it will either be new, ghostless and traditionless, or, if that can't be, at least have been occupied by reasonably happy people. I shall never forget my night at Tomgallon House. And for once in my life I've met a person who could talk me down."

12

Little Elizabeth Grayson had been born expecting things to happen. That they seldom happened under the watchful eyes of Grandmother and the Woman never brighted her expectations in the least. Things were just bound to happen some time...if not today, then tomorrow.

When Miss Shirley came to live at Windy Poplars Elizabeth felt that Tomorrow must be very close at hand and her visit to Green Gables was like a foretaste of it. But now in the June of Miss Shirley's third and last year in Summerside High, little

Elizabeth's heart had descended into the nice buttoned boots Grandmother always got for her to wear. Many children at the school where she went envied little Elizabeth those beautiful buttoned kid boots. But little Elizabeth cared nothing about buttoned boots when she could not tread the way to freedom in them. And now her adored Miss Shirley was going away from her forever. At the end of June she would be leaving Summerside and going back to that beautiful Green Gables. Little Elizabeth simply could not bear the thought of it. It was of no use for Miss Shirley to promise that she would have her down to Green Gables in the summer before she was married. Little Elizabeth knew somehow that Grandmother would not let her go again. Little Elizabeth knew Grandmother had never really approved of her intimacy with Miss Shirley.

"It will be the end of everything, Miss Shirley," she sobbed.

"Let's hope, darling, that it is only a new beginning," said Anne cheerfully. But she felt downcast herself. No word had ever come from little Elizabeth's father. Either her letter had never reached him or he did not care. And, if he did not care, what was to become of Elizabeth? It was bad enough now in her childhood, but what would it be later on?

"Those two old dames will boss her to death," Rebecca Dew had said. Anne felt that there was more truth than elegance in her remark.

Elizabeth knew that she was "bossed." And she especially resented being bossed by the Woman. She did not like it in Grandmother, of course, but one conceded reluctantly that perhaps a grandmother had a certain right to boss you. But what right had the Woman? Elizabeth always wanted to ask her that right out. She *would* do it some time...when Tomorrow came. And oh, how she would enjoy the look on the Woman's face!

Grandmother would never let little Elizabeth go out walking by herself...for fear, she said, that she might be kidnaped by

The Third Year

gypsies. A child had been once, forty years before. It was very seldom gypsies came to the Island now, and little Elizabeth felt that it was only an excuse. But why should Grandmother care whether she were kidnaped or not? Elizabeth knew that Grandmother and the Woman didn't love her at all. Why, they never even spoke of her by her name if they could help it. It was always "the child." How Elizabeth hated to be called "the child" just as they might have spoken of "the dog" or "the cat" if there had been one. But when Elizabeth had ventured a protest, Grandmother's face had grown dark and angry and little Elizabeth had been punished for impertinence, while the Woman looked on, well content. Little Elizabeth often wondered just why the Woman hated her.

Why should any one hate you when you were so small? Could you be worth hating? Little Elizabeth did not know that the mother whose life she had cost had been that bitter old woman's darling and, if she had known, could not have understood what perverted shapes thwarted love can take.

Little Elizabeth hated the gloomy, splendid Evergreens, where everything seemed unacquainted with her although she had lived in it all her life. But after Miss Shirley had come to Windy Poplars everything had changed magically. Little Elizabeth lived in a world of romance after Miss Shirley's coming. There was beauty wherever you looked. Fortunately Grandmother and the Woman couldn't prevent you from looking, though Elizabeth had no doubt they would if they could. The short walks along the red magic of the harbor road, which she was all too rarely permitted to share with Miss Shirley, were the high lights in her shadowy life. She loved everything she saw...the far-away lighthouse painted in odd red and white rings...the far, dim blue shores...the little silvery blue waves...the range lights that gleamed through the violet dusks...all gave her so much delight that it hurt. And the harbor with its smoky islands and glowing sunsets! Elizabeth always went up to a window in the mansard roof to watch them through the tree-tops...and the ships that sailed at the rising of the moon. Ships that came back...ships that never came back. Elizabeth longed to go in one of them... on a voyage to the Island of Happiness. The ships that never came back stayed there, where it was always Tomorrow.

That mysterious red road ran on and on and her feet itched to follow it. Where did it lead to? Sometimes Elizabeth thought she would burst if she didn't find out. When Tomorrow really came she would fare forth on it and perhaps find an island all her own where she and Miss Shirley could live alone and Grandmother and the Woman could never come. They both hated water and would not put foot in a boat for anything. Little Elizabeth liked to picture herself standing on her island and mocking them, as they stood vainly glowering on the mainland shore.

"This is Tomorrow," she would taunt them. "You can't catch me any more. You're only in Today."

What fun it would be! How she would enjoy the look on the Woman's face!

Then one evening in late June an amazing thing happened. Miss Shirley had told Mrs. Campbell that she had an errand next day at Flying Cloud, to see a certain Mrs. Thompson, who was convener of the refreshment committee of the Ladies' Aid, and might she take Elizabeth with her. Grandmother had agreed with her usual dourness...Elizabeth could never understand why she agreed at all, being completely ignorant of the Pringle horror of a certain bit of information Miss Shirley possessed... but she had agreed.

"We'll go right down to the harbor mouth," whispered Anne, "after I've done my errand at Flying Cloud."

Little Elizabeth went to bed in such excitement that she didn't expect to sleep a wink. At last she was going to answer

The Third Year

the lure of the road that had called so long. In spite of her excitement, she conscientiously went through her little ritual of retiring. She folded her clothes and cleaned her teeth and brushed her golden hair. She thought she had rather pretty hair, though of course it wasn't like Miss Shirley's lovely red-gold with the ripples in it and the little love-locks that curled around her ears. Little Elizabeth would have given anything to have had hair like Miss Shirley's.

Before she got into bed little Elizabeth opened one of the drawers in the high, black, polished old bureau and took a carefully hidden picture from under a pile of hankies...a picture of Miss Shirley which she had cut out of a special edition of the *Weekly Courier* that had reproduced a photograph of the High School staff.

"Good night, dearest Miss Shirley." She kissed the picture and returned it to its hiding-place. Then she climbed into bed and cuddled down under the blankets...for the June night was cool and the breeze of the harbor searching. Indeed, it was more than a breeze tonight. It whistled and banged and shook and thumped, and Elizabeth knew the harbor would be a tossing expanse of waves under the moonlight. What fun it would be to steal down close to it under the moon! But it was only in Tomorrow one could do that.

Where was Flying Cloud? What a name! Out of Tomorrow again. It was maddening to be so near Tomorrow and not be able to get into it. But suppose the wind blew up rain for tomorrow! Elizabeth knew she would never be allowed to go anywhere in rain.

She sat up in bed and clasped her hands.

"Dear God," she said, "I don't like to meddle, but *could* You see that it is fine tomorrow? *Please,* dear God."

The next afternoon was glorious. Little Elizabeth felt as if she had slipped from some invisible shackles when she and

Miss Shirley walked away from that house of gloom. She took a huge gulp of freedom, even if the Woman was scowling after them through the red glass of the big front door. How heavenly to be walking through the lovely world with Miss Shirley! It was always so wonderful to be alone with Miss Shirley. What would she do when Miss Shirley had gone? But little Elizabeth put the thought firmly away. She wouldn't spoil the day by thinking it. Perhaps...a great perhaps...she and Miss Shirley would get into Tomorrow this afternoon and then they would never be separated. Little Elizabeth just wanted to walk quietly on towards that blueness at the end of the world, drinking in the beauty around her. Every turn and kink of the road revealed new lovelinesses...and it turned and kinked interminably, following the windings of a tiny river that seemed to have appeared from nowhere.

On every side were fields of buttercups and clover where bees buzzed. Now and then they walked through a milky way of daisies. Far out the strait laughed at them in silver-tipped waves. The harbor was like watered silk. Little Elizabeth liked it better that way than when it was like pale blue satin. They drank the wind in. It was a very gentle wind. It purred about them and seemed to coax them on.

"Isn't it nice, walking with the wind like this?" said little Elizabeth.

"A nice, friendly, perfumed wind," said Anne, more to herself than Elizabeth. "Such a wind as I used to think a *mistral* was. Mistral *sounds* like that. What a disappointment when I found out it was a rough, disagreeable wind!"

Elizabeth didn't quite understand...she had never heard of the mistral...but the music of her beloved's voice was enough for her. The very sky was glad. A sailor with gold rings in his ears...the very kind of person one would meet in Tomorrow...smiled as he passed them. Elizabeth thought of a verse she had learned in Sunday-school..."The little hills rejoice on every side." Had the man who wrote that ever seen hills like those blue ones over the harbor?

The Third Year

"I think this road leads right to God," she said dreamily.

"Perhaps," said Anne. "Perhaps all roads do, little Elizabeth. We turn off here just now. We must go over to that island... that's Flying Cloud."

Flying Cloud was a long, slender islet, lying about a quarter of a mile from the shore. There were trees on it and a house. Little Elizabeth had always wished she might have an island of her own, with a little bay of silver sand in it.

"How do we get to it?"

"We'll row out in this flat," said Miss Shirley, picking up the oars in a small boat tied to a leaning tree.

Miss Shirley could row. Was there anything Miss Shirley couldn't do? When they reached the island, it proved to be a fascinating place where anything might happen. Of course it was in Tomorrow. Islands like this didn't happen except in Tomorrow. They had no part or lot in humdrum Today.

A little maid who met them at the door of the house told Anne she would find Mrs. Thompson on the far end of the island, picking wild strawberries. Fancy an island where wild strawberries grew!

Anne went to hunt Mrs. Thompson up, but first she asked if little Elizabeth might wait in the living-room. Anne was thinking that little Elizabeth looked rather tired after her unaccustomedly long walk and needed a rest. Little Elizabeth didn't think she did, but Miss Shirley's lightest wish was law.

It was a beautiful room, with flowers everywhere and wild sea-breezes blowing in. Elizabeth liked the mirror over the mantel which reflected the room so beautifully and, through the open window, a glimpse of harbor and hill and strait.

All at once a man came through the door. Elizabeth felt a moment of dismay and terror. Was he a gypsy? He didn't look like her idea of a gypsy but of course she had never seen one. He might be one...and then in a swift flash of intuition Elizabeth decided she didn't care if he did kidnap her. She liked his crinkly hazel eyes and his crinkly brown hair and his square chin and his smile. For he was smiling.

"Now, who are you?" he asked.

"I'm...I'm me," faltered Elizabeth, still a little flustered.

"Oh, to be sure...you. Popped out of the sea, I suppose... come up from the dunes...no name known among mortals."

Elizabeth felt that she was being made fun of a little. But she didn't mind. In fact she rather liked it. But she answered a bit primly.

"My name is Elizabeth Grayson."

There was a silence...a very queer silence. The man looked at her for a moment without saying anything. Then he politely asked her to sit down.

"I'm waiting for Miss Shirley," she explained. "She's gone to see Mrs. Thompson about the Ladies' Aid Supper. When she comes back we are going down to the end of the world."

Now, if you have any notion of kidnaping me, Mr. Man!

"Of course. But meanwhile you might as well be comfortable. And I must do the honors. What would you like in the way of light refreshment? Mrs. Thompson's cat has probably brought something in."

Elizabeth sat down. She felt oddly happy and at home.

"Can I have just what I like?"

"Certainly."

"Then," said Elizabeth triumphantly, "I'd like some ice-cream with strawberry jam on it."

The man rang a bell and gave an order. Yes, this must be Tomorrow...no doubt about it. Ice-cream and strawberry jam didn't appear in this magical manner in Today, cats or no cats.

"We'll set a share aside for your Miss Shirley," said the man.

They were good friends right away. The man didn't talk a great deal, but he looked at Elizabeth very often. There was a tenderness in his face...a tenderness she had never seen before

The Third Year

in anybody's face, not even Miss Shirley's. She felt that he liked her. And she knew that she liked him.

Finally he glanced out of the window and stood up.

"I think I must go now," he said. "I see your Miss Shirley coming up the walk, so you'll not be alone."

"Won't you wait and see Miss Shirley?" asked Elizabeth, licking her spoon to get the last vestige of the jam. Grandmother and the Woman would have died of horror had they seen her.

"Not this time," said the man.

Elizabeth knew he hadn't the slightest notion of kidnaping her, and she felt the strangest, most unaccountable sensation of disappointment.

"Good-by and thank you," she said politely. "It is very nice here in Tomorrow."

"Tomorrow?"

"This is Tomorrow," explained Elizabeth. "I've always wanted to get into Tomorrow and now I have."

"Oh, I see. Well, I'm sorry to say I don't care much about Tomorrow. I would like to get back into Yesterday."

Little Elizabeth was sorry for him. But how could he be unhappy? How could any one living in Tomorrow be unhappy?

Elizabeth heard Miss Shirley shriek....

13

The room went around oddly. The furniture nodded and jiggled. The bed...how came she to be in bed? Somebody with a white cap on was just going out of the door. What door? How funny one's head felt! There were voices somewhere...low voices. She could not see who was talking, but somehow she knew it was Miss Shirley and the man.

What were they saying? Elizabeth heard sentences here and there, bobbing out of a confusion of murmuring.

"Are you really...?" Miss Shirley's voice sounded so excited.

"Yes...your letter...see for myself...before approaching Mrs. Campbell...Flying Cloud is the summer home of our General Manager...."

If that room would only stay put! Really, things behaved rather queerly in Tomorrow. If she could only turn her head and see the talkers...Elizabeth gave a long sigh.

Then they came over to her bed...Miss Shirley and the man. Miss Shirley all tall and white, like a lily, looking as if she had been through some terrible experience but with some inner radiance shining behind it all...a radiance that seemed part of the golden sunset light which suddenly flooded the room. The man was smiling down at her. Elizabeth felt that he loved her very much and that there was some secret, tender and dear, between them which she would learn as soon as she had learned the language spoken in Tomorrow.

"Are you feeling better, darling?" said Miss Shirley.

"Have I been sick?"

"You were knocked down by a team of runaway horses on the mainland road," said Miss Shirley. "I...I wasn't quick enough. I thought you were killed. I brought you right back here in the flat and your...this gentleman telephoned for a doctor and nurse."

"Will I die?" said little Elizabeth.

"No, indeed, darling. You were only stunned and you will be all right soon. And, Elizabeth darling, this is your father."

"Father is in France. Am I in France, too?" Elizabeth would not have been surprised at it. Wasn't this Tomorrow? Besides, things were still a bit wobbly.

"Father is very much here, my sweet." He had such a delightful voice...you loved him for his voice. He bent and kissed her. "I've come for you. We'll never be separated any more."

The woman in the white cap was coming in again. Somehow, Elizabeth knew whatever she had to say must be said before she got quite in.

"Will we live together?"

"Always," said Father.

"And will Grandmother and the Woman live with us?"

"They will not," said Father.

The sunset gold was fading and the nurse was looking her disapproval. But Elizabeth didn't care.

"I've found Tomorrow," she said, as the nurse looked Father and Miss Shirley out.

"I've found a treasure I didn't know I possessed," said Father, as the nurse shut the door on him. "And I can never thank you enough for that letter, Miss Shirley."

"And so," wrote Anne to Gilbert that night, "little Elizabeth's road of mystery has led on to happiness and the end of her old world."

14

> "Windy Poplars,
> "Spook's Lane,
> "(For the last time),
> "June 27th.

"DEAREST:

"I've come to another bend in the road. I've written you a good many letters in this old tower room these past three years. I suppose this is the last one I will write you for a long, long time. Because after this there won't be any need of letters. In just a few weeks now we'll belong to each other forever...we'll be together. Just think of it...being together...talking, walking, eating, dreaming, planning together...sharing each other's wonderful moments...making a home out of our house of dreams. *Our* house! Doesn't that sound 'mystic and wonderful,' Gilbert? I've been building dream houses all my life and now one of them is going to come true. As to whom I really want to share my house of dreams with...well, I'll tell you that at four o'clock next year.

"Three years sounded endless at the beginning, Gilbert. And now they are gone like a watch in the night. They have been very happy years...except for those first few months with the Pringles. After that, life has seemed to flow by like a pleasant golden river. And my old feud with the Pringles seems like a dream. They like me now for myself...they have forgotten they ever hated me. Cora Pringle, one of the Widow Pringle's brood, brought me a bouquet of roses yesterday and twisted round the stems was a bit of paper

The Third Year

bearing the legend, 'To the sweetest teacher in the whole world.' Fancy that for a Pringle!

"Jen is broken-hearted because I am leaving. I shall watch Jen's career with interest. She is brilliant and rather unpredictable. One thing is certain...she will have no commonplace existence. She can't look so much like Becky Sharp for nothing.

"Lewis Allen is going to McGill. Sophy Sinclair is going to Queen's. Then she means to teach until she has saved up enough money to go to the School of Dramatic Expression in Kingsport. Myra Pringle is going to 'enter society' in the fall. She is so pretty that it won't matter a bit that she wouldn't know a past perfect participle if she met it on the street.

"And there is no longer a small neighbor on the other side of the vine-hung gate. Little Elizabeth has gone forever from that sunshineless house...gone into her Tomorrow. If I were staying on in Summerside I should break my heart, missing her. But as it is, I'm glad. Pierce Grayson took her away with him. He is not going back to Paris but will be living in Boston. Elizabeth cried bitterly at our parting but she is so happy with her father that I feel sure her tears will soon be dried. Mrs. Campbell and the Woman were very dour over the whole affair and put all the blame on me... which I accept cheerfully and unrepentantly.

"'She has had a good home here,' said Mrs. Campbell majestically.

"'Where she never heard a single word of affection,' I thought but did not say.

"'I think I'll be Betty all the time now, darling Miss Shirley,' were Elizabeth's last words. 'Except,' she called back, 'when I'm lonesome for you, and then I'll be Lizzie.'

"'Don't you ever dare to be Lizzie, no matter what happens,' I said.

"We threw kisses to each other as long as we could see, and I came up to my tower room with tears in my eyes. She's been so sweet, the dear little golden thing. She always seemed to me like a little aeolian harp, so responsive to the tiniest breath of affection that blew her way. It's been an adventure to be her friend. I hope Pierce Grayson realizes what a daughter he has...and I think he does. He sounded very grateful and repentant.

"'I didn't realize she was no longer a baby,' he said, 'nor how unsympathetic her environment was. Thank you a thousand times for all you have done for her.'

"I had our map of fairyland framed and gave it to little Elizabeth for a farewell keepsake.

"I'm sorry to leave Windy Poplars. Of course, I'm really a bit tired of living in a trunk, but I've loved it here... loved my cool morning hours at my window...loved my bed into which I have veritably climbed every night...loved my blue doughnut cushion...loved all the winds that blew. I'm afraid I'll never be quite so chummy with the winds again as I've been here. And shall I ever have a room again from which I can see both the rising and the setting sun?

"I've finished with Windy Poplars and the years that have been linked with it. And I've kept the faith. I've never betrayed Aunt Chatty's hidy-hole to Aunt Kate or the buttermilk secret of each to either of the others.

"I think they are all sorry to see me go...and I'm glad of it. It would be terrible to think they were glad I am going... or that they would not miss me a little when I'm gone. Rebecca Dew has been making all my favorite dishes for a week now...she even devoted ten eggs to angel-cake *twice*... and using the 'company' china. And Aunt Chatty's soft brown eyes brim over whenever I mention my departure. Even Dusty Miller seems to gaze at me reproachfully as he sits about on his little haunches.

The Third Year

"I had a long letter from Katherine last week. She has a gift for writing letters. She has got a position as private secretary to a globe-trotting M. P. What a fascinating phrase 'globe-trotting' is! A person who would say, 'Let's go to Egypt,' as one might say, 'Let's go to Charlottetown'... and *go*! That life will just suit Katherine.

"She persists in ascribing all her changed outlook and prospects to me. 'I wish I could tell you what you've brought into my life,' she wrote. I suppose I did help. And it wasn't easy at first. She seldom said anything without a sting in it, and listened to any suggestion I made in regard to the school work with an air of disdainfully humoring a lunatic. But somehow, I've forgotten it all. It was just born of her secret bitterness against life.

"Everybody has been inviting me to supper...even Pauline Gibson. Old Mrs. Gibson died a few months ago, so Pauline dared do it. And I've been to Tomgallon House for another supper with Miss Minerva of that ilk and another one-sided conversation. But I had a very good time, eating the delicious meal Miss Minerva provided, and she had a good time airing a few more tragedies. She couldn't quite hide the fact that she was sorry for any one who was not a Tomgallon, but she paid me several nice compliments and gave me a lovely ring set with an aquamarine...a moonlight blend of blue and green...that her father had given her on her eighteenth birthday...'when I was young and handsome, dear...*quite* handsome. I may say that *now*, I suppose.' I was glad it belonged to Miss Minerva and not to the wife of Uncle Alexander. I'm sure I could never have worn it if it had. It is very beautiful. There is a mysterious charm about the jewels of the sea.

"Tomgallon House is certainly very splendid, especially now when its grounds are all a-leaf and a-flower. But I wouldn't give my as yet unfounded house of dreams for Tomgallon House and grounds with the ghosts thrown in.

"Not but what a ghost might be a nice, aristocratic sort of thing to have around. My only quarrel with Spook's Lane is that there are no spooks.

"I went to my old graveyard yesterday evening for a last prowl...walked all round it and wondered if Herbert Pringle occasionally chuckled to himself in his grave. And I'm saying good-by tonight to the old Storm King, with the sunset on its brow, and my little winding valley full of dusk.

"I'm a wee bit tired after a month of exams and farewells and 'last things.' For a week after I get back to Green Gables I'm going to be lazy...do absolutely nothing but run free in a green world of summer loveliness. I'll dream by the Dryad's Bubble in the twilight. I'll drift on the Lake of Shining Waters in a shallop shaped from a moonbeam...or in Mr. Barry's flat, if moonbeam shallops are not in season. I'll gather starflowers and June bells in the Haunted Wood. I'll find plots of wild strawberries in Mr. Harrison's hill pasture. I'll join the dance of fireflies in Lover's Lane and visit Hester Gray's old, forgotten garden... and sit out on the back door-step under the stars and listen to the sea calling in its sleep.

"And when the week is ended *you* will be home...and I won't want anything else."

When the time came the next day for Anne to say good-by to the folks at Windy Poplars, Rebecca Dew was not on hand. Instead, Aunt Kate gravely handed Anne a letter.

"Dear Miss Shirley," wrote Rebecca Dew, "I am writing this to bid my farewell because I cannot trust myself to say it. For three years you have sojourned under our roof.

The Third Year

The fortunate possessor of a cheerful spirit and a natural taste for the gaieties of youth, you have never surrendered yourself to the vain pleasures of the giddy and fickle crowd. You have conducted yourself on all occasions and to every one, especially the one who pens these lines, with the most refined delicacy. You have always been most considerate of my feelings and I find a heavy gloom on my spirits at the thought of your departure. But we must not repine at what Providence has ordained. (First Samuel, 29th and 18th.)

"You will be lamented by all in Summerside who had the privilege of knowing you, and the homage of one faithful though humble heart will ever be yours, and my prayer will ever be for your happiness and welfare in this world and your eternal felicity in that which is to come.

"Something whispers to me that you will not be long 'Miss Shirley' but that you will erelong be linked together in a union of souls with the choice of your heart, who, I understand from what I have heard, is a very exceptional young man. The writer, possessed of but few personal charms and beginning to feel her age (not but what I'm good for a good few years yet), has never permitted herself to cherish any matrimonial aspirations. But she does not deny herself the pleasure of an interest in the nuptials of her friends and may I express a fervent wish that your married life will be one of continued and uninterrupted Bliss? (Only do not expect too much of a man.)

"My esteem and, may I say, my affection for you will never lessen, and once in a while when you have nothing better to do will you kindly remember that there is such a person as

"Your obedient servant,
"REBECCA DEW.

"P.S. God bless you."

Anne's eyes were misty as she folded the letter up. Though she strongly suspected Rebecca Dew had got most of her phrases out of her favorite "Book of Deportment and Etiquette," that did not make them any the less sincere, and the P. S. certainly came straight from Rebecca Dew's affectionate heart.

"Tell dear Rebecca Dew I'll never forget her and that I'm coming back to see you all every summer."

"We have memories of you that nothing can take away," sobbed Aunt Chatty.

"Nothing," said Aunt Kate, emphatically.

But as Anne drove away from Windy Poplars the last message from it was a large white bath-towel fluttering frantically from the tower window. Rebecca Dew was waving it.